THIEVES' WORLD™

is a unique experience: an outlaw world of the imagination, where mayhem and skulduggery rule and magic is still potent; brought to life by today's top fantasy writers, who are free to use one another's characters (but not to kill them off . . . or at least not too freely!).

The idea for Thieves' World and the colorful city called Sanctuary™ came to Robert Lynn Asprin in 1978. After many twists and turns (documented in the volumes), the idea took off—and took on its own reality, as the best fantasy worlds have a way of doing. The result is one of F&SF's most unique success stories: a bestseller from the beginning, a series that is a challenge to writers, a delight to readers, and a favorite of fans.

Don't miss these other exciting tales of Sanctuary: the meanest, seediest, most dangerous town in all the worlds of fantasy....

THIEVES' WORLD
(Stories by Asprin, Abbey, Anderson, Bradley, Brunner, DeWees, Haldeman, and Offutt)

TALES FROM THE VULGAR UNICORN
(Stories by Asprin, Abbey, Drake, Farmer, Morris, Offutt, and van Vogt)

SHADOWS OF SANCTUARY
(Stories by Asprin, Abbey, Cherryh, McIntyre, Morris, Offutt, and Paxson)

STORM SEASON
(Stories by Asprin, Abbey, Cherryh, Morris, Offutt, and Paxson)

THE FACE OF CHAOS
(Stories by Asprin, Abbey, Cherryh, Drake, Morris, and Paxson)

WINGS OF OMEN
(Stories by Asprin, Abbey, Bailey, Cherryh, Duane, Morris and Morris, Offutt, and Paxson)

THE DEAD OF WINTER
(Stories by Asprin, Abbey, Bailey, Cherryh, Duane, Morris, Offutt, and Paxson)

SOUL OF THE CITY
(Stories by Abbey, Cherryh, and Morris)

BLOOD TIES

Edited by
ROBERT LYNN ASPRIN & LYNN ABBEY

ACE FANTASY BOOKS
NEW YORK

This book is an Ace Fantasy
original edition. None of the
material in it has been previously
published.

BLOOD TIES

An Ace Fantasy Book/published by arrangement with
the editors

PRINTING HISTORY
Ace Fantasy edition/August 1986

ISBN: 0-441-80595-7

"THIEVES' WORLD" and "SANCTUARY" are
trademarks belonging to Robert Lynn Asprin
and Lynn Abbey.

Ace Fantasy Books are published by The Berkley Publishing Group,
200 Madison Avenue, New York, New York 10016.
PRINTED IN THE UNITED STATES OF AMERICA

CONTENTS

1. Sanctuary
2. Old Ruins (First Settlement)
3. Ranke (Capital of Rankan Empire)
4. Ilsig (Capital of Old Kingdom)
5. (6) Contoured cities, now in Empire
6. Death's Harbor
7. Scavengers' Island
8. The Forgotten Pass

·—··—··—··—··	wanderings of the people
— — — — —	the great road
··········	small roads
• • • • • • •	caravan routes
·—·—·—·—·—·	the generals' route
ᚐᚐᚐᚐᚐᚐᚐ	cliff
⛰⛰⛰⛰	mountains
⟹ ⟹ ⟹	ocean currents
ᴡ ᴡ ᴡ ᴡ	steppes
🌲🌲🌲 🌲🌲🌲	forests
𝚮 𝚮 𝚮 𝚮 𝚮	swamp

1. Governor's Palace
2. Hall of Justice
3. Servants' Quarters
4. Dungeons
5. Officers' Quarters
6. Armory
7. Barracks
8. Stables

9. Hanging/Slave
   Auction Block
10. Bazaar
11. (6) Estates
12. (4) Granaries
13. Lighthouse
14. Ford
15. Cave

← ~1 mile →

BLOOD TIES

Dramatis Personae

The Townspeople

AHDIOVIZUN; AHDIOMER VIZ; AHDIO, *Proprietor of Sly's Place, a legendary dive within the Maze.*

LALO THE LIMNER, *Street artist gifted with magic he does not fully understand.*
GILLA, *His indomitable wife.*
   ALFI, *Their youngest son.*
   LATILLA, *Their daughter.*
   GANNER, *Their middle son, slain during the False Plague riots of the previous winter.*
   VANDA, *Their daughter, employed as maid-servant to the Beysib at the palace.*
   WEDEMIR, *Their son and eldest child.*

DUBRO, *Bazaar blacksmith and husband to Illyra.*
ILLYRA, *Half-blood S'danzo seeress with True Sight. Hounded by PFLS in the False Plague.*
   ARTON, *Their son, marked by the gods and magic as part of an emerging divinity known as the Stormchildren. Sent to the Bandaran Isles for his safety and education.*
   LILLIS, *Their daughter, slain in the False Plague riots.*

HAKIEM, *Storyteller and confidant extraordinaire.*

JUBAL, *Prematurely aged former gladiator. Once he openly ran Sanctuary's most visible criminal organization, the Hawkmasks. Now he works behind the scenes.*
SALIMAN, *His aide and only friend.*

MAMA BECHO, *Owner of a particularly disreputable tavern in Downwind.*

MASHA ZIL-INEEL, *Midwife whose involvement with the destruction of the Purple Mage enabled her to move from the Maze to respectability uptown.*

MORIA, *One-time Hawkmask and servant to Ischade. She was physically transformed into a Rankan noblewoman by Haught.*

MYRTIS, *Madam of the Aphrodesia House.*

SHAFRALAIN, *Sanctuary nobleman who can trace his lineage and his money back to the days of Ilsig's glory.*
ESARIA, *His daughter.*
EXPIMILIA, *His wife.*
CUSHARLAIN, *His cousin. A customs inspector and investigator.*

SNAPPER JO, *A fiend who survived the destruction of magic in Sanctuary.*

STILCHO, *Once one of Ischade's resurrected minions, he was "cured" of death when magic was purged from Sanctuary.*

ZIP, *Bitter young terrorist. Leader of the Popular Front for the Liberation of Sanctuary (PFLS).*

The Magicians

HAUGHT, *One-time apprentice of Ischade who betrayed her and is now trapped in a warded house with Roxane.*

ISCHADE, *Necromancer and thief. Her curse is passed to her lovers who die from it.*

ROXANE; DEATH'S QUEEN, *Nisibisi witch. Nearly destroyed when Stormbringer purged magic from Sanctuary, she is trapped inside a warded house and a dead man's body.*

Others

THERON, *New military Emperor. An usurper placed on the throne with the aid of Tempus and his allies. He has commanded that Sanctuary's walls must be rebuilt by the next New Year Festival.*

The Rankans living in Sanctuary

CHENAYA; DAUGHTER OF THE SUN, *Daughter of Lowan Vigeles, a beautiful and powerful young woman who is fated never to lose a fight.*
DAYRNE, *Her companion and trainer.*
LEYN, OUIJEN, DISMAS AND GESTUS, *Her friends and fellow gladiators.*

GYSKOURAS, *One of the Stormchildren, currently in the Bandaran Isles for education.*

PRINCE KADAKITHIS, *Charismatic but somewhat naive half-brother of the recently assassinated Emperor, Abakithis.*
DAPHNE, *His estranged wife, living with Chenaya's gladiators at Land's End.*

KAMA; JES, *Tempus' daughter. 3rd Commando assassin. Sometime lover of both Zip and Molin Torchholder.*

LOWAN VIGELES, *Half-brother of Molin Torchholder, father of Chenaya, a wealthy aristocrat self-exiled to Sanctuary. Owner of the Land's End Estate.*

MOLIN TORCHHOLDER; TORCH, *Archpriest and architect of Vashanka; Guardian of the Stormchildren.*
ROSANDA, *His estranged wife, living at Land's End.*

RANKAN 3RD COMMANDO, *Mercenary company founded by Tempus Thales and noted for its brutal efficiency.*
SYNC, *Commander of the 3rd.*

RASHAN; THE EYE OF THE SAVANKALA, *Priest and Judge of Sanvankala. Highest ranking Rankan in Sanctuary prior to the arrival of the Prince, now allied with Chenaya's disaffected Rankans at Land's End.*

STEPSONS; SACRED BANDERS, *Members of a mercenary unit founded by Abarsis who willed their allegiance to Tempus Thales after his own death.*
CRITIAS; CRIT, *Leftside leader paired with Straton. Second in command after Tempus.*
RANDAL; WITCHY-EARS, *The only mage ever trusted by Tempus or admitted into the Sacred Band.*
STRATON; STRAT; ACE, *Rightside partner of Critias. Injured by the PFLS at the start of the False Plague riots.*

TASFALEN LANCOTHIS, *Jaded nobleman, slain by Ischade's curse, then resurrected by Haught. His body has become Roxane's prison.*

TEMPUS THALES; THE RIDDLER, *Nearly immortal mercenary, a partner of Vashanka before that god's demise; commander of the Stepsons; cursed with a fatal inability to give or receive love.*

WALEGRIN, *Rankan army officer assigned to the Sanctuary garrison where his father had been slain by the S'danzo many years before.*

The Gods

DYAREELA, *A goddess whose worship in Sanctuary predates the Ilsigi presence and which has been outlawed many times since then.*

HARRAN, *Physician and priest to Siveni Gray-Eyes, now part of her four-fold divinity.*

MRIGA, *Mindless and crippled woman elevated to four-fold divinity with Siveni Gray-Eyes.*

SABELLIA, *Mother goddess for the Rankan Empire.*

SAVANKALA, *Father god for the Rankan Empire.*

SIVENI GRAY-EYES, *Ilsigi goddess of wisdom, medicine and defense, now transformed into a four-fold diety.*

SHIPRI, *Mother goddess of the old Ilsigi kingdom.*

STORMBRINGER, *Primal stormgod/wargod. The pattern for all other such gods, he is not, himself, the object of organized worship.*
JIHAN, *Froth Daughter. His parthenogenic offspring, betrothed to the Stepson's mage, Randal.*

The Beysib

SHUPANSEA; SHU-SEA, *Head of the Beysib exiles in Sanctuary; mortal avatar of the Beysib mother goddess.*

BLOOD TIES

INTRODUCTION

Robert Lynn Asprin

For the first time in over a decade, Hakiem found himself seriously considering leaving his adopted home of Sanctuary.

Leaning out a window on one of the upper levels of the palace, he surveyed the town below as he thought—yet even this depressed him. He had always enjoyed walking the streets, first as a storyteller and later as advisor to the Beysib Empress. The town had always had a rough vibrancy, like the rich organic smell of a swamp, and he drank it in along with the rumors to assure himself of the city's survival. Now, however, he found that he rarely ventured down to the streets to savor it.

Not that he was afraid for his safety, mind you. Whether it was due to his long-standing membership in the community, his well known neutrality and harmlessness, deference to his position as the Beysa's advisor, or a combination of all of these factors, his passage through town was never challenged. Rather, he often hid within the palace shadows and corridors to spare himself the heartache of witnessing what was happening to his beloved Sanctuary.

The spirit of the town he knew had been born of parents named Poverty and Desperation. While he had cursed the crime and filth along with the rest of the citizens, there had also been a secret pride in the inherent toughness of Sanctuary's inhabitants. Like the scrappy optimism of a bright-eyed gutter predator, there had been a certainty that the town would survive regardless of whatever hardships fate or the Rankan Empire could throw at it. Small moments of tenderness or self-sacrificing heroics shone all the brighter here, as uncontestable evidence of the strength of the human spirit.

Then two changes occurred almost simultaneously: the Beysib arrived and Ranke's Stormgod had either died or retreated into oblivion.

As Sanctuary's fortunes literally rose through the influx of

1

Beysib wealth, the Empire's prestige and power had begun to wane—and the very nature of the city altered. Instead of small, vicious fights for survival, the town sank into selfish power squabbles which were proving more deadly and disruptive than anything the citizens had known before. Instead of desperation and poverty, the stench of greed hung over the town and Hakiem found it stifling.

Perhaps he should leave . . . soon, before the current disorder wiped out what few pleasant memories remained. If the new path of the town was fixed, he had no idea to . . .

"You are very quiet, Wise One, for someone who earns his living with his nimble tongue."

Jolted from his reverie, Hakiem turned to find Shupansea, living avatar of Mother Bey and hereditary, if exiled, ruler of the Beysib Empire, regarding him with the delighted smile of a child who has caught his teacher in a spelling error.

"Your pardon, O Beysa. I did not hear you approach."

"There are no others about, Hakiem. Formalities between us are necessary only before unfriendly eyes. Besides, I doubt you would have heard an entire army approaching. Where is the habitual wariness you've tried so hard to instill in me?"

"I . . . I was thinking."

The smile disappeared from the Beysa's face to be replaced with an expression of concern as she laid a soft hand on her advisor's arm. "I know. You seem unhappy of late, Wise One. I've missed the talks we used to have. In fact, I've set aside time today specifically to seek you out and learn your mind. You've helped me so often in the past that gold alone cannot repay it. Tell me, what troubles you? Is there anything I can do to ease your concerns?"

Despite his depression, Hakiem was touched by the sincere concern of this young woman who had been raised to rule an empire and found herself in Sanctuary instead. While a part of him instinctively wanted to hide his feelings, he felt compelled to respond honestly.

"I fear for my town," he said, turning to gaze out the window once more. "The people have changed since the Beysib arrived.

"Not that I blame you," he amended hastily. "You had to go somewhere, and certainly your people have done everything possible to adapt to what I know is a very strange and often hostile environment to you.

"No. What has happened to my town was done by those

who have lived here the longest. Oh, true enough, many of
the changes were forced on them by the Rankan Empire and
its gods—and I know that all things must change. Still, I fear
the townspeople have lost the will and certainly the wisdom to
survive the changes which must follow as surely as a storm
follows lightning. Even now the new Rankan Emperor gathers
troops to—"

He stopped abruptly as he realized the Beysa was laughing
silently.

"I had not intended to be amusing," he said stiffly, anger
flashing just below the surface. "While I know the problems
of a mere storyteller pale to insignificance before—"

"Forgive me, Wise One. I meant no disrespect. It's just
that you. . . . Please, let me be the teacher for once."

To Hakiem's surprise, she joined him at the window, leaning far over the sill until only the tips of her bare toes touched
the cool floor.

"I fear you are too close to the problem," she said
solemnly. "You know so much about Sanctuary and watch so
many of its citizens that you have become overwhelmed by
surface changes and are blind to the currents moving beneath.
Let me tell you what I see as someone new to Sanctuary.

"You underestimate your town, Wise One. You love it so
much that you think that no one else does—but that is incor-
rect. In the two years since my people arrived here, I have yet
to meet a man, woman, or child of Sanctuary who did not,
despite their very loud protests to the contrary, care as deeply
for Sanctuary as you do, though they may show it differently.
And I find, to my surprise, that their feelings are quite conta-
gious."

She caught his surprised glance and laughed again. "Yes, I
find that even with the blood of forty generations of Beysas
and our island empire running in my veins, neither I nor my
goddess has been immune to the lure of your town. At first it
seemed to me to be vicious and barbaric, and it is, but there is
a zest and vigor here that is invigorating and quite lacking in
my own very civilized people. While you may fear that it has
changed or lost, as one watching through new eyes, I can tell
you that it is still there, and if anything it's stronger than when
we arrived. Oh, they may squabble over their new wealth and
power, but this is still Sanctuary. If threatened, the people here
will fight or do whatever is necessary to keep that feeling of
independence and freedom they have toiled so long for. The

Beysib will be at their side, for my people and I are a part of it, just as you and yours are."

After that, she lapsed into silence and, side by side, they studied the town, living symbols of the old and the new Sanctuary. In their own thoughts, they each hoped desperately that she was right.

LADY OF FIRE

Diana L. Paxson

A peach tree grew in the courtyard below Lalo's stairs. It was only a little tree, but Gilla had covered its roots with straw to protect it from cold and dribbled precious water around it when the sun burned in the sky, caring for it as she cared for her children, and through war and wizard weather it had survived. But in the bitter spring of the Emperor's visit to Sanctuary the tree stood barren, with scarcely a leaflet on its twisted branches, and no blooms.

Lalo paused beside it on his way to the palace, wishing that he could breathe life into the tree as he had once breathed life into the work of his hands. But with the destruction of the Nisibisi Globes of Power everyone's magic seemed to have become as strengthless as Master Ahdio's cheap ale; Lalo dared not test his own. And even at his most powerful, he had only transformed symbols, not already living things.

He did not know if he could create anything anymore.

The building behind him was as silent as it had been in the dreadful days when Gilla was Roxane's captive. Latilla and Alfi were with Vanda at the palace. Wedemir was enviously watching the Stepsons maneuver themselves back into shape for campaign, and Gilla herself was at the Aphrodisia House, watching over Illyra's slow recovery from the wound she had taken in the riots when her daughter died.

If Illyra's body had been all that needed healing it would not have been so bad, Lalo thought. But it seemed to him that both women were nursing grief like a child. A pang twisted in his own belly at the memory—his middle son, Ganner, had been struck down, outside the goldsmith's shop where he was apprenticed, in that same climax of disorder that had killed Illyra's girl.

The town was quiet now, but it was the peace of exhaustion—more like a coma than the sleep of healing, and who could tell whether Sanctuary, or any of its people, would awaken to life again?

Lalo shivered and squinted at the sky. Even if it was useless, he ought to get up to the palace before the morning light was gone. As part of a sequence of political and religious negotiations which Lalo did not even try to understand, Molin Torchholder had commissioned him to paint an allegorical mural of the Wedding of the Storm God and Mother Bey. The work was as lifeless as everything else he did these days, but he was getting paid for it. And he did not know what else he could do.

"She was going to be pretty..." said Illyra in an oddly conversational tone. "My Lillis had golden hair like her father's, do you remember? I used to comb it and wonder how anything that pretty could have been born from me...."

"Yes," answered Gilla quietly. "I know." She had only seen Illyra's daughter a few times, but that did not matter now. "Ganner was the fairest of my children..." Her throat closed.

"How can you understand?" exclaimed the half-S'danzo suddenly. "You still have children! But my daughter is dead and they have taken my little boy away! There is nothing left for me."

"Your child was young," said Gilla heavily. "You do not know what she would have been. But all the labor of raising my boy to manhood is wasted. He will never give me grandchildren now. I have buried one infant and lost one from the womb; the boy that was born after Ganner died of a fever when he was six years old. I know the pain of losing them at all ages, Illyra, and I tell you truly that whatever age your child is taken from you is the worst. But I will bear no more. You are still young—you can have other children."

"What for?" Illyra said harshly. "So that this town can kill them, too?" She sank back upon the silken pillows with which the Aphrodisia House furnished even a sickroom and closed her eyes.

From somewhere on the floor below them came a mocking echo of music. The faded silk of the cushions glowed softly in the afternoon light, but to Gilla they seemed as colorless as everything else had been since that terrible day when so many died. Illyra was right—why give more hostages to malicious fate?

Someone scratched hesitantly at the door. When neither Gilla nor Illyra answered, it opened softly and Myrtis, a little thinner, but as impeccably painted and jeweled as ever, came in.

"How is she today?" She gestured toward the half-S'danzo, who lay with her eyes tightly closed.

Gilla got to her feet and moved heavily to meet the older woman—at least one assumed that Myrtis was older, and today she looked it, as if the spells by which Lythande had preserved her famous beauty were fading too. Molin Torchholder's gold had paid for Illyra's convalescence here, but the famous madam of the Aphrodisia House had given them more than a landlady's care.

"The scar is healing, but Illyra grows weaker," Gilla said in a low voice. "I think she does not want to live. And why should she?" she added bitterly.

For a moment Myrtis's eyes glittered. "Do you need a reason? Life is the only thing there is! After all she's survived, and you, too, are you going to give up and let *them* win?" Her gesture seemed to encompass everything outside the room. Then she drew back her hand as if surprised by her own intensity.

"In any case, there are others who need her," she continued more calmly. She moved aside and Gilla saw another figure in the doorway behind her, tall, black-haired, with a lithe poise that the rich gown she wore so awkwardly could not disguise and an energy that made even Gilla give way as she swept into the room past Myrtis.

"What are you doing? She's not well enough—" Gilla began as the newcomer strode to the bed where Illyra lay, and stood looking down at her.

"They say the S'danzo have no gods, and no mages," the woman said gruffly. "Well, the gods the rest of us had aren't talking these days, and the mages are useless. I need information. My old comrades said you're honest. What will you take to See for me?"

"Nothing." Illyra pulled herself up against the pillows, stony-eyed.

"Oh, no—enough of my comrades came to you in the old days that I know you keep to the traditional rule. If you take my coin you are bound to answer me. . . ." She pulled gold from her pouch and held it out. Furiously, Illyra dashed it from her hand.

"Do you know who I am?" the woman said dangerously.

"I know you, Lady Kama, and there is nothing in Sanctuary that will make me See for you!" She caught her breath on a half-sob. "I could not even if I would. When my—in the riots—my cards were destroyed. I am as blind as any of the rest of you now!" She finished with bitter triumph.

"But I have to know!" Kama said angrily. "I have promised to wed Molin Torchholder, but when I ask him about the ceremony he puts me off with theological caveats. And the Stepsons are taking the Third Commando with them on some mysterious campaign—all my old comrades! I could go with them—I'd rather go with them, but I have to know what I should do!"

Illyra shrugged. "Do what you please."

Considering that Molin Torchholder had taken Illyra's other child away, Gilla thought the S'danzo's reaction to this request from his woman mild.

Kama bent suddenly and gripped Illyra's shoulders. "What does that have to do with it? I've sworn oaths—they still bind me even if the gods aren't listening anymore, and I've lost too much blood in this town to just walk away without knowing why. Do you think I've stopped being a warrior because I'm wearing these?" She twitched angrily at the rich folds of her skirts. "I will have answers, woman, if I have to wring them out of you!"

Illyra shook her head. "Can you wring blood from a stone? Do whatever you like to me—I have no answers anymore."

"There may be no blood left in *your* veins," Kama said dangerously, "but what about your husband's? I've learned a lot in this cesspool you call home—will you sing the same song when you see me applying some of that knowledge to Dubro?"

"No . . ." said Illyra faintly. "He has nothing to do with this. You can't make him suffer for me . . ."

"Were you somehow under the impression that life is fair?" Kama straightened and stood looking down at her. "I will do whatever I have to do."

Gilla looked from her to Myrtis, who was watching with a faint half-smile. Had the madam of the Aphrodisia House put Kama up to this in an attempt to shake Illyra out of her depression? She could believe it of Myrtis, but she found it hard to imagine Kama cooperating in anyone else's schemes.

"But I cannot . . ." said Illyra pitifully. "I told you. I have no cards. And I cannot borrow a set—each deck is attuned to the S'danzo who owns it. Mine came to me from my grandmother, and there is no S'danzo craftsman in this town who could paint a new deck for me."

Kama stared at her. Then her gray gaze moved thoughtfully from the S'danzo to Gilla and back again.

"But you know the patterns of the cards—"

Now it was Illyra's turn to stare.

"And *her* husband is a painter who is said to have certain powers . . ." As Kama continued, Gilla read in Illyra's face her own anguished awareness that they both still had hostages to fate.

"Molin Torchholder is the limner's patron. He will order Lalo to come to you, and together you will make a new deck of cards. And then—" Kama's lips twisted in what was intended to be a sweet smile. "Then we will see if there is any magic left in this world."

Lalo pinned another rectangle of stiff vellum to his drawing board. He could feel the tension in his neck and shoulders, and Illyra looked pale, with a sheen of perspiration on her brow. The two cards they had already finished were drying in the sunshine that came through the window.

"Are you ready?" he asked softly through the mask over his mouth he always wore now while working, to keep his breath from accidentally giving life to what he made. "We don't have to do any more today. . . ." Even if he had had the energy to continue, he did not think that the S'danzo woman could go on much longer.

"One more . . ." Illyra winced as she pulled herself upright against the pillows. She was pushing herself. Lalo wondered if she was beginning to feel incomplete without a set of cards, as he always did without drawing materials somewhere at hand, or if she simply wanted to get rid of Kama.

"The next card is the Three of Flames," said Illyra. Her voice altered, developed a peculiarly flat timbre, as if even visualizing the cards was enough to push her into the seer's trance. "There is a tunnel, dark at one end and at the other bright. In the tunnel I see three figures bearing torches. Are they moving toward light or darkness? I cannot tell. . . ."

As if the S'danzo's words had entranced him, Lalo found his hand moving, dipping up dark pigment for the shadows

and red-orange for the three bright flowers of flame. As Illyra
spoke of the meaning of the card, shape and color emerged
from the slip of vellum before him as if his brush were a wand
that made visible what had always been implicit there.

The torchbearers were in silhouette, their faces hidden, but
he could see that one was small, one broad, one wiry and
active. Could the big shape be Molin Torchholder? Lalo finished painting in the number of the card, and in the moment
between the last brush stroke and his return to normal consciousness he thought he saw something of Gilla in the larger
figure. Perhaps the other two were Illyra and himself, then,
but were they moving into deeper shadow or toward the light?

Lalo straightened and looked at Illyra, who lay back
against her pillows with the stillness of sleep, or trance. There
were dark smudges beneath her closed eyes, as if he had
touched her with his paint-stained finger there. He had felt the
power moving through him as he painted, but this time the
meaning of his work was hidden from him even when he came
out of his own trance of creation and looked at the cards.

The three flame-cards that were finished glowed in the
sunlight that came through the window, the colors seeming to
vibrate with their own energy. *I should be grateful,* thought
the limner. *At least now I know that my hands still have
power.* But he did not understand what he had painted, and
something ached in his belly at the anguish he saw in Illyra's
shut face. Carefully, quietly, fearing to disturb her, Lalo began
to put his paints away.

"The cards are beautiful," said Gilla. "So many of Lalo's
recent commissions have been murals, I'd forgotten how
lovely his detail work can be." She laid the root card of Wood
carefully back atop the pile. The rich greens and browns of the
"Forest Primeval" seemed to glow with their own light, like
sunshine slanting through innumerable leaves. Molin Torchholder's demand had for the moment given the marriage mural
precedence over Kama's commission for the cards, even
though the deck was nearly finished now. Illyra was nearly
well now too, in body. But she and Gilla had grown accustomed to each other's company.

"I hate them," said Illyra in a low voice.

Gilla looked back at the couch, an angry defense of Lalo's
work trembling on her tongue. The S'danzo's eyes were

closed, but the slow tears were welling from beneath her shut lids. Gilla stifled her anger and went to the other woman, took a damp cloth, and began to sponge her cheeks and brow.

"My dear, my dear, it's all right now. . . ." It was the instinctive murmur of a mother to a sick child.

"It is *not* all right!" said Illyra in a hard voice. "To See, I must open myself to the Great Pattern—become one with it and channel the part that relates to the question the querent has asked. But I do not believe in the Pattern anymore."

Gilla nodded. Men killing each other was one thing, whether in battle or in the back streets of Sanctuary, but how could there be any purpose in the senseless death of a child? Memory brought her a sudden image of Ganner's eighth birthday, when Lalo had brought him clay and a set of modeler's tools. The light in the boy's face had stamped him and Lalo with a single identity as they explored the new medium. Ganner was the only one of the children to have inherited any of Lalo's skill. But he would never bring beauty into the world now. She swallowed over the ache in her throat and turned to Illyra again.

"More than half the deck is painted now. Kama will force me to read for her when the rest are done and I cannot," said Illyra bitterly. "I will fail her, and then she will take her revenge on Dubro. By all of Sanctuary's useless gods, I hate her! Her, and the rest of those blade-thirsty, swaggering bullies who have destroyed my world!"

"Will you find a sword of your own and go after her?" asked Gilla, trying to channel into scorn the hatred that was making her own belly burn. "Illyra, be sensible. Try to get well, and be thankful that's not your kind of power!"

"My kind of power. . ." said the S'danzo reflectively. "No —when men burn my people for sorcery it's not because they fear the simple power of steel. . . ." Illyra fell silent. Her dark hair swung down across her breast, and Gilla could not see her eyes, but there was something in the other woman's stillness that sent a chill down her back despite the heat of the day.

"It's forbidden . . ." said the S'danzo very softly, "even the little teaching they allowed me said that. But what do I care for anyone else's rules now?"

"Illyra, what are you going to do?" Gilla asked apprehensively as the other woman levered herself painfully off the couch and went to the worktable where the cards that Lalo had finished were piled.

"Everything goes two ways," Illyra said conversationally. "See this card, for instance, the Three of Flames. If it were to come up in a reading, it could mean things getting darker or brighter for the querent, depending on the context. And this one, Steel—" She held up the Two of Ores. "In the usual position, with the swords pointing toward the querent, it's a death card, but reversed it means doom for his enemy."

"So does a real sword," answered Gilla.

Illyra nodded. "So does magic. Power is power. Good or evil lies not in the tool, but in the user's intent and will."

Gilla stared at her. "You can use the cards as a weapon?" Her heart began to pound heavily, and she realized suddenly how she had envied the gifts that Lalo had acquired so inadvertently and used with such trepidation.

Illyra was sorting through the cards that Lalo had completed. "Perhaps—if the right cards are here . . ." She selected one, another, then three more. "When I read, the querent and the cards and I are all linked in the Pattern and the cards that come up reflect his relationship to it. The Pattern is the Cause; the cards are the effect. My Seeing only translates to the querent what is already there."

Gilla nodded, and the S'danzo went on, "But if I were to set the cards into a pattern, and lock it with my will—"

"You could reverse the process?" whispered Gilla. "Make the cards the Cause?"

"I could . . . I would . . . I will!"

Suddenly Illyra gathered up the cards and carried them to a parquetry table in the corner of the room. She held up a card and showed it to Gilla. "Here, this shall stand for the querent and its surrounding atmosphere. . . ." She laid it down.

Gilla squinted, seeing only the sun shining brightly over a painted city. "Which one is that?"

"We call it Zenith—the noonday sun—but your husband has painted a city as well as the sun." Illyra held her hands above it and stood for a moment with brow wrinkled in concentration and eyes closed. "As thou wert Zenith, so thou shalt become *this* city!" she murmured. She dipped her finger into the paint water and flicked a drop upon the card, then bent and breathed upon it. "By wind and water do I name thee Sanctuary, the querent of this reading, and the subject of this casting!"

She shouldn't be doing this, thought Gilla, watching Illyra search through the cards she had selected. There was a focus to her movements that held the attention. Gilla remembered how Roxane had compelled the eye, and shuddered. But she had never understood what needs drove the Nisibisi sorceress, who for all her great knowledge had no part in ordinary women's joys and pains. Illyra, she understood only too well. *We shouldn't be doing this!* she thought then.

Gilla felt the pulse pounding in her temples, tasted the fury of the wolf-bitch whose cubs have been killed. All her life she had known fear, fear of starvation in times of want, fear of theft in moments of affluence. She had grown up listening for the stealthy step behind her as automatically as she watched for movement in the shadows whenever she went out of her door. And then she had borne children, and the fear she felt for them was as much greater than her own personal terrors as the White Foal River was deeper and more dreadful than the sewers of Sanctuary. And there had never been anything that she could do about it! Never, until now. . . .

Ominous as a mountain moving, Gilla's heavy steps shook the floor as she took her place across the worktable from the S'danzo.

"What crosses it, Seer?" she asked.

"The Lance of Ships," said Illyra, "the Narwhale, which may be a card of good fortune, but always means changeability. In this position, it is the good fortune that will disappear!"

"What do we hope for?" asked Gilla, continuing the litany.

Illyra took another card and placed it above the first two. Gilla recognized it—the Two of Ores reversed, with the Steel pointed downward threateningly.

"And this is what we already have," added the S'danzo. "Quicksilver, what some call the Card of Shalpa—the Root of Ores and the Foundation of Sanctuary." The next card was placed below the first two.

"What has gone before is the Face of Chaos—" Illyra held up a card with the images of a man and a woman twisted and distorted as if in some fever dream. She smiled grimly and laid the card down.

"And what is to come, Seer—show me what is to come!" demanded Gilla. She could feel energy flowing from her to the woman on the other side of the table, and knew that more than S'danzo power was going into this casting.

Illyra took another card. "The Zigurrat," she smiled dangerously. "For we shall bring the pride of the destroyers tumbling down."

Gilla looked at the image of the disintegrating tower and thought of the patched up peace that had held the town quiet since the visit of the Emperor. Surely it would take only a finger's push to destroy so uneasy a balance.

"How?" whispered Gilla then. "Seeress, show me how it will be!"

Illyra held the remaining cards fanned out in her thin hand. "First the Lance of Winds—"

The card she set down bore the images of storm and tornado. "This represents our determination to see this done. And this one is for our fear . . ."

She set another card above it, on which a triumvirate of robed and hooded figures stood pointing at a kneeling man. "Justice," came the whisper, and Gilla licked suddenly dry lips, understanding even without explanation that this represented the dead children for whom they sought revenge.

"Our hope is for justice, and therefore I set Sanctuary's tribunal here—" Illyra's voice had a rhythmic resonance, and her eyes seemed to look through the card to some other reality. Gilla realized that the S'danzo was Seeing them as truly as ever she had in a querent's reading, and she wondered suddenly if in choosing just these cards for Lalo to paint first, Illyra had been guided by something more than chance, and if her selection of them now was the result of her will to vengeance, or some subtle working of that Pattern Illyra had denied.

Gilla shivered, for now the S'danzo was wholly entranced, and she felt a heaviness in the air around them as if unseen forces waited around her to see what the final card would be. The magic of the mages had been broken, but, clearly, she and Illyra were drawing now upon deeper powers.

Without looking at the cards still in the pile, Illyra took one and set it above all the rest. Gilla stared at it, her gaze burned by swirling patterns of red and gold, and the beauty of a woman's face staring out of the flames. Even seen upside down that face seared the sight. She forced her gaze away and saw the appalled wonder in Illyra's eyes.

"What is she?" Gilla asked hoarsely.

"The Eight of Flames—the Lady of Fire whose touch can warm or destroy!"

"What will She do to Sanctuary?"

Illyra was shaking her head. "I do not know. I have never drawn Her reversed in a reading before. Oh, Gilla—" The

S'danzo's face twisted in a terrible smile. "*I* did not choose this card!"

In the days that followed, the Lady of Fire came to Sanctuary, not in bolts of flame from heaven as Gilla and Illyra had expected, but silently, insidiously, as a flame that kindled in men's flesh and consumed them slowly from within.

For weeks the weather had been close and still—plague weather, though usually it came to Sanctuary later in the year. In a city whose sanitation system had been designed to move men secretly rather than sewage efficiently, epidemics were an inevitable sign of summer, like the insects that swarmed across the river from the Swamp of Night Secrets. But a dry spring had lowered the water table early, and without enough flow to flush them, the disease bred in the filthy channels and spread swiftly through the town.

It began in the streets around Shambles Cross and moved like a slow fire into the Maze and the Bazaar, where a few corpses more in the morning caused little comment, until the kisses of the drabs who plied their trade in the cul-de-sacs and doorways burned with more than passion's fire, and men began to fall from the benches in the Vulgar Unicorn with their mugs untasted. Soldiers drinking in the taverns carried the plague back to the barracks, and servants going to their work in the great houses of the merchants carried it to the better quarters of the town. Only the Beysib seemed to be immune.

Molin Torchholder realized the danger when his workmen began to drop beside his unfinished city wall and, returning to the palace, found the Prince in a panic and a full-scale crisis on his hands. That morning, the decapitated body of a dog had been discovered in the ruined Temple of Dyareela, with "Death to the Beysib" scrawled in its blood on the altar stone.

Lalo turned, spattering blue paint from the plastered wall past the pillar as the High Priest stormed through the Presence Hall with the Prince and the Beysa hurrying along behind.

"They are saying that Dyareela is punishing Sanctuary because of our betrothal." Shupansea tightened her grip on Kadakithis's hand. "They say that your Demon Goddess is angry because the town has accepted Mother Bey!"

"My goddess!" Both Prince and Beysa fell back as Molin turned on them, looking rather like a Storm God himself with his mantle flaring around him and dust flying from his uncombed hair and beard. Lalo found it hard to believe that this was the same sleek priest who had given him his first great commission so long ago. But then his own changes in the past few years had been even more remarkable, if less obvious. And Sanctuary itself had changed.

"Dyareela's no deity of Ranke, or of the Ilsig either!" Molin's gaze fixed on Lalo and a quick grab hauled the limner out from behind the pillar. "You tell them—you're a Wrigglie! Is Dyareela any goddess of yours?"

Lalo stared at him, more startled than offended by the priest's use of the Rankan epithet. Torchholder's unguarded tongue was the best evidence of the priest's own frustration and fear.

"The Good Goddess was here before the Ilsigi came." He pulled off his mask and answered softly. "She rules the wastelands, and the lost spirits who dwell there. But mostly, men do not pray to Her . . ."

"Mostly?" asked Kadakithis. "When *do* they pray to Her, limner?"

Lalo kept his gaze on the patterned tiles, his skin prickling as if even talking about it could bring the fever on. "I was a boy when the last great plague came here," he said in a low voice. "We worshiped Her then. She brings the fever. She *is* the fever, and She is its cure. . . ."

"Wrigglie superstition," began the Prince, but his voice lacked conviction.

Molin Torchholder sighed. "I don't like to give recognition to these native cults, but it may be necessary. I don't suppose you remember any details of the ceremonies?" His grip tightened on Lalo's shoulder again.

"Ask the priests of Ils!" Lalo shrugged free. "I was a child, and my mother kept me inside for fear of the crowds. They said there was a great sacrifice. They dragged the carcass outside the city to attract the demons away and burned the bodies of the dead and their possessions in a great pyre. What I remember was men and women lying with each other in the streets, with drops of blood from the sacrifice still red on their brows."

Kadakithis shuddered, but Shupansea said that she had heard of similar customs in the villages of her own land.

"That may be so," said the High Priest repressively, "but the theological implications are unfortunate, particularly now. My Prince, I am afraid that your formal betrothal will have to be delayed until this dies down."

"It is the dying I am afraid of," said the Beysa. "They will be sacrificing my people, not stallions or bulls, if you do not do something soon!"

Molin Torchholder's face worked as if he saw the careful edifice of cooperation he had constructed collapsing before him. Without answering, he strode off, and Shupansea and Kadakithis followed him, leaving Lalo staring after them.

Presently he turned back to the mural he had been working on. On the wall of the Presence Chamber, Mother Bey stretched out Her hand to the Storm God against a background of the blue sea. It was no accident that the god looked something like Kadakithis, and the goddess had the bearing and wore the robes of Shupansea, but Lalo had worked from imagination and memory this time, knowing better than to paint the souls of these particular models for all to see.

Technically the work was competent, but the figures seemed lifeless. For a moment Lalo wondered what a little of his breath would do. Then he remembered the wars of Vashanka and Ils, shuddered, and pulled the mask over his nose and mouth again. With Dyareela stalking the streets of Sanctuary, the last thing they needed was two new deities with all the prejudices and failings of the originals fluttering about the town.

He was still struggling with the painting when his daughter Vanda came to him with the news that her sister Latilla had taken the fever, and the Rankans wanted her out of the palace before darkness fell.

There were crowds in the streets outside the Aphrodisia House, but little business inside, men fearing lest the fires of love would ignite a different kind of flame. Their drunken voices sounded like the growling of some great animal. Broken phrases trembled in the still air. "Death to the fish-folk, death and the fire!" At least, thought Gilla, Lalo and the children were safe at the palace, while Dubro was adding his strength to Myrtis's guards downstairs.

Gilla pulled the curtain back across the window despite the airless heat of the evening and sat down again. Illyra lay on

her couch, clutching the coverlet to her breast at every cry, as
if she were cold, despite the sheen of perspiration on her forehead. Gilla looked down at her own clasped hands, red and
workworn, the flesh puffing around the circle of her wedding
band, and tried to tell herself that the plague came nearly
every year. But she knew it did not come this way. She and
Illyra had done this, somehow, with their spell.

A new outbreak of shouting below startled her to awareness again. The building shook as the great door of the
Aphrodisia House slammed, and she heard a mutter of voices
and footsteps on the stairs. It was their door they were coming
to! Gilla got heavily to her feet as it was flung open, and she
saw Lalo framed in the doorway with Myrtis behind him and
Latilla in his arms.

Illyra cried out, but Gilla was already in motion, reaching
out to touch the hot forehead. Latilla opened her eyes then,
focusing with difficulty, and tried to smile.

"Mama, I missed you. Mama, I'm so hot, can't you make
me cool again?"

Throat tight, Gilla took the burning body into her own
arms, whispering words that made no sense even to her. Latilla was so light, her flesh half consumed already by that
inner fire!

"Lay her down on the couch," said Illyra in a strained
voice. "We'll need cold water and cloths."

"I've already ordered them," said Myrtis calmly, "and perhaps these will help as well." She gestured, and one of her
girls brought in two of the plumed fans which they used to fan
away the sweat of amorous exercise from the bodies of their
more important customers, then scurried out of the room.

Illyra had already smoothed the coverlet. Gilla laid Latilla
down and reached out for the first compress without looking
away. But she was aware of Lalo close beside her, and she
drew on his energy as Illyra had drawn upon hers when they
made their spell. After a little, the fanning and the cold cloths
seemed to have some effect, and Latilla fell into an uneasy
doze.

The first crisis over, Lalo had gone to his worktable and
was fussing with his paints, laying them out instinctively as if
work could help him control the chaos of his world.

"Oh Gilla," said Illyra pitifully, "she looks so like my little
girl!" Gilla met her eyes, and the S'danzo flushed painfully.
At her words, Lalo looked up at her.

"Where are the finished cards?" he asked then. "There were only a few to be done—if I complete the deck, perhaps you can read some hope for us now!"

Illyra stared at him, and her face went stark white against the dark masses of her hair. Then her gaze slid unwillingly to the table in the corner, where the cards were still as she had laid them a week ago. Still unsuspecting, Lalo went to it and stood, looking down.

Gilla's flesh had turned to stone. Lalo was no S'danzo, but he was a master of symbol, and he had painted those cards. She tried to read his reaction in the slump of his shoulders, the bent head with its thinning, ginger hair. Surely he must know!

"I don't understand," Lalo said in a still voice. "Did you try to read from an incomplete deck? Is this your Seeing for what is happening now?" Suddenly his hand shot out and he swept the fatal pattern of cards to the floor. He turned and read in their faces the answer to a question he had not even thought to ask.

"You did this?"

"I don't know," said Illyra in a dead voice. "We wanted revenge for our children . . ."

"Blessed Goddess!" breathed Lalo in disbelief.

"No—there are no gods, only Power—" Illyra's laugh scraped the edge of hysteria.

"And you let her—you helped her?" His shocked gaze turned to Gilla. "You still have other children! Didn't you *think—*"

"Did *you* think when you gave life to the Black Unicorn?" she spat back, but her voice broke. She gestured toward Latilla. "Oh, Lalo—Lalo—here is my punishment!"

"No!" he said furiously. "Wasn't losing one child enough for you? *She* hasn't sinned! Why should she suffer for our sake?"

"Strike me then!" Gilla said with a half-sob. Perhaps if he did it would take some of this dreadful pain away.

Lalo stared, and something in his face seemed to crumple. "Woman, if I could hit you I would have done it years ago." As Gilla buried her face in her hands he turned back to Illyra.

"You did this—you make it right again. I have the paints here, and the blanks for the rest of the cards. None of us will sleep tonight in any case. You will describe for me the missing cards, S'danzo, and I will paint them, and then you will read them anew!"

Illyra pushed back her heavy hair with a thin hand.
"Limner, I know what I have done," she said dully. "Take up
your paints and I will give you the designs, for all the help
that will be. I think the gift I abused has gone from me now."

Lalo shuddered, but his face remained implacable as he
went to his worktable and began to unstopper the little jars of
pigment. Gilla stared at him, for it was a face she had never
seen her husband wear before.

"The Seven of Ores is called Red Clay, the card of the
potter, the craftsman," Illyra began as Lalo picked up his
brush. Then Latilla began to whimper, and Gilla forgot to
listen to the S'danzo as she bent to comfort her child.

In the night the mobs began to drag the dead and their
possessions into the streets to burn them, but the sight of
scorching brocades or melting gilt was too much for many of
the more lawless, so the devout took to firing houses without
checking too closely to see whether anyone were left alive
inside. Both the Stepsons and the Third Commando had their
hands full trying to keep the flames from spreading into the
mercantile section of town, while Walegrin and the garrison
guarded the palace from shouting mobs who bayed for the
deaths of Prince Kadakithis and the Beysib whore. By the
time the sun rose like a red eye upon the horizon, the sky bore
a pall reminiscent of wizard weather, but this evil came
wholly from mortals, or perhaps from mortality.

When Lalo finally woke, it took a few disoriented moments for him to realize that his head was throbbing and his
neck stiff not from fever, but from having slept slumped over
his worktable, and that the gray light that filtered through the
curtain was not the cool dimness of dawn, but a dreadful
noon. With a groan he straightened, blinked, and looked
around him.

On the worktable before him were the last of the S'danzo
cards. Illyra lay still in her chair. For one shocked moment
Lalo thought she was dead, and realized that the horror and
hatred he had felt the night before had drained away, leaving
only a hollow despair. Gilla sat by the couch like a monu-
ment, but at his movement her eyes opened, red-rimmed in
her ravaged face.

"How—" The word came out as a croak, and Lalo swallowed, trying to make his voice obey him.

"She's still alive," said Gilla, "but she still burns." She looked at him apprehensively.

Lalo made it to his feet, remembering how he had felt when the Black Unicorn leaped off the wall, and went to her. The Unicorn had been the child of his pride, and it was only one, though the worst, of his sins over the years. But Gilla's only sin had been born of her despair. Perhaps it made them fit mates for each other, but he could hardly say that to her now.

Instead he rested his arm across Gilla's massive shoulders and began to softly stroke her hair. Latilla moved restlessly in her feverish sleep, then stilled again. She was flushed, and it seemed to him that her cheekbones had grown more prominent, so that he saw the skull beneath the skin. His arm tightened convulsively, and Gilla turned her face against his chest.

"You were right about the Unicorn," he said softly then. "But we got rid of it. We'll find some way to deal with this, too."

Gilla straightened and looked up at him, her eyes luminous with unshed tears. "Oh, you ridiculous man! You make me ashamed for all those years when I thought I was the only one with anything to forgive. . . ." She took a deep breath and heaved herself to her feet.

"Yes, we'll do—something! But first we need to wash up and get some food!" The floor shook slightly as she strode to the door and called for the girl who had been waiting on them.

By the time they had finished eating, Lalo felt marginally more effective. In the distance the deep beat of temple drumming mingled with the confused roaring of the mob. Myrtis's servants said that the high priest of Ils had agreed to perform a sacrifice for Dyareela when sunset came. It was hoped that the scent of bull's blood would appease the goddess and the mob. If it did not, the combined might of the garrison, the Stepsons, and the 3rd Commando might be insufficient to prevent royal blood from running where the bull's blood had flowed, and with such provocation, the Emperor was unlikely to wait until the New Year to "pacify" what was left of the town.

Lalo sat before his worktable, eyeing the bright array of cards. It was remarkable, considering his physical and mental state the night before, that they looked like anything at all. But the vision of the seeress had flowed through his hands, and he knew that these cards were artistically far superior to the ones the S'danzo had possessed before. He suppressed the flicker of pride that the thought gave him. He had no memory of painting them—any praise belonged to the power that had impelled his hand. And prettiness would not matter if they could not use the cards to undo the damage they had done.

"I tried to do a reading while you were both asleep," Illyra said when the girl had taken the dishes away. "It's no use, Gilla. The cards kept returning to the pattern we made with them before."

"Then we'll have to try something else," Gilla nodded determinedly.

"Lay them out in another pattern," said Lalo, "a pattern of healing this time."

"I did that too," said the S'danzo helplessly. "But there was no power in it. I could tell."

They did it again, and then another time, but Illyra had told them truly. The cards were no more than pretty pictures making a pattern on the tablecloth. The bright colors glowed mockingly in the lurid afternoon sun.

Illyra was sponging Latilla's face and chest. Lalo sighed, and cut the pack again. The card on top of the deck now was the Archway, a massive gate whose keystone was carved with an arcane symbol whose meaning even Illyra did not know. Beyond it was a mass of greenery, perhaps a garden. Lalo let his gaze unfocus, trying desperately to think of something else to do. Green vibrated in his vision, and he was abruptly aware of a tantalizing sense of familiarity.

He blinked, looked at the card again, and rubbed his eyes. With normal vision he could see nothing, but there had been something. . . . Gilla leaned forward to pour more water into his glass, and the movement of her arm triggered a sudden memory of a white arm pouring wine of Carronne from a crystal flagon into a goblet of gold—it had been the arm of Eshi, in the country of the gods.

"Lalo, what are you looking at?" Gilla asked.

"I'm not sure," he said slowly. "But I think I know where I might find out. . . ."

"You can't go outside," said Illyra in alarm. "Listen!" Even from the Street of the Red Lanterns they could hear the tumult in the city, and Lalo shuddered.

"I don't mean to," he said simply. "I'm going to go inward, through there—" He pointed at the archway in the card. Illyra stared at him, bewildered, but in Gilla's face understanding began to dawn, and with it fear.

"If you mean to go into trance then I'm going with you to

make sure you remember to come back again!" she said tartly. "I don't have the means to compel you the way I did before."

Lalo had no idea what she meant by that, but there was no time to question her now. "If you can, surely you have the right to," he told her, "if either of us can get there that way," he went on, doubting his own intuition suddenly. He propped the card up against the flagon so that they could both see it, and pointed at the other chair.

It creaked as Gilla eased into it. She settled herself, her hands clasped firmly in her lap, then looked at Illyra. "If this works, don't let anyone disturb us, and in the name of your own Lillis, watch over my child!"

The S'danzo's throat worked, then she nodded, her fingers tightening on the damp cloth she held in her hand. "May your goddess bless you," she whispered brokenly, then turned quickly to Latilla again.

"Well?" Gilla's gaze held his. Lalo took a deep breath.

"Randal taught me a little about this," he said slowly. "Make your breathing regular, and try to relax. Look at the card until you have it memorized, then change the focus of your eyes and try to look *through* the gateway into the place beyond. When you can see it, push your awareness toward it and through . . ." He looked at her dubiously. The procedure had seemed reasonable enough when the wizard described it, but he had the awful feeling that he was about to look like a fool.

Then Latilla whimpered again, and Gilla reached out to grip his hand. Lalo took another breath and fixed his gaze on the archway.

Once more the riot of greenery swirled through Lalo's vision. He fought the compulsion to blink, to refocus, and tried to imagine he held a paintbrush in his hand. *See,* he told himself, controlling his breathing. Now all he could feel was the warm pressure of Gilla's hand. Would she keep him earthbound? But even as he thought it, the confusion before him began to resolve into something—green leaves fluttering in the sunlight. . . . He launched himself toward them, and then the garden was all around him, and he was through.

For a moment all Lalo knew was the feel of that springy turf beneath his feet, and the scent of air that was like no breeze that had ever blown through Sanctuary. Then he became aware that someone was beside him. He turned and jerked away, seeing the goddess he had painted on Molin

Torchholder's wall. She smiled, and the face of the goddess
was suddenly that of the golden-haired girl he had courted in
the spring of the world, and then both of them were the face of
Gilla, always and only Gilla, who was looking at him as she
had after the first time they had ever made love.

But the garden, when he looked again, was by no means so
perfect as he had remembered it. Parts of the lawn were with-
ered, while other sections showed the sickly yellow of flood-
ing. The same was true of the oak trees, and some of the
leaves were blotched with a blight like leprosy.

"It's here, too," said Gilla, "the same thing that's been
happening to Sanctuary!"

Lalo nodded, wondering which level had started the trouble. But that didn't matter—what he needed was to learn the
cure. He took her hand and they began to pick their way
across the mottled grass beneath the trees.

After a time Lalo found the pool and the waterfall. But the
clearing where he had feasted with the Ilsig gods was empty
now. Lalo's heart sank within him. If even the Otherworld was
empty, then the magic of Sanctuary had been destroyed indeed! Perhaps the S'danzo were right, and the gods were only
delusions of men. But even as that thought passed through his
mind, his lips were moving in prayer.

"Father Ils, hear me, Shipri All-Mother have mercy! Not
for my sake, but for your people—"

"And for the sake of my child!" came Gilla's voice in his
ear.

A little wind gusted around them and plucked a leaf from
one of the oak trees. Lalo watched, fascinated, as it spiraled
downward and settled at last in the breast of Gilla's gown.
Then a new voice spoke from behind them.

"Why do you call on Ils and Shipri? This is the Face the
people of Sanctuary pray to now!"

Lalo jerked around, flinched as he saw what had answered
them and then stumbled over his own feet, trying to get between it and Gilla. But she had always been broadly built and
big-boned, and she gripped his arm and stayed beside him.

The Thing that had spoken looked on his confusion and
laughed. Lalo stared, realizing in horror that it was female,
wrapped in scorched robes from which pale smoke rose in
ghostly trails, with singed hair that lifted as the wind caught it
and sent up little spurts of flame. It—Her—face glowed like
a lantern, as if the fire that burned Her lay within, and the

features of that face were contorted in a demon's mask.

"Dyareela," he breathed in appalled recognition.

The goddess responded with a terrible smile. "That is one of the names by which men pray to Me, it is true. But it was you who first called Me, daughter." She beckoned to Gilla. "How shall I reward you?"

"Demon, go away!" hissed Gilla in revulsion.

Dyareela laughed. "Still you do not understand! I neither come nor go—I *am!* Only my Faces change . . ."

"Then change your Face again," groaned Lalo.

"Three weddings were promised, and one of them royal, to redeem the land! I would have come to them as Lady of love's fire! But Sanctuary has chosen to see Me otherwise!" Wind whirled around them, and when the falling leaves touched the hair of the goddess they burst into flame.

"Be beautiful, blessed Lady, please be beautiful for us now!" There were tears in Gilla's voice and in her eyes.

"Daughter, in this place I am only a reflection, as you are only a dream. Your words have no power over Me here! If I am to bless you I must be invoked in the world of men!"

The sky seemed to be darkening, and the only thing Lalo could see was the goddess, who glowed like a demon-lantern at the Feast of the Dead.

"We tried," wailed Gilla, "but the cards had no power!"

"The cards *never* had power; they only focused yours. Make the Great Marriage in Sanctuary as has been promised Me! Then I will show you my fair Face again!"

Wind and darkness howled around them. Flaming leaves whirled away and seeded the barren night with stars. Suddenly the goddess was gone, and the oak grove, and even the solid ground on which they had been standing. Buffeted and blown, Lalo lost all sense of who he was and whence he had come, and as awareness left him, the last thing he knew was the firm grip of Gilla's hand

Gilla fell down a long tunnel of darkness into her body again. An eternity later, she tried to move. She was stiff, and so heavy, when she had been moving as lightly as . . . She groaned and opened her eyes.

"Thank the gods!" said Illyra. In the flickering light of the lamps she looked worn and hollow-eyed.

"I thought you didn't believe in them," muttered Gilla. She

was still holding onto Lalo's hand. Carefully she opened her fingers, and set it on his lap with the other. He was still unconscious, but his breathing had quickened. *In a moment,* she thought, *he will waken, and what then?*

The S'danzo rubbed at her forehead. "Right now I'll believe in anything that might help us. I've been listening to the procession—it's gone all around the city and must be nearly back to the ruins of the temple by now. We don't have much time." She lifted her head and stared at Gilla. *"Will* it help us? You both went out like doused candles, but were you asleep, or did you actually get somewhere?"

Lalo shuddered, and opened his eyes. "We got there. We saw the goddess—*a* goddess . . ." He shuddered again. "She's angry. She doesn't want a sacrifice. She wants Shu-sea and Prince Kittycat to get married!" He began to laugh with a soft edge of hysteria that had Gilla instantly on her feet and holding him until the tremors that shook him faded again. At last he pressed his face into her broad breast and groaned. "We've failed," he whispered. "We've failed."

Gilla held him against her and stared over his head, seeing in her mind's eye the glorious young man with whom she had walked in the Otherworld. He had been as handsome as a king. She remembered how lightly she had moved beside him and wondered suddenly, *How did he see me?*

After a moment she focused on the still figure on the couch, and then on Illyra again. "How has Latilla been?" she asked.

The S'danzo's eyes were bright with tears. "She has passed the restless stage of the fever. The sleep she's in now is deeper than yours was. I've tried to cool her, but the cloths dry from the heat of her body as soon as I put them on her. I've tried, Gilla, I've *tried!*" She bowed her head and covered her face with her hands.

"I know you have, Illyra," said Gilla gently. "And now I must ask you to try just a little longer while I do something harder. I must try to make the goddess beautiful."

Lalo pulled away and sat looking at her in wonder as Gilla went over to the bed and kissed her daughter gently on the brow. Then she moved majestically to the door and called for Myrtis.

The madam's eyes widened as she listened to Gilla's requests, but after a moment she nodded, and her eyes began to glow. "Yes, it is true, though there's hardly a respectable woman in Sanctuary who would understand what you mean. Certainly I never expected that *you . . .*" Myrtis left that comment unfinished as Gilla glared at her, smiled, and turned away to give orders to her girls.

I never expected to do anything like this either, thought Gilla, smoothing her hands over the massive swell of her bosom and along the mighty curve of her thigh. *But by the breasts of the goddess I am going to try!*

Sitting in the bath with giggling slave-girls fussing over her, Gilla knew the idea had been ridiculous. She had grown-up children, her blood had ceased to answer the call of the moon two years ago, and Lalo was rarely more than a companionable body in her bed anymore. When she had gotten into the marble bathing pool, her bulk had sent scented water slopping over the side in a tidal wave.

She tried to imagine Lalo's balding head and skinny legs being scrubbed by the girls in the other pool, and thought that he must look even stranger in the midst of all this splendor than she did. She wondered why in the name of the gods he had agreed to it. But of course that *was* why—because of the gods, or one of them, anyway, and because of a picture that he had once sworn she had been his model for.

And then she had a marvelous billowing garment of diaphanous sea-green silk on her back and a garland of sweet-smelling garden herbs on her damp hair, and singing girls were lighting her way to a chamber where the scent of burning sandalwood covered the reek of smoke from distant fires.

The room was paneled in cedar, and behind gauze curtains the windows were screened by marble filigree. What part of it was not taken up by the bed was covered by thick carpet and silken cushions, and there was a rosewood table with a flagon and two goblets of gold. But of course the bed was the point of it all, and Lalo was already waiting beside it, carrying off with more presence than she would have believed possible, a long caftan of jade green brocaded in gold.

He seemed to be memorizing the pattern of the carpet. Gilla thought, *If he laughs at me I will murder him!*

And then he lifted his head, and in his worn face, his eyes were glowing as they had when he looked on her in the Otherworld. Behind her, Gilla could hear the rustle of silk and a giggle cut short as the slave girls backed out of the room. The door clicked shut.

"Health to you, my lord and husband." Gilla's voice shook

only a little as she said the words.

Lalo licked dry lips, then stepped carefully to the table and poured wine. He offered her one of the goblets. "Health to you," he said, lifting the other, "my wife and my queen."

The goblets rang as they touched. Gilla felt the sweet fire of the wine burning down her throat to her belly, and another kind of fire kindling in her flesh as she met his eyes.

"Health to all the land," she whispered, "and the healing fire of love. . . ."

Torches painted the rubble of Dyareela's temple with their lurid glare, dyeing with an even deeper crimson the blood-splattered robes of the priests and the severed head of the sacrifice. The sweet stink of blood hung heavy in the air, and the line of soldiers watched with wary eyes the chanting, murmuring masses of humanity who had crowded into the ruins to see it. The priests were praying now, straining grotesquely toward a darkness of cloud or smoke that blotted out the stars.

"Whatever they're expecting, they'd better get on with it," said a man of the Third Commando. "That kind of babbling won't hold this lot long. They've seen blood, and they'll want more of it soon!"

The man on his right nodded. "Stupid of Kittycat to allow it—anyone could see what would hap—" His words faded to a mumble as Sync's stony eye passed along the line, but his companion heard him add, with a faith that in the circumstances was touching, "This wouldn't of happened if Tempus was here."

"Dyareela, Dyareela, hear, oh, *hear!*" chanted the crowd. *Hear, hear,* or maybe it was *fear, fear,* echoed from shattered pillars and walls. "Have *mercy*—" came the drawn out cry. A shiver of eagerness ran through the crowd and the soldiers stiffened, knowing what was coming now.

Torches flickered wildly in a great gust of wind, a damp wind that came from the sea. The wind gusted again, and the scene grew perceptibly less lurid as several of the torches were blown out. A priest grabbed helplessly as his headdress went sailing away, and the crowd was abruptly distracted from its bloodlust by the struggle for gold thread and jewels. Then somewhere out to sea, thunder rumbled, and the remaining torches were doused by the first splatterings of rain.

Rain hissed in the embers of burned buildings and rinsed

the ashes from the roofs of those houses which had survived.
It scoured the streets and ran clear in the gutters, filled the
sewers and flushed their festering contents down the river out
to sea. It washed the reek of blood from the air, and left
behind it the clean scent of rain. Men who moments before
had growled like beasts stood with faces upturned to the suddenly beneficent heavens, and found the water that ran down
their faces mingled inexplicably with tears.

Grumbling, the priests scrambled to get their finery under
cover, while the crowd dispersed like drops from a fountain,
and presently the bemused soldiery were allowed to break
ranks and seek the shelter of their barracks at last.

All that night the clean rain pattered on the roofs of the
town. Illyra opened her window to let the cool air in and,
returning to Latilla, felt the moisture of sudden perspiration on
the child's tight skin. Her own eyes blurring, she heaped blan-
kets around her, then went fearfully to Lalo's worktable. The
cards fluttered like live things in the damp wind. With beating
heart, the S'danzo began to lay out the Pattern again.

In the morning, the sun rose on a town washed clean.

And there was a new bud on Gilla's peach tree.

SANCTUARY IS FOR LOVERS

Janet and Chris Morris

Down on Wideway by the docks, where a warehouse destroyed by fire was being rebuilt by fish-eyed Beysibs to house a glass-making enterprise as alien as the fish-folk who funded it, a big man in tattered trail gear sat alone on a mud-colored horse and watched the storm roll in from the sea.

Thunderstorms in Sanctuary during summer weren't uncommon. This one, loud as a wounded bear and dark as a witch's eye, cleared the dockside of folk as he watched from shadows thrown by two overhanging roofs: Thunderstorms, these days in a revolution-wracked thieves' world suddenly bereft of the magic that had driven it, meant that a new and feral god called Stormbringer was abroad.

The big man, on the horse whose muddy disguise did nothing to hide its extraordinary girth or the intelligence in its eyes, cared nothing for the god behind the storm—if indeed the chaotic principle named Stormbringer could rightfully be called one.

The man cared more than he wished to admit for that god's daughter—for Jihan, called Froth Daughter, primal expression of Stormbringer's lust for wind and wave, who was betrothed to Randal, the Tysian wizard, and trapped here until the marriage either was consummated or renounced. He'd cared enough to return to Sanctuary, though it was doomed by imperial decree and the folly of its own selfish inhabitants—doomed to eradication at New Year's, when the grace period the new Rankan Emperor, Theron, had given Prince/Governor Kadakithis would have elapsed without order being restored here.

Then the Emperor's troops would come in a multitude—"Even though it be a soldier for every tramp, an arrow for every rebel, a legion if necessary," in Theron's words—and the thieves' world would be a fools' paradise no longer.

Pacifying refractory towns was a passion of Theron's. Pacifying wizard-ridden Sanctuary might once have been an impossibility, but not now: The feuding witches and the greedy priests had, between them, managed to destroy both Nisibisi Globes of Power before spring had sprung, leaving Sanctuary's magical fabric rent and its wards weakened.

At long last, Sanctuary had become what Tempus's fighters of the Sacred Band had long called it: well and truly damned. That this damnation had come from the greedy power plays of its low-lifes, rather than from the pillar of fire which had sprung from an uptown house to affront the heavens, didn't surprise Tempus.

The fact that no one in town save the weakened wizards and a handful of impotent priests knew the truth of it—how Sanctuary had destroyed its own manna and been deserted by the more prudent of its pantheon of gods—*did* surprise even the unflappable Riddler who now headed his horse into the storm and northeast toward the Maze.

He felt no twinge of nostalgia for the old days, when he'd ridden these streets alone as a palace Hell-Hound in Kadakithis's employ, testing the prince's mettle for the Rankan interests who eventually chose Theron in Kadakithis's stead. But he felt a spark of regret when he passed the docks from which Nikodemos, his favorite among the mercenary fighters who followed him, had departed seaward, bound for the Bandaran Islands with two godchildren who might have been Sanctuary's only hope.

As Niko might have been the only hope of a man who'd taken the name Tempus when he realized that his curse caused time itself to pass him by. But hopes were for Sanctuarites, the children of the damned, the dark Ilsigi whom Rankan and Beysib oppressors alike called Wrigglies, and for women touched with Nisibisi wizard blood who sucked purer blood in Sanctuary's steamy summer nights—for anyone but him.

Tempus was relieved of duty here, of all responsibility save what his conscience might impose. And it had brought him back here only to complete preparations under way since winter's end, when Theron had offered him a commission to explore the unknown east and immunity from prosecution to any he chose to hire for the venture.

So once again, and in the east during the trek to come, he would have his Stepsons, the Sacred Band of paired fighters and certain single mercenaries, and the 3rd Commando, Ranke's most infamous cadre, for company.

And if their imminent withdrawal from Sanctuary didn't signal and seal the town's doom, then Tempus hadn't outlived a hundred enemies and their legions. But that wasn't what made him hesitate, brought him down from the capital to ride once more through garbage-heaped streets where the lawless fought each other block by block in open revolt and man by man over matters of eye color and skin hue and heavenly affiliation.

He couldn't possibly care about Sanctuary's survival. The town itself was his enemy. Those who did not fear him for good reason, hated him on principle; those who did neither had left this dungheap long ago.

He could have left the withdrawal to Critias, the Stepsons' first officer, and to Sync, the 3rd Commando's line commander. He could have waited in imperial Ranke's palace with Theron, interviewing chart makers and seamen who told of dragons in the eastern sea with emerald eyes and of treasures in shoreline caves the like of which the Rankan Empire had never seen.

But neither Jihan nor her intended, Randal, understood that their betrothal was the result of a deal Tempus had made with Stormbringer, the Froth Daughter's father—a deal he'd struck in expediency and haste with a god known as a master trickster. Though deal it was, he was no longer certain it was prudent: He'd have use for both Jihan and Randal, the Stepsons' warrior-mage, on the eastward trek, and neither one could leave until the matter was decided.

So he was here, to yea or nay the thing, to make sure that Randal, a Sacred Band partner and one of his men, was not trapped in hell's own bowels against his will, and that Jihan's father did not blow storms of confusion in his daughter's eyes to keep her where He had chosen to abide.

He had come in disguise, as best he was able. His form was heroic in proportion and his face resembled that of a god once known in Sanctuary, but banished now: High-browed and honey-bearded, that face looked upon the gutted ways of the warehouse district with all the disgust three centuries and more of life could impart.

It was the face of Vashanka, now called the Hidden God, that Tempus wore tonight: Selfish and proud, full of war and death, it was the face of Sanctuary itself.

It made him feel at home here, as did the storm descending. In Sanctuary, self-interest never flagged; his presence here upon pressing, private business, was proof of that.

Turning up Shadow Street toward the Maze, he saw deserted checkpoints of some faction who claimed everything from Lizard's Way to the Governor's warehouses as its own.

And because that faction was said to be Zip's Popular Front for the Liberation of Sanctuary (PFLS), as unpopular now as was Zip himself, Tempus reined the horse left on Red Clay Street to reconnoiter despite the gusts and darkening sky and thunderous promise of rain that made the Trôs horse under him shiver and throw its muzzle skyward.

He'd never exchanged a civil word with Zip, whom some said had caused far too much of the springtime carnage—whom Crit said had attempted murder and tried to blame the affair on Tempus's own daughter, Kama.

And since the target of the murderous attack had been Straton, Critias's Sacred Band partner, the pair had teams out night and day, even in the midst of the Stepsons' preparations to withdraw—teams seeking to even the score with Zip's eyes and tongue: an old Band prescription for curing traitors.

Lighting flared, a sheet sky-wide that banished darkness even on Shadow Street, so that Tempus saw backlit figures skulking from garbage heap to doorway in his wake.

This was PFLS territory all right.

The rain that accompanied a peal of thunder so loud it made the Trôs horse flatten its ears and lower its head cared nothing for whom it wet or whom it unmasked: Both Tempus and his horse were only desultorily disguised—the horse with berry juice and trail mud and its rider with dyes no better.

The rain bounced fetlock high on cobbles and ran down the Riddler's oilskin mantle to his sharkskin-hilted sword, where it formed rivulets like spilled blood and just as red from the dye it washed.

The specter of the man and horse (both too large and too well muscled for Sanctuary's own, both streaming water red as blood and splashing it behind, as the man called the Riddler loped his horse, oblivious to the torrent and the spray the horse's hooves kicked up, down the center of Red Clay Street) was one to stop a superstitious heart and make a criminal seek cover.

Yet at the corner of West Gate Street, where the sudden downpour swept seaward to the wharves down the slope so deep and fast that rats and cats and pieces of less recognizable flesh were carried along in its currents as if the White Foal

River had changed its course, three men stepped out from cover, barring his path, knee deep in water, crossbows drawn and blades unsheathed.

A crossbow, in this wind so fierce it blotted out the Trôs's snorts of warning, and in a rain so dense no cat-gut or woman's-hair bowstring could be dry, would shoot awry.

Tempus knew it, and so did the three who stood there, daring him to ride them down.

He considered it, though he'd sought a confrontation, annoyed by the boys with sweatbands around their foreheads and weapons better than street toughs ought to have.

The Trôs, having more sense and being a larger target, stopped still and craned its neck, imploring him with liquid eyes to remember why he'd come here, not just take an opportunity luck offered and waste it to vent some spleen and make his presence known.

Still, this sort should have enough sense to fear him.

That none did, that one stepped forward and said in a thick voice with a trace of gutter accent, "Looking for me, big fella? All your bugger boys are," gave the Riddler time enough to realize that, while he'd been looking for the rebel called Zip, Zip had also been looking for him.

A noise behind, and then more sounds of moving men, gave the mounted soldier and his horse a good estimate of the odds without either turning to see the dozen rebels climbing down from rooftops and up from tunnels and out of cellar windows.

Tempus's skin crawled: Pain wasn't something he sought, and with no death at the end of it, he could suffer infinitely more than other men. But it was his pride that leant him pause: The last thing he needed was to be taken hostage by the PFLS and held to ransom. Crit would never let him forget it.

And the result for the PFLS would then be eradication— total and complete, not the minor harrassment Crit had time to field while busy with a hundred other tasks as he got two fighting units ready to depart a town that had precious little else between it and total anarchy.

So Tempus said to the foremost fighter, "If you're Zip, I am," and slid off his horse, making fast its reins on its pommel: Whatever Tempus was worth, the Trôs was irreplaceable, and would make for the Stepsons' barracks on a whistled command.

But once the Trôs, with teeth and hooves and blood lust

spewing carnage in its wake, made for the barracks beyond the Swamp of Night Secrets, then the die for each and every rebel child was cast.

And children these were, the Riddler realized as he stepped closer: The boy out in front of his compatriots was well under thirty.

The youth held his ground, flickering a hand-signal that brought his troops in closer and made Tempus reassess the discipline and training of the rabble closing on him.

Then the Riddler remembered that this boy had had some little congress with Kama, Tempus's daughter, a woman who was as good a covert actor as Critias and as good a soldier as Sync.

The boy nodded a crisp assent, then added, "That's me, old man. What's this about? You didn't 'accidentally' cross our lines. We won't make peace with Jubal's bluemasks—or with that Bey-licking Kadakithis, who's sold the Ilsigs out twice over." The youth widened his stance and Tempus remembered what Sync had said of him: "The boy's got nearly enough balls, but they override his brains."

So Tempus responded, "No, not accidentally. I want to talk to you . . . alone."

"This is as 'alone' as I'm likely to get with you—you're not half so fetching as your daughter."

Tempus locked his fingers firmly on his swordbelt, lest they cause trouble on their own, seeking a neck to wring. Then he said, "Zip . . . as in zero, nothing, zilch . . . right? Well, despite that, I'll give you a piece of wisdom, and a chance—because my daughter thinks you're worth it." That wasn't true—or at least he didn't think so; he'd never spoken to Kama about Zip: She'd earned the right to choose her own bed-partners, and more.

The flat-faced youth, standing in the rain, barked a laugh. "Your *daughter* lies in with Nisibisi wizards—or at least with Molin Torchholder, who's tainted with Nisi blood. Her idea of who's worth what ain't mine."

The rabble behind and around laughed, but uneasily. The Trôs at Tempus's side pawed the ground and pulled upon its reins to loose them. He put out a hand to soothe the horse and a dozen blades or more cleared their scabbards with a *snick* audible even through the pelting rain, while the three crossbows he could see were centered on his chest.

"The wisdom is: Sanctuary is for lovers, not fighters, this

season. Make peace among you, or the Empire will grind the
lot into dust, and bury your flesh with corn to make it grow
tall."

"Crap, old man. I'd heard you were tough—not like the
rest," Zip spat. "But it's the same garbage I hear from them.
Tell it to your troops—the Whoresons and the Turd Commando: They're the ones causing all the grief."

Tempus's patience was near an end. "Boy, mark me: I'll
call them off you for a week—seven days. In it, you meet
with the other factions and hammer out some agreement, or by
New Year's Day, the PFLS won't be even a memory. Nor will
you live even that long, to verify it."

There was a silence, and in it someone muttered, "Let's
kill the bastard," and someone else whispered back, "We
can't—don't you know who that *is?*"

Tempus peered through the downpour and watched the flat
face before him, emotionless and cold with rain streaking
down it. There was strength in the youth, like the Enlibar steel
some had thought would make a difference here—but, like
the steel, Zip's strength was too little and too late.

Ageless eyes shocked against mortal eyes too sure of their
doom and unwilling to seek favor. But another thing passed
between them: The weariness of the young fighter, hunted by
too many and willing to die against sheer numbers and superior force of arms, had turned to hopelessness; that despair
met its echo in the gaze of the fabled immortal who went from
war to war and empire to empire, taking life and teaching the
wisest something about the spirit's triumph over death.

Tempus, who had created, trained, and fielded the Stepsons, was offering a moratorium, some forgotten hope, where
an ultimatum had been expected.

There was something in Zip's tone when the boy answered,
"Yeah, a week. All right. All I can say is the PFLS will try—I
can't speak for the others. It's got to be enough. Or—"

Tempus had to interrupt. A threat uttered in front of the
youth's followers would be binding. "Enough, for you and
yours. What they sow, they'll reap. You can come out of this
with more than you expect, Zip—an imperial pardon, maybe
a profession, and do what you do best for the good of the town
you say you love."

"The town I'll die for, one way or the other," Zip murmured, because he'd understood what Tempus was saying and

what had been unsaid in their met glance, and wanted the Riddler to know it, before he waved his men back without another word from Tempus.

It took only moments for the intersection where Red Clay Street met West Gate to seem deserted once again. It took no longer to mount the Trôs and head it toward Lizard's Way.

Tempus was thinking, as he rode the Trôs past a pile of refuse that undoubtedly hid at least one hostile youngster, that what Zip might gain, could he do the impossible and show progress toward peace—a coalition of rebel forces, a cease-fire committee, or even a pacification program—was more than the boy's wildest dream: a home.

There were no forces to replace the Stepsons and the 3rd. The Rankan army garrison was just that—Rankan. The Stepsons' barracks, won at so great a cost in life and love five years past, would be deserted; the job the Sacred Band did, undone. There would be a handful of Hell-Hounds to stand against Theron's battalions, Beysib oppressors, and the crime-lords of the town.

If Zip would only let him, Tempus was going to solve a number of problems that had seemed insoluble only minutes before, and do the youth the only favor one man can do another: Give him a start on solving his own problems, a place to stand, a world to win—a fresh start.

If Tempus could keep his own people from killing the charismatic young rebel leader in the meantime. And *if* Zip knew a last chance when he saw one. And *if*, in Sanctuary, where hate and fear passed for respect, Zip hadn't made so many enemies that, no matter what Tempus did, the boy's assassination wasn't as sure as the next thunderclap of Stormbringer's welcome-weather.

When that thunderclap did come, Tempus was already cantering the Trôs down Lizard's Way, headed for the Vulgar Unicorn, where a fiend named Snapper Jo tended bar and word could be spread fast, when a man had rumors he wanted on the wing.

Snapper Jo was a fiend of the gray-and-warty-skinned, snaggle-toothed variety. His shock of orange hair stood out every which way from his head and his eyes looked in both directions at once, causing distress to certain patrons who wondered which orb to fix on when they earnestly begged for credit or leave to pass upstairs, where drugs and women could be had.

Snapper's job of bartending in the day at the Vulgar Unicorn was his most prized accomplishment—save the winning of his freedom.

He'd been the summoned minion of Roxane, the Nisibisi witch called Death's Queen. But his mistress had freed him, after her fashion . . . or, at least, she'd not come around lately to order him to this or that foul depradation.

The fact that Snapper thought of his former existence as a witch's servant as depradacious was central to the fiend's new outlook on life. Here, among the Wrigglies and the mendicants and the whores, he was trying desperately for acceptance.

And he was managing. No one teased him about his looks or shrank from him in fear. They were civil, in the manner of humans, and they treated him as an equal, to the extent that anyone here ever treated anyone else so.

And, in his heart of hearts, Snapper Jo wanted above all to be accepted by the humans—perhaps, someday, *as* a human. For was not humanity something in the heart, not on the surface?

Snapper Jo wanted to believe it so, in this weird inn where pop-eyed Beysibs were hated marginally more than blond and handsome Rankans, where dark skin and uneven limbs and snaggle teeth weren't disfigurements; where everyone was equally oppressed by the wizards from the Mageguild and the priests from uptown.

So when the tall, heroic man with the fearsome countenance, who seemed to be seeping blood—or bloody rain—from every pore, came in and spoke familiarly in a gravelly voice, saying, "Snapper, I need a favor," the day bartender drew himself up to his full height—almost equal to the stranger's—puffed out his spoon-chest, and replied, "Anything, my lord—except credit, of course: house rules."

This, too, was part of being human: caring about little stamped circles of copper, gold, or silver, even though their value was only as great as the demand of the humans who fought and died over them.

But this big human wanted only information: He'd come to Snapper to consult.

The stranger said, while around him the bar cleared for a man's length on either side and behind him certain patrons skulked out into the storm and two serving wenches tiptoed into the back room, "I need to know of your former mistress —did Roxane ever find her way out of Tasfalen's house uptown? Has anyone seen her? You, of all . . . persons . . . would know if she's about."

"No, friend," said Snapper, who used the word friend too much because he'd just recently learned its meaning, "she's not been seen or heard from since the pillar of fire was doused."

The big man nodded and leaned close across the bar.

Snapper leaned in to meet him, feeling somehow special and very favored to be having this conversation with so formidable a human before all the patrons in the Unicorn. Nearly nose to nose, he began to notice, through his right-looking eye, some things about the man which were naggingly familiar: the hooded, narrow eyes that watched him with hot intensity, the thin slash of a mouth whose lips twisted with some private humor.

Then the man said, "And Ischade, the vampire woman—is she well? Down at Shambles Cross? Holding court among her shades?"

"She . . ." Then memory jogged memory, and Snapper Jo raised a crop of goose bumps to complement his warts: This was the Sleepless One, the legendary fighter his former mistress had fought so long. "She . . . is, sire. Ischade . . . *is*. And will be, always. . . ."

Snapper Jo had friends among the not-really-human, the once-dead, the straddlers of the void. Ischade was not one of them, but neither was this man, whom he now knew.

As he knew why the crowd had drawn back, this rabble who knew the players in a game they joined only as pawns and never of their own accord.

Snapper tried not to cringe, but his lips formed words involuntarily, words that whistled out sing-sing, "Mur-der, mur-der, oh there'll be mur-der everywhere and Snapper's so happy without it. . . ."

"When next a Stepson or Commando comes in, instruct him to seek me at the mercenaries' hostel. And don't fail." The man called Tempus lay coins upon the bar.

Snapper could see them glitter with his left-looking eye,

but he didn't pick them up until the big man had gone, leaving behind only creaking floorboards stained ruddy to prove he'd been there at all.

Then the fiend called one of the serving wenches from the kitchen and gave the girl, whom he loved—to the extent that a fiend can love—all the money the Riddler had left him, saying, "See, fear not. Snapper protect you. Snapper take care you. You take care Snapper, too, yes, later?" And the fiend gave a broad and lascivious grin to the woman he favored, who hid her shudder as she pocketed the equivalent of a week's wages and promised the fiend she'd warm his lonely night.

Things were tough enough, these days in Sanctuary, that you took what you could get.

"You want us to *what?*" Crit's disbelieving snort made Tempus frown.

For Tempus, the mercenaries' hostel north of town evoked memories and ghosts as bloody as the rufous walls here, hung with weapons which had won so many days. Here, Tempus and Crit had plotted to flush a witch without thought to the consequences; here, before Crit's recruitment, Tempus had put together the core of the Stepsons and taken command of Abarsis the Slaughter Priest's Sacred Band.

Here, even farther in the past, he'd burned a scarf belonging to a woman who was his most foul curse—a scarf that had been returned to him, magically whole and full of portent; a scarf he wore again around his waist, under his armor and his chiton, as if all between his first days in Sanctuary and the present were but a bad dream.

"I want you to protect, not hunt, this Zip, for one week," Tempus repeated, then added: "If, at the end of that week, there's no cease-fire coalition, no improvement, you can go back to collecting blood-debts."

Crit was the brightest of the Stepsons, a Syrese fighter who'd taken the Sacred Band oath more than once and was now paired with Straton, who in turn was entangled with Ischade, the vampire woman who lived down by Shambles Cross.

No one wanted the Sacred Band out of Sanctuary more than Crit. And no one knew Tempus's heart better, or the specifics of what had transpired while the Emperor was in Sanctuary.

Crit pulled on his long nose and stirred his posset with a finger, staring into it as if it were a witch's scrying bowl. "You're not . . ." he said to the bowl, then looked up at Tempus. "You're not thinking about using that bunch of Zip's as some sort of Sanctuary defense force? Tell me you're not."

"I can't tell you that. Why should I? They're trained, gods know—well enough for this town, anyway. And they're tough—as tough as any we trained ought to be, which most of them are. Niko himself spent some time working with the PFLS leader. And it shouldn't matter to you who we leave in the barracks, as long as it's not Jubal. We can't have crime-lords running things—Theron was very explicit. It'll take locals to police this place, or us."

"That's what I mean: None of us will want to stay to over-see that bunch of murderers—not me, not any of mine. Prom-ise me you won't do that to me again, leave me with an impossible job and an intractable lot of disappointed fighters. The Band wants to go *with* you. I won't be able to hold them here. And Sync's commandos won't take my orders."

It wasn't like Crit to make excuses, so these weren't ex-cuses: These were points the Sacred Bander urgently wanted Tempus to consider.

"Fine. I agree. I just want to make sure that you understand that Zip is more useful alive than dead . . . for one week. And that whatever is between you and my daughter—or not," Tempus held up his hand to forestall Crit's denial, "she's en-tangled with Torchholder, who's Nisi—an enemy. We leave her here. We take Jihan and Randal if we have to drug them senseless to do it, and we get our tails out of here—yours, mine, Strat's, the Stepsons', the Third's—and that's that. We're clear of a degenerating situation. If we can leave some force or other to help Kadakithis, then we're lily-white."

"That's why you came here in person? To cobble together some stopgap that won't hold because Theron doesn't want it to? You know what he wants . . . he wants a tractable, stable Empire's anus. And with the magic screwed up, or down-graded, or whatever it is Randal's been trying to explain to me, he can get it by force of arms. I don't see a winning side for us in that kind of fight, and neither do you . . . I hope."

Tempus grinned fondly at his second-in-command: "Get

Straton disentangled, both from the witch and from his local responsibilities, and—on my explicit order—the two of you personally see that Zip manages to make his contacts. And that none of ours, the Third included, obstructs him. Then we're out of here, back to the capital with the best possible report under the circumstances. And, no, I didn't come down-country for this—I came down for Jihan's wedding: to stop it."

Randal was in the Mageguild, consorting with the nameless First Hazard, trying to make some headway casting a simple manipulative spell to turn the swampy ground between the complex's outer and inner walls to gardens, when Tempus came to call.

The First Hazard was harried, a Rankan of Randal's age who'd assumed the dignity just when it no longer was one: The Mageguild had held the populace in thrall by fear and power for time uncounted. Now that the Nisibisi power globes' destruction had made simple spells uncastable and love potions useless, now that sympathetic magic was no longer so, the Mageguild adepts feared not merely for their income.

When Sanctuary's denizens realized that no wards protected the haughty sorcerers, that spells paid for and tendered wouldn't work, that the Mageguild's collective foot had been lifted from Ilsig and Rankan neck alike, the Hazards' lives would be at risk.

So finding a way to render the grounds and walls malleable to magic was not simply an exercise: The Hazards might need an unbreachable fortress in which to hide from angry clients.

And Randal, whose magic was less affected than the local mages', who had a dream-forged *kris* at his hip and the protection of the very lord of dreams, had been called upon to aid his guild's relatives—though when the guild had been all-powerful, they had not liked the Stepsons' wizard nearly so well as now.

"It's not me, you know," Randal was trying to explain to the First Hazard, whose war name was Cat and who looked more like a Rankan noble than a practiced adept who'd earned such a name. "My magic, such as it is," Randal went on modestly, "is part curse and part dream-spawned—not dependent on whatever forces have been weakened in the south."

The Rankan adept looked at the Tysian wizard narrowly, then wondered aloud, "It's not some power play of Nisibisi origin, then? Nothing Torchholder, Roxane, and the rest of you northern wizards have dreamed up?"

Randal sneezed and wiped his freckled nose on his sleeve, ears reddening in embarrassment: "If I were so powerful as that, couldn't I rid myself of these damnable allergies?" His affliction was back, the one concomitant he'd experienced of the local adepts' distress: Pollen, birds, and especially furred creatures could bring him to a paroxysm of distress. Once he'd had a handkerchief which quelled them, and then he'd had a power which suppressed them. Now he had neither.

The First Hazard's impolitic retort was interrupted by an apprentice who burst in, saying:

"My lords Hazard, a man has breached our wards, a stranger—that is, we think so, but he's coming—up the stairs, now, and he's got his horse *with* him . . ."

The handsome First Hazard hung his head, staring at his twisting fingers in his lap, and lied to the wide-eyed apprentice, "It's a summoning. We were expecting him. Go back to your work. . . . What is it, for dinner? We'll have guests, of course—man and . . . horse."

"Dinner? It's . . ." The apprentice was a witchling girl, thick-haired, short and comely, with a small waist that accentuated breast and hips despite her shapeless beginner's robe. Her face was rosy-cheeked and heart-shaped, and Randal wondered why he'd never noticed her, then banished the thought: He was betrothed, soon to be wed to Jihan, a source of power he never mentioned in this afflicted Mageguild.

The girl, composing herself with obvious effort, said, "Parrots, fleas, and squirrel bunions, m'lords Hazard—a stew, if it pleases."

"What?" snapped the harried First Hazard. Then, when the girl covered her mouth under widening eyes, continued: "Never mind the accursed menu, get out of here. And keep everyone else away until the dinner bell. Go on, girl, *go!*"

As she scurried backwards, a clomping of hoofbeats could be heard, followed by a sound like porcelain crashing on a marble floor.

And then, through the great double doors whence the girl

had just fled, a horse and rider came.

The horseman hadn't dismounted; the horse had eyes of
fiery intelligence and pricked its ears at Randal. Its coat was
mottled, red and black and gray, but there was no mistaking it:
It was the Trôs horse of his commander.

Through a fit of sneezing he miserably endured, Randal
hurried forward, saying, "My lord commander, welcome,
welcome."

And the First Hazard, Cat, behind him, uttered a curse
which bounced around the room in a gray and sickly pall
until, once Tempus had dismounted, the Trôs horse flattened
its ears at the half-manifested ectoplasm and kicked it to
pieces.

"Hazard," said the Riddler to Randal, "and Hazard," to
Cat. "Would you leave us, First Hazard? My wizard and I
need to talk."

"Your wizard" said Cat, still reflexively acting as powerful
as he'd once been. Then his color drained as he remembered
his circumstances and put two and two together. "Oh yes,
your wizard. I see, my lord Tempus. Dinner will be at sundown, if you'd grace us. I'm sure we can find some...
carrots... for your... mount."

Not a word about the desecration of the Mageguild by a
horse, not a single additional attempt to regain control where
all attempts were useless: Cat just chewed his lip.

Even though Randal's eyes were already watering, he felt a
deep and abiding sadness for the handsome young First Hazard, although in former times he had wished, more than anything, to be possessed of so fine a form and face and bloodline
as the Rankan who scurried out of his own sanctum so that
Randal and his commander could confer in private.

It was what you were, not how you looked, that mattered
these days in Sanctuary. And Randal was the only warrior-
wizard in a town that soon would value warriors much more
than wizards.

"You need me, commander?" Randal said, trying to speak
clearly despite the clogging of his nose which proximity to the
Trôs horse was causing.

"Yes, I do, Randal." Tempus dropped the Trôs's reins and
it stood, groundtied, while the big fighter approached the
small, slight wizard, put an arm across his narrow shoulders,
and walked with him toward the First Hazard's purple alcove.

"I need your help. I need your presence. I need your whole attention—now, and always."

Randal felt pride course through him, felt himself grow inches taller, felt his neck flush with joy. "You have it, Riddler, now and always—you know that. I took the Sacred Band oath. I have not forgotten."

Niko had, seemingly, but not even that cloud could block out the light of Tempus's favor—not, at any rate, completely, Randal told himself.

"Nor have we. The Band sets out for Ranke soon, there to meet with Niko and trek east. We want you on that journey, Randal—as a Sacred Bander, purely."

"Purely? I don't understand. It was Niko who broke the pairbond, not—"

"This is not about Niko. It's about Jihan."

"Oh. *Oh*." Randal slipped out from under the Riddler's arm, its weight suddenly unbearable. "That. She . . . well, it wasn't my idea, the marriage. You must know that. I'm not even—good—with women. And she's . . . demanding." The words came out in a rush, now that there was finally someone to tell who would understand the problem. "I've put her off so far, explaining that I can't . . . you know . . . until we're wed. But I'll lose so much . . . power, and there's precious little of that around, these days. She says she'll make up for it, through her father, but I'm not god-bound, I'm bound in—"

"Other ways, I know. Randal, I think I've a solution that might serve to get you off the hook, if you'll help me."

"Oh, Riddler, I'd be so grateful. She's—no offense—more your sort of problem than mine. If you could just get me away from her, as long as it's not taken ill by the Band. I'll sneak away, I'll meet you in Ranke, I'll—"

"No sneaking away, Randal," said Tempus through lips that had parted to bare his teeth.

That smile was one all Stepsons knew. Randal said dumbly, "We can't . . . hurt her—sir. No sneaking away? Then how . . . ?"

"With your permission, Randal, I'm going to woo her away from you—steal your bride from under your very nose."

"Per*mission!*" Oh, Tempus, I'd be so grateful—so everlastingly and abidingly grateful. . . ."

"I have it, then?"

"What? Permission? By the Writ and the devils who love

me, yes! Woo away! And may the—"

"Just your permission will be enough, Randal. Let's not bring any powers into this whose response we can't foresee, let alone control."

The woman was walking alone in the garden while, within the manse beyond, a civilized uptown party was under way. Her hair was blond and curly, bound up in the fashion noblewomen in the capital had adopted this season: held in place with little golden pins hafted with likenesses of Rankan gods.

He came upon her from behind and had his left arm crooked around her neck in seconds, saying only, "Hold, I'm not here to hurt you," while within him a god who shouldn't have been there stirred to wakefulness, stretched, and urged otherwise.

Ignoring the obscene and increasingly attractive suggestions the war-god in his head was making, he gave the woman time to realize who held her.

It didn't take long: She wasn't a typical Rankan woman of blood—no man without Tempus's supernal speed and talent could have caught her unaware.

She stiffened and, every muscle tensed so that his body began taking the god's suggestions literally, pressed back against him—the first move toward putting him off balance, ready to use her own arena-training in weight, feint, and misdirection of attention to try to escape.

"Hold," he said again. "Or suffer the consequences, Chenaya."

"Pork you, Tempus," she gritted in a surprisingly ladylike voice unsuited to the content of her words. He could feel her hands ball into fists, then relax. Behind him, people indoors chatted and clinked their goblets.

"We haven't time for that, unless you're ready." He put his free hand on her hip and spread it, moving it forward to press against her belly and slip downward, putting her in a hold she'd never come up against in a Rankan arena.

"Gods, you haven't changed, you bastard. If it's not my body—for which you'll pay more than it's worth, I assure you—what do you *want?*"

"I thought you'd never ask. It's a little matter of an attempt on Theron's life, yours, I believe—something about boarding the barge. Not a smart move for a member of a decidedly *ex*-royal family: not for you, not for Kadakithis, who'll share Theron's wrath if it's revealed who tried to feed him to the sharks, not for any of what's left of your line."

"Again, halfling, what do you want?"

There were two answers at that point in time, one of which had to do with the god in his head, who was whispering, *She is a woman, and women only understand one thing. She is a fighter. It's long since We've had a fighter. Give her to Us, and We'll be very grateful—and she will be Our willing servant. Otherwise, you cannot trust her.*

To the god in his head, he responded, *I can't trust You, never mind her.* To the woman, he said, "Chenaya, beyond the obvious, which we'll see about"—still holding her tightly enough with his elbow that a slight jerk would break her neck, he began to raise her voluminous white skirt from behind—"I want you to do something for me. There's a faction here that needs a woman whom the gods decree cannot be defeated. What I ask, I ask for Kadakithis, for the continuance of your bloodline, and for the good of Sanctuary. What the god asks, I'm afraid, is another matter." His voice was deepening, and into him was pouring all the long-held passion of Sanctuary's Lord of Rape and Pillage, Blood and Death.

She was a fighter, and god-bound. He hoped, as he began to explain the business that had brought him here and the god in him got out of hand, that she'd understand.

The sentry at the tunnel entrance to Ratfall, Zip's base camp in Downwind, was gagged and flopping in a pool of his own blood.

Zip had slipped in it, then stumbled over the body in the dusk before he realized what he'd stumbled on: Sync's calling card—the sentry's hands and feet had been lopped off.

He thanked the god whose swampy altar he still frequented that he'd come home alone as he raised up on hands and knees and, with his belt dagger, made an end to the quivering sentry's agony.

3rd Commando tactics were meant to terrify; knowing this didn't make it any easier to keep from retching. Knowing that it wouldn't have taken more than a half hour for the sentry to have completely bled out didn't help Zip's frame of mind: Sync's people were probably watching him from the adjacent ramshackle buildings Zip called his stronghold.

The 3rd Commando leader, Sync, said quietly from behind him: "Got a minute, sonny? Some people here want to talk with you."

The words weighed on Zip like burial stones and his own pulse threatened to choke him. Through the entire winter, Sync's rangers had never rousted him. The 3rd's leader had professed autonomy, pretended friendship, left Zip's PFLS to its own devices—as long as it followed an occasional suggestion from the 3rd's cold-blooded leader.

But there had been talk of an alliance then—before Theron had visited Ranke; before Zip's faction had recruited too many and developed factions within its own ranks; before some fools among them had captured Illyra, the S'danzo, and killed a S'danzo child; before an arrow aimed at Straton had been laid at Zip's doorstep; before Kama had left Zip's bed and taken up with Torchholder, the palace priest; before a falling out with Jubal over a slave girl Zip had liberated . . . before things had just gotten too damned complicated, because Zip couldn't hold the territory he'd gained across the White Foal, territory he'd never wanted, like he'd never wanted to be so damned visible (and thus targeted) as Sync's behind-the-scenes maneuvering had made him.

"*Talk* with me? You call this talk?" Zip's voice was shaking, but Sync wouldn't be able to tell whether it was with rage or fear. At that moment, Zip himself couldn't have said which. Blood was all around him, sticky and warm and smelling all too human; the corpse beside him had farted, and worse, once death loosed its bowels.

On his hands and knees in blood and shit, Zip was thinking that this was probably it—the death he'd earned, in circumstances he'd dreamed too often. He waited to see if it was a blade from behind that would do the talking.

A sandal splashed in the blood by his hand; Sync's Rankan-accented voice said, "That's right, talk. If your man here had talked before he acted, he'd be alive now." A gloved hand reached down for him; above it, a bracer with the 3rd's unit device of a rearing horse with arrows in its mouth gleamed—silver, polished, spotless, and whispering of a cruelty so legendary that even the Rankans were afraid to use the 3rd Commando.

Even Theron, who'd come to the throne by way of their swords, if rumor was truth, wanted the 3rd disbanded or under a tight rein. That was why, some said, Tempus, who had created them, had got them back: No one else could control them. Left to their own, they'd slaughter Rankan emperors one by one and auction the throne to the highest bidder—Zip had heard Sync and Kama joke about it when the three were drunk.

Zip let Sync help him up, busy trying to wipe the sticky blood from his palms. He didn't argue about the dead sentry: You didn't argue with Sync, not over something as immutable as the already-dead. You saved it for the plans that could get you killed.

The rest were emerging now: at least twenty fighters—the 3rd never traveled light.

The sight of Kama in her battle dress, with the 3rd's red insignia burned into hardened leather above her right breast and campaign designators scratched below it, made his stomach lurch.

She was unfinished business, would always be. He said, "So, here I am. Talk," and found his tongue unwieldy.

Around her, he realized (as his eyes accustomed themselves to something other than the dead man, handless and footless, who still flopped helplessly in his inner sight), were others of the uptown gangs who masqueraded as authority in Sanctuary: Critias, a covert actionist from the Sacred Band who seldom ventured forth in uniform and never in daylight; Straton, his wide-shouldered, witch-ridden partner; Jubal, black as Ischade's cloak and with a look on his face much blacker; Walegrin, the regular army's garrison commander and brother of the S'danzo whose child Zip's men had killed; and a blond woman he didn't know, who wore arena leathers and had a bird perched on her shoulder.

He ought to be wary, he realized—this sort of crowd hadn't gathered for something as mundane as his execution. But his eyes kept sliding back to Kama and trying to fit the persona of her father over the woman who'd taught him things about lovemaking he'd never dreamed were possible.

And then he realized why these uptown hotshots were down in Ratfall: Kama's father. Tempus's minions, all of these were, some by choice, some by duty, some by coercion. And none of them with a good word to say of Zip, except perhaps for the Riddler's daughter.

Fear sharpened his eyesight, and he looked beyond the

gathered luminaries to their troops, and farther: to where his rebels skulked. None of them would move to save him—the odds weren't good enough.

And neither Ratfall nor Zip were worth saving, not at the kind of price the 3rd Commando would exact, if the sentry was a good example.

And he was. They'd made sure of that, had his visitors.

As he took deep breaths and resolved to tell nothing to this corps of fancy fighters (including the Stepsons' chief interrogator, Strat), Zip realized that something was indeed worth saving here: Behind the men, in the long shed against which 3rd Commando regulars leaned with studied insolence, was a store of incendiaries purchased from the Beysib glassmakers: bottles in which were alchemical concoctions that, once their wicks were lit and the bottles thrown, exploded with such force that the shards and flame and concussion from even one such bottle could clear a street—or a palace hall.

With or without him, the revolution could continue, as long as the Beysib glassblowers took the PFLS's money and Ilsig will-to-fight held out.

So, having determined that he had something to lose, Zip said again, "Talk, I said. What do you think this is, an uptown dinner party?"

"No," said the woman he didn't know, the one with the hawkish bird upon her shoulder, "it's a revolutionary council —a trial, actually: yours."

When Kama came back from Ratfall, her eyes were red-rimmed and she was so disarrayed that she ran up Molin's back stairs, hoping to have the girls draw her a bath so she could get the Zip-smell off her and the straw out of her hair before the Torch saw her.

But Molin was home: She could hear Torchholder's voice, and that of another Rankan, coming from the front rooms.

She froze in horror, realizing suddenly that she couldn't face him—not now, with her thighs sticky and her blood up, and all her father's heritage aroused in her so that she wanted nothing to do with the half-Rankan, half-Nisi who had saved her life, and whom she owed so much.

But was debt the same as love? Zip's faked and fated "trial" had broken her heart thrice over.

The outcome—the verdict of conditional acquittal—was

assured, by Tempus's decree. Zip was the only one who hadn't known it.

It was the cruelest thing she'd ever seen men do to another man, and she'd been a willing part of it, the operator in her fascinated by all she saw, by human emotion and its interplay, by the passions of those who'd lost loved ones, and face, trying to justify the one and regain the other—all because Kama's father had ridden down from Ranke, looked upon the doings of Sanctuary's puny mortals, and not been pleased.

Sometimes she hated Tempus more even than she hated the gods.

And so she'd stayed with Zip, after the others had left, to lick the nervous sweat from his fine young body and to wipe the confusion from his heart in the only way she knew.

Zip was . . . Zip, her aberration: a physical match such as Molin could never be. But that was all. She could never make it more, or let it make itself more, or let Zip convince her it could be more.

He needed help, that was all. And everyone was using him, dangling him this way and that. She felt sorry for him.

So she gave him comfort in the night. It was nothing.

Yet the memory sent her bolting from Molin's doorstep, because the Torch was too intelligent to be fooled by mumbled excuses or headaches, because Kama just couldn't fake it tonight.

She roamed night-hot streets, though she knew better, almost hoping that some pickpocket or zombie or Beysib would accost her: Like her father, when pushed too hard, Kama craved only open violence. She'd have killed a Stepson or a 3rd Commando ranger, one of her own, if any dared cross her this evening.

She stopped in at the Unicorn, half-hoping for a fight, but no one paid attention to her there.

She wandered back streets on a borrowed horse, letting it drift barracks-ward, until she realized that it had brought her to the White Foal Bridge.

And then, as she gave the horse its head and it crossed the river bridge, she began in earnest to cry.

It was Crit she wanted now, whether to hold him or kill him, she couldn't have said if her life depended on it. But Crit was, as Zip would say, old business, and Crit had noticed that she'd stayed with Zip.

Maybe she'd stayed with Zip because of Crit, brushing

hips with his partner, and because even that partner, Strat, had sought warmer company than Critias's—Ischade for warmth that Crit reserved to formed ranks and duty squadrons and the next covert operation on his docket.

So when the sorrel string-horse ambled toward Ischade's funny little gate, as if by habit, Kama brushed her eyes angrily with her forearm and blinked away her tears.

In her nostrils was the rank smell of the White Foal in summer, carrying its carrion to the sea, and the perfume of night-blooming flowers of the occult sort that Ischade grew here.

And the smell of heated horse: Two were stamping, reins tied to Ischade's gate, and one of those was Crit's big black. She recognized it by the star and snip as it turned its head to whicker softly to the mount she rode.

The mare under her gave a belly-shaking acknowledgment and she realized that the horse she rode, and his, were lovers.

Hating herself for resenting even that, for her confusion and her doubts, she dismounted, trying not to think at all.

And walked up to the vampire-woman's gate, and pushed it with a sweaty palm.

Perhaps she was meeting her doom here—Ischade had no reason to cut Kama the kind of slack she allowed Straton, and Crit because of their pairbond, and Kama's father because of some bargain whose specifics Tempus had never revealed.

If Crit was in there, Kama wanted to see him. She focused on that and nothing else.

Love sucks, she told herself, and wondered what he'd say.

She'd knocked upon Ischade's door, which was lit somehow, though no torch gleamed or candle flickered in its lamp, before she'd thought of an excuse to give. She could always say she needed to debrief.

If he was there. If it wasn't a trap. If the necromant wasn't into women this summer.

Then the door opened and a small and dusky figure stepped out, closing it behind her so that Kama was forced to retreat a pace, then take a step down the stoop's stairs.

That put them eye to eye and the eyes of Ischade were deeper than Kama's hidden grief for a child lost long ago on the battlefield and the man who'd refused to give her another chance.

"Yes?" said the velvet-voiced woman who held Strat in thrall.

Kama, who was more woman than she'd have chosen, looked deep into the eyes of the woman who was all any man who'd seen her had ever dreamed of wanting, and felt rough, unkempt, foolish.

"Crit's horse . . . is it . . . ? Is he . . . ?"

"Here? The both. Kama, isn't it?" Ischade's dark eyes delved, narrowed just a fraction, then widened.

"It, I—I shouldn't have come. I'm sorry. I'll just go and . . ."

"There's no harm. And no peace, either," said the vampire-woman who seemed suddenly sad. "Not if your father has the say of it. You want him—Crit? Take care for what you want, little one."

And Kama, who had never known her mother and thought of other women as if she herself were a man, found her arms outstretched to Ischade for comfort, weeping freely, sobbing so deeply that nothing she tried to say came out in words.

But the necromant drew back with a hiss and a warding motion, a shake of her head and a blink that broke some spell or other.

Then she turned and was gone inside, though Kama hadn't seen the door open to admit her.

Suddenly alone with her tears on the doorstep of one of the most feared powers in Sanctuary, Kama heard words within—low words, some spoken by men.

Before the door could reopen, before Crit could see her weeping like a baby, she had to get out of here. She didn't mean it; she shouldn't have come. She needed nobody—not her father, not his fighters, not Zip or Torchholder and, most especially, not the Sacred Bander called Crit.

She'd run down the path and thrown herself up on her saddle before the door opened again.

Anything the man in the doorway might have shouted was drowned out by the mare's thundering hooves as Kama slapped her unmercifully with the reins, headed toward the Stepsons' barracks at a dead run.

There was nothing Crit could tell her that she wanted to hear—except perhaps why she could forgive Zip, who had betrayed her and tried to pin Strat's attempted murder on her, when she couldn't forgive Crit, who had wanted to marry her and have a child with her.

·   ·   ·

Tasfalen's uptown estate had once been luxurious and fine, the centerpiece of one of Sanctuary's most exclusive neighborhoods.

Now it stood alone, blackened and charred but whole, while all around it skeletal remains of burned-out homes teetered for blocks, frameworks leaning on lumps of fused brick, so that occasionally a charcoaled timber snapped of its own weight and came crashing down to break an eerie silence that spread from here to the uptown house where the pillar of fire had once raged, and beyond.

Not even rats ran these streets at night, since the pillar of flame had cleansed an uptown house and all the witchery that once had centered in its velvet-hung bedroom.

But Tempus had called a meeting here, across the street from Tasfalen's front door, in the dead of night—a meeting of those concerned, once all his preparations had been made.

The sleepless veteran was the only one unaffected by the hours he and his had kept this week in Sanctuary.

Crit, who'd born the brunt of delegated tasks, weaved on his feet with exhaustion as he set torches in the rubble of the house across from Tasfalen's; had the light been better, the black circles under his eyes would have told a clearer tale of what he'd been through and what it cost him to petition Ischade for leave to do what tonight must be done here.

Strat, Crit's partner, worked silently beside him, unloading ox thighs rich with fat from a snorting chestnut who didn't like its burden, and oil in child-sized stoneware rhytons, and placing all on a makeshift plinth exactly opposite Tasfalen's door.

Tempus watched his Stepsons work without a word, waiting for the witch to show. Ischade had decreed this meeting be at midnight—necromants will be necromants. She was crucial to this undertaking, so Randal said.

Tempus hardly cared; the god was in him fierce and strong, making everything seem fire-limned and slow: his task force leader; the witch-ridden Stepson, Strat; the horses bearing sacrificial burdens. If he hadn't remembered that he'd thought it mattered, that he'd felt need to leave here owing nothing, he'd have left this stone unturned.

But Ischade owed him this favor—if it really was one. And he, in turn, owed a debt he was loath to carry—a debt to the Nisibisi witch last seen behind that ward-locked door across the street.

Tasfalen's door. It had not opened since the pillar of flame had scoured the neighborhood about it. What might come out of there, not even Ischade was certain. Powers had convened to cleanse the ground here, but stopped just short of the house. Powers that no one thought would ever work together had taken a hand to bar that door—Ischade's sort of powers, and others from deeper hells; Stormbringer's primal fury, and thus those from the sort of heaven Jihan's father ruled.

Or thus, at any rate, Tempus understood it. The god in him understood something different—something of passion inbound and lust unreleased.

There was a *something* in there all right, the god was telling him: something very hungry and very angry.

Whatever it was—Nisibisi witch, a ravening ghost thereof, a demon entrapped, a shard of Nisi power globe—it hadn't survived in there since winter's end on stored foodstuffs and the occasional mouse.

If it was Roxane, behind Ischade's iron wards that not even the rip in magic's fabric could weaken, then the Unbinding would have to be carefully done. If it was Something Else, Tempus was prepared to give it battle—he'd once fought Jihan's own storm-cold father to a draw over matters he had less stake in.

Snapper Jo scuttled up to the Trôs horse by which Tempus stood, the fiend's knuckles nearly dragging on the ground, its snaggle teeth gleaming in the torchlight: "Sire," it grunted, "see her? Snapper can't tell." The fiend, in its distress, ramped like a bear—side to side, side to side. "Mistress won't like, won't like . . . Snapper go now?"

"Did you place the stone, Snapper?" The stone in question was a bluish gem, crazed and fractured, Ischade had given Crit. For what payment, when the stone would help release her enemy and perhaps release Straton, too, for duty to the east, Tempus hadn't asked.

And Crit never made excuses. But there'd been no soldierly cursing, no banter between the Stepsons here this evening. When Randal had come by briefly, to say Jihan would attend, there had been none of the obligatory teasing of the mage that passed for fellowship. Strat hadn't even called Randal "Witchy-Ears."

Tempus knew he was pushing matters, but he had his reasons. And the god, risen in him, was all the sign he needed that his instinct wasn't wrong.

A part of this outrageous enterprise—the freeing of whatever lurked behind Tasfalen's doors—he undertook to right a
balance out of whack. It was something none of those about
him sensed, but Niko, the absent Stepson, would have understood: Tempus labored now for *maat,* for equilibrium in a
town that teetered toward anarchy; and for the Stepsons,
who soon might go where Nisibisi magic was still strong and
had better not, with a debt outstanding to a witch of Nisi
blood.

But the greatest part of this seemingly evil deed—that
Randal had begged him not to undertake and that had troubled
Ischade enough to bring her here—he did because of Jihan,
and her father, and a marriage that, if consummated, would
bind a god to Sanctuary that no little thieves' world could or
should contain.

Three hundred years and more of kicking around this world
of god-inspired battlefields and wizard-won wars had taught
Tempus that instinct was his only guide, that any man's sacrifice went unappreciated unless it was to propitiate a god, and
that the only satisfaction worth having was wrested from the
deed itself—was in the process of accomplishment, never in
the result.

So the sacrifice he was about to make—not the sacrifice of
laying the ox thighs on the oil and sending smoke up to
heaven, but the sacrifice of his own peace of mind—would go
unremarked by men. But he would know. And the god would
know. And the powers who tended the balance which expressed itself in fate and weather would know.

How Jihan's father would react, only Jihan would know.

A movement caught his eye, and the god's eye within him
knew it female. His scrotum drew up, ready to face Jihan in
all her insatiable glory.

But it was Ischade, not Jihan, who came.

Tempus felt a twinge of distress, of uncertainty—something he'd rarely felt in all these years. Could Jihan ignore his
invitation? His challenge? The power in the game he played?
Could Stormbringer have gotten wind of Tempus's intention
and mixed in? Tricking a god wasn't easy. But then, neither
was tricking the Riddler.

Randal had assured him Jihan had said she'd be here. He
knew she thought she was involved with Randal to make him
jealous, to make him fey, to make him come to heel. The
question was, however, whether Jihan herself understood what

she did and why—that Stormbringer had turned her eyes toward Randal.

Tempus wondered, suddenly, whether it would matter to Jihan if she did know. She wasn't human, any more than Ischade, so slight and yet so full of menace, or Roxane.

Jihan was still learning how to be alive; womanhood lay heavy and confusing on her, as it didn't on the witches and the accursed women who fought the witches of blood.

Ischade, no bigger than a child to Tempus, came striding up swathed in black, her face like a magical moon on midsummer's eve, her eyes wide as the hells she guarded.

"Riddler," she breathed, "are you sure?"

"Never," he chuckled. "Not about anything."

And he saw the necromant draw back, sensing the god cohabiting with him, a god the fighters called Lord Storm, whose name had been translated into more languages than the thieves' world knew, but always meant the same: the nature of man to fight and kill for lust and territory. On bad days, Tempus thought that the god who dogged him, chameleonlike, adapting by syncretism to different wars in different lands, was merely an excuse his mind made up—a way to hang his excesses and his sins on others, a faceless repository for all the blame of every death he'd caused.

But seeing Ischade's reaction to the god high in him made him realize it wasn't so.

The necromant took a step forward resolutely, cocked her head, licked her lips, and said, "You jest with me? When He is here?" Then, when he didn't respond, she made a warding sign, withdrawing with a mutter: "Have your witch loosed, then. There's less trouble over there than is right here, with you."

And my fighter, Strat? he or the god wanted to ask, but did not. You didn't *ask* Ischade, you negotiated. Tempus wasn't in a position to negotiate, right now. Unless . . .

"Ischade, wait," he called. Or the god did. And when she came close, he leaned down and let the Lord of Rape and Pillage whisper in the ear of the necromant who commanded all the partly dead and restless dead who never went to Sanctuary's gods.

He tried not to listen to what the god said or what the necromant replied, but it was a bargain they made which concerned him—concerned the flesh of his flesh, and the soul of his Stepson, Strat.

When he straightened up, the frail, pale creature touched his forearm and looked into his eyes. For a moment he thought he saw a tear there, but then decided it was the brightness that passion lent to necromants and their kind.

He could survive what the god had promised Ischade—or at least he thought he could.

It might be interesting to find out . . . if, of course, Stormbringer didn't kick his ass from one dimension to another for meddling in the Froth Daughter's affairs before he had time to make good his promise to spend a night with the necromant.

Disconcerted, as Ischade disappeared—literally—into shadows, he mounted the Trôs and stroked its neck for comfort: his comfort, not its.

Up north, at the Hidden Valley stud farm, a calmer life still beckoned. If he could only be content to do it, he could raise horses and a new generation of fighters to hold the line against the northern wizards with his friend Bashir.

But no matter how he craved a different life at times like these, when battle lines of uncertain composition were drawn, with stakes not so simple as life or death, and opponents whose strength was not corporeal, the god would never let him rest.

Torchholder, the half-Nisi priest, had told him all his curse and godbond were merely habit. It might have been true on the day the priest said it, or true to a priestly eye; but it wasn't true here and now.

And here and now was always where Tempus was, not off somewhere in the realm of Greater Good or Mortal Soul or Eternal Consequence. He'd lost the ability to determine greater good, if there was one; his mortal soul he'd given up on long ago. And as for eternal consequence—he was its embodiment.

So when Jihan finally made her entrance, glowing softly to his god-shared eye, her muscular, lithe form still more feminine than any mortal girl's, her waist too small and breasts too pert and thighs too sleek below scale-armor no human hand had forged, he was more than ready to be just what he was, to lay upon her the consequence of her dalliance, of her games, and of her fate.

She came up to within an arm's length of the Trôs and it backed a pace: It remembered the way she used to curry it until its hide showed bare of hair.

He slipped off its back as her throaty voice, arch and full of childish vanity, said, "You wished to see me, Tempus? I can't imagine why. I did not invite *you* to my wedding."

"Because," he said, reaching out for her with a quick grab and a step forward, "there isn't going to be one."

His hand closed on her arm as hers grabbed for his belt.

They struggled there, and he dropped her by thrusting a leg between her thighs and kicking her balance out from under her.

It was a signal.

As Jihan began to curse and rage and kick beneath him among the charcoal and the bricks, Critias and Strat and Randal began the sacrifice of ox and oil, to pacify the god, while Ischade did whatever Ischade must do to release her wards.

Raping the Froth Daughter wasn't easy: She was as strong as he and just as agile.

He had counted on the lust they shared and the play-rapes in their past to turn her pique into passion and her body into an instrument he could play for best result.

And something of the sort transpired, though who raped whom, he wasn't certain, when they rolled half-naked in the ruins, unconcerned with anything about them, while a witch cast spells and soldiers spoke ancient rituals and Randal, the Tysian wizard, presided over a fiery sacrifice meant to set whatever lurked in Tasfalen's free at last.

Since Tempus was, in his way, that self-same sacrifice to Stormbringer, father of Jihan, and since Jihan's legs were around him and her teeth sunk firmly in his neck, and since the god within him loved the rape-game and Jihan as well— and since Jihan was by then wreaking enough havoc upon his flesh to make him glad the god was in him to bear the brunt of it, he missed the spectacle taking place across the street at Tasfalen's.

As a matter of fact, the fireworks inside his head as the god and he and Jihan and her father came together blotted out the simulacrum of last winter's pillar of fire, rising up to heaven from Tasfalen's home, which had been left unscathed then.

He was later told that, as it rose, the doors and windows of Tasfalen's flew open of their own accord and something fiery —something with huge bird's wings—flew out. And flapped and circled high above the place where Tasfalen lived.

And disappeared into the smoke which billowed every-where—too much smoke to credit to burned ox thighs and jugs of oil; smoke that went up from, or down to, the chimney of Tasfalen's house, as if the light spewing from every window was the light of something burning bright within.

But what burned in Tempus was a light unto itself.

Jihan was his match in all things physical: When they lay quiet, able to hear more than their own breathing and see more than their own souls, she whispered to him, with her head buried in his neck, "Oh, Riddler, what took you so long to come and reclaim me? How could you do this to me? And to Randal?"

"I'll take care of Randal. He'll understand. I want you, Jihan—I want you with me. I . . ." This was hard to say, but he had to say it, not just for Randal's sake, but for the sakes of all who put their faith in him. "I . . . need you, Jihan. We all do. Come north and east and everywhere with me—see this world, not just its armpit."

"But my father . . ." The Froth Daughter's eyes glowed red as the light he was just beginning to notice from across the street.

"Will he not honor his daughter's wish?"

And Jihan's arms locked around his neck in a grip not Tempus, or death itself, could break, and she pulled him down to her. "Then, Riddler, let us show Him that it *is* my wish."

He wasn't sure that, even with the war-god to help, he could manage to prove himself again so soon. But the god was, thanks be to Him, as insatiable as she, and, though Stormbringer began to rumble and to shake the ground in pique, so that soon they thrashed and rolled in a downpour that quenched the fire on the altar and the fire in Tasfalen's house, it was too late for Jihan's father to intervene.

Tempus had wooed Jihan, and won her, and there was nothing even Stormbringer could do to change the Froth Daughter's mind once it was made up.

Zip couldn't believe the trouble he was in, forced into an alliance with so many who had good reason to wish him dead.

Jubal's hawkmasks escorted him out to the Stepsons' barracks to show him around. At least he didn't have to live there—yet.

The deal was, as he understood it, that he spearhead some addled alliance made up of all his known enemies and some he hadn't known he had: One, a bitch named Chenaya, had more balls than half the mercenaries lounging on the white-washed parade grounds and she'd made it clear that she didn't expect the pecking order to hold for long unless she was at the head of it.

Heads tended to get lopped off in Sanctuary, he'd told her, with an exaggerated bow and outstretched hand meant to indicate that she could precede him into any grave, anytime, anyplace.

But Chenaya was some sort of Rankan noble, and didn't realize he was being snide. She's just assumed he habitually bowed and scraped like any other Wrigglie, and let him hand her up into her fancy wagon, telling him she'd see him later.

He'd have felt better about all the changes if Jubal had said Word One to him about settling matters, man to man, or if the Rankan Walegrin hadn't looked at him as if Zip were a goat staked out to lure a wolf, or if Straton wasn't twice his weight and conspicuously absent when Zip was shown the ropes at the barracks.

Yeah, he could hold out in the one-time slaver's estate-turned-fortress. Yeah, it beat the offal out of Ratfall. But somehow, he didn't think he was going to live to move his rabble in here.

And he didn't think the 3rd Commando was going to quit this town, where it was the most powerful single element save gods, wizardry, and Tempus, once the Stepsons were packed off to the capital.

Sync was nobody's fool. And Sync was looking at him funny as the 3rd's commander whistled up a mount for Zip from the string herd and showed him how to put a warhorse through its paces.

It was a bright day, and the horse was sweating, and he was riding around the training ring with Sync like some Rankan kid with his daddy when the arrow whizzed by his head close enough to knick his ear.

He cursed, dove off the horse's wrong side, and rolled toward the fence while Sync bawled orders and men went running about in a fine display of concern.

Zip went after the arrow and found it.

If it wasn't the same one that had been aimed at Straton from a rooftop last winter, it was a perfect copy.

"That doesn't mean that Strat—or any of the Stepsons— are behind this," Sync said, a stalk of hay between his teeth, an hour later as they walked their horses and men came in, sweating and dirty, giving desultory reports of no progress and grinning at Zip, the only Ilsig in the camp, with cold amusement in their mercs' eyes.

"Sure. I know. Probably somebody wants me to think it is. No sweat." And he half-believed what he was saying. If Strat wanted a piece of him, the Sacred Bander would take it with show and ceremony, lots of ritual, the whole exotic Band code enforced so that murder wouldn't be murder once it had been sanctified by the handy murderer's god.

They had an altar to that purpose, out back of the training arena.

Arrow in hand, Zip walked over there with his new horse, thinking about making some kind of statement by kicking the piled stones apart.

Then he changed his mind, swung up on the horse, and loped it out of there.

He didn't really care who'd tried to kill him. From the talk he'd heard while in the barracks, neither did the Stepsons: They were more concerned over walls and the weather.

He'd known that this whole business of putting him at the head of some cease-fire coalition was just a roundabout way of executing him.

Ritual execution, political style, wasn't a nice way to die. But then, Zip had killed enough to know there wasn't one.

He rode all day, through the Swamp of Night Secrets, thinking about his chances—slim—and his alternatives—none.

He was dead the minute he announced he wouldn't play the game; if he was dead a week or two later if he pretended to play along, that was a week or two of living he wouldn't have otherwise.

It wasn't a great shot, but it was the only one he had. He didn't have anywhere to run; he had too many enemies without Tempus added to the list. If he diverged from the "arrangement," he'd have no chance at all of surviving. It would be open season on Zip—for professionals.

He had one hole card, maybe, in Kama. He couldn't imagine she'd get that close with him for any kind of revenge.

He wanted to see her, but by the time he got out of the swamp, the sun was going down and he knew he'd better head for Ratfall.

Though Sync had proved Zip wasn't safe in Downwind, *somebody* had proved he wasn't safe out at the barracks, and he'd known for a long time that he wasn't safer anywhere than his own abilities could make him.

So he went to ground in Ratfall, detouring only long enough to lay the arrow that had nicked his ear on the little pile of stones down at the White Foal River's edge.

He used to bring blood sacrifices there—to something. He wasn't sure what. But it liked them. He thought maybe, if it liked him enough for bringing it presents, it might take offense at whoever had shot the arrow (which had his own blood on it still), and do its single servant a favor.

Because without a god's help, a piece of alley-grime like Zip didn't have a whore's chance of making it through another Sanctuary night unmolested.

Tempus had been right: Sanctuary was for lovers, not fighters, this season.

LOVERS WHO SLAY TOGETHER

Robin Wayne Bailey

Chenaya stretched in her bed as the morning sun centered itself in her east window. A mischievous little grin stole over her lips as she thought again about her encounter with Tempus Thales. Not so imaginative as Hanse Shadowspawn, not half so enchanting as Enas Yorl, and the poor madman had been disappointingly quick. If nothing else, she had added one more of Sanctuary's notables to her personal scorecard, and she was glad to have spotted him sneaking about in that garden, glad she had decided to intercept him.

It had, after all, been a boring party until he showed up.

Of course, he thought he'd raped her, and that only added to her amusement. The impish grin she wore blossomed into a truly wicked smile. What the poor fool didn't appreciate was the price he was going to pay for his brief pleasure.

She sat up languidly, threw back the thin coverlet, rose, and pulled on a sleeveless robe of pale blue silk. On a small, ornately carved table beside her bed lay a bronze comb. She picked it up, began idly to tease it through the thick mass of her blond curls as she crossed the room and sat on the window sill. The sun felt wonderfully warm on her flesh. It would be a scorching day.

She shut her eyes and leaned back. Her thoughts turned to the strange meeting in Ratfall. It was the first time she'd met or even seen Zip, the leader of the so-called Popular Front for the Liberation of Sanctuary. She smiled at the irony of the name. Zip wasn't particularly popular with anybody right now, and if Sanctuary wanted liberation from anything it was from the bloody terrorist tactics of his night-running faction.

Somehow, in her imagination and from the stories she'd heard, she'd always thought of Zip as closer to her own age. Probably because everyone called him *boy* all the time. It had surprised her to see that the rebel was older by some years. She called up her memory of him again: dark-haired, with that cute sweatband above his eyes, pleasant to look at. He hadn't cared much for her, though. That had been clear enough in his eyes.

Tempus had made more than one amusing proposal to her in that garden. Both his Stepsons and the 3rd Commando were leaving Sanctuary, he'd told her. That would leave the city virtually defenseless unless someone seized control of the PFLS and used it to forge a unified force of all the other factions.

"Use your gift," he'd grunted in her ear as he fumbled with her skirts. "You can't be defeated. Be the one to take control."

Control, indeed. It was she who'd been in control even as he'd pushed her to the ground. She smiled at that. It was a morning for her to smile, it seemed.

Tempus had even tried to blackmail her into accepting his proposition. Apparently, he'd realized it was she and her gladiators who had attacked Theron's barge when the cursed usurper had unexpectedly come to Sanctuary. Unfortunately, the wily old crown-thief had possessed the foresight to dress some luckless fool in his raiments while he saw to business elsewhere. Her attack had been successful; she'd just aimed at the wrong man.

Still, there was merit to the Riddler's idea, and a plan had come to her in the night, like a dream, like the voice of Savankala himself guiding her. She opened her eyes, glanced at the sun thoughtfully, and resumed her combing.

Things had not gone well between her and Kadakithis lately, and Chenaya knew she had caused the breach by returning her cousin's missing wife to Sanctuary. It hadn't been a charitable act, by any means; she'd done it to prevent a marriage between him and the Beysib Shupansea. Despite a Rankan law forbidding divorce among the royal family, Kadakithis clearly intended to announce his betrothal to the Beysa at summer's end.

Chenaya set the comb in her lap and leaned back. Unless she made some effort the breach might never heal. She couldn't bear to have her Little Prince angry with her, and she resolved to face the fact that she might even have to make peace with the fish-eyed bitch he wanted to marry.

Tempus, bless his inadequate little self, had handed her the means to do so. She stared upward at the sun and uttered a hasty prayer: *Thank you, Bright Father, thank you for filling the world with such an abundance of fools.*

She smiled yet again, rose, and began to dress. It was
going to be a good day, full of events sure to entertain her.

The door to her quarters opened without so much as a
knock to announce her visitor. The dark-haired beauty who
strode toward her wore a sullen look and the garments of a
Rankan gladiator. Sandalled heels clicked smartly on the un-
carpeted floor stones. She gave Chenaya a look of disapproval. Then, all the starch went out of the young woman; her
shoulders sagged; she sighed, fell backward with great drama,
and sprawled on the bed. "Up at the crack of dawn, you've
told me a score of times, and out on the practice field ready to
work." Another sigh rose from those pouty lips, and a delicate
ivory finger pointed accusingly. "You're not ready, mistress."
Her last words dripped with mockery and accusation.

"Daphne, your bad attitude can do nothing to spoil this
day," Chenaya replied as she pulled on a scarlet fighting kilt
and buckled on a broad leather belt that gleamed with gold
studs.

"Since Daxus," Daphne whined, "you've given me no
more throats."

Chenaya tied the straps of her sandals and lied patiently.
"I've told you before. The only other names I could give you
would all be Raggah. Daxus sold information about your caravan to that gods-cursed desert tribe. They're the ones who
sold you to the pirates on Scavengers' Island. There was no
conspiracy to dispose of you. It was just business as usual for
the Raggahs."

It wasn't the truth. But those others in Sanctuary who had
plotted to destroy Daphne's caravan were too important—
given the threat posed by Theron—to let Daphne carve them.
Despite Chenaya's promise, Daxus was the only throat
Daphne was going to get.

"Right," Daphne snapped. "Business as usual. They just
happened to land themselves a princess of Ranke—Kadakithis's wife. Nothing personal. How stupid do you think I
am?"

"I'm sure I haven't begun to plumb your depths." Chenaya
lifted her sword from a wooden chest at the foot of her bed.
"If you've got nothing better to do than bitch about life's un-
fairness, then get up and head for the practice field. Leyn will
instruct you today."

Daphne sat up, startled, angry. Then, her face recomposed
itself into a familiar frown. "Leyn?" she cried. "Where's

Dayrne? He's supposed to be my trainer."

"He left on a mission last night," Chenaya told her newest student. "He's attending to some business for me that will take him to various parts of the Empire. While he's gone, Leyn will be your trainer." She pointed a finger at Daphne. "And no complaints. You've whined enough this morning. Even the least of my men has plenty to teach you. Now, on your way, Princess." She put special emphasis on the title, a not-so-subtle reminder that Daphne's rank counted for nothing while she wore fighting garb.

Daphne rose with deliberate slowness, giving a haughty toss of her waist-length black hair. "As the mistress commands," she answered with false meekness as she moved toward the door. But before she passed through and out of sight she added, just loud enough for Chenaya to hear, *"bitch."*

It was one more cause for Chenaya to smile. After all, she didn't train automatons—she trained gladiators. And fighters without some spit in their souls would never be worth a damn. She'd kept a close eye on Daphne; for a princess she was coming along just fine.

Chenaya headed for the practice field, but before she got much farther than her door she bumped into her father. "Ummm, pardon me," she said, leaning one hand on the door he had just closed. "Isn't this Aunt Rosanda's room?" She batted her eyelashes in mock innocence, knowing how such an expression usually irritated him.

But this time Lowan Vigeles imitated her, batting his own eyelashes. "I knew all those expensive tutors were a fine investment." He tapped her on the forehead with a fingertip. "I brought your aunt a breakfast tray. Nothing more lascivious than that."

She just stood there, looking up at him, grinning, batting her lashes.

Lowan drew a deep, patient breath, his usual silent invocation to the god of parenthood, and pushed open the door. Lady Rosanda flashed them a startled look of embarrassment from her bed as a strip of cold meat fell from her lip to the tray on her lap. She chewed hurriedly, hiding her busy mouth with one hand.

Lowan pulled the door closed once more and regarded his daughter with the look of an unjustly wronged man.

Chenaya brushed at her hair with one hand and refused to look repentant. "What a selfish bastard you are, Father," she accused. "Too saintly to offer what we both know you've got? Have pity! The only man she's seen in years is Uncle Molin." Chenaya faked a shiver.

Lowan Vigeles took her by the arm and led her from Rosanda's door and down a broad staircase to the floor below. "I saw Dayrne off," he said, changing the subject. "He bears a writ from me that should speed our cause. Later today, I'll hire artisans to start the barracks and outbuildings. I'll set Dismas and Gestus to constructing the training machines."

"Not those two," she contradicted. "I'll need them myself today. Have Ouijen see to it, and Leyn when he has time. But there's no rush. It'll be a few weeks at least before anyone arrives. Assuming any will answer the summons."

Lowan shook his head as they left the manse and stepped out into the rear garden where nearly a score of falcons were elaborately caged. "That's not an assumption, Daughter. My school in Ranke produced most of the finest *auctorati* ever to fight in the games. They will come when I call. And Dayrne carries enough money to purchase any other fighters he deems worthy."

She nodded. She would miss Dayrne's presence at her side, but when it came to choosing trainees and fighters there wasn't a better judge of manflesh. And except for herself or Lowan there was no other she would trust with such a mission.

"I have to get to the field, Father," she said suddenly. She raised on tiptoe and gave him an affectionate peck on the cheek. "Then, I'll be gone most of the day. Don't worry if I'm not back tonight."

Lowan batted his lashes, turning her own coy expression against her.

She punched him playfully in the ribs. "Nothing so lascivious," she said, adopting his line. "This is business." Then, she looked thoughtful and amended her remark. "Well, some of it's business. Some of it will be pure pleasure." She reached up and scratched his chin: "That mare of yours, is she still hot?"

Lowan Vigeles eyed her suspiciously. "Changing the subject? Don't want to talk about tonight's boyfriend?" He sighed. "Yes, the mare's still hot. I've taken pains to keep *her* away from any boyfriends. It spoils them for riding when they swell."

She said no more to her father. He'd forgive her, after a

few days, when he found out what she'd done. Tempus, on the other hand . . .But who cared about him? She grinned, relishing the delightful mood she felt today. Had she said *pure* pleasure? She chuckled aloud.

Lowan looked at her strangely. She patted his hand, winked, and headed for the practice area where Daphne and eleven of the best gladiators ever to set foot in the arena were already hard at work and sweaty.

The sun was nearing its zenith when Chenaya called a halt to the workout. She sent Daphne, Leyn, and the others back to the manse, but called Dismas and Gestus to her side. The two were a team, almost never apart. Lovers, they even resembled each other with their sandy hair, close-cropped beards, and exaggerated musculature.

"Interested in a little game, friends?"

The two looked at each other, then at her, and said nothing. They had a good idea what she meant. They'd helped her with other *little games* before.

"Nobody can sneak around like you two," she continued. In fact, they'd been the shiftiest pair of thieves and burglars in Ranke before they were finally caught and sentenced to Lowan's school for arena training. "And very few are faster on their feet."

Dismas folded his arms, repressing a grin. "Save the grease, mistress," he said in clipped Rankene. "It's too hot to stand here and exchange flatteries, even true ones."

Chenaya sidled up to Dismas and rubbed her body against his. "Aren't you taking good care of him these days?" she said teasingly to Gestus. With a knuckle she tapped the leather groin guard under Dismas's kilt. "He's so grumpy today."

"N'um faults," Gestus answered with a shrug. That was the odd thing about this pair. So alike in everything else, Gestus had never mastered Rankene. Dismas, on the other hand, spoke it like a court noble.

She stepped back again and turned serious. "There's someone I want you to watch for me, and something I want you to do. You'll have a fat purse of coins to spend. If your quarry goes to a tavern, so do you. If he goes to a brothel . . ." She hesitated, scratched her temple. "Well, you'll think of something." Gestus folded his arms, too, and grinned. Clearly, she'd caught their interests. "Just make sure you don't attract notice." She flipped a finger against their studded belts. "Wear something less identifiable."

Dismas unfolded his arms, so Gestus did, too. "The name of our fox?" he said conspiratorially.

"No fox," she cautioned. "A deadly mountain cat. Mind you, don't cross him. Just keep an eye on him and inform me of his movements." She beckoned them closer, and they bent to hear. She made a show of glancing in all directions, then put a finger to her lips. "Now here's the fun part. Before sundown I want one of you back here with half a brick of krrf."

That raised eyebrows.

As she'd predicted, the day turned scorching, too hot for her usual fighting leathers. Yet she'd wanted to make sure she attracted attention, so she'd donned trousers and blouse of shining black, loose-fitting silk and spit-polished boots that rose almost to her knee, not quite high enough to conceal the hilts of the daggers stuck in each one. Over one shoulder she wore a leather strap to which a number of Bandaran throwing stars were attached; a simple twist easily freed them from their stud mountings. On her right hip she wore one more weapon —a gladius whose golden tang was fashioned to resemble the wings of a bird. Lastly, because she'd seen Zip do it, she'd tied a sweatband of clean white linen above her eyes.

Every gaze turned her way as she strode brazenly across Caravan Square on her way to Downwind. She smiled and winked at the gawkers, sometimes lightly brushing the hilt of her sword. Only a few had balls enough to smile back; most glanced quickly in some other direction and passed on.

As she approached the bridge that crossed the White Foal River a gaggle of grubby street urchins surrounded her. She smiled at their play, dipped a hand into the purse on her belt, and tossed a fistful of coins over her shoulder. The children lost interest in her and began scuffling for the glinting bits of metal. She laughed heartily, started past the deserted guard-post and across the bridge.

As she set foot in Downwind two men appeared to block her path. "Mebbe y'ud be s'free wi' the rest o' yer spark," croaked the one on her left. The point of his sword indicated her purse.

"An' wit' yer other charms, too," his partner suggested.

A disdainful smirk flickered over Chenaya's features as she heard two more slide up behind her, heard the soft susurrus of steel slipping from sheathes. They wore no armbands, so they weren't part of Zip's group. From the rags they wore she guessed they followed Moruth.

That suited her fine. Moruth—the beggar king—was one of the faction leaders that had dared to oppose the PFLS. Well, she hadn't come to Downwind to win Moruth's favor. Unfortunately for His Beggar-Majesty, she had come to win Zip's.

She didn't bother turning to see the two behind her. They gave away their positions by their breathing and by their constant foot-shuffling. "You'll make perfect offerings," she informed them gruffly. "I'll pour your blood as a libation to the leader of the PFLS."

The man who had spoken first tuned pale, but he held his ground, tapping his blade against his palm. "You part o' Zip's group?" he asked suspiciously. "You got no band on yer sleeve."

"Spoils the silk," she answered. She waited a brief moment, daring them with her haughty gaze to make their move or to scatter from her path. The man on her left stopped his incessant sword tapping; the one beside him chewed his lip. Yet they were unwilling to back away from her, a mere woman.

"She mus' think she's purty good wit' that sticker," said one of the men behind her.

Chenaya had no more time to waste. "Watch carefully," she advised with impatience. "I don't often give lessons to scum."

Her hand was almost a blur. Bright steel flashed through the air. A soft *thunk;* a groan of surprise and fear sounded as a throwing star embedded in the first man's throat. His sword tumbled into the dirt, followed instantly by his lifeless body.

Even before the star scored, Chenaya had her sword free. She ran screaming at the man on her right. In stark terror he raised his sword to protect his head. Her blade crashed down twice against his, then arced down and across, opening his belly. On the backswing she knocked the sword from his grip, severing several fingers.

There was no time to watch him fall. She whirled, settled in a deep forward stance to meet the remaining two. But these were beggars, not seasoned warriors. Still, they knew the better part of valor. She watched their departing backs as they ran

for shelter beneath the bridge. Laughing, she hurled a second
star with all her arena-trained skill. A scream ripped from one
of the fleeing beggars; he tumbled headlong through the
weeds, down the bank, and into the river. Sputtering, screaming, clutching at the four-pointed agony behind his knee, he
dragged himself onto the bank and scrambled after his
comrade.

She laughed again, a bitter and challenging sound that rat-
tled in her throat, and she glanced around in time to spy the
street urchins who had gathered at the far end of the span to
watch. They melted away like shadows in the sun. On the
Downwind side, too, figures faded into alleys and doorways,
unwilling witnesses. Chenaya bent and wiped her blade on a
dead man's garments, retrieved the first star, and cleaned it,
too.

She had no doubt that Zip would hear of this. She wanted
him to hear. It was why she had come to this stink-hole side of
town. Sheathing her sword, she walked on, giving no further
thought to the bodies in her wake.

Come to me, Zip, she willed, *come to me.*

There were taverns in Downwind, or places that professed
to be taverns. Only Mama Becho's, though, could legitimately
claim to be such. Even so, there were lifelong drunks in Sanctuary who wouldn't deign to spit on its threshold, let alone
consume its questionable product.

Chenaya stepped through the low, doorless entrance, her
vision swiftly adjusting to the dim light. A dozen pairs of eyes
turned to examine her. Quite a different crowd from the one
that frequented the Unicorn. There the faces were full of menace or scheming or general disinterest. The eyes at Mama
Becho's reflected only desperation and despair.

It was like no place she had ever seen before, and she
thought of the men who had met her at the bridge, men like
these, men with the same desperate eyes. They had wanted
her gold and had gone down for it. She saw in Mama Becho's
men who would have done the same and welcomed the death
she gave. And why not? For such as these, life had little to
offer, little to hold them.

She thought of the bridge again, of men who poured their
blood into the dirty street for a handful of spark, and for one
moment, Chenaya hated what she had done.

Fortunately, the moment passed. She reminded herself she had come to this cesspool on business.

"You want somethin', honey, or you jus' come to see the sights?" A mountainous woman in a tattered smock leaned one elbow on the board that served as a bar and leered at her. She wiped at the interior of an earthen mug with a grimy rag that hadn't seen a rinsing in weeks. Wisps of grizzled hair floated about her thick-jowled face as she worked.

"Uptown bitch," someone muttered into his cup. Pairs of eyes began slowly to turn back to their drinks, to the private fantasy worlds found only in foul brews.

"Honey," Chenaya said smiling to Mama Becho, "I want a couple of things. First, a cup of some decent beverage, Vuksibah if you've got it in this dump." The eyes all turned her way again, whether at her mention of the expensive liquor or because of the insult, she didn't know or care. "A respectable wine or cool water if you don't." She leaned on the board facing the fat proprietor and felt it sag under their combined weights. The old woman's breath was worse than fetid, but Chenaya managed to force a grin. "Then I want Zip."

That got their attention. She reached into her purse, drew out another handful of coins. Not bothering to look at them or judge their value, she threw them over her shoulder, all but one which she placed on the board. It was a gleaming soldat.

"I'm betting somebody here knows how to contact him," she said, still addressing Mama Becho, well aware that everyone could hear. "And when he walks through that door I'll scatter another fistful of coins."

"An' what if we jus' take yer spark, lady?" said a lean, twisted man who squatted in a gloomy corner against the wall. He fingered one of the silver pieces that had fallen his way.

"Shet up yer mouth, Haggit," Mama Becho snapped. "Can'tcha see we got us a fine noblewoman here? Mind yer manners!"

Chenaya cast the soldat to the one called Haggit; he caught it with a deft motion. "I give my gold where and when I see fit. Two who tried to take it are still cooling at the foot of the bridge." She gave him a hard, penetrating look. "Now, I want to see Zip, and I'll pay fairly to find him. Play me any other way, Haggit—" Chenaya winked at him and nodded her head "—and you'll do all the paying."

Haggit glared at her for a long moment, bit into the soldat with his front tooth, then rose and went out. One by one all the other customers drifted out, too. Not one of Chenaya's coins remained on the floor.

"Now ye've scared away my business," Mama Becho complained. She still scoured the same mug with the same filthy rag. "Might as well get comfy, honey." She waved at the cloth-covered furniture that served in place of stools and tables. "No tellin' when Zip'll turn up. Thet boy comes an' goes as he pleases."

Chenaya remained where she was as the old woman disappeared to fetch her wine. She took a deep breath and let it out. Zip would turn up, she had no doubt. She'd spread enough wealth to insure that; she'd killed his enemies, too. He'd come all right, if only out of curiosity.

She took another deep breath and held it. What was that odor? She glanced at the doorway Mama Becho had gone through. An old, worn blanket hung across it; a thin, tenuous smoke wafted around the edges.

Krrf smoke.

She wet her lips slyly and wondered how Gestus and Dismas were faring.

Two bitter cups of wine and one cup of water later, the man she had come to find mercifully walked in, leaving, by the sound of things, a couple of his cronies standing guard in the alleyway. Mama Becho made a discreet nod of greeting and headed for the back room.

"Don't bother listening through the curtain or one of the cracks in the wall, Mama," Zip called and waved his hand to draw her back. "Up here—where I can keep an eye on you, too." Mama Becho put on a look of wounded innocence and reached for another mug to polish.

Zip walked calmly up to Chenaya; his gaze ran unabashedly up and down her body.

"There's a lot more swagger in your step than when we met in Ratfall," she commented wryly.

His gaze met hers with unconcealed arrogance. "You've got a lot less muscle with you this time," he answered bluntly. "What do you want, Chenaya? Did Tempus send you?"

She laughed. Her hand reached out to touch his shoulder, drifted down over his chest, then resumed its place at her belt. Hard, lean muscle beneath his clothing, she'd discovered, no fat. "Tempus Thales isn't quite the puppeteer he thinks himself."

Zip leaned on the board, close to her, giving her a long

look. "I wouldn't tell him that—not me."

He had a nice face, she realized. Young and rugged, crowned by a mop of dark hair. Sweat-tracks lined his brow and cheeks, and there were circles of dirt around his neck where the flesh showed above his rough-woven tunic. He smelled, but it was a man's musky odor, not the stench of Downwind. She stared brazenly into his eyes and chuckled.

"Oh, I've taken his measure," she said, "and he comes up short."

"He hears the voice of the Storm God," Zip cautioned with an enigmatic, taut, little smile.

"He hears voices, all right." She caught a piece of his tunic and pulled his face close to hers. In conspiratorial tones she whispered, loud enough still for any to hear, "But the Storm God?" She shrugged meaningfully. "Between you and me and these others, I suspect he's just a crazy, common madman. He uses the so-called *voices* to excuse his perversions and aberrations. After all, he can't be blamed—and needn't take responsibility for his actions—if *divine voices* compel him. He's only a poor avatar."

Chenaya didn't actually believe it; she had little doubt of the veracity of Tempus's relationship with the Storm Gods. Her own experiences with Savankala were proof enough that such god/mortal alliances evolved. Still, it was a delicious rumor to start.

Zip picked up the mug of beer Mama Becho had placed at his elbow. He took a long drink, regarding Chenaya over the rim. He set the vessel down between them. "You threw away a lot of money to find me, woman," he said finally. "Why? Not just to gossip about the Riddler."

She gave him her look of mock-innocence, picked up his mug, and drained the contents. "But I did want to talk about Tempus," she replied. "At least about a proposal Tempus suggested to me."

She crooked a finger, beckoning him close again. "Your Riddler wants me to seize control of your PFLS. He thinks I can shape it into an adequate defense force to replace his Stepsons and the 3rd Commando when he leads them out of Sanctuary."

A hint of red colored Zip's cheeks. He straightened, took a step away from her. "You play dangerous games, Rankan." His eyes glinted. "So you'll just take over? You think it's that easy?" He chuckled at her.

She threw a fist at his face. Zip raised an arm to block it. But her move was only a feint. Chenaya caught his rising arm at the elbow, tugged, and kicked his foot when he tried to catch his balance. Zip fell heavily, stunned. She straddled him, sat on his chest, and brought one of her boot daggers to rest at his throat.

Then, she smiled at Zip, and suddenly her lips crushed down on his. There was power in her kiss; it didn't surprise her at all when he began to return it. She sat up, wiped her mouth, grinning.

"Just that easy, Zip, my love," she told him. "And Tempus knows it. That's why he approached me." She tangled her hand through his hair and kissed him again.

When she sat up, the point of her blade flashed downward to bite deeply into the boards near Zip's ear. She left it quivering there while she loosened the laces at the neck of his dirty tunic. "But I'm not interested in running your little social club," she whispered, "and what Tempus wants is unimportant." She dragged her nails teasingly over the exposed portion of his chest. "However, I have some proposals of my own. Would you like to hear them?"

His eyes reflected so much: uncertainty, defiance, curiosity, lust—all half-hidden behind a facade of nonchalance. Zip drew a breath. "Get the frog off of me." The knife was still there by his ear. He could have gone for it—his eyes slid that way—but he didn't.

She patted his cheek. "Soon, lover, when we have an agreement. But right now, Mama Becho is going to bring us a couple more drinks, right, Mama?"

The old proprietor said nothing, but waddled over with two mugs of bad wine. It was too far for her to bend over and place them on the floor, so Chenaya reached up to accept them. Mama Becho grumbled incoherently and backed away.

"I'm supposed to drink from here?" Zip asked caustically.

Chenaya moved one of the mugs near to his head, dipped a finger in it, and held it to his lips. After a moment's hesitation, Zip's tongue poked out and licked away the red droplets, their gazes remaining locked all the while.

"I know the funds from your Nisi supporters have dried up lately." Chenaya dipped her finger again and held it for him to suck. "The PFLS needs money, like any group, and I've got plenty of that. We've also got mutual enemies, so it's only natural that we should join our efforts." She paused long enough to swallow a draught from her own cup. "You want to free Sanctuary from the Rankans and Beysibs." She tapped his chest. "I want to drive out the Beysibs, too. But it looks like I've got to get rid of a Rankan to do that."

One of Zip's men slipped through the door and made a move toward his leader. A throwing star flashed briefly through a random sunbeam that spilled through a crack in the ceiling and *thunked* into the wall. The man leaped back. Chenaya clucked her tongue and wagged her finger, and he leaned uncomfortably against the doorjamb.

"Kadakithis?" Zip guessed. "But isn't he your cousin?"

She spat. "He's going to marry that fish-eyed slut, Shupansea, in defiance of Rankan law. Bad enough that he allowed them to land here without a fight. Bad enough that he beds the silly carp. But to marry one? To make her part of the royal family, a princess of Ranke?" She spat again. "Blood is only so thick, lover."

"I'd 'preciate it if ye'd stop that," Mama Becho snapped. "Someone's gotter mop up when yer gone now."

Zip shifted beneath her, locking his hands together behind his head, an arm cocked around her dagger. He tried to look innocent and almost achieved it. But his face was full of suspicion. "All right, lover," he mocked her. "What you got in mind?"

She pulled the dagger from the floorboards and returned it to her boot, rose, and extended a hand to help Zip to his feet. Unsurprisingly, he declined her offer and got up on his own. He made a show of brushing Mama Becho's dust from his clothing.

"Tomorrow night," she told him, "meet me with as many of your men as you have—the entire PFLS—at the old stables near the granaries."

Zip frowned, bent down, and picked up the mug of wine that yet remained on the floor. He turned it in his hands without drinking. "That's right across from the dungeons."

Chenaya taunted him with a nasty grin. "Don't get nervous, Zip. I heard you were a man of action. Well, action is what I'm going to give you." Let him interpret that as he wished, she thought wickedly. "I happen to own the guard who works the Gate of the Gods tomorrow night—he has a very expensive krrf habit—and a word from me will open that passage. It's a very brief run from there to a side entrance into the palace itself." She pushed back her hair with one hand, raised herself from the floor with the other, and poured the last of her own bitter wine down her throat. Her hand opened then, and the earthen mug shattered at her feet.

"Now," she challenged, "you and your playmates can go on butchering helpless shopkeepers and limp-wristed nobles and getting nowhere with your so-called revolution . . ." She took the cup he'd been fidgeting with, raised it in a silent toast to him, and drained it, too, regarding him over the rim. An instant later it joined the first one in pieces on the floor. ". . . or the PFLS can at last strike a meaningful blow. What do you say?"

Zip looked thoughtful. "With Kadakithis dead we'd still need some kind of defense for when Theron returns." He scratched his chin, frowning.

"Theron will probably thank you," she pointed out. It was safe to gamble that Zip had never met the usurper, knew nothing of the subtle workings of the old general's mind. Theron wanted Sanctuary for a bastion on Ranke's southern border. Nothing would convince him to release the city from the Empire's iron grip. Not even the execution of the legitimate claimant to the very crown he had stolen.

But Zip wouldn't understand that. He was a fighter, no politician.

"No need for all my men," Zip argued. "A small force— two or three—just enough to sneak in and do the job."

Chenaya stepped closer. She was almost as tall as Zip, almost as broad through the shoulders. Again, she inhaled the smell of him and bit her lip. "A small force for the prince and his fish-faced consort," she agreed, nodded her head as a patient teacher might with a dim-witted but struggling pupil. "The rest will take care of every other Beysib in the palace— and anyone else who gets in the way."

Plainly, Zip's thoughts were churning. He glanced at his man by the door. He'd heard every word; eagerness gleamed in his face, though he kept his silence. Zip began to pace back and forth, crushing pottery under his tread. "And the garrison?" he asked. "What about a way out? Armed resistance inside?"

Chenaya scoffed at his endless questions. "Tempus told me you were a man who knew when to act, yet you sound like Molin Torchholder with your endless queries."

Zip shut up, but continued to pace.

"Would you do it with Tempus to lead you?"

He stopped in mid-stride, regarded her through narrowed eyes. Still he said nothing, but questions hung on his lips.

She spat again, but this time for Mama Becho's sake the wad landed squarely on Zip's boot. "I'm everything that Tempus is, lover," she said, grim-voiced, mocking his trepidation. "And more. You don't believe that yet, but you will." She turned her back to him, went to the serving board. To Mama she said, "Got a pair of dice?"

The old woman reached up onto a shelf and found a pair of yellowed ivory cubes. She set them on the counter with a rude grunt. Chenaya crooked a finger at Zip. "Roll 'em," she ordered. "High number wins."

He paused, studying her, their gazes locked in a game of dare and challenge. Finally, he swept up the cubes and tossed them. "Eleven," Chanaya announced. "Not bad." Then, she rolled them. "Twelve." Zip seized the dice again and beamed when eleven black dots showed up once more.

Chenaya didn't even bother to look as she gathered and dropped the ivory bits.

Zip blinked.

Twelve.

"I can't be beaten," she assured Zip, never taking her eyes from his. "Not at anything."

"Kind of takes the fun out of life, doesn't it?" Zip said, dead-pan.

She flicked a glance over her shoulder. "Call your man," she instructed him.

Zip did. The man she'd nearly shaved with the throwing star took a step forward. "The black smudge on the far wall," she suggested. The man threw his belt dagger. One of the daggers from her boot followed. Two good throws, but hers was clearly nearer the center of the mark. "Not at anything," she repeated.

"So you have luck and skill," Zip conceded. "That doesn't mean squat against the Riddler's god—or his curse, or whatever it is."

She rolled her eyes; a long sigh hissed between her teeth. "I'll bet you another kiss," she said at last. "You've played guess-the-number?" She waited for him to nod. "Go to the far end of the bar, take your knife, and carve any number between one and ten. No, wait. Let's make it fun—between one and twenty-five."

Mama Becho waddled up, her gray hair flying. "Oh, no,

ye don't!" she cried. "Yer not cuttin' on my fine board, yer
not. Not easy to come by good wood. An' I've jus' about
enough of this spittin' and breakin' mugs an'—"

Chenaya pulled her purse free and upended it on the
counter. Coins spilled everywhere. She dropped the empty
leather bag on the top of the pile. "Mama," she said softly,
"shut up."

"All right," Zip announced from the other end, covering
his scratching with one hand, flipping his knife nervously and
catching it.

"Forty-two," she answered smugly. "Cheater."

Zip stared at the number he'd carved into the wood, at his
knife, at his men, at her. Without another word, he went to
Chenaya and made good on his bet.

The glaring sun had long since disappeared beyond the
western edge of the world, and beautiful Sabellia, resplendent
in her fullness, scattered diamond ripples over the ocean's
surface. Chenaya dangled her feet over the end of Empire
Wharf, stared at the glistening water, and listened to the
muted sounds of a nearly silent thieves' world. The old pilings
creaked gently, rocked by the relentless surf; the riggings and
guy wires of nearby fishing ships hummed and sang in the
night wind. There was little else.

It was one of the places she went when she was troubled.
She couldn't say for sure exactly what it was disturbed her,
but she felt it like a gloomy darkness on her soul. She tried to
dismiss it. The water often made her melancholy. But the
mood lingered.

She touched the bag that was tied to her belt. It contained a
mixture of sugar and the high-grade krrf Gestus had obtained
for her. She squeezed it and grinned. No, it certainly wasn't
that which bothered her. She planned to enjoy her little prank
on Tempus.

What then?

Far out on the water something flashed in the moonlight.
There was a muffled splash. She peered, straining to see, and
spied the silver gleam of a dorsal fin as it cut through the
waves. Briefly visible, it submerged and was gone. A dol-
phin, she wondered? A shark?

The world—particularly this thieves' world—was full of
sharks. She thought of Kadakithis and Shupansea hidden away

in their palace, and she thought of Zip and Downwind. She
thought of the betrayal she planned.

She knew, then, the cause of her dark mood.

But it must be done, she swore. *Sooner or later, it would
be done.*

Chenaya extended her arm; the metal rings of her manica
shone richly under Sabellia's glory. She pursed her lips, gave
a thin, piercing whistle.

It was impossible in the darkness to see Reyk; she didn't
even hear the beat of his pinions, leading her to guess he had
been circling overhead and had simply plummeted in response
to her call. She felt only a sudden rush of air on her cheek and
then his weight and the tension of his talons on her forearm.

She stroked the falcon very lightly down the back of his
head and between his wings. "Hello, my pet. Did you feast?"
She had expected to find traces of beyarl plumage between his
talons. Several of the sacred birds had skimmed the water
earlier. But Reyk's claws were clean. She took a jess from her
belt and slipped it around his leg.

Together, they sat quietly and watched the goddess's argent
chariot sail over the ocean. Chenaya didn't even mind that the
moon seemed to watch her, too. The light seemed to ease her
troubled spirit, and eye to eye, she thanked Sabellia for that
small relief.

Reyk stretched suddenly to full wing-span. Talons tightened on her arm; he emitted a single, sharp note.

The falcon's keen eyes had spotted Dismas before Chenaya
had heard his footsteps on the wharf. Reyk calmed immediately, recognizing the gladiator as he padded with a burglar's
swift stealth toward his mistress. "Now, lady," Dismas whispered urgently. "It's the perfect time and place. We may not
get a better chance."

Chenaya squeezed the bag of krrf and sugar again, feeling
her pulse quicken. She had waited at the wharf a long time for
Dismas to report. "What of Walegrin and Rashan?" she asked,
getting to her feet.

"They should already be on their way to Land's End.
Gestus carried your message and returned to keep watch while
I came for you."

She removed Reyk's jess and returned it to her belt one-
handed. "Where is he?"

The huge gladiator hesitated only a moment and swallowed. "With the vampire-woman, Ischade." He wiped a

trickle of sweat from his brow. "Not far, but a good run. We should hurry. He's been there an hour already."

"Then up, pet." She sent Reyk aloft. His pinions beat a steady rhythm as he climbed into the night sky and disappeared. She squeezed the krrf bag once more. "Let's go," she called, tapping her friend on the arm in comradely fashion. There was more than a hint of glee in her voice.

Dismas led her down the Wideway, up the Street of Smells and along a narrow road she didn't know. The road rutted out; they were in undergrowth denser than any she'd imagined this side of the White Foal. They stopped in a wide ditch.

"There," he whispered.

The windows were dark; no light spilled out. Nothing told that anyone was within. Yet Tempus Thales' huge-muscled Trôs horse was tethered to the gate.

"An hour, you say?" she questioned Dismas. "Where's our other partner?"

He pointed silently to the deeper brush.

She smiled and stole a peek at Tempus's magnificent mount. A very rare breed, Trôs horses. No other steed could match them for strength, endurance, intelligence. She had seen only two others in her lifetime. It was a cause for wonder that Tempus had left the beast unguarded.

Yes, a rare breed, Trôs horses, and she meant to have one.

"Get Gestus and make for Land's End as quick as you can. Have everything ready at the family stables when I arrive. Have Walegrin and Rashan there, too."

"But, mistress," Dismas protested. "The vampire and the Riddler—you may need our help."

Chenaya shook her head sternly. "I can handle them. Do as you're told and have everything ready. Discreetly, too. I don't want my father to know anything about this." She smacked his chest with the flat of her hand and gave him a little shove. "Go!"

She watched as he faded back into the night, then leaned back in the shadows and drew a slow breath. With her friends gone she could safely get on with her little prank. It would have been an insult to two good men if she had explained why she sent them on. But she knew Tempus Thales, and she knew the stories about Ischade. If anything went wrong with her plan she didn't want her men to pay the price.

Chenaya took the bag of krrf and sugar from her belt, loosened the strings that held it shut, and moved toward the dark house. The Trôs horse, she suspected, had been trained to recognize warriors. She would have trained it to do so, and she expected no less of Tempus. But she was a woman and had left her weapons at home this night. Reyk was weapon enough—and her god-spawned luck.

She approached the beast slowly, mumbling soft words. The Trôs eyed her with suspicion and snorted once. It kept still, though, and that encouraged her. She reached into the bag and extracted a handful of powder. Holding her breath with excitement, she took the final step that brought her within reach of the horse.

The Trôs smelled the sugar but not the raw krrf. He licked it eagerly from her hand and whickered for more. Chenaya gladly obliged. There was enough drug mixed in the sugar to kill several big men. Enough, she hoped, to make this creature very, very happy.

Handful by handful, the beast consumed the entire contents of the bag. Chenaya cast cautious glances over her shoulder from time to time, watchful of the doors and windows in Ischade's home, ready to bolt if anyone peered out.

The horse's eyes quickly glazed over. It slurped the last of the powder from her fingers and palms and gave her a look that almost made her laugh aloud. If a horse could go to heaven, this one was on its way.

Have a good time, horsie, she thought, grinning, *and don't give me any trouble*.

She didn't actually underestimate Tempus or his pride; unguarded as the horse might appear, it wouldn't easily be stolen. Carefully she untied the reins and stroked the horse along the withers while muttering in its ear. The Trôs didn't move or make a sound. She held her breath and locked her fingers around the pommel, levering herself quickly into the saddle. The animal trembled; its ears twitched. She paused, then settled herself more comfortably, smiling.

Then her head snapped back, rolled around on her shoulders, threatening to rip off first to the left then the right. Her spine folded backward; whipped forward. Her right leg came free of the saddle and she kneed herself in the eye.

The world spun crazily. Were those bright stars in the heavens or in her head? She squeezed with her thighs as tightly as she could, clung to the saddle with one hand, to the reins with her other.

There was a metallic creaking and breaking. The Trôs

stumbled and lurched, making a ruin of Ischade's fence and
gate. The beast reared, pounding the twisted wrought iron
with its shod hooves. It reared again, screamed, raced away
from the house, and collided with a good-size tree.

It staggered back a pace; stared with huge, wet eyes at the
offending obstacle. Dazed, confused, it took a side step, then
another, and stood still.

Chenaya hesitated, afraid to let go of saddle or rein. Her
heart thundered against her ribs, a trickle of blood ran down
her chin; she had bitten her lip. Finally, she dared to let go of
the saddle. With her free hand, she rubbed the small of her
back. Breath held much too long hissed between her teeth.
She glanced back at Ischade's fence, let go a low chuckle,
then reached down and stroked the Trôs's powerful neck.

"That looked like fun. Do it again."

Chenaya knew that voice by now. Her gaze rose to find her
observer. He looked down at her from a comfortable notch in
the very tree the Trôs had struck.

"Does the Riddler know you're stealing his horse?" Zip
asked sardonically.

She put a finger to her lips and glanced back at Ischade's
darkened windows. "I think he's too busy *knowing* the vampire woman, if you get my meaning," she answered, matching
his lighthearted tone. "Are you doing anything tonight? How
about a date?"

Zip swung his legs back and forth absent-mindedly, much
as she had done earlier at the wharf. The similarity struck her
as odd.

He rubbed his chin, a barely visible shadow against the
starlit night. "It has been rather dull. Nothing I'd like more,"
he said in his most affected Rankene. "You're so easy to follow."

"When I want to be," she acknowledged. "I figured you
couldn't keep your eyes off me." She stared upward, craning
her neck, guessing what was going through his mind as he
rose to stand in the notch. She admired his daring, if not his
sense, as he balanced above her.

"A date, you say?"

She stroked the Trôs again. "How about a ride?" She put
on a big grin. Zip wore the shadows like a cloak, but she was
limned in Sabellia's light. She knew he could see her smile.
"You can help me with my prank on Tempus Thales. Make up
your mind, though." She cast another glance over her shoulder

at the darkened estate. It occurred to her to wonder why all the racket had roused no one. She didn't particularly care to wait around to find out—not on Zip's account. "This isn't a very good neighborhood, I'm told, and a lady has to guard her reputation."

"You expect me to ride behind you?" His voice was incredulous. "After what I just saw?"

Chenaya leaned forward, scratched the horse between its ears. "It's all right," she assured. "We're good friends now, aren't we, horsie?" The Trôs didn't contradict her.

Zip hesitated. She wondered if he had ever ridden before, or if he was daunted by the fact it was Tempus's horse he was being invited to help steal? In either case, she couldn't wait around for Zip to find his balls. Dismas had assured her that Tempus was inside Ischade's house. At this very moment he might be struggling into his breeches, reaching for his sword. . . .

She blew Zip a kiss. "Sorry, lover," she called. "It's *yes* or *no* and no time to think about it—that's the way it is with me." She gathered the reins in both hands. "But how about tomorrow night?" She nudged the Trôs with her heels and clicked her tongue. The horse raced through Shambles Cross and turned onto Farmer's Run before Zip could say another word.

Though Lowan Vigeles's properties extended all the way to the Red Foal River, the major portion of the estate was ringed by a massive, fortified wall. Along the southern rampart, with gates of their own, stood the stables. It was through this gate that Chenaya rode. Dismas held it open, hailed her, then leaped frantically clear before the Trôs trampled him into the dirt.

Chenaya jerked on the reins with all her might. The warhorse's hooves tore up chunks of earth. It reared, nearly throwing her again, then stopped, completely still, trembling.

She blew an exhausted breath, swung one leg over the Trôs's neck, and slid to the ground. Dismas, Gestus, Walegrin, and Rashan hurried to her side.

"Damn beast nearly gave it to me!" Dismas mutterred, brushing dust from his sleeves, looking as if he'd eat the Trôs if given time to build a fire.

Chenaya pushed the hair back from her eyes. Her golden

mane was a tangled mess; sweat and dirt streaked her cheeks. She wiped her face with the back of her hand and passed the reins to Gestus. "Put him in the pen with Lowan's mare. Hurry! She's in heat, and this one's got enough krrf in him to incite the lusts of an army." She swatted the Trôs's rump as the gladiator led him away. "Rashan, I want you to invoke Savankala's blessing on this union. The mare must conceive. I want a strong foal from her."

The priest's eyebrows shot up. "You want me to bless copulating horses?"

"You're a priest, aren't you, the Eye of Savankala?" She embraced him and gave him a quick peck on the cheek. Rashan had lived at Land's End while he oversaw the building of her private temple on the shore of the Red Foal. They had shared many late night discussions, and he had taught her much.

"Very well," he agreed, rolling his eyes. "But we must speak this night before we part." He turned to follow Gestus, but continued talking over his shoulder. "I've had another dream. You must hear the message. It was the voice of the Thunderer himself."

She watched him go, saying nothing. But his words disturbed her. His walk and bearing were those of a warrior, not a priest, and his body was developed as befitted a Rankan. Yet a priest he was, and first among Savankala's hierophants. Yet, lately, Rashan had been having dreams, messages from the god, he claimed, visions that foretold Chenaya's future and her destiny. All through the winter they'd argued the meaning of his dreams. Not messages at all, she'd tried to convince him. Just the wishful thinking of an old man who saw his nation decaying around him.

She clung to that argument now as he disappeared inside the stables with Gestus and the Trôs. There could be no truth to his dreams. She was not the Daughter of the Sun. That was only a name, an appellation pinned on her by arena spectators and fellow gladiators. Nothing more.

There was movement on her right side. She had forgotten her other guest.

"Lady," Walegrin said uneasily. "It's the middle of the night. Your man said it was of the direst importance that you speak with me, that I come dressed thus out of uniform. Because you are Lord Molin's niece I hastened, but the morning—"

She cut him off with a curt gesture. "If you came only because of Uncle Molin, Commander, then you may leave again." She looked him straight in the eye, not at all intimidated by his towering height. "If you came, though, to enhance your own career or to do good service to your prince, then stay and hear me out."

His eyes grew wide in the moonlight, but she turned her back on him and spoke to Dismas. "There's a sectarius of red wine on a peg in the stables. Bring it."

A sudden din from the stables interrupted her. They all looked toward the building. There came a crashing and cracking of wood, the challenging cry of the Trôs horse, the lamentation of the mare. There was cursing from Gestus, and Rashan's shouted prayers soared over the whole.

"Bring the wine," she repeated, touching Dismas's arm in comradely fashion. "There's parchment and ink there as well. Bring them along, too."

She turned back to Walegrin when they were alone. "You command the garrison in this garbage pit," she said, folding her arms over her chest, regarding him evenly. "And the closest thing to a police force in Sanctuary is your men. I'm not going to hold it against you that you've been keeping company with that scheming uncle of mine. We all seek advancement by the fastest means, after all."

"If your uncle schemes," Walegrin broke in defensively, "he does so on Sanctuary's behalf."

Chenaya threw back her head and smiled scornfully. "Molin Torchholder does nothing except in his own behalf. But I didn't call you here to argue my uncle's lack of virtue. As you pointed out, it's late." She rubbed her backside. "And I've had a rough night."

Walegrin folded his arms, unconsciously imitating Chenaya's aggressive stance. He looked down at her. "Then what did you call me here for?"

"You're the police," she said over the noise from the stables. "What's the biggest problem you've got in the city right now?"

He scratched his chin and considered. "Right now?" He pursed his lips, put on an expression of intense seriousness. "I'd say it's finding the thief who stole Tempus's horse before he takes the town apart."

She stared disdainfully at him, gave him her back, and headed after her friends. "Go back to your bunk, Commander.

I picked the wrong man. I'll take care of Kadakithis myself as I've always done."

He came after her, caught her by the shoulder. Chenaya whirled, knocked his hand away. "Wait," he pleaded as she started to leave him again. "What about Kadakithis? If there's some trouble, let me help."

She ran her gaze up and down his rangy height, taking his measure. She'd kept an eye on him during her time in Sanctuary and generally considered him one of the few honest men in the city. Reportedly, he was competent with his weapons, though not a brilliant fighter. He did seem, however, to have the loyalty of his men, and that counted for much.

She not only *needed* his help, she *wanted* it.

"The PFLS," she said at last, drawing a deep, calming breath. "They started out murdering Rankans and Beysibs in cold blood. Men, women, children—armed or unarmed, it didn't matter. They began a reign of terror that ended up carving Sanctuary into sections like a big pie, and their terrorist activities have earned them the animosity of nearly every citizen in town." She paused, thinking suddenly of Zip. "Their leader still harbors dreams of Ilsig liberation, but the rest kill and kill simply for the feeling of power it gives them when they grind someone else into the dirt."

Dismas came back bearing the sectarius of wine, the parchment, and the inkpot. "Keep those," she told him, taking the leather vessel. She unstoppered it, swallowed a mouthful, wiped her lips, and passed it to Walegrin who followed her example. "How goes it in there?" she asked Dismas, nodding toward the stables.

The gladiator looked askance and grinned. "Such a mating as I've never seen. Hear for yourself how the mare enjoys her pleasure. I thought they were going to tear the stalls down, but they've taken more than a liking to each other."

"I thought I heard Gestus cursing." She took the wine from Walegrin, offered it to her man. Though her gladiators called her *mistress*, she treated them fully as equals.

Dismas lifted the bottle and swallowed. "He got kicked in the hand," he explained. "He tried to unsaddle the Trôs, but the mare already had her tail in the air."

"I've met men who similarly couldn't wait to undress," she quipped. "I guess you're all part horse." She hesitated purposefully, then added, "or some part of a horse." She slapped her rump and winked.

"The PFLS," Walegrin reminded her, trying to remain patient. "And Kadakithis. Is there some threat?"

The noise from the stables suddenly ended. A few moments later, Rashan emerged and started across the lawn. She waited for the old priest to join them and offered him the wine. He drank deeply, then accepted the parchment and inkpot from Dismas. He gave Chenaya an inquiring look.

"Tempus came to me with a proposal," she said to Walegrin. "One with implications for all of Sanctuary. You know that Theron has promised to return at New Year's and make this city what he wants most—a bastion for the Rankan Empire's southern border." She glanced at Dismas and a silent message passed between them. "You also know that I have no love for Theron."

Walegrin surveyed the faces of those around him. "It was you and your gladiators who attacked his barge and killed his surrogate." He said it with absolute calm and certainty.

Chenaya reached up and tapped his forehead exactly as her father would have done to her. She had never attempted to make a secret of it, just as she had never thought to fail. In fact, she hadn't failed, just shot her bolt at the wrong target. The man in Theron's robes hadn't been Theron at all, and the Usurper had gotten out of town before she could try again.

Her mouth shaped itself into a smirk. "Tempus was stupid enough to try to blackmail me with information that seems to be common knowledge. He'll be leaving soon with his Stepsons and the Third Commando." Walegrin nodded. The imminent departure of the two groups was not news. "Well, he had an idea that I should take control of the PFLS and use it to weld the various factions into a Sanctuary defense force." That much of her speech was the truth, then she added her own thoughts and plans. "And use it to resist Theron when he returns."

The garrison commander rubbed his chin, his nose, an ear, wishing he hadn't heard that tidbit, thinking about what he'd have to do with it. "You realize you're accusing him of a treasonous offense?"

Chenaya shrugged, took another drink of wine, passed him the sectarius. "I wouldn't try to make it stick," she advised. "Tempus owes more loyalties than you and I can begin to guess. He joins Theron but plots against him. Who can know his motivations?" She shrugged again. "Anyway, I thought there was some merit to the idea—but not the way he formulated it. Take a look around, Walegrin. You don't expect this city to become just another good little satellite obedient to the Empire, do you? Something's brewing here. Call it rebellion."

Rashan spoke up, passing the wine to Dismas. "If you expect resistance when Theron returns," he said softly, "then Sanctuary will need a defense force. Theron is a murderer and a usurper. Loyal Rankans *should* rise up against him."

Chenaya waved a hand, dismissing his speech. "Loyal Rankans have little to do with this," she said. "But Sanctuary is a different matter entirely, a melting pot of many interests, none of which favor Theron. Yes, Tempus had the right idea, but because he is Tempus Thales, and a fool, he overestimates the importance of his Stepsons and commandoes. Even without them Sanctuary is far from defenseless. And we don't need the PFLS to take their place, either."

She held up her fingers and began to tick off a few numbers. "The Beysibs have a good five hundred warriors; that doesn't include the Harka Bey, who are an unknown quantity. The garrison houses at least sixty men-at-arms, almost all of them raised and recruited locally. There are the Hell-Hounds, who feel the Empire has deserted them; I think they'll fight for us. There are Jubal's minions—they have nothing to gain and much profit to lose if Theron should pacify this region." She tapped her chest with one hand, rapped the knuckles of her other on Dismas's shoulder. "Then I have my twelve gladiators, the finest arena-flesh in the history of the games. And by the New Year I'll have a hundred more, the best fighters ever to come out of Rankan schools."

Walegrin looked thoughtful, seeming to forget that, as he spoke, he was also committing a treasonous offense. "We could dredge up more from the streets," he observed, "and we have our wizards. Sanctuary is full of wizards."

"What we don't need," Chenaya continued, encouraged by his participation, "is the PFLS. That group has caused too much dissension, actually fostered the factionalism that has cost so many lives. The swiftest thing we can do to unify those factions is to put an end to Zip and his bloodthirsty band."

The garrison commander nodded slowly, perceiving the truth in her words. Even Zip's own people, most of the Ilsigi population, had turned away from the ideas espoused by the PFLS when it became general knowledge that the group was backed by Nisibisi insurgents who wanted only to stir up trouble on Ranke's rear border while their demon-spawned sorcerers pushed their conquests from Wizardwall through the surrounding kingdoms.

"Without the Third Commando liaison, we've never been able to lay hands on Zip," Walegrin complained. "What makes you think that's going to change? They're like rats. And it's not just Ratfall that they call home; the Maze and Downwind belong to them as well."

Chenaya took another swallow of wine when it came her way again. "Any rat can be lured out of its hole with the right cheese," she said. "I've already set the trap. I only need you to help spring it."

Gestus emerged from the stables leading the Trôs by the reins. The big creature seemed completely bewildered, still in the krrf's embrace. Chenaya could almost swear the beast was grinning. She pointed to the parchment and the inkpot that Rashan held. "Write for me, Priest, " she instructed. "Use your finest calligraphy."

Rashan looked over his shoulder, located the full moon, and positioned himself in the best light. He took the stylus from the inkpot and held himself poised for the first stroke.

"Write . . ." Chenaya paused, thoughtful. "Thanks for the stud service, lover." She laughed then, remembering her garden encounter with the Riddler. "Sign my name in big letters."

Rashan gave her a disapproving look, the kind Lowan Vigeles would have given her. She paid him as much attention, and he wrote. When he was done she took the parchment and gave it to Gestus. "Fix it to the saddle," she instructed, "and let the Trôs go."

The gladiator looked shocked. He was, after all, a thief, and he thought he'd taken part in a very clever and daring theft. A good thief didn't give back the booty. "Let go horse?" he mumbled.

"Let it go?" Walegrin echoed in better speech.

Chenaya repeated herself. "I'm no fool, Commander. Though I enjoy pricking Tempus's bubble a little, I don't underestimate him. In a short time, the marc will have a foal, then I'll have a half-Trôs of my own to ride. I can wait a couple of years. Keeping this one could lead to a direct conflict between the two of us." She glanced up at Sabellia floating serenely in the dark sky. "Who knows what cosmic forces that would unleash, what war among the gods would result?" She shook her head. "No, when I risk that, it will be for something far more important than a horse, even a Trôs."

Rashan made the sign of his god. "Let us hope Tempus has as much sense. You know him better than he knows you, child."

Gestus led the Trôs toward the gate. But before he got beyond it, a penetrating and high-pitched whistle sawed through the night. Chenaya cried out in pain, clapped hands to her ears to stop the sound. Through tear-moistened eyes she watched her companions do the same. The Trôs reared unexpectedly, jerking the reins from her gladiator's hand. It whinnied and sped out of sight, as if in response to the strange whistle, the sound of its hooves adding thunder to the shrill, knife-edged keening.

Abruptly, the sound ceased, and Chenaya straightened. Despite the ringing in her ears, she found strength to smile. "I don't know what that was," she said, "but I think our living legend finally missed his mount." She rubbed her ears and the side of her neck. "I hope the note doesn't fall off."

A look of utter confusion lingered on Walegrin's face. He whispered to the priest in an overly loud voice. "What was she talking about? Gods and cosmic forces, all that? I'm beginning to think Molin is right. You're all insane!"

Rashan shook his head, doing his best to calm the excitable commander. "You'll learn soon enough," he said, low-voiced. "Tempus is hundreds of years old, they say. Imagine all his power, maybe more, in the person of such a young woman." He made a bow in Chenaya's direction. "She is truly the Daughter of the Sun."

Chenaya ground her teeth. "Shut up, Rashan. I told you, I'm tired of that title and your little fantasy. Now leave us. You've done your part this night, and I've got plans to discuss with the commander."

Rashan protested. "But the dream," he reminded her. "We've got to speak. Savankala summons you to your destiny."

She waved him away, her irritation growing. Such talk was disturbing enough in private. Before Walegrin, she felt a genuine anger. "I said leave us," she snapped. "If I'm really who you think I am, you don't dare disobey me. Now go!"

Rashan stared sorrowfully at her, not angry, not disappointed, patient. "You don't believe," he said gently, "but you will. He will show you. When you look upon his face, you will know the truth." He raised a finger and pointed at her.

"Look upon his face, child. See who you are." He turned, strode toward the gate and beyond.

She sighed, her anger turned suddenly upon herself. Rashan was her friend, and he meant well. She resolved again not to let his delusions interrupt that friendship. In such troubled times and in such a city as this, trustworthy comrades were hard to come by.

She put fingers to her lips and gave a high whistle of her own. While he was free and unjessed, Reyk was trained to follow wherever she went. The falcon dropped from the sky to perch on her arm. She took the jess and a small hood from her belt, stroked her pet a few times, and passed him into Dismas's care.

Then she took Walegrin by the arm. "Come up to the house, Commander. There's more wine and a bite to eat." She called back to the two former thieves. "Wake all the others," she instructed. "Daphne, too. They're all involved."

These were treasonous times, and it was time to talk treason.

Eight men. That was all that remained of the Popular Front for the Liberation of Sanctuary, Zip assured her. There were no more. And looking him straight in the eye, she believed him.

They were a rag-tag lot, some even without sandals or boots. But they carried good Nisibisi metal or equally well-crafted weapons recovered from Rankans and Beysibs they had murdered. They were young, the eight, but as they huddled in the deep shadows of the old stables off Granary Road, their armament was cold reminder of the treachery and chaos they had inspired.

It was time, though, for her treachery, and she led them swiftly down Granary Road, past a corner of her own estate to the Avenue of Temples. Noiselessly, they stole up to the Gate of the Gods, wide-eyed rats, eager for a taste of cheese.

She looked at Zip's face, barely visible in the shadows, feeling something that bordered on regret. He, of all these cutthroats, seemed sincere in his quest for Ilsig liberation. But he had murdered Rankans—her people—and so many others, done such evil in freedom's name. She turned away from him and rapped quietly on the sealed gate, glad that Sabellia had not yet risen to shine on this moment.

The gate eased open a crack. From beneath the metal brim of a sentry's helm, Leyn peered out. He cast a suspicious gaze over Zip's band, playing his part well, and held open his palm. "The other half of my payment, lady," he whispered slyly. "It's due now, and the gate is yours."

Chenaya took a heavy purse from the place where it rested between her leather armor and her tunic. It jingled as she passed it over. Leyn weighed it, considering, frowning, chewing the end of his mustache.

Zip pressed forward impatiently. "Move it, man, while you've still got a hand to count with!" The others, too, pressed forward, demonstrating that the gate would be breached whether the guard was satisfied or no.

"You sure it's all here?" Leyn grunted. "Then inside, and damn you all, and damn the filthy Beysibs." He tugged the gate wide and stood out of the way, waving them in with a bow full of mockery. "Blood to you this night, gentlemen, much blood."

Chenaya led them, hurrying, crouched low, across the courtyard toward the governor's roses, toward a small entrance in the western palace wall. She had come here once before, her first week in Sanctuary, to save Kadakithis from an assassin. By this very way she had come. She found that a bitter irony.

Because she listened for the sound, she heard the gate close behind them, heard the sturdy iron lock click into place.

Zip heard it, too. His sword slid serpent-quick from the sheath as all around them shadows rose up from the ground where they had rested flat in the gloom. There was horror in his eyes when he faced her, and anger. But worst of all was the look of betrayal. In an instant, he knew her for what she was, and she knew he knew.

That didn't stop her. Furiously, Zip lunged, his point seeking her heart. Chenaya side-stepped, drew her gladius. In the same back-handed motion she smashed the pommel against his brow as he passed her. The rebel leader fell like a stone at her feet and didn't move.

"Sorry, lover," she muttered honestly, meeting the nearest man with balls enough to try avenging Zip. Blades clashed in a high arc, then she dropped low and raked her edge over his unarmored belly. As he doubled, screaming, she cut upward through his throat.

A manic yell went up from the PFLS as her gladiators

crashed into their ranks, hacking at their foes. The Rankans let out their own cry, a vengeful paean full of rage for all their slain kindred. There was no mercy in them and no thought of surrender in Zip's band. Blades clashed and clanged, throwing blue-white sparks. Blood fountained, thick and black in the night. Cries and groaning and grunting filled the palace ground. Walegrin's men came running.

Then hell erupted. All around, flame spumed upward. Within the bright geyser a Rankan screamed, threw his arms up uselessly, and ran like a crazed demon trailing fluttering fire.

Another incendiary exploded. Fire spread like a deadly liquid across the earth. Rankans and PFLSers alike shrieked and burned. Someone ran screaming toward her, swathed in fire. Foe or one of her own, she couldn't tell, but she gave him a quicker death.

She had thought to stay by Zip, to guard and keep him alive through this carnage. But now she whirled about, searching for the bomber. He was the paramount threat.

She spied him then, as he lobbed yet another bottle of the strange fluid. The flash dazzled her vision; heat seared the left side of her face. The smell of singed hair crept malodorously into her nostrils—her own hair, she realized with a start. And though she knew she could not die thus—Savankala himself had shown her the manner of her death—in that moment she tasted a small bite of fear.

She gripped her sword more securely and started toward him.

But the bomber's eyes snapped suddenly wide; his mouth opened in a horrible scream. His hands went up as if to supplicate the heavens. Then, he toppled forward, dead.

Daphne eyed her mistress across the courtyard, her sword running red with the bomber's blood, a mad grin spreading over her small face. Knowing Chenaya watched, the Rankan princess threw back her dark-haired head and laughed obscenely. Again and again she hacked at the body until the torso was a scarlet mass.

Chenaya glanced over her shoulder at the palace. Lights flared in the windows where darkness had been before. Heads peered out at the slaughter. Armed Beysibs, barely dressed, surged out to join the tumult.

It ended quickly after that. Gladiator, garrison soldier, naked Beysib looked around for new foes and found none.

Taciturn as ever, the fish-folk wiped their blades on whatever was at hand and went back to bed. Walegrin gave orders; his men began to drag away the corpses.

Leyn rushed to Chenaya's side and returned her pouch of gold. He had thrown aside the sentry's helm or lost it in the conflict. His curly blond hair shone with the glow of the fires that still burned. "Mistress," he said softly, "we lost two of our own." He told her the names.

Chenaya drew a deep breath. "Fire or sword?" she asked.

Leyn turned his gaze away. "One to each."

She winced, full of grief for the one who had burned. It was no way for a warrior to die. "If you can, get the bodies from Walegrin. We'll give funeral rites ourselves at Land's End and scatter their ashes on the Red Foal."

Leyn moved away to carry out her order. Alone for a moment, Chenaya fought back tears of anger. All of her gladiators were hand-picked men, all completely loyal to her, and she had led two of them to their deaths. Death itself was nothing new to her, but this responsibility for other men's lives was. Suddenly, she found it a heavy yoke to bear.

She gazed up at the sky, wishing Sabellia would come to brighten up her world. There were but twelve links on her chain now—no, only ten. But soon there would be a hundred. One hundred bonds to bind her.

She went back to Zip's unconscious form. Already, a bruise had appeared where her pommel had struck him. She knelt and felt for a heartbeat, fearing she had hit too hard.

"Is he alive?"

She looked up at Walegrin. The garrison commander was smeared with blood, though apparently none of it was his own. He was a grisly sight. The color and smell of it had never bothered her before, but this time she turned her gaze away.

It was then she saw her own hands. They, too, were dyed the same mortal shade.

"He lives," she answered at last. "I meant for him to live." A light breeze stirred Zip's black curls. Unconscious, there was almost an innocence about his features, so composed, peaceful. "He should stand public trial for his crimes," she said, disturbed to the core of her soul. "People must know that the PFLS's long night of terror has come to an end. Then we can start putting the pieces of this town back together."

A lamb, she thought of Zip suddenly. *The sacrificial offer-*

ing that will make us well and whole again. She took one of his still hands in hers, then pulled away. For the second time that night she tasted fear. Zip had fallen on his sword. There was a long cut across his palm. It relieved her to find no more serious wound.

Literally now, his blood was on her hand.

She rose, trying to wipe her fingers clean on her armor. "Take him," she said to Walegrin, "and say this to Kadakithis and Shupansea"—she looked at Zip's quiet face as she spoke, almost as if her words were meant for him—"that Zip is my peace offering to them and to this city. I will feud with the Beysa no more, but it's they who must pull the factions of Sanctuary into one unified whole." She hesitated, swallowed, went on. "Say also that they cannot do this from behind the palace walls. It's time for them to come out into the midst of their people and lead as leaders should."

She looked away from Zip's face and surveyed the courtyard. The dead were being arranged in separate groups: those that could still be recognized, those that could not. The stench of scorched flesh permeated the air. Her gladiators worked beside the garrison soldiers. Even a few Beysibs who had not gone back to bed lent their hands.

"Otherwise," she said to Walegrin, "all this will have been for nothing."

She left him then, and Leyn, who still had the key, let her out through the Gate of the Gods. When no one could see her, the tears at last spilled down her cheeks, and hating the tears, she began to run. She didn't know the streets she took, nor did she know the time that passed before her grief and anger subsided. She wound up on the wharf again where she had been the night before, sitting, dangling her feet over the deep water as Sabellia began her journey through the sky.

She could still feel Zip's eyes upon her back, watching her as he had last evening.

She shuddered and hugged herself and wished for Reyk to keep her company. But the falcon was in his cage, and she was alone.

Alone.

As alone as Tempus Thales?

IN THE STILL OF THE NIGHT

C. J. Cherryh

Haught opened the sealed window ever so carefully, in this nightbound room of shrouded furniture, the hulking, concealed chairs and table like so many pale ghosts reverted only then to furniture, pretending in the shadows. He made no sound. He made no trial of the wards which sealed the place, nor even of the vented shutters which closed the outside. But a wind breached those barriers effortlessly. The first breath of outside that had come into the mansion in . . . very long, stirred the draperies and the sheets and brought a sultry warmth to the dank, sealed staleness in which he had lived.

That wind stirred the few grains of dust that were about. (It was an astonishingly clean house, for one sealed so long, from which servants had long since fled.) It swept down the halls and into another room, and touched at the face of a man who slept . . . likewise very long. In that darkness, in that silence in which the mere arrival of a breeze was remarkable, that cold and handsome face lost its corpselike rigor; the nostrils widened. The eyes opened, long-lashed, mere slits. The chest heaved with a wider breath.

But Haught knew none of these things. He was drawn. He felt the exercise of magics like a tremor in the foundations, a quivering in his bones. He felt the power coming from that ruin across the street, where most of an entire block of Sanctuary's finest houses had mingled all in one charcoaled wreckage of tumbled brick and stone and timbers; and he felt it rush elsewhere, tantalizing and horrific and soul-threatening. He bent down to peer through the vents of that window, careful to shroud himself, which was his chiefest Talent, to go invisible to mages and other Talents. To that, his magic had descended. He spied on the working of magic that he could not presently command. He longed after power and he longed after his freedom, neither one of which he dared try to take.

He saw the coming together of his enemies out there in the

98

dark, saw looks directed toward the house, and felt the straining of spells which the witch Ischade had woven about his prison. He shivered, as he stood there and inhaled that wind redolent of old burning and present sorceries and exorcisms, of revenge; he suddenly knew this house the target of all these preparations, and he felt an overwhelming terror: and trembled with his hatred. He felt the power build, and the wards flare with a moment's dissolution—

And he was paralyzed, frozen with doubt of himself, even while that dreadful force came all about the house and burst the wards in a great flare of light.

He screamed.

Elsewhere the sleeper started upright, and convulsed, and smoked from head to foot, which smoke streamed in a flash toward the hall, and the chimney, and aloft, in a moment that all living flesh in the house was battered with light and sound and pain.

The sleeper fell back again, slack-limbed; Haught collapsed by the window in the front room, and by the time he was conscious enough to lift himself on his arms and assess the damage, all the air seemed still and numb, his hearing blasted by a sound which never might have been sound at all.

He gathered himself up and clung to the sill, and lifted himself further, trembling. He stood there in that condition till it was all quiet again, stood there till the shadowed figures went their way from the ruin across the street, and he dared finally move the window and shut it again.

A hand descended on his shoulder and he whirled and let out a scream that made it very fortunate that the party across the street had dispersed.

The calm, handsome face that stared so closely into his— smiled. It was not the smile of the man who had owned the body. It was not that of the witch who lived there now. *Nothing* sane was at home within that shell. Haught was a mage, still. Against another threat he might fling out some power, even with the crippling of magic throughout the town; he was still formidable.

But what slept behind those eyes, what wandered there sometimes sane and sometimes not, and sometimes one mind and sometimes another . . . was death. It had reasons, if it remembered them, to take a slow revenge; and to hurl magic against the wards (he felt them restored) which held that soul in—

Haught prayed to his distant gods and cringed against the shutters, made an unwanted rattle and flinched again. Ischade had been there. Ischade had been near enough long enough that perhaps this thing that looked like Tasfalen would pick that up; and remember its intentions again in some rage to blast wards and souls at once.

But the revenant merely lifted a hand and touched his face, lover's gesture. "Dust," it said, which was its only word; daily Haught swept up the dust which infiltrated the house, and sifted it for the dust of magics which might linger in it, the remnant of the Globe of Power; with that dust he made a potion, and dutifully he infused it into this creature, stealing only a little for himself. He was faithful in this. He feared not to be. He feared a great deal in these long months, did Haught, once and for a few not-forgotten moments, the master mage of Sanctuary; he suspected consequences which paralyzed him in doubt. Because he had choices he dared none of them: his fear went that deep. It was his particular hell. "It's all right," he said now. "Go back to bed. Go to sleep." As if he spoke to some child.

"Pretty," it said. But it was not a child's voice, or a child's touch. It had found a new word. He shuddered and sought a way quietly to leave, to slip aside till it should sleep again. It had him trapped. "Pretty." The voice was clear, as if some deeper timbre had been there and now was lost. As if part of the madness had dispersed. But not all.

He dared do nothing at all. Not to scream and not to run and not to do anything which might make it recall who it was. He could read minds, and he kept himself from this one with every barrier he could hold. What happened behind those eyes he did not *want* to know.

"Here," he said, and tried to draw the arm down and lead it back to bed and rest. But it had as well be stone; and all hell was in that low and vocally masculine laugh.

The slow hooffalls echoed in the alleyway, off the narrow walls; and another woman, overtaken alone in this black gut of Sanctuary's dark streets, might have thought of finding some refuge. Ischade merely turned, aware that some night rider had turned his horse down the alley, that he still came on, slowly, provoking nothing.

In fact, being what she was, she knew who he was before

she ever turned her face toward him; and while another woman, knowing the same, might have run in search of some doorway, any doorway or nook or place to hide or fight, Ischade drew a quiet breath, wrapped her arms and her black robes about her, and regarded him in lazy curiosity.

"Are you following me?" she asked of Tempus.

The Trôs's hooves rang to a leisurely halt on the cobbles, slow and patterned echo off the brick walls and the cobbles. A rat went skittering through a patch of moonlight, vanished into a crack in an old warehouse door frame. The rider towered in shadow. "Not a good neighborhood for walking."

She smiled and it was like most of her smiles, like most of her amusements, feral and dark. She laughed. There was dark in that too: and a little pang of regret. "Gallantry."

"Practicality. An arrow—"

"You didn't take me unaware." She rarely said as much. She was not wont to justify herself, or to communicate at all; she found herself doing it to this man, and was distantly amazed. She felt so little that was acute. The other feeling was simply awareness, a web the quiverings of which were always there. But perhaps he did know that, or suspect it. Perhaps that was why she answered him, that she suspected a deeper question in that comment than most knew how to ask. He was shadow to her. She was shadow to him. They had no identity and every identity in Sanctuary, city of midnight meetings and constant struggle, constant connivance.

"I heal," he said, low and in a voice that went to the bones. "That's my curse."

"I don't need to," she said in the same low murmur. "That's mine."

He said nothing for a moment. Perhaps he thought about it. Then: "I said that we would try them . . . yours and mine."

She shivered. This was a man who walked through battlefields and blood, who was storm and gray to her utmost black and stillness; this was a man always surrounded by men, and cursed with too much love and too many wounds. And she had none of that. He was conflict personified, the light and the dark; and she settled so quickly back to stasis and cold, solitary.

"You missed your appointment," she said. "But I never wait. And I don't hold you to any agreement. That's what I would have told you then. What I did, I did. For my reasons. Wisest if we don't mix."

And she turned and walked away from him. But the Trôs started forward as if stung, and Tempus, shadowlike, circled to cut her off.

Another woman might have recoiled. She stood quite still. Perhaps he thought she could be bluffed, perhaps it was part of a dark game; but in his silence, she read another truth.

It was the challenge. It was the unsatisfiable woman. The man who (like too many others) partly feared her, feared failure, feared rejection; and whose godhood was put in question by her very existence.

"I see," she said finally. "It isn't your *men* you're buying."

There was deathly silence then. The horse snorted explosively, shifted. But he did not lose his control, or lose control over the beast. He sat there in containment of it and his own nature, and even of his wounded honesty.

Offended, he was less storm and more man, a decent man whose self-respect was in pawn: whose thought now was indeed for the lives and the souls he had proposed himself to buy. He was *two* men; or man and something much less reasonable.

"I'll see you home," he said, like some spurned swain to the miller's daughter. With, at the moment, that same note of martyred finality and renunciation. But it would not last at the gate. She did not see the future, but she knew men, and she knew that it was for his own sake that he said that, and offered that, in his eternal private warfare—with the storm. Man of grays and halftones. He tormented himself because it was the only way to win.

She understood such a battle. She fought it within her own chill dark, more pragmatically. She staved things off only daily, knowing that the next day she would not win against her appetites; but the third she would be in control again; so she lived by tides and the rhythms of the moon, and knowing these things she kept herself from destructive temptations. This man served a harsher, more chaotic force that had no regular ebb and flow; this man warred because he had no peace, and no moment when he was not at risk.

"No," she said, "I'll find my own way tonight. Tomorrow night. Come tomorrow."

She waited. In his precarious balance, in his battle, she named him a test of that balance and she knew even the direction his soul was sliding.

He fought it back. She had not known whether he could,

but she had been sure that he would try. She knew the silent anger in him, one half against the other, and both suspecting some despite. But there was the debt he owed her. He backed the Trôs and she walked on her way down the alley unattended.

Another woman might have suffered a quickening of the pulse, a weakness in the knees, knowing who and what eyes were staring anger at her back. But she knew equally well what he was going to do, which was to sit the Trôs quite still until she had passed beyond sight. And that he would wait only to prove that he could wait, when the assaults would come on his integrity, not knowing any tide at all.

He touched her, in a vague and theoretical way. She respected him. She took a monumental chance in what he proposed for payment, not knowing whether either of them might survive it. Perhaps he knew the danger and perhaps not. For herself, she felt only the dimmest of alarms. It was the dreadful ennui again, the sense of tides.

The fact was that she missed Roxane. She missed her own household of traitors. She missed them with the feeling of a body totally enervated, the ancient ennui the worse to bear because for a little while, so long as there had been an enemy and a challenge, she had been alive, for a little while she had been stirred out of a still and waking sleep.

Only her lovers could touch her when the ennui was heaviest. It was not the sex for which she killed. It was the moment of anguish, of terror, of power or of fear or sorrow—it never mattered which. It never lasted long enough even to identify. There was only the instant that had to be tried again and again, to try to know what it was.

Perhaps (sometimes she wondered) it was the only moment she was alive.

The Trôs horse thundered from the alley, the rider never looking back; and Straton, Stepson, pressed himself flat against the streetward wall, staring after Tempus until horse and rider merged with the night.

And turned abruptly and looked down the dark and empty alleyway, knowing that Ischade would have gone.

That she would blast him to hell for spying on her business.

He heard rumors of her—heard!—gods, he had *heard* a

thousand whispers without hearing them, not truly. Then—
then he had taken a bad one, then he had spent long enough in
hell to shake any man from his confidence in himself, in his
choices, in the fool gesture that had sent him blind angry onto
a street without his cautions or his wits. Now for the rest of
his life there might be the small twinges of pain, all unexpected, that shot through his shoulder when he moved his arm
at the wrong angle, an unpredictable pain that enraged him
when it would come shooting through and he would stop in a
certain reach, at an angle. It came so quickly and so indefin-
ably that he could not feel whether it was the pain of scarred
tendons and joint running up against their limit and freezing
dead, or whether it was only the pain that froze the arm, in an
eyeblink of flinching that he was not man enough to master.
He tried with exercise and with dogged resistance when it did
freeze; but still it betrayed him at bad moments.

It was his confidence that had died in that street, before
Haught had ever gotten his hands on him. It was the shattering
of a body he had always taken businesslike care of, and
treated well, and gotten hale and whole to this end of his life
when he had begun to look on shopkeepers and merchants and
their wives and their brats with a kind of forlorn envy; merc
service was a young man's game and he had begun to think of
another kind of life, still with his body and his wits intact, still
with his resources and his experience and his contacts—

Until a single careless act wrecked him and flung him
down on a curbside under the eyes of all of Sanctuary; left a
flinch in his shield arm and a knotted fear in his gut—not the
nightmares that waked him sweating, not that fear. It was the
suspicion that he had deserved it, and that Crit was right: His
whole world was a construction of cobwebs and moonbeams.

The woman whose face he saw in the act of love, the beautiful, dusky face, the black hair scattered in silk webs across
the pillows—the face that mused and smiled her thoughtful
smile above him in the soft light of a fire and candles—

—he could not equate with the one who walked the alleys.
With the one who took lover after lover in the most sordid
byways of Sanctuary, indiscriminate—killer.

He followed her the way he drove at the arm, to find the
limits of the pain and to control it, to exorcise it—like the
other evil. He had seen things he could not forget. He had
leaned toward sanity, toward Crit, and leaving her when the
Stepsons rode out from this town; he would not look back; he

would dream about it less and less. The arm would heal and he would recover himself somewhere, some year.

But this betrayal he had not imagined, this . . . *double* . . . betrayal, her with his commander.

Damn them both. Damn them. He thought that he had felt all there was to feel. He had not put together until then, that he had been a real power in Sanctuary even before she had taken him to her bed. That she had made him almost a great one. But that was changed. He was useless to her, at a critical time. So she threw out her nets and gathered in one more apt for her purposes.

He flung himself around the corner, down the walk, and flinched. It was the same street. It was the same blind rage. Reprise, replayed. The bay horse was waiting for him; it always waited, a mockery of faithfulness, her gift to him, that would never leave him. He left it stabled. In the mid of nights he heard its hoof-falls on the cobbles beneath his window. He heard it pacing, heard its breath, the shift of its body in his dreams. And there was this small patch on its rump which . . . was not there. There was nothing of color about it. It was just a flaw, a place that, if one stared at this coin-sized spot, one imagined one saw no horse at all, but cobbles, or the wall beyond, or some shimmer behind which the truth might be visible. He began, in his loss of confidence, to find terror in its faithfulness and its persistence.

He went to it now and gathered up the trailing rein and put his left arm about its neck, again, his left, to see if it would hurt; and hugged and patted the sleek warm neck to see if it would turn with its teeth and prove itself some thing out of hell. There was pain now, a muddle of ache and anger in his chest and in his throat and behind his eyes, and he was a damned fool out on the street where a sniper had found him before.

"Strat."

He spun about, a rush of cold fear and then of outrage. "Damn you, what are you doing here?"

His partner Crit just stood there and looked at him a moment. He had left Crit down the block, down by the burned houses.

"How'd I get this close?" Crit asked him. "You don't know. *That*'s what I'm doing here."

"I want to find the bastard that shot me," he said. "I want to find that out." There was a connection. Crit could put most

things together. That was what Crit did in the world, add little
pieces and make big patterns. Crit had made one that said he
was a fool. That was the man Crit saw tonight. He wanted to
show Crit another one. He wanted to show Crit the old Straton
back again, and to take care of his business and seal up the
pain and not let it interfere with his working any longer.

Take care of his business and finish it so that he could ride
out of this murder-damned town when the Stepsons pulled
out, and not go with the feeling that he was driven.

Go out of town under Tempus's order, riding in the same
company, with his mouth shut and his business all done. That
was all he wanted.

The bay horse nosed him in the ribs, lipped his hand with
velvet, insistent in its devotion.

There was no relief, no breath of wind, through the slit of a
window, which overlooked nothing but the narrowest of air
shafts down to a barren court. Somewhere a baby cried. A rat
squealed in some fatal moment, in the jaws of some other
predator of Sanctuary nights. The loft just above rustled with
wings, disturbance among the sleeping birds that cooed and
bickered and scratched by twilight and now ought to have
slept. Of a sudden they started, all at once, a great clap of
wings and avian panic; and Stilcho flinched, standing naked at
that window in the dark. Wings fluttered, battering at the narrow opening overhead that gave the panicked flock an escape;
gray wings took to the night, day birds put to rout by something that hunted above. He shivered, hands clutching the sill;
and looked back at the woman who lay sprawled, coverless on
the ragged sweat-soaked sheet. A body did not so much sleep
in this third floor hellhole as pass out; the air was fetid and
stank of human waste and generations of unwashed inhabitants. It was as much resource as they had, he and Moria. He
was alive, but barely. Moria had sold everything she had, and
plied her old trade, which terrified him; they hanged thieves,
even in Sanctuary, and Moria was out of practice.

She stirred. "Stilcho," she murmured. "Stilcho."

"Go to sleep." If he came to her now she would feel the
tension in him, and know his terror. But she got up, a creak of
the rope-webbed underpinnings, and came up behind him, and
pressed her sweaty, weary self against him, her arms about

him. He shivered even so and felt those arms tense.

"Stilcho." There was fear in her voice now. "Stilcho, what's wrong?"

"A dream," he said. "A dream, that's all." He held her arms in place, cherished her sticky, miserable heat against him. Heat of life. Heat of passion when they had the strength. Both had returned to him, along with his life. Only the eye that Moruth had taken—kept seeing. He had fled Ischade, fled mages, fled the agencies that used him as their messenger to hell. He was alive again, but one of his eyes was dead; and one looked on the living, but the other—

A third shiver. He had seen into hell tonight.

"Stilcho."

He put his back to the window. It was hard to do, his naked shoulders vulnerable to the night air; and worse, his face turned to the room, with its deeper dark in which his living eye had no power. Then the dead one was most active, and what moved there suddenly took clearer shape.

"They've let something loose, oh gods, Moria, something's gotten loose in the town—"

"What, what thing?" Moria the thief gripped his arms in hands gone hard and shook him for the little she could move him. "Stilcho, don't, don't, don't!"

The baby squalled and shrieked, from the window down the shaft. The poor shared their violence and their tempers, lived in such indignities, the noise, the raised voices audible from apartment to apartment.

"Hush," he said, "it's all right." Which was a lie. His teeth wanted to chatter.

"We should go back to Her. We should—"

"No." He was adamant in that. If they both starved.

But sometimes in not-quite dreams, in that inner vision, he felt Ischade's touch, plainly as he had ever felt it, and suspected in profoundest unease that she knew precisely where her escaped servants were.

"We could have a house," Moria said, and burst into tears. "We could be safe from the law." She burrowed her head against him and hugged him tight. "I came from this. *I can't live like this, it stinks, Stilcho, it stinks and I stink and I'm tired, I can't sleep—"*

"No!" The vision was there again. Red eyes stared at him in the black. He tried to shift his sight away from it, but it was more and more real. He tried to push it away, and turned to the little starlight there was and clung to the sill till his fingers ached. "Light the lamp."

"We haven't—"

"Light the lamp!"

She left him; he heard her rattling and fussing with the tinderbox and the wick and tried to think of light, of any pure, yellow-golden-white light, of sun in mornings, of the burning summer sun, anything that had the power to dispel the dark.

But the sun he limned in his one living eye, there in the dark, reddened, and became paired, and lengthened, winking out in a blink as deep as hell and reappearing in slitted satisfaction.

The lamp glow began slowly, brightened, profligate waste. He turned and saw Moria's face underlit, haggard and sweaty and fear-haunted. For a moment she was a stranger, a presence he could no more account for than he could account for that vision which had waked him, of a thing launched into the skies over Sanctuary and hurtling free. But she moved the lamp and set it on the little niche shelf, and it made her body all shadows and flesh tones, her hair all wispy gold, all over. The magic that Haught worked had been thorough. She had still the look of a Rankene lady, however fallen.

She needed him, in this place. He persuaded himself of that. He needed her, desperately. At times he feared he was going mad. At others he feared that he was already mad.

And at the worst times he dreamed that she might wake and discover a corpse by her, the soul dragged back to hell and the body suffering whatever changes two years might have wrought in it, in its natural grave.

Day, brutal heat in the still air that settled in over Sanctuary since the rains. Shoppers at market were few and listless; merchants sat fanning themselves and keeping to the shade, while vegetables ripened and rotted and the remaining few fish did the same. There was trouble in the scarred town. The rumor ran up from Downwind and down from the hill, and all the byways murmured with the same names, furtively delivered.

High up on the hill an officer of the city garrison met with higher authority, and received orders to carry elsewhere.

In Ratfall there was a certain stirring, and certain merchants received warnings.

And a furtive woman went out on the streets to steal again, in gnawing terror, knowing her skills were not what they had been, and knowing that the man she had taken up with was approaching some crisis she did not understand. For this woman there must always be some man; she was adrift without that focus, shortsighted, on some life that made hers matter; she wanted love, did this woman, and kept finding men who needed her—or who *needed,* at any rate . . . and who lacked something. Moria knew need when she saw it, and went to that in a man like iron to a lodestone, and never understood why her men always failed her, and why she always ended giving away all she had for men who gave nothing back.

Stilcho was the best, thus far, this dead man who, whenever he could, gave her more gentleness than anyone had ever given but a strange doomed lord who still filled her dreams and her daydreams. Stilcho held her gently, Stilcho never demanded, never struck her. Stilcho gave something back, but he took—Shipri and Shalpa, he took; he drained her patience and her strength, waked her at night with his nightmares, harried her with his wild fancies and his talk of hell. She could not provide enough money to get them out of this misery, and a single mention of seeking help from Ischade drew irrational rage from him, made him scream at her, which in her other men had ended with blows, always with blows. So she flinched and kept silent and went out again to steal, her bright Rankene hair done up in a brown scarf, her face unwashed, her body anonymous and all but sexless in the ragged clothes she wore.

But desperation drove her now. She thought again and again of the things she had known, the luxuries she had had in the beautiful house, the gold and the silver that would have melted in the fire that ended that life. And even among Sanctuary's brazen thieves there was a notable reluctance to venture into that charred ruin; they came, of course. But none of them knew building from building or where the walls had stood, or where certain tables had been.

So when evening fell she went back again and began her sooty search, furtive as the rats which had become common in this stricken district, hiding from other searchers. She had

never yet found a thing, not the silver, not the gold, which
must exist as a flat puddle of cold metal somewhere below;
but she had tunneled for weeks into the sooty ruin, and
searched what had been the hall.

That was why she came late home. And this time—gods,
she trembled so with terror in the streets that her legs had
practically no strength left for the stairs—this time she
brought a lump of metal the size of her fist; and to Stilcho's
anxious, angry demand where she had been, why she was
besooted (she had always washed before, in the rainbarrel,
and wiped it all to general grime on her dark clothes) and why
she had let wisps of her yellow hair from beneath her scarf—

"Stilcho," she said, and held out that heavy thing which
was, for all the fire and its changing, too heavy to be other
than what it was. Tears ran down her face. It was wealth she
had, as Sanctuary's lower levels measured it. Where she had
rubbed it, it gleamed gold in the dim light from the lamp he
had burned waiting for her.

Finally, to one of her desperate men, she had given something great enough to get that tenderness she had longed for.
"Oh, Moria," he said; and spoiled it with: "Oh gods, from
there! Dammit, Moria! Fool!" But he hugged her and held her
till it hurt.

The river house waited, throwing out light from one un-
shuttered window, across the weed-grown garden, the trees
and the brush and the rosebushes which embedded the iron
fence and the warded gate.

Inside, in the light of candles which were never consumed,
in a clutter of silks and fine garments that lay forgotten once
acquired, Ischade sat in her absolute black, black of hair, of
eye, of garments; but there was color in her hands, a little
lump of blue stone that had also known that fire. She had
gathered it out of the ash in a moment's distraction—she was
also a thief, by her true profession; and if her hand had suffered burns from the ash, the stone had sucked all the heat into
itself, and rested cool in unscarred, dusky fingers.

It was the largest piece of what had been the globe. It was
power. It had associated with fire, and flame was the element
of her own magic, fire, and spirit. It was well it reside where
it did; and it was best if no one in Sanctuary were aware just
where it resided.

Hoof-falls sounded outside, echoing off the walls of the warehouses which faced her little refuge, while the White Foal murmured its rain-swollen way past her back door. She closed her hand till flesh met flesh; and the blue stone was gone, magician's trick.

She opened the outer gate for her visitor and opened the front door when she heard his steps on the porch. And looked around from where she sat as she heard him come in.

"Good evening," she said. And when he stood there disregarding the invitation and too evidently in a hurry about their business together: "Come sit down—like my proper guest."

"Magics," he said in his lowest tone. "I'll warn you, woman—"

"I thought—" She made her voice a higher echo of his, and with a taint of slow mockery: "I did think you were in better control than that."

He stood there in the midst of her scattered silks, the littered carpet and scarf-strewn chairs. And she shut the door at his back, never stirring from where she sat. He stared at her, and a little spark of reckoning flickered in his eyes. Or it was the disturbance of the candles that sent shadows racing? "I did think your hospitality was better than this."

The fire was there, inside her, it always was; and it stirred and grew in that way that, last night, should have sent her on the hunt. "I waited for you," she said. "I'm quite at my worst."

"No damned tricks."

"Is this how you pay your debts? I *can* wait, you know. So can you, or you'd be prey to your enemies. And you've so much vanity." She gestured at the wine on the tables. "So have I. Will you? Or shall we both be animals?"

He might have attempted rape, and then murder; she felt the tilt in that direction. And she felt him pull the other way. Surprisingly he smiled.

And came and sat down across from her, and drank her wine, in slow silence there at the empty hearth. "We'll be pulling out," he told her in the course of that drinking, amid other small talk. "We'll leave the town to—local forces. I'll be taking all of mine with me."

That was challenge. Strat, he meant. She stared at him from under her brows and let her mouth tighten ever so slightly at the corners. Her hand came to rest by the base of the wineglass. His covered it, and it was like the touch of fire.

He sat there, his fingers moving ever so delicately, and let the fire grow—*Wait, then. Enjoy the waiting.* Till it was hard to breathe evenly, and the room blurred in the dilation of her eyes.

"We can wait all night," he said, while her pulse hammered at her temples and the room seemed to have too little air. She smiled at him, a slow baring of teeth.

"On the other hand," she said, and let her leg brush his beneath the table, "we could regret it in the morning."

He got up and drew her up against him. There was no time for undressing, no thinking of anything more, but a tending toward the couch close at hand, a hasty and rough passage of feverish hands. He did not so much as shed the mail shirt; it resisted her fingers and she clenched her hands into his outer clothing. "Careful," she said, "slow, go slowly—" when he thrust himself at her. Warning him, with the last of her sanity.

The room went white, and blue and green, and thunder cracked, spinning her through the dark, through warm summer air, through—

—nowhere, till she came to herself again, lying dazed under a starry sky, with the ramshackle maze of Sanctuary buildings leaning above her. She felt nothing for a while, nothing at all, and shut her eyes and blinked at the stars again, her fingers exploring what should have been silk, but was instead dusty cobblestone. The back of her head hurt where she had fallen. She felt bruised along her whole back, and where he had touched her she felt a burning like acid.

He never lost consciousness. For a moment he was clearly elsewhere, then lying stunned on pavement with a curbside against his ribs. He had hit hard, and he ached; and he likewise burned, not least with the slow realization that he was not in the riverside house, that he was lying in a midnight street somewhere in the uptown, and that he hurt like very hell.

He did not curse. He had learned a bloody-minded patience with the doings of gods and wizards. He only thought of killing, her, anything within reach, and most immediately any fool who found amusement in his plight.

When he had picked himself up off his face and gained his balance again there was no question which direction he was going.

• • •

It was a long tangle of streets, a long, limping course home, in which she had abundant time to gather the fragments of her composure. Her head ached. Her spine felt quite disarranged. And for the most urgent discomfort there was no relief until she rounded a corner and came face to face with one of Sanctuary's unwashed and ill-mannered.

The knife-wielding ruffian gave her no choice and that contented her no end. She left him in the alley where he had accosted her, likely to be taken for some poor sod dead of an overdose of one of Sanctuary's manifold vices. His eyes had that kind of vacancy. In a little while he would simply stop living, as the chance within his body multiplied by increments and everything went irredeemably wrong. The poor and the streetfolk died most easily: their health was generally bad to begin with, and his was decidedly worse even before she left him lying there quite forgetful that he had been with any woman.

She was, therefore, in a more reasoning frame of mind when she arrived on the street by the bridge, and walked up the road which most ignored, to her hedge and her fence on this back street of Sanctuary. But she was not the first one.

Tempus was already there, walking sword in hand about the perimeter, up along the fence; and he stopped in his tracks when she came from beyond the trees, into the feeble glow of the stars overhead and the light from between her shutters. There was rage in every line of him. But she kept walking, limping somewhat, until they were face to face. He looked her up and down. The sword inclined its point to the ground, slowly, and hung in his fist.

"Where were *you?*" he asked. "And where in hell is my horse?"

"Horse?"

"My horse!" He pointed with the sword to the front of the fence and the hedge, as if it were perfectly evident. In fact there was no horse in sight and he had ridden in; she had heard him. She gathered her forces and limped on to the front of the en-hedged fence, where the ground, still soft from the rain, was churned and trampled by large hooves.

And where one of her rosebushes was trampled to splinters.

She stood there staring at the ruin, and the light inside her shuttered house flickered brighter, glowed with a white incandescence. It died slowly as she turned. "A girl," she said. "A girl is the thief. At my house. From my guest."

"This wasn't your doing."

His voice was calmer, restrained.

"No," she said in soft and measured tones, "I do assure you." And drew herself up to all her height when he reached for her. "I've had quite enough, thank you."

"It threw you too."

"To the far side of the mage quarter." She drew in a hissing breath through wide nostrils. It smelled of horse and mud, trampled roses, and bitch. And there was wrath and chagrin both in this huge man, wrath that began to assume a certain embarrassed self-consciousness. "Our curses are not compatible, it seems. Storm and fire. And we were so well begun."

He said nothing. His breathing was rapid. He walked past her to the trampled ground and gave a whistle, piercingly shrill.

She caught it up for him, reached inside and flung it to the winds, so that he winced and faced her in startlement.

"If that will bring him," she said, "that will carry to him."

"That will bring him," Tempus said, "if he's alive."

"A young woman took him. Her smell is everywhere. And krrf. Don't you smell it?"

He drew in a larger breath. "Young woman."

"Not one I know. But I will. My roses come very dear."

"A bloody young bitch." It sounded particular and specific, his eyes narrowing in some precise identification.

"In frequent heat. Yes."

"Chenaya."

"Chenaya." She repeated the name and stored it away carefully. She waved the gate open. "A drink, Tempus Thales?"

He slid the sword into its sheath and walked with her, a light touch beneath her arm, steadying her as she walked up the steps, and wished the door open, a blaze of light into the dark thicket of the yard.

"Sit down," he said when they were inside; his voice was a marvel of self-restrained gentleness; he poured wine for her, and then for himself. Then: "I owe you an apology," he said, as if the words were individually expensive. Then further: "There's mud in your hair."

She gave out a breath of a laugh, and breathed larger and wider and found herself awake. It was not a pleasant laugh, as the look on Tempus's face was not a pleasant one. "There's mud on your chin," she said, and he wiped at it, with a hand likewise smudged. They both stank of the streets. He grinned suddenly, wolflike. "I'd say," Ischade said, "we were fortunate."

He drank off his glass. She poured another round.

"Do you get drunk?" he asked, directly.

"Not readily. Do you?"

"No," he said. There was a difference in his tone. It was not arrogance. Or pride. He looked her straight in the eyes and it was clear that tonight, this moment, it was not a man-woman piece of business. It was similar perspective. It was a rare moment, she sensed, that a man got this close to Tempus Thales. And a woman—perhaps it was the first time.

She recalled him in the alley, on the horse, that something-to-prove manner of his.

But defeated, robbed and offended, he was being astonishingly sensible. He was going far to excess in it, and again she felt that precarious balance, polar opposite to the direction black rage insisted he go. He smiled at her and drank her wine, issues all forever unresolved.

One expected a man of vast lifespan to be complex. Or mad, at least to the limited perspective of those who lacked perspective. It was vitality of all sorts which was his curse, healing, sex, immortality.

Annihilation was hers. And the apposition of their curses was impossible.

She laughed, and leaned her elbow on the table and wiped her mouth with the back of a soiled hand.

"What amuses you?" There, the suspicion was quite ready.

"Little. Little. Your horse and my roses. Us." As distant hooves echoed in the streets, within her awareness. "Shall we dice for the bitch?"

He had heard the horse coming. He recovered himself, as she had guessed, became the stranger again, and headed for her door.

Well enough.

She came out a moment or two later, when the horse had come thundering up, and brought a cloak which had lain underfoot for months. It was velvet, soiled, and a horse which had run the width of Sanctuary was bound to be sweated. "Here," she said, joining him at the open gate. "For the horse." Which was rolling its eyes and lolling its tongue and reeking of krrf as he worked at the cinch. Tempus snatched the skewed saddle off, jerked the cloak from her hands, and used it on the Trôs.

"Damn," Tempus said over and over.

"Let me." She moved in despite the hazard from both, put out a calm hand, and touched the Trôs's bowed forehead; it was a little exertion. Her head throbbed and it cost her more than she had thought. But the horse steadied, and his breathing grew more regular. "There."

Tempus wiped and rubbed, walked the horse in a little circle on the level ground. And never said a word.

"He's all right," she said. He knew her magics, that they could heal—others with some skill; her own hurts with less effectiveness. He had seen her work before.

He looked her way. She demanded no gratitude, nor expected any. There was a sour taste in her mouth for this abuse of an animal. Their personal discomfiture she could find irony in. Not this.

She stood with her arms folded and her cloak about her while Tempus carefully, without a word, threw the sweated blanket and the saddle on. The Trôs ducked its head and scratched its cheek on its foreleg, as if abashed.

He finished the cinch and gathered up the reins, looked once her direction, and then swung up.

And rode off without a word.

She heaved a sigh, the cloak wrapped about her despite the steamy warmth of the night. Hoofbeats diminished on the cobbles.

The wide focus had disappeared, along with the ennui. Dawn was lightening the east. She walked back along the path and closed the gate behind her, opened the door, arms folded and head bowed.

Her perspective had vanished, together with the ennui, from the time that they had met in the alley. And since that encounter in the ruin, something had nagged at her which said danger, which had nothing to do with human spite. It did have something to do with what they had carried out uptown, some misfortune which encompassed her and perhaps Tempus.

Since the Nisi Globes of Power had dispersed their influence over the town, surprising things happened. Mages missed, sometimes: far more of chance governed magics than before, and common folk had more of luck in their lives than they were wont, amazing in Sanctuary; but dismaying for the town, mages who worked the greater magics found their powers curtailed, and sometimes found the results askew.

Therefore she abstained from the greater workings, until she let herself be talked into an exorcism, principally by the Hazard Randal, whose professional and personal honesty she counted impeccable—rarest of qualities, a magician of few self-interests.

Now she simply had that persistent feeling of unease, exacerbated, perhaps, by the experience of being hurled from one side of Sanctuary to the other, by the bruises and the throbbing in his skull. *Fool!* to have tried such a thing, such a damned, blind trial of a curse that had been, for a while and in the height of Sanctuary's power, manageable.

The headache was just payment. It could have been much worse.

It would have been worse, for instance, had she kept Straton, had this blindness and execrably bad judgment brought him back to her bed, opened that old wound.

And morning seen him dead as that drunken fool in a Sanctuary alley, who was by now neither drunken nor any longer a fool, nor able to see the dawn in front of his eyes.

"We can't both leave," Stilcho concluded. Sleep eluded them both. They were hoarse and blear-eyed and exhausted, sitting opposite each other at the rickety little table. "I can't leave you here alone with that thing."

"I *found* it, dammit." Moria wiped back a stringing lock and brought the hand hard onto the table. "Don't treat me like a damn fool, Stilcho, don't tell me how to manage! I carried it clean across town! We melt it—"

"What *with,* for godssakes? On the damned little firepot we cook on? We just get a damned hot lump of—"

"Hsssssst!" Her hand came up out-turned toward his mouth, her face twisted in fury. "These walls! These walls, dammit, how many times do I have to tell you keep your voice down! I'll *steal* us the stuff, how do you think we come by *anything* lately, except *I* steal it, and *you* live on it! Don't you tell me what to do! I've had it all my life, and I'm not taking it, I'm not taking any of it, not from you and not from anybody!"

"Don't be a damned fool! You go flashing gold bits around

this town you'll get your throat cut, this isn't silver, dammit, listen. *Listen!* You——" Of a sudden, even in the gray morning light filtering through the window, the vision of the lost eye shifted in, stronger than the living one. He stopped, his heart laboring in terror.

"Stilcho?" Moria's voice was higher, frightened. "Stilcho?"

"Something's wrong," he said. In that inner eye, soiled, filmy shapes went streaming like smoke through the gates, the gates—the fires, the lost reaches. . . . "A lot of people just died." He swallowed hard, tried to calm his shaking, tried to get back the sight of Moria across the table, and not that black vision where Something waited, where by the riverside—in the woods—

"Stilcho!" Her nails bit into his hand. He blinked and tried again to focus, succeeded finally in seeing her, beyond a veil like black gauze.

"Help me. M-moria—"

She rose and her chair overset, crashing down so violently she came and grabbed him and held on to him with all her might. "Don't, don't, don't, dammit, don't, come back—"

"I don't want to go down there, I don't want to die again —oh *gods,* Moria!" His teeth would not stop chattering. He could shut his living eye. He had no such power over the dead one. "It's in hell, Moria, a piece of me is in hell and I can't blink, I can't shut it, I can't get rid of it—"

"Look at me!" She jerked his head by the hair and looked him in the face. Another jerk at his hair. "Look at me!"

His sight cleared. He caught her around the waist and hugged her tight, his head against her breast, in which her heart beat like something trapped. Her hand caressed his head, and she whispered reassurance; but he felt her heart hammering fit to shake her small body. No safety. As long as she was with him there was none for her, and there was nowhere any for him.

Get out of here, he would tell her. But he dreaded the day he would slip and Moria would not be there to pull him back; he dreaded the solitude in which he might then go mad. If he were a brave man he would tell her go. But not today. They would climb out of this pit together; for that much they needed each other—he needed her skill and she needed his restraint and his protection to use the gold; but after that, after she was set up and he had a chance as well, then he would find a way to let her go.

• • •

"Damn!" Crit hissed. The news had come down the hill with the swiftness only bad news could manage; but Straton said nothing at all. Straton headed out the barracks door and whistled up the bay, which came; of course it came. It made trouble in the stables, it cleared the stable fence like a gull in flight, and nothing held it. It came to him in this early dawn, and he went to the tackroom to get what belonged to it.

"Where are you going?" Crit asked him, meeting him outside as he came out into the dusty yard, his right hand hauling the saddle, the treacherous left unburdened with anything but the bridle and the blanket. Crit was careful with him nowadays, uncommonly patient, a perpetual walking on eggshells.

"Town," Strat said. He cultivated patience, too. He saw Crit's analytical look, the inevitable reckoning what small house lay on his way. And he had not thought of that till he saw Crit think of it; then it got its claws into his gut, and the thought began to grow that of powers in Sanctuary which ought to be warned, which might exert a calming influence on the town—

—damn, she had contacts in all the right places. With Moruth the beggar-king; with the rats in the very walls when it came to that, the rabble that was most like to take the slaughter uptown very hard indeed. Zip arrested. *That* would not last long. Best he *be* arrested till someone had a chance to talk sense to him. Likely Walegrin.

"Stay off riverside," Crit said, and laid a hand on his arm, delaying him a moment. In months past that would have gotten a shrug-off, at best a surly answer. But Crit was fighting for Strat's soul, and Strat had gotten to know that, in a kind of fey gratitude for a friend with a lost cause, or at best a cause that was not worth the effort Crit spent on it. *I'm crippled, dammit, you got me back, you risked your damn neck pulling me out, but you have to get another partner, Crit, one who won't let you down in a pinch, and you know it and I know it. The fire's dying and I'm not going to be again what I was, when I get the twinges I know that. Tomorrow I'll tell you that. When we're out of this damned city I'll tell you that. And you'll tell me I'm a damned fool, but neither of us is. Time we split. Leave me to fend for myself: you don't have to go on carrying me, Crit.*

Crit's hand dropped. There was a worried look on his face.

Strat's stares could put it there, lately. And that usually got
Crit's temper up when other provocations failed. This time he
just stood there.

"Yeah," Strat said. "I'm going to drop out a few hours on
the way back, expect it: I'll be pulling in a few contacts." He
hung the bridle on his shoulder, flung the blanket over the
bay's back, not—not looking more than he must at that coin-
sized patch just by the bay's hipbone. "I may talk to her.
Figure I can walk out of there, too. It's all cooled down; she's
got her choices, I have mine." He slung the saddle up, and the
bay never offered to move. It had as well been a statue that
breathed and smelled like a horse. "She's sleeping around. We
got corpses to prove it."

"Don't be a damn fool."

"Hey." He turned his head and looked at Crit. "Trust me to
do what needs doing. All right? You're not my mother."

Crit said not a thing.

*Damn mistake, Crit. Say it. My mind's like the damned
shoulder, on and off, I never know when. I can't think, I can't
know when I'm on target, can't know when I'll flinch.*

She's got herself another lover. One I can't match, can I?

*I can meet her and ride away again. You don't know how
easy it is. I've seen her in the streets, Crit. Like the rest of the
whores. With a pox that'll kill you.*

He slipped the bridle on, cinched up, and hurled himself
into the saddle without the least twinge from the shoulder.
"See you," he said, and rode for the gates.

"Where?" Tempus snapped, just arrived on the hill, just
arrived inside Molin's offices. It was not a good day for Molin
either, but Tempus was clearly begun on a worse one. "When
and who?"

"About six of the piffs. Zip survived. He's in lockup, for
his own sake. And the city's. Walegrin's going to have a talk
with him."

"Who did it?"

Molin drew a careful breath and told him.

The headache had diminished. The malaise persisted, and
discouraged attempts at philosophy; Ischade kept to her house,
her hair immaculate, the mud scrubbed from her person, the

salvageable roses off the damaged bush decorating a vase on the table, not for the beauty of them (they were black and the moisture-beads which stood on their petals from their watering shone blood-bright red in certain lights), but as a reminder of a task she did not want to undertake in her present mood and with her headache.

Having power, she set limits to it; having the ability to blast an enemy, she refrained from it for no altruistic motives, but because killing was very easy for her, and very seductive, and led to untidy consequences which resisted solution.

She had taken rare inventory of her stores, and tidied up a bit (rarer still). Haught had kept things in some order. Stilcho had tried. She missed them, missed them today with outright maudlin melancholy, which both would have found bewildering.

Stilcho had fled, vanished. She might, she thought, find him.

The thought, as she paused with broom in hand, became quite inviting. Stilcho had shared her bed—many a night.

And died and waked. But that had been when her magic was unnaturally great. To do it now would risk him. And he had been loyal, he had saved Strat's life, he had deserved some choice in his fate, which was patently and sanely not to come back to her.

A presence came near her garden gate. She knew it, a little thrill along her nerves, in all the noon coming and going up and down the street just beyond.

She suddenly knew who it was even before she heard the horse distinctly, or felt someone touch the ironwork. She set the broom aside, flung the door open, and walked out onto the porch against her habit, in the full summer daylight.

"Go away," she said to Strat, and held the wards against him. "Out!"

"I've got to talk to you. It's business."

"I have no business with you."

He held both hands in plain sight. "No weapons."

"Don't try me. I warned you. I told you you'd be no different than the others."

"Fine. Open the gate. I don't want to shout from the street. This is trouble. Hear me?"

She wavered. The gate gave to his push against it, and creaked open when he shoved. He came walking up as far as the porch, his face all sullen and thin-lipped. "Well?" she said.

"There's been a murder uptown. A lot of it."

"I haven't been up to much this morning."

"Six of the piffs. You understand me."

She did understand. Faction war broken open again. With the Empire's hand already heavy on the town. "Who?"

"Can I come in?"

It was not wise. Neither was it wise to ignore the news. Or to fail to use the contacts she had, this one no less than the rest. She turned and went in, leaving the door open, and he followed her.

Night again. A shambling figure staggered among the reeds and the brush of riverside, snuffling at times and swatting at the midges and other insects that thrived here. One who knew Zip might not have recognized him beneath the swelling, the cuts and bruises: one eye was shut and puffed, even the good one running a trail down his face. His nose ran: that was the swelling. Or perhaps he was crying. He himself had no idea. He sniffed and wiped his nose on a muddy arm, the hand of that arm already caked in mud where he had fallen.

Run for it, the Stepson escort had told him, when they had brought him near the bridge, at twilight. He expected an arrow in the back, but he had no third choice: Walegrin had said they would let him go. So he ran for his life when they gave him the chance, raking through the undergrowth and tearing his lacerated face on thorns and brambles and branches. He had run until he slipped and sprawled on the slick bank, and run again, till his side hurt too much and he took to walking in the dark.

Man, something said to him, just that word, over and over, and direction which was the same as the direction he went, so that he hardly needed keep his good eye open, only to fend the branches away with his hands and to go toward that voice that led him. *Revenge,* it said then; and that was, in his delirium and his pain and his blindness, even better.

He did not know where he was until he had found the tumbled stones of an ancient altar. He did not know it at first sight, but stood there snuffling and tasting the thin constant seep of his own blood in his mouth, blinking at the haze and trying to focus; but it was his personal place, it was the altar where he had laid offerings to vengeance, because he was

Ilsigi and the old gods the Rankans let exist among the temples were quislings all. Ilsig had had a wargod once. A god of vengeance. And if all of them were dead and the statues only statues, he had still had a feeling about this old place that no Rankan had ever touched it, no force but earthquake ever tumbled these old stones, no Rankan ever knew its name to defile it. So he worshiped it, and gave it human flesh: that was the way he was in those days. It never answered him. But in those days it was all he had had, till he had ruled a quarter of Sanctuary.

Now Rankans killed his brothers, other Rankans turned him out with apologies, and he was here, fallen on his knees back at his beginnings, his ribs hurting, his face one mass of agony, his elbows bruised on the stone like his knees when he had hit the pavings in the massacre. He wept, and snuffled and wiped his nose and his eyes, trying to catch his breath.

Revenge, something whispered to him. He lifted his head and drew in a hoarse breath, hearing a murmuring and a rumbling in the earth. Something was there, in the dark just across the altar, facing him, a horripilating conviction of presence and a voice in his throbbing skull.

He blinked again. Two red slits appeared in that dark, and the same glow limned the flare of humanish nostrils and the seam of a humanish mouth, as if there were fire inside an utterly dark face. It smiled at him.

My worshiper, it said.

And whispered other things, about power, and how it had been shut in hell until it gained its freedom. The pain ebbed down. But not the cold.

"I'm going," he told it. "I got to get to my people, I got to tell them—"

Tell them they have a god. What would you give—for Ilsig to rise again? You paid lives. You'd pay yours. But it's worship I want. None of this business about souls. I want a temple. That's all. Whatever kind of a temple you want to make over there on the Avenue. That's where we can begin. Small. Till we have things in hand.

Zip wiped his nose and wiped it a second time. He ought to be running, except that he had no strength left. Except that this thing *was* real, and in a world where magery and power ruled, it was talking about Ilsig, and power of a sort Ranke had had a monopoly on too damned long.

Me, he thought. *Me. With this thing.* He was not sure what it was. God did not quite describe it, but it assuredly had ambitions to be one.

A temple Ilsigis might build. A priesthood other than those damned eunuchs and temple prostitutes the Rankans called state-approved Ilsigi gods. A priesthood with swords. And real power.

He sniffed and swallowed down the taste of blood, licked a bruised and swollen mouth. "If you're a god," he said, "tell my followers come to get me. If you're a god, you know who they are. If you're a god, you can call them here for me."

Do you really want them here, yet? We should talk strategy, man. We should make plans. You made one expensive mistake. Don't gather all your forces in one place. Cooperate with these foreigners. With everyone. Get your information in order. Deal only with authorities or use subordinates. You have to learn to delegate.

"Prove to me—"

Oh, yes. The red slits crinkled at the corners, the mouth stretched in a wide, wide smile. *Of course you'd come to that.*

Chenaya screamed, in the dark, in a sudden nowhere as if the world had dropped away. She fell and fell . . .

. . . hit a bruising surface that wrapped about her and bubbled past her and folded in on her with a terrible pressure. Water drove up her nose and filled her mouth and ears, threatening to burst her eyes and eardrums. Instinctively she tried to move her limbs and swim, but the momentum was too great, until she had gone deep, deep, and the pressure mounted.

Asleep in her own bed, her brain tried to tell her.

But the cold and the crushing force increased in one long narrowing rush downward after the impact, till she slowed enough to kick and the natural buoyancy of her body began to hurl her inexorably toward the surface. Salt stung her eyes and her throat; her lungs burned for air and her stomach was trying to crawl up her windpipe as she struggled with arms gone weak and legs kicking against too much water pressure.

. . . not going to make it, not going to make it, consciousness was going out in red bursts and gray and her lungs were clogged, needing to expel what they had taken in, in a spasm which would suck water in after it, and finish her.

Savankala! she wailed.

But nothing hastened her rise. She stroked and kicked and stroked, and her gut spasmed; she forced the last few bubbles out her nose, trying to gain time, fought with all instinct demanding to intake air where there was no air: she would faint, was going out, and her body would breathe by that instinct—

Her hand broke surface, and she grabbed at it with that hand and the other, one last desperate effort that got her face half clear and a froth of water and air sluicing down nose and throat. She coughed and spasmed and flailed, trying to spit up water and take in a clear breath while her temples ached to bursting and her gut racked itself in internal contractions. Stroke by flailing stroke she gained on life, gulped clear air and vomited, swam and gulped and choked in the toss of waves. Her sight showed her nothing but dark, abysmal dark.

"Help!" she yelled, a raw, animal sound. And gasped a mix of air and water as the chop hit her in the face and washed over her. Her voice was small in the wind and the night sky.

She gained enough strength to cast about her then, and blinked at the lights that she saw when she turned in the water, the distant line of the wharf, the Beysib ships riding at anchor. She had not a stitch of clothing. She was chilled and bruised and half-drowned, and she had no idea in the world how she had come there, or whether she had gone mad.

She started to swim, slow, painful strokes, until she remembered that there were sharks in these waters. Then she threw all she had left into the drive across Sanctuary's very ample harbor, toward the distant lights.

NO GLAD IN GLADIATOR

Robert Lynn Asprin

Chenaya shivered, part from her damp nakedness, part
from fear, as she clutched the threadbare blanket more tightly
about her. Fear? No, rather nervous anticipation.

The whole thing so far had a surreal, dreamlike quality to
it. First the rude awakening, sans clothes, deep in Sanctuary's
less-than-fragrant bay, and then the long swim to shore, wor-
rying all the while about the hunger and size of aquatic preda-
tors lurking below. There had been men waiting for her on the
pier, three of them, one bearing the blanket she now wore.
Nervousness made her declare her identity unasked, including
all her ranks and titles, yet they seemed as unimpressed and
unmoved by her station as they were by her nakedness. The
blanket itself was a silent statement of friendship, or at least
sympathy, however, so it seemed natural to follow without
protest as they hurried her through a bewildering maze of back
streets and alleys to the room where she now sat waiting.

Ignoring the scattering of candles and oil lamps which cast
flickering shadows about, she glanced again at the large chair
which dominated the room. All signs indicated that she was
finally going to meet the man she had been trying to contact
since she reached town. Well, her requests *had* said a time and
place of his choosing.

Her thoughts were cut short by the entrance of a man
through a door she had not seen in the shadows. Although his
features were obscured by a blue hawkmask, she had no difficulty recognizing him. Tall and lean as he was dark, she had
applauded him often in the Rankan arena, and stood near him
in the "tribunal" that Tempus had convened on Zip.

"Jubal," she said—more a statement than a question.

He had been studying her covertly as she waited, and admired her spirit despite himself. Naked and alone, she showed

no sign of fear, only curiosity. It was clear to him that this conversation would not be an easy one to control.

Neither acknowledging nor denying his name when she uttered it, he set one of the two clay bottles he was carrying within her easy reach.

"Drink," he ordered. "It's better against the night chill than your blanket."

She started to reach for the offering, then hesitated, her eyes going to him again as he settled himself in the thronelike chair.

"Aren't you supposed to taste this in front of me? A hospitable gesture to guarantee against poison? I was told it is a local custom."

He took a long drink from his own bottle before favoring her with a mirthless smile. "I'm not that hospitable," he said. "The wine I'm drinking is of a notably better vintage than yours. I swore off that slop when I left the arena, and I don't intend to break that vow just to make you feel better. If you don't trust it, don't drink it. It makes no difference to me."

He watched her quick flash of anger with amusement. Chenaya was indeed a Rankan noble, unused to being told that her actions were a matter of indifference to anyone. Jubal half expected her to throw the wine in his face and stalk off . . . or at least try to. The girl proved to be of sterner stuff, though. Either that, or she wanted this meeting more than Jubal had realized.

Defiantly, she raised the bottle to her lips and took a long pull. It was the coarse red wine given to gladiators.

"Red Courage," she said, using the gladiators' nickname for the drink as she wiped her mouth with the back of her hand, letting the blanket slip to expose one bare shoulder. "Sorry to disappoint you, but I'm not shocked. I've had it before . . . and liked it. In fact, I've developed a taste for it and drink it often with my men."

Jubal shook his head.

"I'm not disappointed. Puzzled, perhaps. Arena slaves drink that swill because they can't get any better. That or they've never had anything to compare it to. Why someone who is highborn and raised to finer things would choose to drink Red Courage when there are more delicate beverages to be had is beyond me. Of course, you've always been one who preferred being coarser than is necessary."

His words were intentionally insulting, but this time Chenaya seemed unmoved.

"I bow to the master," she smiled. "Who knows more of crudity and coarseness than Jubal?"

Unknowing, her riposte stuck Jubal in his most vulnerable spot: his vanity.

"I was born a slave," he hissed, leaning forward angrily in his chair, "and in that station crude living and no morals are a way of life. I learned to lie and steal and eventually to kill as a means of survival, not as a sport. I didn't like it, but it was necessary. Once I won my freedom, I did everything I could to rise above my beginnings . . . not far by noble standards, but as high as I have been able. I'm told I have a contempt for those below me who have not matched my efforts, let alone my success. That may be so, but I have more regard for them than for one who is highborn and wallows in the gutter by choice!"

Jubal caught himself before he said more and inwardly cursed his lack of control. The purpose of this interview was *not* to show Chenaya how to get him to lose his temper. Such information could be dangerous in the wrong hands.

Fortunately, the girl seemed more taken aback than alerted by his outburst.

"Please," she said in an uncomfortably contrite tone, "I don't wish to insult you or to fight with you. I . . . I made it known that I wanted to meet with you because I hoped we might work together."

This was more to Jubal's liking. He had anticipated this request when he first heard that she was trying to get in touch with him.

"Unlikely," he replied grimly. "I've had you watched since you arrived in town, as I do anyone who has the potential of influencing or disrupting the balance of power in this town. So far, your actions have been those of a spoiled brat: alternating malicious pranks with tantrums. I have heard of nothing that would give you value as an ally."

"Then why did you have me brought here?"

Jubal shrugged. "When I heard of your predicament, I thought perhaps the sudden demonstration of your vulnerability might shock you into thinking. Now that you're here, however, I see that you're still too full of yourself to listen to anyone else, or even talk to them instead of at them. Your value remains zero, however great the potential."

"But I have much to offer. . . ."

"I have no need of a slut or a horse thief. The streets are full of them, and most are better at it and smarter about plying their trade than you seem to be."

Jubal expected an angry retort to this, or at least an argument as to her value as an ally. Instead, the girl lapsed into silence, her thoughts obviously turning inward before she answered.

"If you are uninterested in me as an ally," she said, choosing her words carefully, "then perhaps I can impose on you as an advisor. You've been monitoring my actions, and know what I have and what I can do. But where I see strength, you will only acknowledge potential. Could I ask you to share your thoughts with me that I might learn from your experience?"

The crimelord studied her as he drank from his bottle. Perhaps Chenaya was wiser than he had given her credit for.

"That's the first intelligent thing you've said in this meeting. Very well, if for no other reason than to encourage your newfound humility, I'll answer your questions."

The girl took another sip from her own bottle as she organized her thoughts, unconsciously grimacing as if the sour bite of the wine was no longer pleasant to her tongue.

"I have nearly a dozen gladiators under my command and am currently recruiting more. I've always believed that gladiators, such as you yourself used to be, were the finest fighters in the Empire. Am I wrong?"

"Yes."

Jubal came out of his chair in a fluid motion and began pacing. "Every fighting force or school sincerely believes that its style is the best. They have to in order to muster the necessary confidence for combat. Your father trains gladiators, so you've been raised believing that a gladiator can defeat any three fighters without similar training."

He paused to regard her steadily.

"The truth is that there are certain individuals more suited to combat than others. Poor fighters die early, whether they're gladiators or soldiers. The survivors, particularly those who survive numerous battles, are the best by virtue of the process of elimination, but it's more a tribute to the individual than to the training."

"But my agents have been specifically instructed to recruit experienced gladiators," Chenaya interrupted. "Professionals who have survived numerous bouts. Doesn't that insure that I'll be getting the best fighters?"

Jubal fixed her with an icy stare.

"If you'll allow me to finish, perhaps you will hear the answer to that question. I thought you wanted to hear my opinions, not your own."

Chenaya wilted under his gaze, and nodded mutely for him to continue.

The crimelord waited a few more moments, then resumed his pacing. "As I was saying, it is the individual's abilities that dictate how good a fighter he can eventually become. Training prepares him for a specific type of combat. Gladiator training is fine for arena-style individual combat, but it doesn't teach a fighter to watch the rooftops for archers the way he'd need to in street fighting, or to deal with maneuvering groups of fighters the way the military does. Then again, even military maneuvers are useless in some situations, like when the mobs were forming during the plague riots. Any training will be of limited value when taken out of its element.

"As for your so-called professional gladiators, I don't like them, and would never endanger my name and reputation by hiring them to represent me. Regardless of what you might think, being a gladiator is not a desirable profession. A soldier or a thief can have a long and successful career and see little, if any, actual combat. By the nature of his livelihood, a gladiator must risk his life in open combat on a regular basis. If you are a slave, as I was, it's a dubious way to earn your keep, but to choose it freely as your 'professional gladiators' do is unthinkable. They are either fools or sadists, and neither are known to be particularly controllable."

"So you think I'm foolish to hire gladiators?"

"If that's your only criterion. At the very least I would advise that you look beyond training and arena records and study the individuals. Some of the men currently in your employ have questionable backgrounds. You might start looking into that before you place too much trust in them. Further, I would suggest that you find a trainer who can drill your troops in tactics more suited to the street than the arena. They'll stand a better chance of winning."

"I . . . I'll have to think on it," Chenaya said slowly. "What you say makes sense, but it's all so contrary to what I've been raised to believe."

"Take your time." Jubal smiled. "The time to think is before, not after you've committed yourself. Sending men into combat isn't a game."

She looked at him sharply. "I think I hear a hidden warning in that last comment. I take it you've heard of my special talent: the fact that I never lose. It's not potential, and I should think it would count heavily in my favor as a leader . . . or an ally."

The crimelord averted his eyes as he sank into his chair.

"I've heard of it," he confirmed. "In my opinion, it makes you both arrogant and vulnerable. Neither of which are traits I would want in someone leading me, or guarding my back."

"But . . ."

"Let's assume for the moment that you're right . . . that you'll never lose. I'll contest that later, but for now we'll take it as a given. You'll win every contest. So what? Start thinking like an adult instead of a child. Life isn't a game. An arrow out of the dark that takes you in the middle of the back isn't a contest. You can retain your perfect win record and still be just as dead as any loser."

Instead of arguing, Chenaya cocked her head quizzically.

"That's the second time you've mentioned archers or arrows, Jubal. For my own curiosity, were you behind the arrow that nicked Zip?"

Jubal cursed himself inwardly. He would have to stop underestimating this girl just because she was young. Her mind was quick to pick up unrelated conversational points and weave them into whole fabric.

"No," he said carefully, "but I know who was. The eye behind that arrow used to work for me, and unless her skills have degenerated badly since her departure, if his ear was hit, that was the target."

He noted the sudden lift of her eyebrow and realized too late that he had inadvertently given away the gender of the archer. It was time to steer conversation back to less sensitive subjects.

"We were speaking of your infallible luck. You seem to feel that if you never lose, you'll never fail. That kind of thinking is dangerous, both for you and anyone who sides with you. There is no such thing as an unstoppable attack or an impenetrable defense. Believing in one or the other only leads to overconfidence and disaster."

"But if I never fail in battle . . ."

". . . Like your attack on Theron?" The crimelord smiled.

"The attack was a success. We just chose the wrong target," she argued stubbornly.

"Spare me the rationalizations. Anyone who deals with magic or gods gets quite adept with excuses. All I know is that supernatural intervention exacts a price dearer than most intelligent people are willing to pay."

"Of course, you speak with the authority of one who has had a wide range of experience with gods and magic."

In response, Jubal swept his mask off with one hand.

Vanity made him conceal his unnaturally aged features from all but his closest associates, but at times like this his appearance could be far more eloquent than words.

"I have had one dealing with magic," he said grimly, "and this was the result. Years lost off my life was the price I paid to keep from becoming a cripple. While I do not regret the trade, I would think long and hard before entering into further bargaining. Does it ever occur to you that sooner or later *you* will have to pay for your luck . . . for ever dice roll that you do so casually to show off your so-called talent?"

The demonstration had the desired effect on Chenaya. She shook her head in mute admission, averting her eyes from the sight of the now-old man she had once cheered.

"Your noble birth gave you a natural arrogance," the crimelord continued relentlessly, deliberately leaving his mask off, "and your belief in your own infallibility has escalated it to proportions that try the patience and the stomach. You seem to believe that you can do whatever you want, to whomever you want, without regard to consequence or repercussion. Perhaps the most arrogant assumption of all is that you think that your undisciplined behavior is not only acceptable, but admirable. The truth is that people find your antics alternately amusing and offensive. If they either tire of being tolerant, or if you ever actually succeed in putting something together that is seen as a genuine threat, the real powers of this town will squash you like a bug, along with anyone who stands with you."

His taunting stung Chenaya out of her shock. "Let them try," she snapped. "I can . . ."

Jubal smiled, watching her face as she stopped in midsentence, hearing her own arrogance for the first time.

"You see? And that's while you're sitting there in a blanket after being dumped in the middle of the bay. My guess is that whoever did it to you was merely annoyed. If they had been really mad, they would have dropped you farther out. Yet still you persist in feeling that it doesn't matter who you offend."

Chenaya was hunched forward now, hugging the blanket about her as if it could ward off words and ideas as it had the chill. "Am I really that disliked?" she said without looking up.

Jubal felt a moment of pity for the girl. He had also gone through a period when he wanted friends desperately, only to find that his efforts were ignored or misinterpreted. A part of him wanted to comfort Chenaya, but instead he bore on relentlessly, taking advantage of her sagging defenses.

"You've given people little reason to like you. There is new wealth in town from our new Beysib residents, but the citizens still remember how hard money is to come by. You flaunt your wealth, deliberately inviting attack from those who are still desperate, then use your skills or your luck to kill them. Were one of them to succeed in slitting your throat some dark night, I doubt there would be much sympathy expressed anywhere. Most would feel that you deserved it, were asking for it in fact. I would hazard a further guess that there are even those who are secretly hoping it will happen, to teach an object lesson to Rankan nobles who underestimate the dangers in this town. Then, there is your sexual appetite. The tastes in this town are varied and often jaded, but even the lowest whore walking the streets near the Promise of Heaven can approach a man without grabbing his crotch in public."

"You're just saying that because I'm a woman," Chenaya protested. "Men do it—"

"That doesn't make it admirable," Jubal interrupted firmly. "You consistently take the worst models for your behavior. You've chosen to ignore the subtleties of femininity in favor of the blunt coarseness of men. What's more, you've tried to pattern yourself after the worst of men. I assume you've watched the gladiators when they're given women the night before they enter the arena. Remember that gladiators are viewed as animals by most, including themselves. What's more, they know there is a good chance they will not live through the next day, so they have little concern for thinking of the future or making a good impression on their partners. Then again, there's the minor detail that a gladiator's usually dealing with imprisoned whores or slaves. If he tried his pre-fight advances on a free woman in a tavern, I doubt he would find them acceptable to the lady or the other patrons. If you want someone to like you or admire you, you don't do it by embarrassing them in public . . . or in private, for that matter. Rape isn't admirable, no matter which sex perpetrates it."

"But Tempus is respected, and he's a known rapist."

"Tempus is respected as a soldier, in spite of . . . not because of his ways with women. I have yet to hear anyone, including his own men, describe his sexual habits as admirable. Remember what I was saying about paying a price for dealing with magic? If my information is correct, part of the cost Tempus pays for being 'favored of the gods' is only being able to take a woman by force. At least, that's the excuse he gives for his conduct. What excuse do you have for yours?"

Jubal had time as he spoke to reflect on the irony of him defending Tempus. "Forgive me if I seem to harp on my criticism of arrogance," he said, "but I firmly believe it's the most dangerous characteristic one can have in Sanctuary. You asked a moment ago of my experience with magic. Well, arrogance is something I am very experienced with; I've had to learn of its dangers the hard way."

Unbidden, images from the past rose up in his mind. Images that usually confined themselves to his dreams.

"Once, before your cousin came to town, I and my hirelings ran Sanctuary. The governor and the garrison were corrupt and ineffectual, and the power was there to be had by anyone strong enough to seize it and hold it. We were strong enough, but it led us, and me in particular, into believing that we were invincible. Consequently, we swaggered through the streets, flaunting and occasionally abusing our power, eager to have everyone acknowledge our strength. The result was that when Tempus arrived in town, we were the obvious targets, first for his individual attention, and then for the Stepsons when they joined him. My holdings were seized, my force scattered, and I was left with the wounds that cost me so much to have healed. All that from one man, the same one you are so willing to provoke with petty games."

"Yet you respect Tempus and are willing to ally with him?" Chenaya wondered out loud.

Jubal was suddenly aware of how far astray his memories had led him.

"You miss the point," he said brusquely. "The fault was mine. It was my open arrogance that brought attention of a sort I neither expected nor wanted. If you willingly lay your hand in a trap, do you hate the trap for snapping shut, or curse your own stupidity for placing your hand in jeopardy?"

"I should think you'd want to avenge yourself on the one who cost you so much."

"I'll admit that I have no great love for Tempus. If at some point in the future I have the opportunity to pay him back, I'll probably take it," Jubal observed, allowing himself a brief flash of the hatred he fought so hard to suppress. "What I won't do is devote my life to it. Revenge is a tempting side street which usually turns out to be a dead end. All it does is lure you farther away from your original path. You would do well to remember that in your schemes to deal with Theron."

"But he had my family murdered!"

"Isn't that part of the risk of being a noble?" he said, raising an eyebrow. "Remember what I was saying about everything having a price? Your family led a comfortable existence, but the price was linking your future to the existing power structure in the Empire. When it fell, so did your family. It was a gamble. One you lost. Do you really want to spend the rest of your life hating and pursuing the winner?"

"But—"

The crimelord held up a hand to still her protests. "I still haven't finished talking about my own arrogance. If you'll indulge me?"

Chenaya bit her lip but nodded.

"I thought I had learned my lesson. When I rebuilt my force, I contented myself with covert operations and maintained a low profile to avoid attention. To a large extent it worked, and the various factions in town turned their energies on each other. I watched them stacking bodies and licked my lips . . . yes, and even worked to keep them at each others' throats. It was my thought that eventually they would grow so weak that I could again rule Sanctuary."

He paused to take another sip of wine, a part of him wondering what there was about this girl that led him to confide his thoughts and plans to her.

"It wasn't until I was criticized by someone, an old man whose opinions I've grown to respect, that I realized that I had again fallen into the trap of arrogance. The Empire has changed and Sanctuary has changed. Things will never be as they were, and I was foolish to think otherwise. I will never again control this town, and all my machinations to weaken my rivals have only made it more vulnerable in its inevitable confrontation with Theron. That's why I was willing to go along with Tempus's plan to negotiate a truce among the warring factions. There is more at stake here than personal vengeance or ambition."

He noticed Chenaya was looking at him strangely. "You really care for this town, don't you?"

"It's a hellhole, or a thieves' world if you listen to the storytellers, but I'm used to it the way it is. I wouldn't like to see it changed at the whim of a new emperor. To that extent, I'm willing to put my personal ambition and pride aside for a moment, for the good of the town."

Chenaya nodded, but Jubal suspected that his attempts to make light of his feelings for Sanctuary had not deceived her in the slightest.

"Tempus wants me to organize the town's defenses once he and his forces leave town."

Jubal grimaced at her statement as if someone had placed something unpleasant on his plate.

"Unlikely. As shrewd as he may be militarily, Tempus still doesn't know the heart of Sanctuary. He is an outsider as you are. The townspeople resent your coming in and clanging the mission bell to tell them how to solve their problem. Even his own men are beginning to rebel against his high-handed ways after so long an absence. The truce was agreed to because it made sense, not because Tempus proposed it. I doubt *you* could effectively unite the locals because you are an outsider. Any cooperation you got would be grudging at best."

He considered pointing out that her betrayal of Zip made her decidedly untrustworthy in the eyes of any who knew of it, but decided against it. They were closing on one of the main reasons he had granted this audience, and he didn't want the conversation to veer off on unwanted tangents.

"Who, then? You?"

"I told you before that I'll never control this town again," he said, shaking his head. "I'm a criminal, and an ex-slave to boot. Even if those difficulties were overcome, too many of the factions have old grievances with me and mine. No, they might fight beside me, but they'd never willingly follow me."

"Then in your opinion, the best leader would be . . ."

She let the question hang in the air. Mentally, Jubal took a deep breath and crossed his fingers.

"Your cousin, Prince Kittycat. He's been here long enough to be considered one of the locals, and he's very popular with those common folk who've had any direct contact with him.

More importantly, he's probably the only figure of authority who has not directly opposed any of the necessary factions. If that isn't enough, he has closer dealings with the Beysib than anyone in town with the possible exception of the fishermen. The town will need the support of the fish-eyes, both financially and militarily, if we're going to stand against Theron. The proposed betrothal between Kadakithis and Shupansea will cement that alliance better than—"

"I know. I just don't have to *like* it."

Chenaya was on her feet and Jubal knew he was close to losing her.

"My cousin will never marry that bare-breasted freak! But gods, he's of royal birth—"

". . . As is she," he snarled, rising to his feet to match her anger with his own. "Such an arrangement would not only be for the good of the city, it might well be necessary. Think on that, Chenaya, before you let your childish jealousies rule your tongue. If you continue to oppose the union, you might just become enough of a danger for the powers of Sanctuary to test your invulnerability."

"Are you threatening me?" Fear and rebellion mixed in her voice as their gazes locked.

"I'm warning you . . . as I've been trying to do through this entire meeting."

For a moment the rapport between them teetered on the brink of disintegration. Then Chenaya drew a ragged breath and exhaled noisily.

"I don't think I could give my blessings to the marriage, no matter how good it might be for the town."

"I'm not suggesting that you have to encourage it, or even approve," Jubal said soothingly, trying not to let his relief show. "Simply cease opposing the marriage and let events take their natural course."

"I won't oppose it. But I have much to think on."

"Good," he nodded. "You're long overdue for some thinking. I think you've had enough advisement to fuel your mind for one night. My men outside will see you back to your estate . . . and tell them I said to find some clothes for you. It's not seemly for someone of your station to parade through the streets in a blanket."

Chenaya nodded her thanks and started to go, then turned back.

"Jubal, could I . . . will you be available in the future for additional counsel? You seem willing to tell me things that others avoid or overlook."

"Perhaps you are simply more willing to listen to me than to your other advisors. However, I'm sure our paths will cross from time to time."

"But if I need to see you at a specific time instead of waiting . . . ?" she pressed.

"Should anything urgent arise, leave word at the Vulgar Unicorn, and I will find a way to contact you."

It was a simple enough request, Jubal told himself. There was no reason at all that he should feel flattered.

"So, overall, what do you think of her?"

Saliman had joined Jubal now, and they were sharing the wine, the good vintage, as they discussed Chenaya's visit.

"Young," Jubal said thoughtfully. "Even younger than I had anticipated in many ways. She has much to learn and no one to teach her."

The aide cocked an eyebrow at his employer.

"It would seem that she impressed you."

"What do you mean?"

"For a moment there you sounded almost paternal. I thought you were out to appraise a potential ally or enemy, not looking for someone to adopt."

Jubal started to snap out an answer, then gave a barking laugh instead.

"I did sound that way, didn't I?" he grimaced. "It must be my reaction to misguided youth. So little could make so much difference. But you're right, that has nothing to do with our goals."

"So I repeat the question: What do you think of her? Will she be able to provide leadership in the future?"

"Eventually, perhaps, but not soon enough to be of immediate use."

"Which leaves us where?"

Jubal stared at the wall silently before answering.

"We cannot afford to have Tempus and his troops leave Sanctuary just yet. Something will have to be devised to keep them here. If we cannot arrange it through others, we may have to commit ourselves to the task."

Saliman sucked in his breath through his teeth.

"Either way, it could be expensive."

"Not as expensive as an ineffectual defense. If the town opposes Theron, it will have to win. To try and fail would be disastrous."

"Very well," the aide nodded. "I'll have our informants start checking as to who's available and if their price is gold or anger."

"The other thing I haven't mentioned regarding Chenaya," Jubal said casually, "is that I've agreed to advise her in the future. I felt it would be wise to be sure that her development followed patterns suitable to our goals."

"Of course," Saliman nodded. "It's always best to plan for the long term."

They had been together a long time, and Saliman knew better than to point out to Jubal when he was using logic to try to hide his own sentimentality.

THE TIE THAT BINDS

Diane Duane

Pillars of fire and other such events notwithstanding, people in Sanctuary have routines, just as they do everywhere else in the world. Dawn comes up and thieves steal home from work, slipping into shambly buildings or into early-opening taverns for a bite and sup or some early fencing. Brothel-less whores slouch out of the Promise of Heaven, or make their way up from the foggy streets by the river, to go yawning back to their garrets or cellars before the sun makes too much mockery of their paint. And people of other walks of life—fullers, butchers, the stallkeepers of the Bazaar—drag themselves groaning or sighing out of their beds to face the annoyances of another day.

On this particular summer morning, one fragment of routine stepped out of a door in a much-rundown house near the Maze. People who lived in the street and were going about their own routines knew better than to stare at her, the tall handsome young woman with the oddly fashioned linen robes and the raven hair. One or two early travelers, out of their normal neighborhoods, did stare at her. She glared at them out of fierce gray eyes, but said nothing—merely slammed the door behind her.

It came off in her hand. She cursed the door, and hefted it lightly by its iron knob as if ready to throw the thing down the filthy street.

"Don't do it!" said a voice from inside; another female voice, sounding very annoyed.

The gray-eyed woman cursed again and set the door up against the wall of the house. "And don't kill anyone at work, either!" said the voice from inside. "You want to lose *another* job?"

The gray-eyed woman drew herself up to full height, producing an effect as if a statue of some angry goddess was about to step down from her pedestal and wreak havoc on

140

some poor mortal. Then the marble melted out of her, leaving her looking merely young, and fiercely lovely, and very tall. "No," she said, still wrathful. "See you at lunchtime."

And off she went, and the people in the street went about their business, going home from work or getting up for it. If you had told any of them that the woman in the linen chlamys was a goddess exiled from wide heaven, you would probably have gotten an interested inquiry as to what you had been drinking just now. If you had told that person, further, that the woman was sharing a house with a god, another goddess, and sometimes with a dog (also divine)—the person would probably have edged away cautiously, wishing you a nice day. Druggies are sometimes dangerous when contradicted.

Of course, every word you would have said would have been the truth. But in Sanctuary, who ever expects to hear the truth the first time . . . ?

"She hates the job," said the voice from inside the house.

"I know," said another voice, male.

The house was one of those left over from an earlier time when some misguided demi-noble, annoyed at the higher real-estate prices in the neighborhoods close to the palace, had tried to begin a "gentrification" project on the outskirts of the Maze. Sensibly, no other member of the nobility had bothered to sink any money in such a crazed undertaking. And the people in the mean houses all around had carefully waited until the nobleman in question had moved all his goods into the townhouse. Then the neighbors had begun carefully harvesting the house—never so many burglaries or so large a loss as to drive the nobleman away; just many careful pilferings made easier by the fact that the neighbors had blackmailed the builders into putting some extra entrances into the house, entrances of which the property owner was unaware. The economy of the neighborhood took a distinct upward turn. It took the nobleman nearly three years to become aware of what was happening; and even then the neighbors got wind of his impending move through one of his servants, and relieved the poor gentleman of all his plate and most of his liquid assets. He considered himself lucky to get out with his clothes. After that the property fell into genteel squalor and was occupied by shift after shift of squatters. Finally it became too squalid even for them; which was when Harran bought it, and moved in with two goddesses and a dog.

"Whose turn is it to fix the door?" Harran said.

He was a young man, perhaps eighteen years of age, and dark-haired . . . a situation he found odd, having been born thirty years before, and blond at the time. His companion was a lean little rail of a woman with a tangle of dark curly hair and eyes that had a touch of madness to them, which was not surprising, since she had been born that way, and sanity was nearly as new to her as divinity was. They were standing in what had been the downstairs reception room, and was now a sort of bedroom since the upper floors were too befouled as yet to do anything with at all. Both of them were throwing on clothes, none of the best quality. "Mriga?" Harran said.

"Huh?" She looked at him with an abstracted expression.

"Whose turn is it to fix the door? . . . Oh, never mind, I'll do it. I don't have to be there for a bit."

"Sorry," Mriga said. "When she's angry, I get angry, too. . . . I have trouble, still, figuring out where she leaves off and I begin. She's out there wanting to throw thunderbolts at things."

"This is unusual?" Harran said, picking up a much-worn shirt and shaking it hard. Rock dust snapped out of the folds.

"It should be," Mriga said rather sadly. She sat down on one of their pieces of furniture, a large bed with multiple sword hacks in it. "I remember the way things were for her when she was a goddess for real. A thought was all it took to make the best things to wear, anything she wanted to eat, a god's house to live in. She didn't have to be angry then. But now . . ." She looked rather wistfully to one side, where a huge old mural clung faded and mouldering to the wall. It was a scene of Ils and Shipri creating the first harvest from nothing. Everywhere there was a wealth of grain and flowers and fruit, and dancing nymphs and gauzy drapery and ewers of out-poured wine. The wood on which the mural was painted was warped, and Shipri had wormholes in her, in embarrassing places.

Harran sat down beside her for a moment. "Do you regret it?"

Mriga looked at him out of big hazel eyes. "Me myself? Or she and I?"

"Both."

Mriga put out a hand to touch Harran's cheek. "You? Never. I would become a goddess a hundred times over and give it up every time, to be where I am now. But Siveni . . ."

She trailed off, having no answer for Harran that he would want to hear. Perhaps he knew it. "We'll make it work," he said. "Gods have survived being mortals before."

"Yes," Mriga said. "But that's not the way she had it planned."

She looked at a bar of sunlight that was inching across the bare wood floor toward the other piece of furniture, a table of blond wood with one leg shorter than the three others. "Time to be heading out, love. Do we all eat together today?"

"She said she might not be able to make it . . . there's something going on at the wall that may take extra time. An arch of some kind."

"We should take her something, then."

"Always assuming that I get paid."

"You should hit them with lightning if they renege on you."

"That's Siveni's department."

"I wish it were," Mriga said. She kissed Harran goodbye and left as he was looking for a hasp to rehang the door.

Mriga walked slowly toward her own work, threading the streets with the unconscious care of a lifelong city dweller. It had been a busy year for all of them . . . for her in particular. One day Mriga had been just another madwoman . . . Harran's bedwarmer and house servant, good for nothing but mindless knife-sharpening and mindless sex. The next, she had been awake, and aware, and divine—caught in the backwash of a spell Harran had performed to bring back Siveni from whatever oblivious heaven she and the other Ilsig gods had been inhabiting. Harran had been one of Siveni's priests, the healer-servants of the divine patroness of war and crafts. He had thought he would remain so. But the spell had caught him, too, binding him and Siveni and Mriga together through life, past death. That was no mere phrase, either, for the three of them had been in hell together, and had come back again to what should have been a cheerful, delighted life together . . . long years rich with joy.

Mriga stepped over the sewer runnel in the middle of a street and reflected that even the gods were sometimes caught by surprise. The trouble had started with Stormbringer's pillar of fire; the banner of a new power in Sanctuary, one that was

going to diminish all others that were already there. She could
still remember the night she woke in terrible shock to Siveni's
anguished screams, and to the feeling of something fiercer
than life seemingly running out of her bones, as godhead wavered and sank within them both like a smothered fire. And
then the Globes of Power were destroyed, and what little in-
nate power was left to the three of them began to go awry. She
and Siveni had said they were willing to be mortal, to die, for
Harran's saké. Now it appeared they would have a chance to
find out just how willing. Meantime, a god (or goddess) without a temple needed a place to live, and food to eat....

Mriga walked across the bridge over the White Foal
(briefly holding her breath against the morning smell) and
headed into the Bazaar from the south side. Most of the stallkeepers were setting up their canopies, muttering to one another about prices, wholesalers, arguments at home: the usual
morning gossip. She made her way over to the side near the
north wall.

There was Rahi, her stallmate, setting up as usual ... a
large, florid, corpulent man, fighting with the canopy poles,
sweating and swearing. Rahi was a tinker who did a small side
business in small arms, knives, and the like. He boasted that
he had sold knives to Hanse himself, but Mriga doubted this;
anyone who really had would be too cautious to cry the man's
name aloud. At any rate, apart from his boasting, Rahi was
that astonishing phenomenon, an honest tradesman. He didn't
mark up his wares more than a hundred percent or so, he
didn't scrape true gilt off hilts or scabbards and substitute
brass, and his scales had trustworthy weights to them. Why he
chose to be such an exception, he usually refused to explain
... though one night, over a stoup of wine, he whispered one
word to Mriga, looking around him as if the Prince's men
were waiting to take him away. "Religion," he had said, and
then immediately drank himself drunk.

Their association, odd though it might be, satisfied Mriga.
When she had been job hunting and had passed through the
Bazaar one day, Rahi had recognized her as the crippled
former idiot-girl who used to sit there and hone broken bits of
metal on the cobbles until they could split hairs, until Harran
took her home to sharpen Stepsons' swords and his surgical
tools. Rahi had offered her a spot in his stall—for a small cut
of her profits, of course—and Mriga had accepted, more than
willing to take up her old trade. Swords got dull or notched

quickly in Sanctuary. A good "polisher" never starved . . . and Mriga was the best, being (these days) an avatar of the goddess who invented swords in the first place.

"'Bout time you got here," Rahi bellowed at her. Various people close by, sweetmeat sellers and clothiers, winced at the noise, and off in the cattle pens various steers lifted up their voices in mournful answer. "Day's half gone, where you been, how you gonna make your nut, I hafta kick you out, best spot in the Bazaar, eh lady?"

Mriga just smiled at him and unslung her pouch, which contained all her tools: oil, rags, and five grades of whetstones. Others in the city worked with more tools, and charged more, but Mriga didn't need to. "There's no one up but us and the birds, Rahi," she said. "Don't make me laugh. Who's been here with a sword this morning that I've missed?"

"Eh, laugh, sure, sometime some big guy from the palace, you'll laugh then, charge him big, but no, he'll be uptown and you, not a copper, out on the stones again, you be careful!" He rammed the last canopy pole into its spot and glared at her, sweating, smiling.

Mriga shrugged. Rahi traditionally spoke in a long gasp with a laugh at the end, and dropped out words as if he was afraid to run out of them some day. "Hey, Rahi, if it gets slow over here I can always go over to the wall and sharpen the chisels, eh?"

Rahi was shaking out the canopy, a six-foot rectangle of light cotton with some long-faded pattern just barely visible in the weave. "No good'll come of that, mark," he said, "didn't need the wall until now, what for? But to hold out armies, or hold people in. Put a lock on a door and people start thinking there's things to steal, sure. That—the Torch—" He was plainly unwilling to say Molin Torchholder's name aloud. That was no surprise; many people were. Sanctuary was full of ears, and there was frequently no telling who they belonged to. "Playing kingmaker, that one. If he doesn't get us burnt in our beds . . ." Rahi trailed off into grumbling. "Your man, how about him, eh?"

"He's doing all right. Word's been getting about that there's a good barber to be had in the Maze. We haven't even been robbed yet. . . . They let us be, seeing as how it might be Harran that has to patch one of them up some night after a job goes sour."

"Doesn't do to have the barber mad at you, no indeed;

pots! Pots to sell!" Rahi shouted suddenly, as a housewife with a thumbsucking child in tow went by the stall. "Other lady, the tall one, she learns that too? No? 'Spose not, doesn't seem the 'prenticing type, too proud, she."

Mriga silently agreed. While still active in the Ilsig pantheon, Siveni had invented many a craft and passed them on to men. Medicine, the sciences, the fine arts, the making and using of weapons, all had been hers. Trapped in the world Siveni might be, but what she knew of the spells and arts of medicine was far more than the best of her priest-healers had known; and Harran had been only a minor one of those. "No," Mriga said, "she's on the wall. She does well enough."

She took out a favorite knife, a little black-handled thing already fine-edged enough to leave the wind bleeding, wiped it with oil, and began absently to whet it. More people were coming into the Bazaar. In front of them Yark the fuller went by with his flat cart. On top of it one of the Bazaar's two big calked-straw pisspots lurched precariously, making ominous sloshing noises. "Any last-minute contributions?" said Yark, grinning.

Mriga shook her head and grinned back. Rahi made an improbable remark about Yark's mother, the last part of which Mriga lost as a young man passing by paused to watch her work. She lifted the knife, a friendly gesture. "Have anything that needs some work, sir?"

He looked dubious. "How much?"

"Let's see."

He stepped closer, reached under his worn tunic and pulled out a shortsword. Mriga looked at him covertly as she turned over the sword in her hands. Young, in his mid-twenties, perhaps. Not too well dressed, nor too poorly. Well, that might be a relief. People had been doing better lately; the Beyfolk's money was making a difference. The sword was of a steel that had forge patterns like those in Enlibrite, and it was darkbladed with rust, and had notches in it. Mriga tsked at the poor thing, while sorting other impressions . . . for even though swathed in flesh and trapped away from heaven, a goddess has senses a mortal has not. A dubious blade, this, with the memory or the intention of blood on it. But in this town, what weapon hadn't killed someone? . . . That was after all what they were for. "Dark or bright?" she said.

"What?" The young man's voice was very raw and light, as

if it might still tend to crack at times.

"I can polish it bright for you, if it needs to be seen," she said. "Or leave it dark in the blade, if it needs not." She had learned that delicate phrasing quickly, after accidentally scaring away a few potential customers whose work required that their blades be inconspicuous. "Either way, the edge is the same. Four in copper."

"Two."

"You think you're dealing with a scissors grinder? The Stepsons brought their blades to me, and the Prince's guard do still. The thing'll be able to slice one thought from the next when I'm done with it. Always assuming that you can keep it out of the tables at the Unicorn after this." That got his attention; that much Mriga had been able to pick up from the blade itself, though it wasn't talkative as steel went. "Three and a half, because I like your looks. No more."

The young man screwed up his face a little, slightly ruining those looks. "All right, do it dark. How long?"

"Half an hour. Take mine," she said, and handed him her "loaner," a plain, respectable longknife with quillons of browned steel. "Don't 'lose' it," Mriga said then, "so I don't have to give you a demonstration with this one."

The young man ducked his head and slipped into the growing crowd. Rahi said something not in a bellow, and it got lost in the increasing noise of people crying fish and cloth and ashsoap.

"What?"

"You ever have to demonstrate?" he wheezed in her ear.

Mriga smiled. Siveni, so long unprayed-to by mortals, had been losing her attributes. And as such things will, one attribute—the affinity for things with edges—had slipped across into mortality and into the person best equipped to handle it: Mriga. "Not personally," she said. "Last time, the knife did it itself. Just lost its balance all of a sudden . . . slipped out of the thief's hand and stuck her right—well, whatever. Word got around. It's not a problem now."

Yark the fuller went by with the cart again. This one was sloshing. "Last chance!" he said.

"Pots," Rahi bellowed beside her, "pots! Buy pots! You, madam! Even a fish—sorry—even a Beysib needs a pot!"

Mriga rolled her eyes and began to whet the new knife.

●　●　●

When Molin Torchholder let it be known that he was going to complete the walls of Sanctuary, the noise of merriment about the new jobs that would become available was almost as loud as Stormbringer's fireworks had been. There were, of course, quieter conversations about what the old fox was up to this time. Some dared to say that his sudden industriousness on the Empire's behalf had less to do with his desire to keep Sanctuary safe for the Imperials, as to keep it safe from them. Some day, not too far off, when Sanctuary's own trade was well enough established, when it had enough of its own gold, and was secure in its gods again . . . then the gates could swing shut, and Molin and others would stand on the walls and laugh in the Empire's face. . . .

Of course those who said such things said them in whispers, behind bolted doors. Those who did not lost the tongues that had spoken them. Molin didn't bother himself with such small business; his spies tended to it. He had too many things to take care of himself. There was his new god to placate, old ones to assist out of existence, Kadakithis and (in a different fashion) the Beysa to manage. And there was the wall.

As an exercise in logistics alone it was trouble enough. First the plans, argued over for weeks, changed, changed again, changed back; then ordering the stone, and having it quarried; then hiring people enough to move such weights, others to work on the roughed-out stones, trimming them to size. Overseers, stonemasons, mortarers, caterers, spies to make sure everything was working. . . . Money was fortunately no problem; but time, all the things that could go wrong, were riding on Molin's mind. The vision of what it would be if all went well—security against enemies, against the Empire, power for himself and those he chose to share it—that vision was barely enough to counter the murderous work of it all. He took any help he could find, and didn't scruple to use it to the utmost thereafter.

He hadn't scrupled on the morning several months or so back when the first courses of stone were being laid on the southern perimeter, and there was trouble with the foundations, dug too deep and uneven to boot. The plans were spread out on a block on undressed northern granite, and he was speaking to his engineers in that soft voice that made it plain to them that if they didn't set things to rights shortly, they would be very dead. And in the middle of the quiet tirade, he had become aware of someone looking over his shoulder. He didn't move. The someone snorted. Then a slender arm poked down between his shoulder and the chief architect's and said, "Here's where you went wrong. The ground's prone to settling all along this rise; using that for your level-strings threw all your other measurements off. You can still save it, with cement enough. But you won't have time if you stand here gaping. That ground dries out, a whole city's worth of cement on top of it won't hold firm. And mind you put enough sand in it."

He had turned around to see the ridiculous, the laughable. It was a tall young woman, surely no more than twenty-five, with cool clean features and long black hair, and a most peculiarly draped white linen robe with a goatskin slung over it. He looked at her with annoyance and amazement, but she was ignoring him—which was also ridiculous; no one ignored him. She was looking at the plans as if they had been drawn in the mud with a stick. "Who designed this silly heap of blocks?" she said. "It'll fall down the first time an army hits it."

Beside him, Molin's chief architect had turned a ferocious shade of red, and then began shifting from foot to foot as his gout started to trouble him. Molin looked at the gray-eyed woman and said, in the deadly soft voice he had been using on the engineers, "Can you do better?"

The woman flicked eyebrows at him in the most scornful expression he had ever seen. "Of course."

"If you don't," he had said, "you know what will happen."

She gave him a look that made it plain that his threats amused her. "Parchment, please," she said, knocked the plans aside into the mud, and sat down on the block like a queen, waiting for the writing materials to be brought her. "And you'd better do something about that cement right now, before the ground dries. That much of your wall I'll keep. You—" She pointed at one of the engineers. "Send someone to the biggest glassmaker in town and ask for all the cull they've got."

"Cull?"

"Broken glass. Pound it up fine. It goes in the cement. . . . What's it for?! You want rats and coneys tunneling under and undermining the wall? Leaving holes for people to pour acid in, or something worse? Well, then!"

The engineer in question glanced at Molin for permission, then hurried away. He turned to her to say something, but the parchment and silverpoint had already been brought, and the woman was sketching with astonishing swiftness on the smooth side of the skin—drawing perfectly straight lines without rulers, perfect curves without tools. He had to fight to keep the scorn in his voice. "And who might *you* be?" he had said.

"You may call me Siveni," she had said, not looking up, as if she were royalty doing a beggar a favor. "Now look here. That curtain wall was all wrong; it would never bear crenellations. And of course you are going to crenellate at some point. . . ."

He entreated her politely, for the moment, to speak quietly; crenellation was forbidden by the Empire except under very special circumstances, and he had been planning to do it . . . just not now, when it was important to seem not to be having any thoughts of autonomy. Even as he entreated her, though, he found himself becoming uneasy. It was not as if Siveni was an uncommon name in Sanctuary; it was not. But every now and then he was troubled by the memory of how the abandoned temple of the goddess of that name had had its bronze doors torn right off and thrown in the street a while back; and from all indications, they had been broken out from the inside. . . .

Siveni, of course—knowing all these thoughts of Molin's, in a goddess's fashion, as if from the inside—was amused by the whole business. It amused her, the inventor of architecture, to be building for mortals; to be building for the man who had cast her priests out of Sanctuary; to be confusing him, and unnerving him, and at the same time doing something worthwhile with her time. Like many gods, she had a flair and taste for paradox. Siveni was indulging it to the point of surfeit.

Such indulgence was one of the few pleasures she had these days, since she and Mriga and Harran had come back from hell. Harran had been dead, killed by one of Straton's people in the raid on the Stepsons' old barracks. The two of them, with Harran's little dog Tyr, and Ischade as guide on the road, had gone down and begged his life of hell's dark Queen, and (rather to their surprise) had gotten it.

The arrangement was peculiar. Harran (playing the barber even past death) had picked up the wounded soul of a mind-dead body, so that his own soul had somewhere to live again. The Queen had let them all out of hell on condition that from

now on they should divide Harran's hell-sentence among
them, and take death in shifts. Tyr was in hell presently, en-
joying herself a great deal, to judge by the vague impressions
Siveni occasionally received. Hell's Queen had made a pet of
her. But how the rest of the arrangement would function now
—even if it was still intact—Siveni had no idea. Hell's gate
was closed. The magics that had made Ischade free of the
place were severely curtailed since the loss of the Globes of
Power.

And heaven's gate, it seemed, was closed, too; the Ilsig
gods were locked away from the world by Stormbringer's sudden terrible assertion of power. Originally, Siveni's plan and
Mriga's had been to take Harran straight back to heaven with
them, to her tall, fair temple-house in the country beyond the
world's time. But they had dallied too long in the mortal
world, while Harran got his bearings and got used to his new
body . . . and then one night had awakened to find that
heaven's gate was shut on them, and no way back. They were
marooned. . . .

So Siveni walked the mortal world without her armor,
without her army-conquering spear, and built city walls, and
pondered vengeance on Molin Torchholder. Some ways, this
was all his fault. Harran would never have been moved to
summon her out of the terrible calm of the Ilsig heaven had
not the Torchholder banished her priesthood from Sanctuary.
And now, she thought—looking down between the fourth and
fifth courses of new stone at a little tunnel being built between
them—now he would pay for it. Or perhaps not now; but as
gods reckon time, soon enough.

"Yai there, Gray-Eyes," came a shout up to her from one of
the stonemasons. "We're ready for the next one!"

She grimaced, a look she was glad the mason couldn't see
through the kicked-up dust of the hot day's work. Gray-eyes,
they all called her; but it was a joke. There was no telling
them who she was. It hadn't been too long ago that she sat
cool and calm in her house in heaven, hearing her name called
in reverence, smelling the uprising savor of good sacrifices,
stepping down in power to help those who called on her. No
more of that.

Love she had now, yes; she had never had that before—
certainly nothing so immediate. But was it as good . . . ?

"Right," she shouted back. "Kivan," she shouted in another direction, "get the crane around, man, the mortar's wet!

It's three in a row here. Yes, those three. Get them up on the hoist. Where the hell are the draggers?"

She watched them haul the stone in question into place and wrap the crane's ropes around it. While they were grunting and straining she let herself go unfocused for a moment, and listened. Knife-grinding, she "heard"; and someone screaming, while sure hands worked over them and other hands held them down; and more faintly than the first two impressions, a clear sense came of being rubbed in the good place behind the ears. Siveni smiled to herself. She had always been a single goddess, being too busy inventing things to bother splitting off alternate personae, dyads and trinities and whatever. Now, after Harran's spell, and their trek past hell's gate, she was not only a trinity, but one with four members. Interesting, it was. And very unsettling.

And was it worth it . . . ?

A shadow fell over her as she leaned on the last-laid stone. "Molin," she said.

"How do you do that, mistress? Know how someone's coming behind you, I mean."

She stiffened a bit. "In sun like this," she said, "it would take a blind woman not to see your shadow's shape. Has that new stone come in yet? We'll need the softer stuff for the arrowshot wall."

"It's in. Come take a cup of something cold with me."

She stepped down from the stone, wondering about the odd tone in his voice, schooling herself to show no reaction. Carelessly she walked in front of him to the tent he'd had set up at the site, so that he could watch the workers, and her, in comfort. She flung one flap on its door aside. Silk, she thought. And not because it makes the best tents, either.

There were only two chairs, too close together for her taste. She took the better of the two and sat waiting for Molin to pour for her. Massive and splendid, he sat down in the other chair and looked at her for a long moment before reaching out to the decanter and glasses on its table between the chairs. Alarm, his mind sang to Siveni. Curiosity growing. Thought winding around itself, choking like ivy growing up sheer cold stone. . . .

"Why do you live in that little hole in the Maze?" Molin said, pouring, and passing her the cup. "You could certainly afford better, with what I'm paying you."

She took the cup and looked at him, unsmiling, wishing

she had her spear with the lightnings sizzling around it; he would not be daring to ask her questions. "It'd be too much bother to move in the middle of a work like this," she said.

"Ah, yes. Another question I wish you would answer, with your obvious expertise. What other jobs have you done?"

Better ones than you're doing now, Siveni thought as she lifted the cup and smelled, very deep in the bouquet of the wine, an herb she recognized. She had invented it; and this was one use for it that she had never approved. "Stibium," she said, answering his question and naming the drug, both at once. "Torchholder, for shame. The preparation has to be started weeks in advance if you intend to have someone drink it and then spill out their life's secrets to you. Though perhaps you just mean my next flux to be painless. A kind thought. But I manage that for myself. And I'm pained that you don't trust me."

"You live with a common barber and a woman who was an idiot once," said Molin. "She's whole now. How did that happen?"

"Good company?" Siveni said. Oh, for my lightnings; oh, for one good crack of thunder out of a clear sky, to back this impertinent creature down! "I'm no sorceress, if that's what you're thinking. Even if I were, what good would it do me these days? Most magicians are lucky if they can turn milk into cheese now. Your problem," she said, "is that I seem to have come out of nowhere, and you have no hold over me . . . and at the same time, no choice but to trust me; for I've saved your wall from the rotten ground it stands on four times now, and will keep doing so until it's whole."

He gazed at her as levelly as he could, and made a point of drinking from his own cup. "You've taken arthicum, I imagine," she said. "Mind that you don't eat anything made with sheep's milk for the next day or so; the results would be unfortunate. At least, inconvenient, for a man who has to spend more than an hour without running off to ease himself."

"Who are you?" he said, very conversationally.

"I am a builder," Siveni said. "And the daughter of a builder. If it pleases me to do a masterwork while living in a slum, that's my business. Think, if you like, that I'm making this city safe for my family to live in in future years. Have you had anything to complain of about my work so far?"

"Nothing," said Molin. He sounded as if he would rather have had complaints.

"And have you not been checking the actual building against the plans each day and each night? And have you or your spies found one stone out of place, or anything not just as it should be?"

Molin Torchholder stared at her.

"Then let me do my work and take my wage in peace." She looked at him merrily. "Which reminds me," she said; "there are stones out there waiting for our attention at the laying. Come on." And Siveni drank off the cup and set it down appreciatively.

"It *does* add something to the flavor," she said, and got up. "Come, sir."

She went out into the bright hot day, Molin following. Alarm was still singing in his mind; and now in hers, too.

He suspects something . . . even though there's nothing to suspect. He'll do Harran and Mriga some harm if he must, to find out the truth. Wretched mortal! Why can't he leave off meddling?

I must think of something to do.

I never had these problems when I was single!

"Yai, Gray-Eyes! You ready?"

"Coming, Kivan," she called, and headed down along the stone course, feeling the Torchholder's eyes in her back, like spears without lightning.

"I'm sorry I couldn't have let you sleep through that," Harran said to the man he had been cutting. "But with the wound so deep in the hand, if you were asleep and I hit a nerve, we would never have known it, and the hand might have been useless an hour later, though the poison was out."

The joiner—Harran had forgotten his name, as he always forgot his patients' names—groaned a little and eased himself up to sit, his wife helping him. Harran turned away for a moment, busying himself with cleaning his tools and not noticing his surroundings. He had been a priest, used to clean, open temples, fresh air, scrubbed tables, light. Cutting someone on a kitchen table that until five minutes ago had had chicken dung on it was not unusual—not anymore—but he would never like it.

The few chickens in the mean little hut walked about the floor, scratching and singing, oblivious to the blood and pain of the last half hour. The joiner had driven a nail through his hand while working, and had yanked the thing out and thrown it away, going on with what he had been doing. Then the wound had festered, and there were signs of the beginning of lockjaw when Harran had finally been called in. He had had to run like a madman down to the flats by the river for the plant to make the lockjaw potion; luckily, even now, the small medicinal magics seemed to work—and then, once that was in the joiner, and the poor man was flushed and sweating from its effects, then came the cutting. He had never been terribly fond of that part of any surgery, but the suppurating wound had to be drained. It was drained, though it nearly turned his stomach, which was saying something.

Now the hand was bound with clean linen, and Harran's tools were clean and in their satchel. The man's head was lolling to one side, an aftereffect of the lockjaw remedy. Timidly, his wife came to Harran and offered him a handful of coppers. She tried to be nonchalant about it, but it was too plain from her eyes that they were all she and her man had. Harran considered, took one, for form's sake, and then professed great interest in one of the chickens, a rather scrawny red hen that looked good for soup, if nothing else. "How about her, eh?" he said. "Looks like there's nice pickings on her."

The joiner's wife saw instantly what Harran was trying to do, and began protesting. But the protests were feeble, and after a while Harran walked out of the hut with a copper, and a copper-colored chicken, and blessings raining on his back. He walked as fast as he could out of that particular corner of the Maze. It was always the blessings that embarrassed him the most.

The only good thing about them, Harran thought as he made his way toward the Bazaar, was that they made it unnecessary for him to cry his wares like a streethawker. In the old days, as Siveni's priest, people had known where to come for healing, and had done so without any fuss. Even in the Stepsons' barracks, they had known. It had galled him, after the return from hell, to have to go hunting the sick and injured like some grave robber in a hurry. . . .

Graves. . . . It was a thought. There was an old friend he had not seen since shortly after he got back from hell. He began a detour, and stopped in a wine shop for a pot of cheap red, then headed across town toward the charnel house.

The day was leaning toward noon; the sun burned down

and the streets stank under it. What did I ever see in this foul
place? he wondered as he went. The answer was plain enough;
Siveni's priesthood, which had been all the life he wanted.
But then the priesthood was banishcd as Molin Torchholder
went systematically about making the smaller Ilsig gods un-
welcome. Then he had started making the best of things,
working with the Stepsons, and with their poor replacements,
until the real ones came down on the stand-ins' barracks and
slaughtered them wholesale.

And Harran with them.

Alive again now, in a new body, he had rather hoped that
the memory of being dead would go away. Instead it got
stronger. Images of hell laid themselves pale and chill over
daylight Sanctuary—the cold-smoking river, the silences broken only by the abstracted moaning of the sleepwalking
damned. More remotely, through the bond he shared with
Siveni and Mriga, and even with Tyr, he saw things he had
never seen himself. The great black pile of the palace of hell's
rulers; hell's gate burst inward by a spear that sizzled with
lightnings; Ischade the terrible, coolly leading them down the
path into darkness; Tyr flying in splendid rage at the throat of
a monster ten times her size. And one image, brief but clear,
of the cold black marble floor of that dark palace seen as if by
one who groveled upon it . . . while just out of eyeshot,
Siveni's bright helm rolled on the floor where it had slipped
off her as she bowed her proud power down, begging for
Harran's life.

For him . . . all that done for him. He could never get used
to it. And no matter how many times Mriga and Siveni protested that it was nothing, that they would do it again, he
could not believe them. Oh, they believed it when they said it.
But their faces from day to day, as Siveni came home looking
drawn and grim from the job she had made for herself, as
Mriga looked at her goddess-sister with pity, and at Harran
with helpless, slightly sorrowful love—their faces betrayed
them. They were exiled from the heaven where they belonged,
and condemned to this wretched hole of a town, for his sake.

There must be something I could do, he thought.

The breath went out of him in annoyance as he sighted the
charnel house not far away. He had been something of a sor-
cerer once; most of the priests of Siveni had been, since there
was as much use for magic in the healing and building arts as
anywhere else. But since Stormbringer arrived, all other gods'

powers were diminished—that was half his problem—and after the globes were destroyed, spells tended to fall to pieces or produce unlikely results.

Just ahead of him, a small ragged man crouched in an alleyway, wearing a furtive look. He glanced up at Harran, looked very cautiously around him, and whispered, "Dust? You want some dust, mister?"

Harran stopped and glared at the dustmonger, who shifted uneasily under the stare. "I don't want anything of Storm-bringer's," he said. "As if that stuff does anything . . . which it doesn't." And he brushed past and made for the charnel house.

The amazing smell of the place briefly drove everything, even his annoyance at the dustmonger, out of his head. Farmers came from all over to get at its muckheap, and barbers and surgeons came here for corpses to practice on. Harran had other reasons. He choked his way through the long low building and prayed for his nose to turn itself off quickly.

Close to the end of the building, by the big pickling vats where innards were thrown until they could be buried, he found Grian. Grian had worked with Siveni's priests in the old days, supplying corpses for their anatomy classes, and he knew the last of Siveni's priests in Sanctuary rather better than Harran wanted to admit. He looked Harran up and down, noted the winepot under one arm and the chicken under the other, and a look of dull delight came into his eye. He tossed the paunching knife he was using to the slab where his present project lay, and said, "Lad, where you been this month and more? Thought you'd died. Again."

Harran had to laugh. "Not sure I could."

Grian moved his big red-headed bulk over to a bench where jars with secondhand stomachs and intestines were waiting for the sausagemakers. He pushed the jars off to the side, and Harran sat down next to him and offered him the winepot. The chicken, released, fell to scratching with great interest in the straw on the floor.

They spent a little while just drinking in companionable silence. Finally: "Home life keeping you busy?" Grian said.

"Not home so much. Work. There are too many sick people in this town, and only one of me." He took another drink. "Same as usual. You?"

"Business, business." Grian waved around him, where ten other men and women were handling the day's supply of dead bodies. "Had to hire on more help for the summer. Putting in a new muckpit, too, 'n' a new ossuary. Old one's full up. Muckpit kept overflowing. Neighbors complained." Grian laughed, a rough cheerful sound, though Harran noticed that his friend didn't breathe too deeply in the process. "They piffles, they're ruffling about trying to get the better of things again. No good. They kill somebody now and the noble-folk, the Imperials, everybody 'n' his brother comes down on 'em like bricks. Half the people in here are piffles this morning. Arrowshot, knifed, you name it. People in the city gettin' tired of them. About time, *I* say."

Harran agreed, passed the winepot back. Grian took a long one. "This new body," he said, elbowing Harran genially in the ribs, "working OK? Eh? Be interesting to get inside it one day, see what makes it tick."

Harran smiled again. Grian's humor never strayed far from his work. "I wonder myself, sometimes."

"Don't hold with such things myself," Grian said in cheerful disapproval. "Magic, eh, who needs it? Hear it's gone sour, and good riddance to it. So many magicians in this town, man can't spit without hittin' one. Unnatural. City should have done something long time ago. But now they don't have to, eh? They got other problems." Grian swigged at the pot again. "They puttin' less in these than they used to. Your gray-eyed lady—hear she and Molin are getting friendly. Work crew brought down some more heart-seizes from the Wall today, saw her sitting there in his fine tent, drinking his wine."

Harran's heart turned over in him. Not jealousy—of course not—but concern. Through the bond among them she could feel, too often, a clear cool regard turned on Molin Torchholder, a sense of vast amusement, vast satisfaction. And Siveni held a grudge better than anyone else alive. "Eh," Grian said, nudging him again. "You be careful, huh? Life's hard enough."

"Grian," Harran said, surprising himself—perhaps it was the wine—"have you ever been in a situation where you got everything you wanted, *everything*—and then you found out it's no good?"

Grian looked in mild perplexity at Harran and scratched his head. "Been so long since I got anything I wanted," he said softly, "I couldn't say, I'm sure. You got trouble at home?"

"Sort of," said Harran, and held himself quiet by main

force for several minutes, letting Grian drink. He had started this whole thing. The thought of bringing an Ilsig goddess back into the world to set things to rights, that had been his idea. And the later, crazier idea of serving that goddess personally—the stuff of fantasies—had been his idea, too. His idea it had been to bring a little knife-whetting idiot-stray home from the Bazaar as servant and casual bedwarmer. Now the idiot was sane, and not very happy; and the goddess was here, and mortal, and even less happy; and his dog was in hell, and though she was fairly happy, she missed him—and he missed her fiercely. And Harran himself was not completely mortal any more, and was also the cause of all of them having the promise of heaven snatched out from under their noses. His fault, all his fault. In this world where death wins all the fights and things run down, his fantasies had accomplished themselves and then promptly turned into muck.

Something had to be done.

Something *would* be done. He would do it.

"I have to go," he said. "Keep the wine."

"Hey, hey, what about these cord-twins here I been saving in pickle for you? Fastened together in the funniest place, now you come look a moment—"

But Harran was already gone.

"Here now," Grian shouted after him, rather hopelessly, "you forgot your chicken!"

Grian sighed, finished the wine, and picked up his paunching knife again.

"Oh, well. Soup tonight. Eh, chickie?"

The three did not meet at lunchtime, and dinner turned out to be very late. It was midnight when Siveni came in, all over dust and grime, and sat down at the table with one short leg and stared at it moodily. Mriga and Harran were in bed. She ignored them.

"Eat something, for pity's sake," Harran said from under the covers. "It's on the kettlehook."

"I am not hungry," Siveni said.

"Then do come to bed," said Mriga.

"I don't want that either."

Harran and Mriga looked at one another in mild astonishment. *"That's* a first."

Siveni shrugged off her goatskin and threw it over a chair.

"What's the use of losing my virginity," she said, "if I keep getting it back every morning?"

"Some people would kill for that," said Mriga.

"Not me. It hurts, and it's getting to be a bore. If I'd known what being a virgin goddess was going to mean down here, I would have gone out for being a fertility deity instead."

Mriga sat up in bed, wrapped a sheet around her, and swung her legs over the edge. "Siveni," she said, very quietly, "has it occurred to you that maybe we're not really goddesses anymore?"

Siveni looked up, not at Mriga, but at the poor mouldering mural, where Eshi danced in her gauze, and Ils was godly-splendid, and everything was youth and luxury and divine merriment. The look was deadly. "Then why," Siveni said, just as quietly, "do we share this wretched heartbond, like good trinities do, so that all day I can hear you both thinking how unhappy you are, and how sorry for me you are, and how you miss the dog, and how we're trapped here forever?"

Harran sat up, too, tossing the other end of the sheet across his lap. "We're something new, I think," he said. "A mixture. Divine without being in heaven, mortal without—"

"I want to go back."

The words fell into silence.

"After this job," she said. "Harran, I'm sorry. I'm not one of those dying-and-reborn gods who makes the corn come up, and shuttles back and forth between being mortal and divine; I'm just *not!* It's not working for me! I've been fighting it, but the truth is that I was made for a place where my thought becomes fact in a second, where I shine, where I'm worth praying to. I was made to have power. And now I don't have it, and you're all suffering for my lack." She sat down against the table. It shifted under her weight, and the broken bit of dish propping the short leg crunched and broke with a sound that made them all start.

"I've got to go back," she said:

Mriga looked unhappily at her. "How?" she said. "Nothing's working. You can't make so much as heat lightning these days."

"No," Siveni said. "But have we tried anything really large?"

"After what happened to Ischade . . ."

Siveni shrugged, a cold gesture. "She has her own problems. They don't necessarily apply to us."

"And Stormbringer. . ." Harran said.

Siveni cursed. The dust on the table began to smoke slightly with the vehemence of it. Siveni noticed it and smiled, approving. "Come on, Harran," she said. "The situation was no different when you called me out of heaven, and Savankala and the wretched Rankene gods were running things. You brought me out in their despite. This new god is too busy chasing Mother Bey to care a whit about us hedge-gods." The smile took on a bitter cast. "And why should He care what we're doing? We'd be *leaving* his silly city, not meddling with it further. I think He'll be glad to see the back of us."

"We," Harran said, and looked sober all of a sudden.

Both Mriga and Siveni looked at him in shock. "Surely you'd be coming with us," Mriga said.

Harran said nothing for a moment.

"Harran!"

"There is *nothing* here for you," Siveni said. "You've thought it a hundred times, you've cried about it when you thought we don't notice. You've seen hell, you've glimpsed heaven through us; how can mortal things possibly satisfy you anymore? Any more than they satisfy me? Or you," she said, looking at Mriga.

Mriga stared at the floor.

"Come on!" Siveni said, sounding a touch desperate. "You were born a clubfooted idiot, you went through a whole life being used as a slave or a pincushion, living like a beast—and what do you do that's better now? You grind knives in the Bazaar as you always did, and take a little copper for it, but where's the joy in that? Where's the life you were going to lead with *him* in the Fields Beyond? All the peace, the joy? You expect that in *Sanctuary?*"

Harran and Mriga looked at each other. "There's something to be said for life," Harran said, as if doubting the words as they came out. "In heaven everything bends to suit you. Here, you bend—but you come back stronger sometimes—"

"Or you break," said Siveni.

Silence. The firelight and candlelight wavered on the mural; Eshi seemed to sway a little.

"I'm going back," Siveni said. "I know the spells. I *wrote*

them. And you two—are you going to sit here and be miserable for all your short lives, on the off chance that it'll make
you stronger?"

Mriga let out a long breath. "Harran?"

His eyes were for Siveni, as they had been so many times
before, in statuary or the flesh. "I wanted you," he said.

They waited.

"It does seem selfish to want it all my way," he said. "All
right. We'll try it."

Mriga sat back down on the bed. Siveni shifted her weight
again, and again the table crunched and sagged.

"When will the Wall be done?" Harran said.

"Weeks yet," Siveni said, looking thoughtful. "It must be
done before the frost sets in, or the mortar won't set. But they
have the plans. They hardly need me to complete them." And
she began to laugh softly, so that the table creaked.

Harran and Mriga exchanged looks. "You have to have
known," Siveni said. "There are passages hidden in those
walls already, alterations I made in the building that don't
show in the plans. The wall is as full of holes as a bubble-
cheese. No one knows—not even Molin. I was most careful.
He'll think himself all secure, and until I choose to put the
word in some oracle's ear, he will be. But that day—let Sanctuary look to its walls."

"Well," Harran said, "one thing only. What about Tyr?
She's in hell. No one can go there anymore, from what I
hear."

"But people can come out," Siveni said. "She's of us.
Where we go, she'll go also, if she wants."

It seemed likely enough. "At any rate," said Siveni, "I
shan't wait for the walls. All the work that I needed to handle
myself is done. Let's get together the things we need and be
gone tomorrow night. Not the mandrake spell, Harran. The
older one, that you didn't have materials for the last time—
the one that uses bread and wine and a god's blood. There'll
be no accidents this time. We'll storm heaven, and settle down
once and for all, and leave this poxhole to its own devices."

Harran shuddered once.

Mriga sighed and climbed back into the bed. "Come and
get some rest, then," she said.

"Oh, all right," said Siveni, looking at them both with a
lighter expression. It became apparent that rest was suddenly
not on her mind.

Harran's ironic young face got lighter, too. He slid under the sheet and said, "Well, since it *is* my last night on earth..."

Siveni threw her chlamys over his head and put the candles out.

The old Temple of Siveni Gray-Eyes, near one end of the Avenue of Temples, was not what it once had been. Its brazen doors, struck down by its annoyed patroness's spear, had been taken away and melted down as scrap. Its old storerooms had been looted, first by its last priest, then by everyone in Sanctuary who could not resist an open door. Even the great gold-and-ivory statue of Siveni, armed and armored in splendor, had been stolen. Glass lay in bright shards on the dirty floor, fallen from the high windows; spiders wrought in every corner, and rats rustled here and there. There were fire-scorches in the corners from squatters' fires, and the bones of roast pigeons and cats.

Also still there, visible by the light of their one shuttered lamp, was an old round diagram traced on the floor in something black—bitumen, to judge by the scrape marks where curious feet had kicked at it through a year's time. Curious signs and letters and numbers in old languages were scribed smudgily there, and there was a brownish mark in the middle on the white marble, as if blood had been shed.

Harran put the lamp down, being sure its shutter was open no more than a hairsbreadth, and turned away from the street. "I wish the doors were still here," he said.

Siveni sniffed, putting down the bag she had been carrying. "Late for that now," she said. "Let's be about our business; it will take a while as is."

Mriga stepped up behind them and put down another bag, quietly beginning to sort through its contents. "The wine was something of a problem," she said. "Siveni, you owe me two in silver."

"What?"

"I thought we were splitting this expense three ways."

Siveni somehow managed to look indignant, even when there was no light to do it in. "You goose, we don't need money where we're going! I'll make you a whole house out of silver when we get there."

"Deadbeat."

Harran began to laugh softly. "Stop it. What kind did you get?"

"Wizardwall red," she said. "A half-bottle each of wine of our age. Enough?"

"Plenty. The wineseller say anything?"

"I told him it was for a birthday party. What about the bread?"

"It rose. You needn't have worried about the yeast. The worst part was grinding the wretched stuff. I think it's going to have pebbles in it from the flints."

The gongs of one of the temples down the way spoke midnight, a somber word that echoed in the summer-night stillness. There was no breath of wind tonight, and the heat seemed to have gotten greater after the sun sent down, rather than less. A fat bloated moon, gibbous and a day from full, was riding high, its pallid light slanting down through the shattered windows and striking gemlights from the broken glass on the floor. Echoes tinkled down from the high ceiling as Siveni kicked the stuff aside.

Harran looked up, brushing away a piece of glass that Siveni had kicked at him. "Siveni—are you really sure this is going to work?"

She looked at him haughtily. "All those spells that have gone awry have been done by mere practitioners of magic. Not authors of it. I helped Father Ils write this spell; I taught the bread and wine what to mean. All the dying gods who come back to heaven on a regular basis swear by it. Really, Harran, we'll never make a decent mage out of you if you don't learn to trust your materials."

"Have you ever actually *done* the spell? Yourself?" Mriga said under her breath as she got a rag out of her bag and began scrubbing some of the old markings off the floor.

"Not myself. I gave it to Shils to test; it worked all right. In fact, they started to wish in heaven that I *hadn't* given it to him. He's a terrible bore, and now there's no getting rid of him. Throw him out of heaven and a second later he's back."

They worked in silence for a few minutes, Harran laying out the bread, Mriga finishing her scrubbing, then uncorking the wine and setting out the various cups into which it would have to be poured by thirds and mixed with blood, Siveni writing with a bit of yellow chalk inside one of the areas that Mriga had cleaned off. At one point she stopped and looked critically at one graceful phrase. "I never did like that letter after I invented it," she said, "but after Ils sent it out to men, it was too late to call the wretched thing back."

Mriga sat back on her heels and laughed at her almost-sister. "Is there anything you *didn't* invent?"

"The rotgut they distill in the back of the Unicorn. That's all Anen's fault."

A few minutes' more work and they stood up, finished. "Well enough," Siveni said. "Are you sure of the words?"

They could hardly avoid it, being in some ways Siveni themselves, and hearing her mind nearly as clearly as their own, at the moment.

"Then let's be about it. The sooner I see the inside of my house again, the happier I'll be."

"Our house," said Mriga, in a warning tone.

Siveni began to laugh. "Harran, we used to have the best fights—the house would change its nature every other minute. How the neighbor gods stared...." Her eyes flashed, even in that light so dim as to make expression impossible. For a moment Harran looked at her and saw again the crazed hoyden goddess he had fallen in love with; and Mriga smiled, remembering many fights won best two falls out of three, while the noise scandalized the divine neighbors. "If this works..." she said.

"If?" Siveni reached out for the bread. "Give me that."

They took their places. The diagram was a triangle within a hexagon within a circle, and other lesser figures were traced in the apertures. At each point of the triangle they stood, each with a cup and a small round loaf of bread in front of them—the cup washed in wine and upended, the bread baked in a fire struck by the same flints that ground its grain. In the center stood an empty cup, this one of glass. If all went well, at the end of all this it would be cracked and they would never hear the sound; the heavens would have cracked open for them at the same moment.

"I call, who have the right to call," Siveni said, not too loudly. "Powers above and below, hear me; powers of every bourne; shapes and strengths unshapen, Night and Day Her sister; steeds of morn and evening, you forces that clip the great world round about; all thoughts and knowledges that live in elements; hear now my words, the law laid down, the rule enforced, the balance set aright..."

Harran was beginning to be upset. He knew this spell by reputation, though it was one that the younger priests had never been let near. He knew perfectly well that even now, at the first invocation, terrible quiet should have fallen around them, all light should have been extinguished, even the cold moonfire falling through the window should have hit the ensorcelled marble and gone dark. But none of that was happening.

". . . new law, part with the Worlds and parcel; for I that was of times beyond and fields beyond, now go again unto my own. Death has taken hold on me, and failed; life has run my veins, and failed; and having conquered both, now I will to journey once again where time moves not, where the Bright Mansions stand, and my place is prepared me among the Deathless as of old . . ."

There were rats watching them from the walls. No living thing outside the circle should have been able to be so close to the wards without falling unconscious. Harran sweated harder. Did I put too much honey in the bread? Did one of them misdraw something . . . ?

". . . and all Powers I call to witness as I open the gates for my going, by the means ordained of Them of old. By this bread baked in its own fires, as my body lives and is fueled of its own burning, I do call Them to witness; that by its eating, it becomes of me, and myself of it, in the old circle that is the way of gods, and both become immortal forever more . . ."

They all three took up their loaves of bread and began to eat them. Harran reassured himself that there was not too much honey in the bread. In fact, it had risen rather nicely. In the great silence left after he had eaten the little cake, he noticed abruptly how very silent it was getting—

"And likewise behold ye this wine of my age, burning under the sun in the grape as my blood has burned in lifelight in my veins all my days of this world, and turned to wine of its own virtue as the blood and thought of mortalkind turneth to the divine of its virtue and in its time. Now do I drink and make it so part of me, and myself part of it, both alike immortal . . ."

Harran drank the lovely old vintage, reassured, feeling it slide down his throat like velvet fire as the spell took, made it more than wine, in token of his and the others being more than merely mortal. Across the circle, Siveni made a face at the taste of wine only nine months old; Harran was hard put not to grin and spill his own. The silence was thick. At the sides of the great room, frozen eyes shone dulled in the spell-light that was rising about them. Harran's heart grew fierce inside him. It was going to work. Those bright fields that he had glimpsed, that long peace, that eternity to love in, to work in, to be more than mortal in—his, *theirs*, at last—

". . . and these tokens offered up, these rites enacted," Siveni said, her voice becoming terrifyingly clear though she had not raised it a whit, "as last sign of my intent I offer up my blood, come of gods in the olden time, returned to them at last; wherein godhead resides past time or loss, and wherein it may be regained . . ."

They stepped forward, all three. The night held its breath as Mriga picked up the cup, half full of a mixture of the three wines of their age. From her belt she slipped out her loaner knife. It gleamed like a live thing in the spellfire, and throbbed as if it had a heart. Siveni put up her arm.

". . . that we may drink of it, as the law has always been, as I have made it, and so be restored to our own. By this token let gates be opened to us . . ." She never flinched as the knife slit her wrist the short way, as the blood ran down and into the wine. ". . . let night and day part for us, let time die for us; let it be done!"

She passed Harran the cup. He drank, thinking to ignore the taste, and finding that it was more as if the taste ignored *him;* the liquid in the cup was full of such power that his senses drowned in it. He staggered, seeking light or balance, finding neither. He felt as transparent as its glass. Blindly he reached out, felt Mriga take the cup from him. He felt her own drowning as if it were his. Then Siveni took it, and drained it; the great uprushing clarity that leapt into her mind was a blinding thing, and Harran nearly fell to his knees. He thought he had seen the heavens. He saw now how wrong he was. Something clutched at him: Mriga. He held onto her slender arms as if she were the last connection to reality. He was seeing things now, though not with the eyes. Other eyes there were, that watched them all from within the circle; not dull beasts' eyes like the stupefied rats', but eyes that danced and were glad, and glowed in a small dog's head, waiting for them to break through to touch the owner—

"Let all be open," Siveni cried, "let the way be prepared for us; we pass! We pass!" And Harran felt her lift the cup, to dash it against the written marble and open the way; and he felt her hesitate; and he felt her sway.

His eyes were working again, much against their will.
There was moonlight where there should not have been, and
Siveni stood bemused, looking at her wounded arm, watching
the blood run down.

"It's wrong," she said. "It shouldn't hurt."

And she fell to the floor, and the cup went flying out of the
circle and crashed in the wrong spot, all its virtue spilled in a
black pool under the moon.

Harran fell down beside her. The edges of the wound were
dark and inflamed. He looked at Mriga in horror. "The
knife . . ."

"Poison," she said, her face in anguish. "But it never left
me all day—"

"Yesterday," Harran said.

In Mriga's shocked mind he saw the young man, with his
knife with death in it. One of the Torchholder's spies.

They started up in horror together, neither sparing more
than a look for the fair young form of Siveni, that had lived
thousands of years as an Ilsig goddess, and had now had those
thousands of years catch up with her in one withering second.

That was when the silvertipped arrows came whistling in,
and feathered them both. They fell.

When the backwash of the spell had died down a bit, in
behind his men came Molin Torchholder, who missed nothing
in this city, especially nothing done by those whom mere
silly love made careless. Stormbringer, too, was not quite settled yet, and had spoken a word in his ear about rogue deities
climbing over his walls, in one direction or another. Molin
carefully broke the circle, kicked the shattered glass of the cup
of blood and wine about, and nudged with his toe the skin-
and-bones body of his erstwhile architect.

"I do wish people wouldn't try to cheat me," he said.
"Idiots, anyway, trying spells anymore. Nothing of this intensity works right."

With a sigh he turned. "Clean up this mess," he said to one
of his men, "and tomorrow detach a work detail and raze this
place. We can use the stone."

Then he went away to get some sleep. He had a long day
tomorrow, on Stormbringer's business.

His men took the bodies away to the charnel house and left
the place in darkness. One thing they did not take: one small

form, wholly there now, in the darkness of the shadows beyond the moon; a shape like a small delicate dog, with too many lives sitting behind her eyes.

Tyr snarled, and got up, and walked out into the night to consider her vengeance.

SANCTUARY NOCTURNE

Lynn Abbey

Walegrin had his back to Sanctuary—vulnerable, unconcerned. One foot rested on a broken-off piling; his folded forearms rested on his upraised knee. His eyes were empty, staring at the still, starlit harbor, watching for the faint ripple that might mean a breeze coming up.

A thick blanket of sun-steamed air had clung to the city these last four days. Last winter they—the powers in the palace—had told him to paint false plague-signs along the streets. Then, in a dry spring, pestilence had erupted from the stagnant sewers and only luck, or divine intervention, had saved Sanctuary from a purging. Now, as the dank, foul air leeched vitality from every living creature, plague season had come in earnest and the nabobs were worried. Worried so much that they fled from the palace and their townhouses to outlying estates, some no more than Ilsigi ruins, to await a change in the wind. Improvements to the city's long-neglected ramparts had ground to a halt, as stone, brick, and work-gangs were openly diverted to providing comfort and security to those rich enough, or powerful enough, to afford it.

But if plague did break out, their walls, atriums, and shaded verandas wouldn't protect them. So they told *him*, the garrison commander, to keep the guards out and alert. His men grumbled, preferring to slouch over a desultory dice game in the barracks, but he welcomed a chance to get away from the walls that trapped the heat of summer as surely as they did the frigid dampness of winter.

Sanctuary itself was quiet. No one was moving an unnecessary muscle. The Street of Red Lanterns, which he had patrolled, had been almost deserted. Few men would pay to touch sweat-slicked flesh on a night like this.

It was ironic, in a way, that after a year or more of wizard-witched weather, the Street talk was about the failure of magic. Most of the brothels—the big houses like the Aphrodisia, anyway—usually bought cool night breezes from the journeymen up at the Mageguild, but this summer (a summer that was really no worse than any other) the big magic-banded doors stayed shut and the Hazard-mages, when they were seen at all, were sweating through their robes like any common laborer.

Rumor said the worst was over and the magic was coming back, though only to the strongest, or the cursed, and as yet too unpredictable to sell at any price. Rumor said a lot of things, but Walegrin, who did Molin Torchholder's direct bidding, got the truth of them sometimes. Stormbringer's pillar, which had purged Sanctuary of its dead and deadly, had sucked away the ether that made magic work. It would be a dog's year before Sanctuary's Mageguild sold anything but charlatan spells or prestidigitation regardless of the hazardous ranking of its residents.

The black harbor water diffracted into diamonds of starlight; a breeze moved whisper-weak across the wharf. The ragged-eared cats with slitted sickly green eyes were stretched out along the damp planks. A mouse, or young rat, skittered up a mooring rope past a cat that didn't care enough to twitch its tail. If a man held still, like the cats—breathing slow, keeping his mind as calm as the water—he could forget the heat and slip into a timeless daze that was almost pleasant.

Walegrin sought that oblivion and it eluded him. He was a Rankan soldier, the garrison commander, self-charged with patrolling the city. Such pride as he had stemmed from his ability to fulfill his duties. So his mind churned forward, pursuing the thoughts he'd lost before sunset. He had an appointment to keep: the true reason why tonight, more than any other, *he* rather than one of his men was making the rounds of Sanctuary's alleys.

The summer had seen a change in the city's social fabric that was as profound as it had been unexpected: Official protection had been extended to, and accepted by, the besieged remnants of the PFLS after their leader was betrayed and nearly killed within the palace walls. Gutter-fighters like Zip, whose lives had been measured in hours and minutes at the season's beginning, now dwelt in the Stepson barracks beyond Downwind and sweated hot and cold under the tutelage of Tempus's lieutenants.

And the cause of this change? None other than Prince Kadakithis's once-favorite cousin and Molin's never-favored niece: Chenaya Vigeles, a young woman of considerable talent and little sense. A young woman who had propositioned him with treason and upon whom, with the knowledge and permission of his superiors, Walegrin now spied.

Once, not so long ago, he had discounted the influence of women both in his own life and in the greater realities of the universe; then he had returned to Sanctuary. In this gods- and magic-cursed place, the worst always came from a woman's hand. He'd learned to hold his tongue and his liquor with women whose naked breasts stared back at him; women whose eyes glowed red with immortal anger and women whose love-play left a man dead in the dawn light—and all of them were saner than Chenaya.

Rumor said, and the Torch confirmed, that she was favored of Savankala himself. Rumor said she couldn't lose, whatever *that* meant, because she and the few frightened remnants of an unlamented Imperial dynasty had fled the Rankan capital after Theron's takeover and wound up here in Sanctuary which had never been known to attract anything or anyone but losers. But it meant something—Walegrin knew that personally. And out at the Land's End estate, where she lived with her father, a small horde of gladiators, and the disaffected members of what had been the city's Rankan upper crust, there was a god-bugged priest who was determined to make a mortal goddess of her.

He'd seen the shrine Rashan was building, with stones pilfered not only from the ramparts but from long-neglected, best-forgotten altars. He'd passed the word along to Molin and watched his mentor seethe with rage, but he hadn't managed to pass along the danger—the awesomeness—he felt when Rashan made his Daughter-of-the-Sun speeches or when Chenaya took him into her confidence and arms.

The water diffracted again, broken as a school of minnows scattered through a larger, slow-spreading circular ripple. Walegrin shed his reverie and stretched himself erect. His leather baldric, all he wore above the waist, slimed across his spine; the illusion of equilibrium between his flesh and the air vanished. He wiped the sweat-sheen from his forehead then wiped his hand on the limp homespun of his kilt. A nya-fish spread its fins, arching above the water to outrace the fleeing minnows. Walegrin slid the baldric into position and turned back to the city.

If there was an afterlife, if Sanctuary wasn't hell itself, then maybe he'd spend eternity as a nya-fish chasing minnows. At least fish didn't sweat.

The narrow, convoluted streets of the Maze held the heat. Turning down Odd Birt's Dodge, Walegrin passed through invisible walls of hot, stagnant air. He sniffed the air, thought about plague, and knew he'd have to send men in here to check the alleys for bodies come morning. From up on the rooftops, he heard the sounds that said love, or lust, had gained a momentary victory over the weather, but otherwise the Maze was uncommonly quiet for this hour.

Hand on his sword, he backed into a portico and put his shoulder against the half-hinged door. Picking his way across the rubble-strewn floor of what had been, until recently, one of the PFLS safe-houses, he approached the window casement, leaning away from the gray starlight, and tried to guess what route Kama would use to reach their rendezvous.

Kama.

Buoyed by the heat, Walegrin's mind drifted back in time and a few hundred yards deeper into the Maze; back to Tick's Cross and another night almost as hot as this one when he'd taken the midnight patrol. The night he'd agreed to let Zip live—at least until Tempus had ridden beyond Sanctuary's new gates.

He'd heard the horse first, moving too fast through the rutted muck that passed for paving stones hereabout, and made his way to the cross in time to see its rider go ass over elbow to the ground. The horse was well-trained and came to a shame-faced stop not five paces from its motionless rider. Walegrin grabbed the loose reins and led it back to the moonlit intersection.

Kama lay on her back, knees splayed and angled up—a posture more becoming a whore than a 3rd Commando assassin. Walegrin had looked only long enough to be sure it was her before turning discreetly, uncomfortably, away.

"It would be you. That's *twice*—damnit all," the husky voice had said, reminding him of the time his men had hauled her out of a malodorous cistern. "I've killed better men for less."

He had stared at her, knowing the absolute certainty of her claim and yet, for one wild, reckless moment able to see the absolute absurdity of her position. "Better for less?" he'd repeated in a bantering tone he used infrequently, even with his own men. "Better for less? Kama, either I'm the best or you'll have to kill me right now"—and immediately wished that someone had taken the trouble to cut his tongue out long ago.

But Kama, absorbing the picture she presented, had thrown her head back and laughed heartily at some private joke. She'd extended her filthy hand toward him and, using him as a brace, jumped to her feet.

"Buy me a drink, Walegrin; buy me a tun of the sourest wine in the Maze and you can be the best."

They said magic had vanished from Sanctuary, but there was a cold, bright spark of magic that moment as they led the lame horse from Tick's Cross, Kama listing against his shoulder—her laughter a quaver short of hysteria.

Molin Torchholder trusted her, including her in any strategy session her other duties allowed her to attend, and frequently accepting her opinions about Sanctuary's darker byways without question. She had been the one to convince them to go along with Tempus's PFLS schemes when he, Molin, and half a dozen others had demanded Zip's last drop of blood. But she was also Molin's woman. She shared his bed—and not simply because the Torch's betrothal offer had gotten her out of a tight spot with the Stepsons. There was genuine passion between them as well as a mutual understanding of intrigue that gave anyone who had known either individually a shiver of apprehension whenever they were seen talking intensely to each other.

So Walegrin used his privileged position as a keeper of Sanctuary's peace to wring not sour wine, but carefully aged, wicker-wrapped flasks of brandywine from one of the town's better-off innkeepers. Then, still leading her horse, they'd hiked beyond the walls to an abandoned estate, now occupied by one of the Beysa's innumerable female cousins. She'd sluiced the worst of the muck off her leathers in a still icy stream while he got started on the first flask and reminded himself ten times over that she was more dangerous than beautiful.

They'd talked until dawn: bragging, swapping anecdotes, and finally exchanging the stories they'd sworn no other living soul would hear. Toward dawn, when she was lying on her back again, watching the stars fade, magic passed between them again; Walegrin could have set aside his baldric and undone the damp laces of her tunic. He forbore, contenting himself with one agonizingly chaste kiss as a red-gold sliver of sunlight flashed above the eastern horizon.

"I always wanted a brother," she'd said in a whisper he wasn't sure he was supposed to hear.

There was a flicker of motion on the rooftops; nothing he could focus on, nothing that was repeated, but he knew she was coming in from above. Moments later the stairs creaked softly and she stood opposite him in the starlight. The supple leather of her tunic hung loosely from her shoulders and her face was matte-shadowed.

"Futtering gods below—you're not even sweating!" he greeted her.

"There *are* places worse than Sanctuary—and I've lived in most of them."

"I spent five years with the Raggah on the Sun's Anvil—it wasn't as bad as this and I *still* sweat like a pig."

Kama laughed and slid down the wall until her spine settled against the floor. "Say it's something I get from my father."

Walegrin, having once acknowledged that Tempus at his best was a heavier burden than his own father had been at his worst, redirected his conversation to the reason for their meeting. "It's getting bad at Land's End, Kama. Since they fished her out of the harbor Chenaya's like one of those damned Beysib fire-bottles. She's got herself a head full of schemes and any one of them would rip us apart. The Torch's going to have to do something."

"He's going to have to wait his turn, isn't he? Ischade's not satisfied yet; neither is Tempus and the rest haven't even launched their attacks. I hear it was Jubal's men that fished her out and that he gave her a lecture that dried the water right off her. You know Molin; He's not one to waste energy when so many others are willing to—"

"It's not just Chenaya, Kama, it's Rashan, that pet priest of hers. Rashan and his crawling little altar out there. He sits out in the heat for hours and stares at Savankala's shadow. He's god-bugged—and he's got no love for the Torch."

"God-bugged?" she asked, her body tightening.

Walegrin stammered. It was his own phrase; one he'd first used for Molin himself when Stormbringer had been after him. He used it to describe a man's face after the gods had been in his mind—when he went about his business as if a nest of fire-ants raced under his skin. When he was not only unpredictable but nigh invincible. Walegrin had witnessed those changes more than once and had only one word for them: god-bugged.

"Yeah, god-bugged," Kama repeated after he had lapsed into silence. "Crit'd like that; maybe I'll tell him sometime. You think Rashan's god-bugged, too?"

"Even if he isn't, he's doing a good job of convincing Chenaya that she's got the gods' own work to do in Sanctuary."

"Savankala's not all-powerful down here, you know," she reminded Walegrin.

"I didn't say Savankala. The frogging priest's god-bugged. It could be any one of them. He's going out in the middle of the night stealing old stones from who knows where and piling them against his altar."

"You're starting to sound like Molin," Kama mused. "All right, I'll try to convince Molin to take Rashan seriously. Anything else?"

She pulled her legs in and started to rise.

"If he doesn't listen, we'll have to do something... ourselves."

Kama stopped in mid-ascent, her weight perfectly balanced on one bent leg, then sank gently back to the floor. "Like what?"

Walegrin swallowed hard, the tension in his throat bringing pain to his ears. "Like... take him out."

"Shit."

She stared past him. He hoped he had judged her right and she'd come to the same conclusion he'd already reached; hoped her affection for and loyalty to Molin Torchholder was strong enough. She laced her fingers through her hair and, unconsciously, brought it around as a curtain to hide her face as she thought.

"Yeah, if it comes to that. *If.*"

Her hair fell back from her face which reflected that faint starlight. She was sweating now and needed to tug her tunic away from sticky skin like any other mortal.

"How's your sister, Walegrin?" she asked, sitting beside him in the casement now, seemingly eager to place some other thoughts in the front of her mind.

"The same, I guess."

Illyra had recovered from her wounds better than they had dreamed possible. A quick glance at her sitting under the shade of the forge awning and no one would suspect that she had lain near death for over a week with a suppurating gouge in her belly where the PFLS ax which had slain her daughter had come to rest. But her spirit—that was another matter.

"She never smiles, Kama. There's only two memories in her mind: the day Lillis died and the day the ship sailed for Bandara with Arton on it. It's gone beyond mourning."

"I tried to tell you both that in the spring."

The tension went out of Walegrin's neck; his chin slanted toward his breastbone. It was a delicate subject among them. Molin had used his own fortune to provide for Illyra's healing and when the seeress's mind proved more injured than her body he'd prevailed upon Kama's near-legendary talent for dissimulation to provoke the S'danzo's recovery. No one wanted to discuss it but it seemed likely that Illyra's damaged mind had both started and then mercifully aborted the spring plague outbreak.

"And we didn't listen." His voice was as despairing as his half-sister's ever was.

Kama twisted her hair through her fist. "Look, I wasn't sure, either. It bothered *me* that one woman, who wouldn't ever hurt anybody, was suffering more than anyone else in this whole filthy, stinking town. Gods below, man, the last thing I ever want to know is my destiny—but I'd belt myself into one of Rosanda's old gowns again and stand outside that forge in the midday heat if I thought it'd make a difference—"

"But it won't. She's healed wrong—like Strat."

"Maybe another child," she mused, ignoring Walegrin's remark about the stiff-shouldered Stepson. "It wouldn't make her forget—but she'd have one to care for, to keep her going from one day to the next until she didn't feel the pain so sharply."

The ebony-haired fighter stared out the window as she spoke. Walegrin knew what had passed between herself and Critias. Knew about the unborn child she'd lost up along Wizardwall and her secret fear that now there could never be another one.

"Gods below, her husband's a big man. He's thought about it but she's too soon recovered," Walegrin said, trying to force humor into his voice.

It worked better than he'd expected. Kama's lips twisted into a lewd, lopsided smile. "There're other ways than that, my man."

Walegrin was grateful that such light as reached down into the room fell on her rather than him. His face burned and his groin tensed. He hadn't *always* known, hadn't really suspected much one way or another until recently. Chenaya took far greater pleasure from her ability to astound and stupefy him than she did from any of his own exertions.

Sensing either his embarrassment or his detachment, Kama made ready to leave the room. "I'll talk to him, Walegrin, but you're still his only eyes and ears out at that place and he won't want to lose you. Maybe we'll take the priest; I've got the stomach for that, but we can't touch *her*. Even if she didn't have some sort of divine protection, she's still Kadakithis's cousin and he'll crucify anyone who rids him of her."

"I know that. I tell it to myself over and over whenever I'm with her. She's using me all the while she pretends to listen or care. When we're alone there's hate and disgust. It's unnatural."

Kama paused at the foot of the stairs. "The only thing unnatural about it is that she's a woman and you're a man— otherwise many men think it's a most natural, and satisfactory, arrangement."

Bitterness and anger had pushed the taste of bile into his mouth. He almost asked about the men of the 3rd, or the Stepsons, or her father who could not lie with a woman, only rape one. In the end, though, he swallowed and stared out the casement, away from her.

"It helps, sometimes, to bathe, to scrub yourself with a coarse cloth until you've shed your own skin," she added in a gentler voice as she disappeared up the stairs.

He waited until he was certain she was gone before making his own way back through the twisted streets. There was an old Ilsigi bathhouse between the garrison barracks and their stables. Cythen made use of it frequently, regardless of the season, often getting his lieutenant, Thrusher, to help her build the fires and haul the water. He had generally ignored them; indulged them, if the truth be known, because they were shy about the time they spent together. Perhaps he would join them . . . no, not that, but learn how the fires were built and follow Kama's usually wise advice.

The narrow streets of the Maze gave way to the Street of Smells, which more than merited its name these days. He crossed it and made his way into the Shambles where the charnel houses, infirmaries, and butchers plied their trades. A year ago this had been where the dead dwelt: an area of Sanctuary given over to magic and other worlds. For a while, after the spring plague, the Shambles had been almost completely abandoned, but they were occupied again.

Theron had proclaimed his command to rebuild Sanctuary's walls throughout the Empire. Singly, in pairs and in small groups, men had begun to come to the Imperial anus to make their fortunes. Roustabouts, seventh sons, and exiles from the ongoing Wizardwall skirmishes took over the empty buildings of the Shambles and took their places on the work gangs. They drank, whored, and otherwise indulged themselves in ways that made longtime residents smile uncomfortably, for these men had great expectations that, so far, Sanctuary had not beaten out of them.

They had their own taverns as well—the Broken Mallet, Tunker's Hole, and Belching Bili's—laid out in a row, spilling sound and light onto Offal Court despite the night's heat. Walegrin watched as a man staggered out one bright doorway and relieved himself in the street before choosing another route. The newcomers didn't get into much trouble—yet.

The charnel houses were busy. Sacks of lime were stacked hight against the buildings. Moonlight turned the dust a glowing, yellow-green. It reflected off the carapaces of the nightflies, the jewel-colored insects which had recently appeared here and which were too beautiful to be vermin. He'd heard the Beysib glassmakers were having some success instilling the colors in their work and that traders were taking egg cases to aristocratic gardens all over the Empire.

Walegrin watched their swirling dance. Its ethereal beauty took the stench and the heat from his mind, but spared him enough awareness to know he was, suddenly, not alone. Tensing imperceptibly, he located the sound and let his fingers hook casually over his belt—and his sword hilt. He spun around into an armed crouch as the intruder hailed him.

"Whoa! Commander?"

He recognized the voice and wished to the gods he didn't. With his sword still at the ready, he straightened up.

"Yeah, it's me. What do you want, Zip?"

The Rankan waited while the PFLS leader came down the street. There was an ugly shadow across the young man's face—courtesy of the treachery he'd found at Chenaya's hands. He'd been proud that Sanctuary had never marked him. Those days were probably over.

"You keepin' your promises, Commander?"

Walegrin shifted his weight nervously and with evident distaste slid his sword back into its scabbard. "Yeah, I'm keeping promises. You got a problem you can't handle?"

There was no love lost between these men. Zip had wielded the ax that had hacked Illyra's gut open and broken her daughter in two. They'd meant to fight to the death that day—only Tempus's accidental intervention had stopped them. Walegrin judged it extremely likely that he'd finish the job someday; someday after Tempus was gone and Zip's absence wouldn't raise embarrassing questions.

"Not me personally—unless you lied to your priest and the Riddler both. Well, you coming with me?"

Liking it not at all, Walegrin fell in step behind Zip and followed him into the alleyways. The truth was, and the garrison commander knew it, that Zip's feelings were never very personal. He and Illyra had had a run-in more than a year ago and he'd stabbed her then—but that had had nothing to do with his attack on her daughter and neither had meant that Zip felt any more strongly about her than he felt about anyone. Tempus's Ratfall farce had probably secured Zip's loyalty and good behavior about as well as it could be secured.

There wasn't really any reason for Walegrin's sweat to go cold as they tunnelled through another cellar and he knew he'd not get back to a street he recognized without help before sunrise.

They were at another of the PFLS safe-houses, an old, uninviting structure whose only doorway opened on a blind courtyard. Glancing at the rooftops, Walegrin knew they weren't a stone's throw from the Wideway—but he'd never imagined this house and its courtyard existed. He wondered how many other boltholes like this the PFLS retained and if even Tempus truly had them under control.

"It's upstairs," Zip called and vanished through the half-ruined doorway.

It took a few moments for Walegrin's eyes to adjust to the faint-shadowed darkness of the house. By the time they had, he'd heard the groaning and flailing about in the upper room—the room to which Zip was leading him. The Torch had offered to keep Zip and the two other piffles who had survived Chenaya's ambush in sanctuary at the palace until their wounds had healed. Zip had refused for both himself and his men; Walegrin figured he regretted it now.

Certainly the smell of blood was strong enough in the air-less room they were crowded into. A lump-tallow candle provided sputtering, smoky light. Walegrin took the sconce from the wall and studied the place. He shoved a smaller man aside and headed for the corner where the whimpering was coming from, then brought himself up short.

"It's a woman!"

"It usually is," Zip replied. "She's been like this for three days. Around sunset we thought she was going to have it, finally. But it's only gotten worse. You gonna help?"

Walegrin knelt down and had his worst suspicions confirmed. This was no hell-cat PFLS fighter; this wasn't even the result of a private quarrel; no, this was a girl, a child really, lying on the filthy wood, her clothes long since torn and discarded, laboring to get a child out of her belly.

"Sweet Sabellia's tits," he swore softly.

The girl opened her eyes. She tried to say something to him but the sounds that came from her were too ragged for him to understand.

"I could stitch up a cut, maybe. Maybe get Thrush. . . . Shit on a stick, Zip—I can't do anything for her. I'm not a god-damned midwife." He stood up and took a step away.

"She needs a midwife," another voice told him, the man he'd pushed aside who was no more a man than the girl in the corner was a woman.

"She needs more than a midwife. She needs a bloody miracle!"

"We'll settle for a midwife," Zip countered.

"You're crazy, Zip. Three days she's been here? Three days? Maybe two days ago; maybe even at sunset she needed a midwife. You can't possibly move her; she's half-dead already."

"She's not!" the youth shouted, his outrage turning to tears. "She needs a midwife—that's all." He turned to Zip, not Walegrin. "You said—you said you'd find someone."

The PFLS leader's facade of uncaring arrogance cracked a bit—enough so the garrison commander could recognize a familiar despair. You made your men trust you so you could ask them to do the impossible and get results, but then they turned around and asked you to do the impossible as well. Walegrin didn't need to like, or even respect, Zip to sympathize with him.

"What about it? You know anyone?" Zip asked.

"Who'd come here? At this hour?"

Walegrin twisted his bronze circlet free, pushed the loose hair off his forehead, and blew a lungful of air through his teeth. The unborn baby chose that moment to send its mother into a back-wrenching arc of pain and terror. As she thrashed about Walegrin saw more than he wanted to see: a tiny leg dangling below the girl's crotch. Even he knew babes were supposed to enter the world the other way around.

He locked stares with Zip and racked his memory for a competent, but foolhardy, midwife.

Molin Torchholder had told him, back when he'd begun taking orders from the priest, that in the Rankan Empire a place's population was usually about fifteen times its tax roll. Until the coming of the Beysib, the Prince had collected taxes, or tried to collect taxes, from some four hundred citizens: Say 6,000 people in the city, not counting Beysibs and new-comers, and Walegrin knew, or could recognize, most of them.

He had a memory for faces and names; had made a hobby of it since his childhood right here in Sanctuary. Moreover his mind was sufficiently flexible to recognize people years after he'd last seen them. He'd recognized Zip, remembering him as a street tough about his own age—always surrounded by followers, always fighting, never winning. He'd recognized another not long ago: a lady living in moderate style and comfort near Weaver's Way.

"Maybe," he told them and headed for the door.

"I'll be going with you," Zip countered and preceded him down the stairs.

They left a different way than they'd come, squat-walking through a gap Walegrin would not have noticed without Zip to lead him. The safe-house shared a wall with a dilapidated warehouse. A warehouse which should have been empty, judging by the way Zip recoiled when they confronted the burning lamps and the little man coming toward them.

"Muznut!" Zip shouted and the bald little man came to a shame-faced stop.

Dressed in drab Sanctuary rags, it took Walegrin a moment to realize he was actually looking at a Beysib who was well-known to, if not exactly friendly with, the PFLS leader. He didn't recognize the foreigner, but he'd know him the next time they crossed paths.

"We share with them, for a price," Zip tried to explain.

"Some fish want to get out of the water." He turned to the Beysib and snarled: "Get back to your tub-boat, old man. You've got no business here after sundown!"

The man's eyes went wide and glassy, like he'd seen a ghost, then he turned and ran. Zip stood staring after him.

"Umm," Walegrin said, pretending disinterest. "I thought we were in a hurry. If this is your shortcut to Weaver's Way, I don't think much of it." He sniffed disdainfully, as the locals expected the Rankans to do, and took note of the smells in the air. Only one was worth remembering: distilled light oil such as he had smelled when Chenaya ambushed the PFLS and they'd retaliated with their fire-bottles.

"Can't trust those fish," Zip said as they approached the door the Beysib had left open in his haste to leave the warehouse.

"Ain't that the truth," Walegrin agreed, and wondered if Zip were truly preoccupied enough to believe that a Rankan soldier hadn't figured out where the oil and glass for his fire-bottles was coming from.

The PFLS leader set a good pace along the Wideway. Sweat came up and clung to the both of them. Once they crossed the Processional, though, and entered Sanctuary's better neighborhoods, Walegrin took command with Zip walking nervously beside him.

"You sure about this place?" the dark-haired man demanded.

"Yeah. I'm no fool. You'll owe me one."

Zip stopped, touching Walegrin's arm as he did, so the two men stood facing each other.

"Pork all, Walegrin. It's for the girl back there, not me."

"That's part of the job. You owe me for keeping quiet about your warehouse back there and your fish glassblower."

"They're shit-dumb, man. He thinks we own the place, so we charge him rent."

"It's not going to wash, Zip." Walegrin watched as the other man went white and furious in the moonlight. "Now look: You're dealing with the guy who brought Enlibar steel to this hole. You got yourself a nice advantage there, but right now you don't need it, correct? Everybody's at peace; you're one of us. And, now that I've got the pieces in my head— well, I can get to better Beysib than your Maznut.

"But let's say I don't want to. Let's say I don't trust some of my allies any more than you do, but the time comes, maybe, that I need a fire-breathing hero, then you come running, Zip—or Shalpa's cloak itself won't hide you from me. Understood?"

Zip weighed his options in silence.

"Maybe you can find another warehouse," Walegrin bantered easily. "Maybe something will happen to me before it happens to you. I remember you from the Pits, long before Ratfall, and I'm betting you want to be a hero just once in your life. But you don't swear right now, and you'll tear Weaver's Way apart looking for her . . . and you won't find her." He smiled his best triumphant smile.

"What do you get out of it?"

"Maybe I'm going to need a home-grown, fire-breathing hero," Walegrin replied, thinking of Rashan and the altar out at Land's End and hoping that Kama would approve.

Zip gave his word and they continued in silence, alone on the streets, until they reached Weaver's Way.

"Keep out of sight," Walegrin told his companion before he climbed the steps to rap loudly on the door.

"Be gone wi' you!" a voice called from inside.

"It's the Prince's business! Open up or we'll break through the door."

There was a long silence, the sounds of two heavy bolts being drawn back, then the door cracked open. Walegrin smacked the heel of this hand against the upper part of the door and threw the weight of his hip against the lower. It gave another few inches but not enough for Walegrin to enter. He looked down at the house guard.

"I want to talk to the Mistress zil-Ineel. Call her." He emphasized his request with another shove, but the house guard was braced as securely as he was and the door didn't budge.

"Come back in the morning."

"Now, fat man."

"Let him in, Enoir," a woman called from the top of the stairs. "What's Eevroen done now?" she asked wearily as she descended.

Walegrin gave the hapless Enoir a leering smile and pushed his way into the open room. "Nothing unusual," he told the woman. "I'm here to see you."

"I haven't done anything to warrant a midnight visit from the garrison," she retorted with enough fire to convince Walegrin that he had indeed come to the right house.

He softened his stance and his voice. "I need your help.

Or, rather, a young girl in the Shambles needs your help."

"I . . . I don't know what you're talking about."

"You're Masha zil-Ineel; you were Mashanna sum-Peres t'Ineel until your uncles went bankrupt and married you off to Eevroen. You lived on Dry Well Street in the Maze until somehow you got lucky, disappeared for almost a year, and came back to buy this place."

"I came by my good fortune the hard way: honestly. I've paid my taxes."

"When you lived in the Maze, Masha, you worked as a midwife—with a doctor present east of the Processional, without one the rest of the time. The girl in the Shambles— she's been in labor for three days, in this heat. Once upon a time visiting the Shambles was moving up for you; I'm hoping you won't be afraid to go there tonight."

Mash sighed and let her lamp rest on the handrail. "Three days? There won't be much I can do."

But she would come—the answer showed on her face before she said anything. Enoir protested and insisted he accompany her but she ordered him to remain at the house and retreated upstairs to dress. Walegrin waited, politely ignoring Enoir's barbed glances.

"You have an escort in the street?" Masha asked when she returned, one hand pulling a prim, but almost transparent, shawl around her shoulders and the other carrying a battered leather chest.

"Of course," Walegrin replied without hesitation as he, rather than Enoir, held the door open.

He called for Zip as soon as the door had shut behind them.

"That is your escort?" Masha sneered, the edge in her voice trying to cover her discomfort and fear.

"No, that's our guide; I'm the escort. Let's get moving."

Whatever Masha zil-Ineel was doing now that she had money, she hadn't let it soften her. She let the shawl drape loosely from her shoulders and kept pace with them along the Path of Money. The heavy chest seemed not to slow her at all and she refused to let either man carry it. The moon set; Walegrin bought a brace of torches from the Processional night-crier and they continued along their way, avoiding the Maze though all of them knew the secrets of its dark passages. They came into the Shambles and halted.

A knot of torch fires was headed toward them, bobbing, even falling, as their bearers shouted into the still, hot air. It reminded the three native Sanctuarites of the riotous plague marches that told the city's better-off citizens when death had erupted in the slums. Silently Zip melted back into the shadows, pushing Masha and her white shawl behind him. Walegrin slipped the straps off his green-steel sword and shoved the stump of his own torch into a gap in the nearest wall.

A gang of newcomer workmen emerged from the darkness. They staggered and stumbled into each other and their shouting proved to be the once-tender chorus of a love ballad. Walegrin shrugged a good deal of the tension from his shoulders but held his ground as they took note of him and lurched to a halt.

"A whorehouse, off-sher, where the wimmen're pretty?" their ersatz leader requested, drawing the outline of what he considered an extremely attractive woman in the air between them. His cohorts broke off their singing to whistle and laugh their agreement.

Walegrin rubbed the loose hair from his forehead and tucked it under his bronze circlet. If he waited a few more moments at least two of the newcomers were going to pass out in the dust and their whole expedition would come to naught. But the men who worked on the walls were being paid daily in good Rankan coinage and the Street of Red Lanterns was suffering from the weather. He did his civic duty and pointed them out of the Shambles toward the Gate of Triumph where, if they did not fall afoul of Ischade, they would eventually find the great houses.

Zip was at his side before he had the torch pulled from the wall.

"Porking, loud fools," he snarled.

"Maybe we should give up our respective trades and build walls or unload barges for a living," Walegrin mused.

"Listen to them. They must be halfway into the square and you can *still* hear them! They'll get eaten alive."

The garrison commander raised one eyebrow. "Not while they're traveling in packs like that," he challenged. "You backed off quick enough."

And Zip stood silent. There were big men in Sanctuary. Tempus was about the biggest; Walegrin and his brother-in-law, Dubro, weren't exactly small-boned either. But, save for the Stepsons, the newcomers were the biggest, best-fed men Sanctuary had seen in a generation or more. Even if they were only common laborers, another man—a native man like Zip —would have to think seriously before bothering them.

"They're ruining the town," the PFLS leader said finally.

"Because they work for their bread? Because they pay fairly for what they need and save to bring their families here to live with them?" Masha interjected. "I thought you were bringing me down here to see a woman."

With a half-glance back toward the square, where the newcomers were still singing, Zip grabbed the torch from Walegrin's hands and plunged into the Shambles backways.

The safe-house was ominously quiet as Zip doused the torch and led the way to the deeply shadowed stairway. He stopped short in the doorway to the upper room; Walegrin bumped into him. The girl was still lying in the corner silent and motionless. Her young lover squatted beside her, his face shiny with unmanly tears. The garrison commander scarcely noticed as Masha shoved him aside. Her movements did not interrupt the invective he privately directed to such gods and goddesses as should have taken a care in these matters. Like many fighting men, Walegrin could understand the sudden death that came on the edge of a weapon but he had no tolerance for the simpler sorts of dying that claimed ordinary mortals.

He watched, and was faintly curious, as Masha took a glass horn from her kit and, with the solid stem of it to her ear and its open bell against the girl's skin, performed a swift, but precise, examination.

"Get the torch over here!" she commanded. "She's still breathing; there's hope, at least, for the babe."

None of the men responded. She stood up and grabbed the nearest, the young man who had been crying.

"There's hope for your child, you fool!" She shook his tunic as she spoke and a glimmer of life returned to his eyes. "Find a basin. Make a fire and boil me some water."

"I . . . we have nothing but this." The young man gestured at the crudely furnished room.

"Well, find a basin . . . and clean rags while you're about it."

The young man looked at Zip, who stared blankly back at him.

"Your fish-eye, Muznut—next door," Walegrin suggested. "He'll have all that, won't he? Even the rags, I imagine."

Zip's face twisted unpleasantly for a moment, then, with a

sigh, he turned back to the stairway, and the warehouse. The other men followed.

Masha hung her delicate shawl over a huge splinter in one of the wall beams and began unlacing her gown. There was messy work to be done and no sense to ruining her own clothing as well. She tore off the bottom panel of her shift and used one strip to bind her already dripping hair away from her face. With the rest she mopped up as much of the blood as she could and plotted the tasks before her.

They built a fire in the courtyard using some of Muznut's fine charcoal and such burnable rubble as was scattered about. The flames turned the ruined gardens into an inferno but the men stayed close by the fire, returning to the upper room only when Masha demanded fresh water or cloths. They said nothing to each other, choosing positions within the courtyard that allowed a clear view of the midwife's flickering shadow and yet shielded them from each other's casual glance.

Toward dawn the bats returned to their normally deserted lairs, their shrill peeps echoing off the walls and the men themselves as they protested the occupation of their homes. The day-birds took flight as well and the small square of sky above them turned a dirty gray that betokened another round of oppressive heat. Walegrin wanted a beaker of ale and the limited comfort of his officer's quarters in the palace wall, but he remained, rubbing his eyes and waiting until Masha was through.

"Arbold!" she called from the window.

The young man looked up. "Water?" he asked, giving the neglected fire a prod.

"No, just you."

He headed into the house. Walegrin and Zip exchanged glances before following him. Masha had expected them and was at the doorway to block their entrance.

"They've only got a few moments," she said softly.

The midwife had washed the new mother's face, smoothed her hair, and surrounded her with the last of Muznut's fine-woven fuse-cloth. Her eyes were bright and she was smiling at both her swaddled child and her lover. But her lips were ashen and her skin had a milky translucence in the dawn light. The men in the doorway knew Masha was right.

"The baby?" Zip whispered.

"A girl child," Masha replied. "Her leg is twisted now, but that may come right with time."

"If she has—" Walegrin began.

A final spasm racked the girl's body. A red stain spread swiftly across the cloth as she closed her eyes and gasped one more time. The child she had cradled with her waning strength slipped through her limp arms toward the floor; Arbold was too stunned to catch it.

"It killed her," he explained, his hands balled into fists at his sides, when Masha tried to place the infant in his arms. "It froggin' *killed* her!" His voice ascended to screaming rage.

The infant, which had been sleeping, awoke with the short-breathed cries peculiar to the just-born. Masha held her protectively against her own breast as the young man's rantings showed no sign of abating.

"Killed her!" she shouted back. "How should an innocent child be held accountable for the chances of its birth? Let the blame, if there is any, fall on those fit to carry it. On those who left her mother here without care for three endless days. On the one who fathered her in the first place!"

But Arbold was in no mood to consider his own part in his lover's death. His rage shifted from the infant to Masha and Zip moved swiftly across the room to restrain his comrade.

"Is there one you trust to care for this child?" Masha asked Zip. "A mother? A sister, perhaps?"

For a heartbeat it seemed there might be two irrational men in the cramped, death-ridden room, then Zip emitted a short, bitter laugh. "No," he answered simply. "She was the last. No one's left."

Masha continued to hold the infant tightly, rocking from side to side across her hips like an animal searching for a bolthole. "What then?" she whispered, mostly to herself. "She needs a home. A wetnurse—"

Walegrin chose that moment to step between them. He looked down at the infant. Its hands were red and impossibly small—scarcely able to circle his forefinger; its face was dark-mottled as if it had taken a beating just in entering this life—which it probably had.

"I'll take her with me," Masha concluded, daring Zip or Arbold to challenge her.

"No," Walegrin said—and they all stared at him in surprise.

"Is the garrison commandeering babes-in-arms now?" Zip sneered.

The blond man shrugged. "Her mother's dead; her father

refuses to acknowledge her: That makes her a ward of the state—unless you're thinking of raising her yourself."

Zip looked away.

"Now, Mistress zil-Ineel's an upstanding woman—but she's raised her own children and's not eager to raise another."

His ice-green eyes bore down on the midwife until she, too, looked away.

"I know a woman whose children have been taken from her. You know her too, Zip—know her *very* well."

"Gods. No." Zip inhaled the words so they were barely audible.

"You'd gainsay me?" Walegrin's voice was as cold as his eyes.

"What? Who?" Arbold interrupted.

"The S'danzo. The one in the alley. You remember: the pillar of fire and the riots afterward?" Zip replied quickly, never taking his eyes away from Walegrin, whose hand rested on the exposed hilt of the only sword in the room.

"What would a S'danzo want—" the young man began.

"You'd gainsay me, Zip, now or ever?" Walegrin repeated.

The PFLS leader shook his head and extended an arm across Arbold's chest, pre-empting any untoward response from that corner.

"Say goodbye to your daughter, pud," Walegrin commanded, lifting his hand from the sword-hilt and fumbling through his belt pouch instead. "This is for you," he dropped a silver coin in Masha's hand, "for the birth of a healthy child. And this is for *her*," he gestured to the dead woman before dropping similar coins in Zip's palm, "to buy a shroud and see her properly buried beyond the walls."

His hands were empty now; he reached out for the infant. Masha had already assessed his determination and placed the squirming bundle gently in the crook of his off-weapon arm.

"Shipri bless you," she whispered, pressing her thumb against the child's forehead so it left a white mark when she lifted it, then she spun her shawl off the splinter and tucked her leather chest under one arm. "I'm ready," she told Walegrin.

They left before the two piffles could say another word. Walegrin was more nervous about dropping the child than about having Zip at his back. He could feel it struggling against the bands of cloth and the awkwardness with which he held it. Once they had clambered through the courtyard and warehouse to the Wideway, he offered to swap burdens with the midwife.

"Never held a hungry newborn before?" Masha guessed as she settled the infant under her breast. Her companion grunted a noncommital reply. "I certainly hope you know what you're doing. Not every man's mistress is eager to take a foundling."

Walegrin adjusted the sweaty hair under his circlet and glanced at the rising sun. "We're taking the child to my half-sister in the Bazaar. Illyra the seeress—her own child was slain and she took Zip's ax in her belly in the fire riots last winter. And I have no idea if she'll want to keep it at all."

"You *are* a bold one," she averred, shaking her head in amazement.

The heat was affecting the Bazaar as it affected the rest of the city. Most of the daily stalls were shuttered or deserted and the vendors who made their homes in the dust-choked plaza were standing idly by their wares, making little effort to confront potential customers. Lassitude had even touched Illyra's husband, Dubro. The forge was still banked although the sun was well above the harbor wall.

The smith saw them coming, took another bite of cheese, then came forward to meet them. The months since Illyra's injury had seen a mellowing of the uneasy relationship between the two men. Dubro, who blamed his half-brother-in-law not only for the absence of his son but for all the flaws of the Rankan Empire, had been forced to admit that Walegrin had done all any man could do to save his wife and daughter. He missed his son, mourned his daughter, but knew that he cherished Illyra above all else. He greeted Walegrin and Masha with a puzzled smile.

"Is Illyra about?" Walegrin asked.

"Abed, still. She sleeps poorly in this heat."

"Will she see us?"

Dubro shrugged and ducked under the lintel of his home. Illyra emerged moments later, squinting against the sun and looking nearly twice her natural age.

"You said you were patrolling nights until this heat broke."

"I was."

He explained the night's events to her—at least those that accounted for his presence with a midwife and infant. He said nothing about his conversation with Kama or the anger that had swept over him when he saw the newborn girl's life being bartered among unwilling patrons. Illyra listened politely but made no move to take the infant from Masha's arms.

"I'm no wetnurse. I can't care for the child, Walegrin. I tire too quickly now, and even if I didn't—I'd look at her and see Lillis."

"I know that; that's why I've brought her," her half-brother explained, with a sincere tactlessness that brought fire to Dubro's eyes and a sigh through Masha's lips.

"How could you?"

They were all staring at him. "Because her mother's dead in some stinking room in Shambles Cross and no one wanted her. She didn't ask to be born any more than Arton asked to become a god or Lillis asked to die."

"No other baby can replace my daughter, don't you understand that? I can't take her in my arms and tell myself that all's well with the world again. It isn't. It won't ever be."

The elegance and simplicity of logic that had allowed him to face down Zip and the child's father ceased to support Walegrin as he stared back at his half-sister's face. Words themselves failed him as well and a crimson flush spread quickly from his shoulders to his forehead. In desperation he grabbed the infant himself and thrust it into her arms as if physical contact and the sheer force of his will would be sufficient.

"No, Walegrin," she protested softly, resisting the burden but not backing away from it. "You can't ask this of me."

"I'm the only one stupid enough to ask it of you, Illyra. You need a child, Illyra. You need to watch someone laugh and grow. Gods know it should have been your own children and not this one. . . . " He turned to Dubro. "Tell her. Tell her this mourning's killing her. Tell her it's not good for any of us when she doesn't care about anything."

So it was that Dubro, after a long moment's hesitation, put his arms under Illyra's to support the child. The girl child did not immediately stop struggling within her swaddling nor did the oppressive weather vanish, but, after she sighed, Illyra did smile at the infant and it opened its blue-gray eyes and smiled back at her.

SPELLMASTER

Andrew Offutt and Jodie Offutt

*Wear weapons openly and try to look mean. People see the
weapons and believe the look and you don't have to use them.*

—*CUDGET SWEAROATH*

One thing led to another and swords came scraping out of
their sheaths. Fulcris knew he was in trouble. The two men
facing him with sharp steel in their fists had left the caravan
yesterday afternoon when it halted here, just outside Sanctuary. They had gone on down into the town for a little of the
partying he had denied them en route from Aurvesh. Now, just
after midday, they'd come the short distance back out here to
the encampment. Looking for trouble.

Fulcris wasn't the sort to pretend not to see them and be
somewhere else, however wise that would have been. They
had obviously been drinking their lunch. That was bad; these
two, still cocky adolescents at thirty or so, were mean as sat-
on spiders to begin with.

He spoke quietly and calmly and everything he told them
was true. They chose not to accept any of it. Furthermore,
they chose to push it. All three men knew that part of the
reason was the sword-arm of caravan guard Fulcris. Only a
few days ago he had taken a wound, high up near the
shoulder. It still bothered him. The arm and its muscle were
weakened, a little stiff. That made him a good man for two
men to pick a fight with. Or a good victim.

Now their sword-hands had made it clear that they were
through talking and he'd better be, too. His choices were two:
he could run or he could defend himself. The fact that it was
not fair because of his arm was not important to them and it
had better not be to Fulcris. Besides, the choice did not exist
for him. He couldn't run. He was a caravan guard. To flee
from attackers, whether two or four, days-old wound or no,
would ruin his reputation and the life he hoped for in this new
town.

With only the slightest of winces, well hidden behind
clenched teeth, he reached across his belt buckle. He made

193

sure that when he drew his sword, the blade swished audibly and blurred as it rushed across him into readiness.

The man in the green tunic blinked at that and his arm wavered. Fulcris remembered his name: Abder.

His companion kept coming, though, and so Abder did, too.

Just feint at the green tunic, Fulcris told himself, *going high, and try to get the more dangerous one on the backstroke, down. Abder will waver. If I can hurt his crony, it will be over.*

If I don't, they'll kill me.

Damn. What a way to end a good life. And just when I was thinkin' about trying to settle down. He whipped his sword back and forth, strictly to make a bright flash and an impressive *whup-whup* noise that should give third thoughts to Abder, who had already had second ones about this encounter.

Uh. The exertion started the wound leaking. He felt the trickle of blood, warm on his upper arm.

"You son of a bitch," snarled the one in the grayish homespun tunic.

One more step, Fulcris thought, knowing the name-calling stage was about to end. The homespun man was worked up just about enough. For the first time in a long while, Fulcris knew fear. *One more step. Then either I end it or they do.*

"Yo!"

Fulcris ignored the hail. He kept his gaze on his assailants. They glanced toward the source of the call. A solitary traveler was pacing his large dun-colored horse toward them, trailing a pack-animal. His hair was invisible within the odd flapped cap he wore, leather left its natural shade. Fulcris could have taken out both of them, then. He didn't.

"You two fellows need help with this mean-looking criminal?"

"No business of yours," homespun said, while that big dun-colored horse kept coming at him, just pacing.

"That's true," the newcomer said in a quiet voice, staring levelly. Not menacingly, or with a mean expression; it was just a steady look.

Fulcris allowed himself a glance. He saw what they saw: a big man with a big droopy moustache, sort of bronzey-russet. A great big saddle-sword, and another sheathed at the man's left thigh. A shield, looking old and worn and bearing no markings whatever. His dusty, stained tunic was plain undyed homespun with an unusually large neck. Its sleeves were short enough to show powerful arms.

A horseman coming alone, with seeming consummate confidence, from the northeast—Aurvesh? A man of weapons. He kept his mount pacing easily, while his calm gaze remained on the two men before Fulcris. He never glanced at Fulcris at all.

An *experienced* man of weapons, Fulcris thought.

"Just interested," the quiet voice said equably. "No blow's been struck but his arm just started leaking. Got yourself a man with a recent wound, hmm. Two of you. You calling him opponent or *quarry?*"

Abder of the green tunic said, "Huh?"

Homespun said, "Listen, you—"

And then he had to back a couple of paces, because the big-dun colored horse paced right in between him and Fulcris. Fulcris was on the horse's left. The mounted man stared down at homespun. Abder tried to be unobtrusive about backing two more paces.

"Came here to ask a favor. You with the caravan?"

The two men exchanged a look, homespun having to turn a little because his companion had backed farther away. Homespun looked back up at the interfering newcomer.

"Naw. He is."

"Mind if I tock with him, then?" He had said "talk," but part of his accent was that the *aw* sound came out as short *o*.

Abder moved away from his companion. His arm hung straight down; the one with the sword in it. Homespun exchanged stares with the nosy newcomer a while, then glanced at Abder. He was surprised to see that the latter was several paces behind him and well to his right.

"Huh! Leaving me alone, huh, Ab?"

"Pardon us," the mounted man said, "while we tock." On Fulcris's side the newcomer's left hand moved in a little waving gesture.

When the dun horse began pacing forward again, between Fulcris and his accosters, Fulcris paced too. He noticed that the newcomer never so much as glanced at him. They took about twenty steps without anyone's saying a word. By that time, the other two were well behind them. The newcomer leaned back to swing a big-thighed leg over the pommel of his saddle, which was molded in the shape of a turtle's head. He dropped to the ground a foot from Fulcris. Surprisingly blue eyes looked into the very brown ones of the caravaner. They were about the same height. The traveler was bigger.

"You a caravan guard?"

"Aye. Those two—"

"Mean on strong drink. You took a wound a few days ago?"

"Aye. You just—"

"I could sure use some wotter, and your arm could use something."

Not much for talking, Fulcris thought, and nodded. "Right. Just over here."

"Uh. Wait here, Jaunt."

Fulcris assumed that was the name of the big man's horse. He tried not to talk as they walked toward his old tent of faded blue and dull yellow stripes, but just now that was impossible.

"I started with the caravan in Twand. Those two joined us in Aurvesh. Just a little trouble the first night, and me'n another guard had to forbid them anything stronger'n water. Caravan stopped here to break up; sort ourselves out. You know. They went right on into Sanctuary last night lookin' for what we kept from them. They obviously had some more this morning."

"Um."

Sure not a talker, Fulcris mused. "Oh—name's Fulcris."

"Strick."

Guess that's his name, Fulcris thought. And didn't this man speak quietly and in an unusually matter-of-fact voice, no matter what he was saying or talking about! "The arm's not bad, but it could've made a difference. Thanks, Strick. Here."

His gesture indicated the interior of his tent; the flap was open and fastened back.

Strick glanced back to see the two men, swords sheathed, heading toward the city's wall. He nodded. "Saw it all. Noticed the arm." Ducking his head, he entered.

"Uh-huh. You notice a lot, don't you."

"Only one of 'em was dangerous. I never glanced at the other. He cot that: contempt. When I called, you kept your eyes right on them. You know what you're doing, Fulcris. Might want to be careful, in Sanctuary."

"Cot" was "caught," Fulcris realized. "You too! They don't like either of us, now. Here you go." Fulcris started to pass Strick the cloth-wrapped water skin, then changed his mind.

He decanted cool water into the tin cup he had carried for years. The cup showed it. "You didn't think I was a 'mean-lookin' criminal'?"

Strick shrugged. He drank, uttered the predictable "ahh," and drank some more. "I wanted to interrupt and that was something to say. Didn't want to come galloping and embarrass you. Let's see about that arm."

"It's all right."

"Wouldn't have started leaking if it was all right. Clotted now. Hmm." Strick had pushed up the other man's sleeve and bent a little closer to peer at the wound. "Spear cut. Not one of those two?"

"No. Little trouble just this side of Aurvesh, four days ago. Six idiots thought we looked attackable and played bandit. Two of them got away. One of the dead ones gave me this. It's all right."

"Looks all right. Give me some wine, though, so I can give you a sting."

After Strick had re-reopened the wound and treated it with wine—it stung—he rearranged and re-tied the bandage. "It will be fine in two days," he said with casual confidence. "Won't leave a scar, either."

More like another week, and there will *be a scar,* Fulcris mused, but certainly didn't say it. Instead: "Saying 'thanks' is getting to be a habit. What about putting some of that wine on the inside?"

"I wouldn't mind."

Fulcris filled the tin cup. Noticing that Strick asked no questions, he decided to emulate that, though naturally he wondered where the big fellow was from and why he'd come here. From how far, alone? He even managed not to volunteer his own business. After a couple of minutes he remembered:

"Oh. You mentioned a favor."

Strick looked at him, lowering his cup. The lines around his eyes, Fulcris thought, put the big man up in his thirties. Maybe forty, depending upon how much of his life he'd spent traveling. Fulcris was thirty-eight, but years of escorting caravans had lined his face so much that he could pass for forty-nine or fifty.

"I'd like to leave my horse here, along with the shield and saddle-sword." His eyes gazed straight into Fulcris's and his moustache writhed in a smile it concealed. "Don't want to ride into a town looking like a dangerous man of weapons."

"Who rode here alone, from . . . someplace that gave you an accent I can't place."

Strick shrugged. "True. Will you name me a charge for keeping my horse for a few days?"

"You looking for work as a—for weapon work? There's a merc camp not too far from here, and another in the city."

"No, that's not what I want to do. You know a few things about this town."

"Just a few," Fulcris said, thinking that the man was not telling the truth but that he even lied well, in that same matter-of-fact way. "You learn things from people you pass on the road, and I listened, up in Aurvesh. This town's had a real mess in the past year or so. Fire, flood, a war among witches trying to take over and the Stepsons—mercenaries under someone named Tempus who has sort of taken over 'defense' and peace-keeping; and all the while the town's really been taken over by some odd invaders from oversea. The Empire's not as strong as it was."

"Ranke?"

"Right."

"So I heard. Odd invaders?" Even "odd" sounded odd; this man's short *o* was *extremely* short.

"Freaks, or half-humans, or something. Guess we'll find out. Listen, you know I'm not going to charge you to take care of your gear and horse for a few days. But here's a thought, unless you're in a hurry. A man and a couple of women are riding into town later, and they've already asked my caravan master if he'd give them an escort. He asked me. Sure; that trio's rich!" Fulcris flashed a smile and noticed that the other man only nodded. "Anyhow, if you care to rest here while I see to a few things I have to do, the five of us can ride in together. You'll be a lot less noticeable—people will take you for another from the caravan."

"Fulcris, well met and I thank you. I can waste some time knocking the dust off and leaving the shield and big sword—here?"

"Of course. Just consider the tent yours while I take care of business. Have some more of that, if you want."

"I don't."

I didn't think so, Fulcris thought, and left the tent.

•   •   •

He was surprised, a couple of hours later, at sight of his new friend. Fulcris had seen him an hour ago, putting his stripped pack-animal into the temporary enclosure the caravaners had set up.

Now Strick's tunic of drab, undyed homespun had given way to a considerably nicer one in medium blue wool. He had buckled on his sword again, an unremarkable weapon with a brass-ball pommel in a worn old sheath, but he had replaced his worn old belt with a newer one, black with a silvered buckle. Never mind the dagger. That was an everyday utensil no one saw as a weapon until one came at him. Strick's was plain of handle and pommel. Merely utilitarian; a working man's tool. The stained leather leggings were gone, replaced by snugly fitting cloth, dun-colored. What calves and thighs the man had! His light boots were medium brown, and well worn.

Aside from his bronze-red moustache and ruddy face, a quite drab man despite the handsome tunic of Croyite blue. He still wore that odd, flapped skull-covering cap, too.

Jaunt stood nearby, saddled and bridled anew—with worn old leather that had been unremarkable even when new—and wearing a smaller version of the traveler's pack. Shield and the big sword were not in evidence.

"Left a few things inside," he said, so quietly and half apologetically.

"Good," Fulcris said, and introduced the wealthy man and the two women.

All three of them looked dressed for court. The not-unhandsome man in matching tunic and leggings of yellow-green silk wore a fine cloak of a blue so pale it was nearly white—not from age or wear. Strick was polite, greeting each woman with a little inclining of his head, speaking quietly as ever. The bosomy, steatopygous one in pink to the collarbones, along with garnets set in silver, was the wife of this Sanctuarite nobleman. Chest on her like a shelf for displaying fine glassware, Fulcris thought. The lean, dimply young blonde in blue, Fulcris saw, was interested in Strick. Despite both his and Strick's efforts to avoid it, she rode beside the big man with the bronze moustache as they walked their horses the sixth of a league or so to the city walls.

"Where are you from, Strick?" Her voice was girlish and her dimples glorious.

"North."

She shot him a look. "Oh. Do you intend to settle in Sanctuary?"

"Might."

After a few moments of silence, she tried again: "Will you, uh, go into business here, Strick?"

"I'm considering it."

Riding in front of them beside the wealthy Noble Shafralain of Sanctuary just back from a lengthy stay in Aurvesh, Fulcris smiled. The Noble Shafralain's doubtless noble wife was chattering away about what sort of shape the house might be in. The lean young blonde had gone silent, doubtless wracking her brain for a way to get Strick to converse. Politeness forbade her pursuing any of the previous questions, since he apparently was not minded to volunteer any information on those subjects.

At last her voice piped again: "Do you know where you plan to stay, Strick?"

"I don't know, my lady. Perhaps—"

"Oh goodness, Strick, do call me Esaria!"

A glance to his left showed Fulcris how Noble Shafralain's well-molded face went grim in disapproval. From behind them the quiet voice spoke as if Strick had seen that expression:

"Perhaps you could suggest an inn, my lady Esaria. It need not be the city's fanciest!"

"Oh. Father—would you recommend an inn to this traveler from afar?"

"My dear," the silken-cloaked man beside Fulcris said stiffly, "we do not know this foreigner's means. The prices of Sanctuary's inns vary as greatly as the quality of their food. The Golden Oasis, I should say, is our best."

"Oh darling, it's been so long—let's do take dinner there tonight!"

"A moment, Expimilia," Shafralain said, with mild impatience.

"I am from Firaqa to the northwest, Noble Sir, and hardly of your means. What are second- and third-best?"

Fulcris smiled.

"Could we do that, darling? I really don't relish opening the house just in time to have to eat there! Who knows what the servants have done with the place—and what shape the larder's in!"

Fulcris's smile broadened at Lady Expimilia's importunings.

Her husband continued to stare straight ahead, chin nobly high. Without turning so much as his head in replying to the man riding behind him where Shafralain doubtless thought he belonged, he named two other inns.

"A grateful foreigner's thanks," Strick said, with only the hint of stress on the third word.

"Are we going to sup at the Golden Oasis, Father?"

"For all we know," Shafralain said, this time with a slight turning of his head, "the Golden Oasis has been destroyed, or sadly damaged."

"I'd be glad to ride straight there and have a look," Esaria said. "I'd be perfectly safe, too; Strick would ride with me, wouldn't you, Strick?"

"That," her father said, "will not be possible."

They rode in silence, approaching the wall of Sanctuary. Abruptly the nobleman's noble wife turned partway around and spoke in a determinedly pleasant voice.

"Well, Strick of Firaqa, will you please escort *me* to the Golden Oasis? Yes, Esaria, you may come along. Aral," she said to her husband in a different voice, "we will be fine and will join you later at home."

The Noble Shafralain gave his wife a long, slow stare.

"My lady," Strick said softly, "I regret that I already have other plans."

"*Oh-h!*" Esaria said, in clear exasperation. Obviously Strick had chosen diplomacy and deference to her father over touching off family problems.

For the first time, Shafralain turned to give the foreigner a fleeting glance. It was not an unpleasant look.

"Firaqa," he said, turning back. "Firaqa . . . oh. That where the pearls come from?"

"Aye."

"Freshwater pearls," Expimilia exclaimed. "Of course! Firaqan Souls of the Oyster!" Abruptly she half-turned to look at the quiet man. "You didn't come here to sell any of those beauties, did you?"

Shafralain snorted. Strick made a chuckling noise. "Sorry, my lady."

They entered the city and within a few hundred feet were accosted by two young men. Each wore a cloth band of the same color around his upper arm and bore a crossbow in addition to sheathed sword.

"Welcome to Sanctuary! You will need a pass in this area, gentle travelers," one glibly told them. "We offer five armbands for two pieces of silver."

"A *pass!*" Shafralain snapped. "Likelier you'll be ridden down! Since when does the Noble Shafralain need to wear a dirty patch of cloth in order to move through his own city?"

The faces of their accosters underwent unpleasant changes. The one who had not spoken stepped back and showed that his crossbow was cocked. Passersby were carefully not-seeing the tense encounter. Most wore brassards matching those the two youths wore and offered for sale.

"Since quite awhile, Noble," the spokesman said. "Maybe you left town when things got nasty last year and're just coming back, hmm? See, citizen security is sort of divided up amidst serveral pertection groups, and we just can't garntee yer safety here without but you're wearing onea these handsome armbands."

"Oh, I think they're quite pretty armbands really," Esaria said.

Her mother said, "If it's what people are wearing this season . . ."

Shafralain, however, was Shafralain: "You *threaten* us, fellow?"

"Here is a piece of silver," a quiet voice said. "It should suffice. See that nothing happens to these people, whether they consent to wear your armbands or no. I will."

"So will I," the surprised Fulcris heard himself say, even as they heard the ring of silver off a thumbnail and saw the young man before him throw up a hand to catch Strick's coin.

He examined it. "Huh! Never seen onea these before. What's this on it, a fire? Whur's it from at?"

"Firaqa," Strick told him. "Way up northwest. Not part of Ranke's Empire. Mints its own coins, with the sign of the Flame. It will spend; it's silver."

Immediately after his last word came the sound of his clucking to his horse. Fulcris swallowed, but at once made the same sound in his cheek. That worked; the horses moved forward and the two accosters stepped back on either side. The speaker extended a number of armbands.

"Pleasure doing business with you," he told Strick, as the latter accepted the "passes."

"Fulcris," Strick said, and passed one to the caravaner. "Noble Shafralain?"

The nobleman would not turn or glance at the proffering hand. "I had far rather chop the arm off that arrogant snot than put one of his dirty rags on my arm!"

"Me too," Strick said, equably as ever. "But while we did that, the other would have flicked his trigger and sent a crossbow bolt into . . . one of us."

"Those boys?! Likelier he'd have missed!"

"Father-r . . ."

"Agreed," the quiet voice said from behind stiff-backed Shafralain, "and alone, Fulcris and I might have taken that chance. I'm very aware of being in the presence of a noble of this city—and of two women."

The only way out of that one was for Shafralain to take offense by pretending to have been accused of cowardice. Either he chose not to do or he didn't think of it. "Hmp," he muttered. "What has become of my city while I have been out of it?"

Coincidence or that goddess known as Lady Chance chose to let Strick and milady answer in chorus: "We had better find out," and she went on, "and be careful the while."

"Good advice, my Lord," a nervous Fulcris said. He was beginning to wonder how soon a caravan might be heading east and need a guard. Or north, or west either. Or even south, right into the sea.

Abruptly Shafralain's arms tightened. "Whoa," he said, and turned—with stiff dignity—in the saddle to look back at the big man beside his daughter. After studying him for a moment, the noble asked, "Can you use that sword, foreigner?"

"Name's Strick. From Firaqa."

The two men gazed at each other, each maintaining a practiced serene look from wide-open eyes that each had learned obtained this or that result. The moment stretched on, with four people watching the lean, thin-moustached face of Noble Shafralain with its high cheekbones and sculptured brows. Suddenly those features moved in a small smile.

"I was hoping you would answer my question. Can you use that sword, Strick of Firaqa?"

Stick shrugged and made a depreciatory gesture. "When I must."

"Until we know more about the situation in *my* city," Shafralain said, "we shall not be going to the Golden Oasis or anywhere else save our home. My family and I can *not* stoop to giving aught to scum who demand 'protection' money with crossbows. I would like to double what you gave that scum if you would ride with us, Strick of Firaqa."

Strick nodded.

"Good, then. Let us—"

"Perhaps you could change a few of these Firaqi coins for me," Strick said, just as Shafralain started to turn back to face front. "Collector's items for you, and I attract less attention as a *foreigner*. If we exchanged ten for ten, I believe I'd owe you a difference; a few coppers."

Shafralain clicked in his cheek while jiggling his reins of shining red leather. His horse paced a few feet before being reined about so that its rider could face the man from Firaqa.

"Difference! A few coppers! I just heard astonishing honesty! Certainly you are not a banker! But . . . do you have ten silver coins, Strick?"

Strick nodded lazily.

"We will exchange ten for ten as soon as we reach my home, sir!"

"Your pardon, Noble, but—let's do it now. Just in case."

Shafralain cocked his head. "Just in case of what?"

Strick tapped the armband he had slipped on. Even below his elbow, it was snug. "Just in case your home is in another *area of protection*."

"*Damn!*"

"Agreed."

While Fulcris watched, more astonished than nervous now, the two men solemnly exchanged ten coins of silver, while sitting their mounts on a street in Sanctuary. At least they were as discreet as possible about what they were doing. In daylight, in the street. In the town called Thieves' World!

Shafralain turned to Fulcris. "Caravaner," he said, "thank you and good fortune."

Since that was an obvious dismissal, Fulcris touched a finger to his forehead, nodded, and started to rein away.

"Meet you at the Golden Oasis at noon tomorrow for a cup of something," the by now familiar voice said quietly, and Fulcris nodded and smiled as he rode on into a city suddenly sinister. Wearing a cloth brassard as "protection."

Strick was right about the city's "security" zones. By the time they reached the imposing mansion on its walled estate, they had collected another set of armbands and the noble owed more silver to the quiet man from Firaqa.

That was how it came about that on his first night in Sanctuary the foreigner dined with the Noble Shafralain and family in their fine big manse, waited upon by silent servants in beige and maroon. He did an amazingly superb job of telling little about himself and wandering around the outskirts of questions and answers, and he would not stay the night. Shafralain was glad of that, considering his marvelously dimpled daughter's fascination with this unusual and quite mysterious fellow.

Strick knew that. It was precisely why he declined the invitation and departed to walk alone through the darkness of that divided city.

Although Fulcris walked into the Golden Oasis before noon next day, he found Strick there before him. The reason was simple: Strick had spent the night here. He had risen relatively early to descend for breakfast. Since then he had done no talking, asked few questions, and done a lot of listening. Seated privily at a small, shining table in the well-kept main room, the two newcomers sipped watered wine and shared new-gained knowledge of a damned city.

The place was a mess. Too many people had grabbily tried to treat it as their own and, greedy for power and control, indiscriminately introduced too many random factors. Meanwhile supposed rulers, anointed and otherwise, took no firm stand and failed to exercise the control they were supposed to have and wield.

"Sanctuary," Fulcris said, "is ruled by King Chaos."

"Black magic," Strick said morosely, looking ill. "The bottomness of humanity's inhumanity."

Sanctuary had not even recovered from or grown accustomed to Rankan rule before the seaward invasion of the folk called Beysins. Both men had by now seen examples of that strange womanish sea-race with the unblinking eyes equipped with nictitating membranes.

They merely turned up one day "in about a million boats," as a man had told Strick at breakfast, and after that it was essentially "Hello: Welcome to the Beysib Empire!" That turned the city on its ear—on its rear, as Fulcris put it. The Beysin gynecharch, the Beysa, moved herself right into the palace. No one in power did anything. About ten minutes later, out of the gutters crawled something called the Popular Front for the Liberation of Sanctuary: a rabble organization of the unorganizable led by a feisty-swaggery street-lord-and-dolt. His avowed dedication was to throwing out the invaders and their (god-related?) lady boss with her twining snakes and bare jigglies, along with her people's ghastly habits with small, preposterously lethal serpents.

What he and his PFLS accomplished was a great deal of mischief and murder and discomfort among his fellow Ilsigs. The fish-folk flourished.

"Ilsigi," Strick corrected Fulcris. "It's plural and possessive both. No *s.*"

Next came still another group, this one with the unlikely name of the Rankan 3rd Commando, whatever that meant. By then the staggering town was divided some four ways and none of the rival groups could claim to be in charge.

All did.

Meanwhile gods wrangled and rassled, people murdered each other indiscriminately, and consumption of alcoholic spirits increased dramatically. An apparently brutish fellow named Tempus and his herd of nomadic womanless warriors-for-hire stayed just long enough to make things worse for the people they despised as "Wrigglies." Then they decamped, to leave behind a vacuum that led to more struggling and more murder of guilty, guiltless, and innocent alike. Decent, normal citizens cowered about their daily business. As a matter of fact so did indecent and abnormal citizens. Daily business had come to mean a striving to continue living.

To what purpose, none could be sure.

Speaking of the abnormal and indecent, the next advent was of a vampire witch and a necromant—or maybe it was a necromant and a vampire witch; everyone was confused because it was all too much—along with acres of walking dead. The two witches juggled people and Balls of Power and did everything but dice for poor pitiful Thieves' World. The rule of females in Sanctuary became absolute. The founder-god seemed to have abdicated. Tale-tellers tried using female names for their characters, even when they were transparently male. That did not work; the storytellers bogged down and received fewer coins because reality was beyond their imaginative abilities.

Dead men wandered about and acted and a dead horse clop-clopped the streets of a city surely forsaken by all gods.

Meanwhile intelligent natives, smart people such as Shafralain, got the hell out.

Fifteen or so minutes ago Fulcris had learned why the ruler
—the youthful Rankan governor—wasn't ruling; he was busy
playing house with the fish-eyed snake-lady with the naked
turrets. Even his fellow Rankans sneered at this Kadakithis,
calling him by a contemptuous nickname.

All right, so she wore her turrets *partially* covered these
days. Because of the invasion of her striding dykish females,
décolletage was very much in vogue. Sanctuarite breasts were
bared just short of the nipples—while skirts were long and
flounced and saddlebagged.

"I've no-tisssed," Strick said, and Fulcris chuckled.

"Me too. The skirts are stupid and ugly but I do love all the
jiggle above!"

A demonic monoceros had run rampant, goring people and
wrecking real estate.

"They have a low inn or dive called the Obscene Monoceros," Strick said, shaking his head.

Fulcris stared for a moment, then fell back laughing. "Vulgar Unicorn!" he corrected.

Strick shrugged. "Blackest magic," he muttered, staring
into his cup. "This city is damned and abhorred by all gods,
surely."

"Yet why do gods or people allow it," Fulcris said, and
drank. "You heard about the dead (?) warrior-god—female,
of course—some fool revived to terrorize streets and citizenry?"

Strick countered with the fact that another someone had
broken into the palace, impossibly, and (impossibly) made off
with the head snake-lady's wand or something, and she had
done not a bloody thing about it. Incredible!

A nasty adolescent boy in a female body was going about
in the garb of a Rankan arena-fighter, insulting and threatening everyone in sight, including the ones she whorishly lay
with. Five well-trained soldier-bodyguards from Ranke were
reduced to guarding cattle or goats or orchards, while a street
tale-teller was in the palace, wearing silk robes. The Rankan
highest priest was apparently giving more time to personal
romance—despite his being married—than priesting.

And King Chaos waved his scepter over Sanctuary.

Street skirmishes erupted into street war. Blood flowed in
the gutters and someone started a fire that burned a good bit of

real estate—mostly the homes of the poor, of course. After that Sanctuary was assaulted by a few years' worth of rain, all in a few days. Every creek, river, and sewer decided to back up.

"Sorcery," Strick muttered. "Abhorrent black magic. Ashes and embers, what poor pitiful people in need of help!"

A burned town was washed off and hoisted off its foundations on swirling flood waters. Somewhere in there the high-civilization bisexual mercs of Tempus had come back and barbarously massacred a band of men in "their" barracks. More innocents had of course perished in *that* private war. Meanwhile in Ranke someone did away with the emperor and the new one—up from field general, hurrah!—dropped over to Sanctuary to say hello. Apparently he did naught else.

Yet perhaps it was he who pushed it along: the war against the witches/vampires/Things had grown, and a whole fine estate-mansion had burned in a towering pillar of fire for days or maybe it was weeks. When the fire went out the place was still there but no one dared go near it.

"Still is," Fulcris said. "Furthermore, one of the witch-women-Things is still about, living peacefully just outside town, and none of these poor excuses for humanity is doing a bloody thing about it."

"Black magic," Strick muttered, staring into his cup. "All black magic, on and on. By the Flame, but these people need relief, help, an advocate! A little surcease from agony and blackness in their lives!"

While Fulcris was still blinking at that strange utterance, their attention was drawn to the door. It had opened to admit a good-sized fellow in a light tan tunic whose skirt- and sleeve-hems were decorated with maroon bands, and with a maroon bar running over each shoulder and down his torso. His high buskins were dark red. He bore a sword and long dagger in maroon sheaths, and he looked competent. Just inside, he swept the common room with a bleak gaze. It lingered for a moment on Strick and Fulcris before passing on. He backed a pace, nodded to someone outside, and stepped in to stand to the door's left. Rather stiffly, in the manner of a sentry.

Through the doorway, all bright and summery in white and yellow, bustled a beaming Shafralaina Esaria. Smiling and dimpled, she came straight to the two men. Strick continued looking past her long enough to note the other man outside, also in her family's livery.

"Strick! Fulcris! Well met!"

"What a coincidence," Strick said drily, as both men rose.

"Don't be silly! I came here to see you! I'd have been here earlier, but first I had to convince father that I needed to *shop*, and then I had to wait while he gave detailed instructions to no less than two 'escorts' to accompany me. What's in those cups?"

She had a breathless, girlish way of talking that Strick could not despise. The tallish, lean girl with the pale hair was too fresh, too charming. Soon she was seated with them, also with a cup of water-weakened wine. Well met indeed, Strick soon learned, when he mentioned that he wanted information as to where he might "open a place of business." Flashing those bemazing dimples, Esaria was delightedly able to help. A cousin of her father's, it seemed, was a civil servant whose customs job had remained secure through the various administrations. That was partially because of his sideline: he remembered everything and conducted scrupulously private investigations.

An hour later Fulcris was on his way back to the remnant of the caravan and Esaria was introducing Strick to her second cousin. Then she took her leave to buy something or other to prove to her father that shopping had indeed been her goal.

"And what about the report those dangerous-looking bodyguards give him?" Strick asked, smiling a little.

"Oh, they tell him what I tell them to tell him. They do exactly as I tell them."

Strick thought this an opportune time to say, "I am not that sort of man, Esaria."

White teeth flashed and dimples sprang into bold evidence. "Can't I just see that, O Mysterious Foreigner!" And with a wave, she was gone.

Still smiling that close-mouthed smile of his, Strick turned to her Second Cousin Cusharlain.

"Second Cousin Esaria is . . . taken with you, Strick."

"I know. That's why you just heard me warn her. I am being careful, Cusharlain, and not encouraging your noble and wealthy cousin's dotter, believe me. Now let me tell you a little about my plans, and the sort of information I need."

Confident that Cusharlain was working on his behalf, Strick wandered. Passing snatches of conversation informed a tourist who used his ears as well as his eyes.

Carrying a bag formed of a dirty sheet trailing dirty laundry, he studied the palace while Beysin guards studied him with little interest. He went on his way, and soon bought a third armband. When it would not fit around his upper arm, he was apologetic about returning it. The "protectors" chuckled after him as the foreigner, apparently chicken-hearted for all his size, went on his way. Having strolled to the very end of Governor's Walk, he had a look at Sanctuary's main temples. He noted destruction, and the busywork of reconstruction. No, he learned, there was no Temple of the Flame or any kind of fire in Sanctuary. About every other deity imaginable was represented here, though, including a little chapel to Theba.

The foreigner nodded. The death goddess was of no interest to Strick of Firaqa.

He took the Street of Goldsmiths down to the Path of Money, noting among the well-off citizenry more décolleté dresses too busy below the waist. He found the moneyhandler Cusharlain had recommended.

They held a bit of converse, during which both men learned this and that of interest to each. Then, in private, Strick opened the dirty-sheet bag to reveal its other contents, carefully pressed together and snugly wrapped to prevent their clinking.

The banker was delighted to make the acquaintance of Torezalan Strick tiFiraqa and his foreign gold.

Strick left in possession of several documents and carrying the bag that now held only dirty laundry. Two doors down and across that showily clean street, he entered the establishment of the second moneyhandler Cusharlain had mentioned. While that individual might have been uninterested in a foreigner with so little taste as to carry his soiled clothing along the street called Money, he was experienced enough to know that eccentric people came to him with treasures in eccentric disguises. He acceded to a private interview and was rewarded.

From his underwear the foreigner in the strange skullcap took a small felt bag. It did not jingle, but it did contain two gleaming examples of the largesse of Firaqa's Pearl River. They were worth over twenty horses, or much gold.

Strick departed with several more documents, less weighty underclothing, and carrying the bag that now held only dirty laundry.

He stopped in at the Golden Oasis to get something done

about the latter and to visit his horse. He left bearing a smaller, cleaner bag. It contained food and wine. Ever listening, he walked down the Processional to Wideway. Here he noted that most damage to the ever-important docks had been repaired. He saw workmen, fisherfolk and their boats, and Beysib ships. Ambling easily, keeping his face wide open and his eyes large, he observed, listened, asked carefully unpointed questions, and listened. He noted some flood damage, rather less décolletage among these working people, and some damage from fire.

Three workmen were astonished at the offer of the strange big man who spoke so quietly. Naturally they accepted: They joined him on a loading dock for a bite and a bit of wine. This time he learned the location of the dive called Sly's Place; two of these men knew of it. He was in the wrong section of the city, though close. He was advised to stay out of that area of town, and he thanked the adviser.

Only after he had meandered off on his way, leaving the rest of the wine, did they realize that they had learned little from him while he had learned much. No matter. What a fine nice fellow he was, with his funny accent!

Strick, meanwhile, was wandering some more, observing and listening.

"Well. Here's a new face! I'm Ouleh. Buy a girl a cup, good-lookin'?"

Strick looked up at the woman who materialized beside his corner table in this noisy place. She was a "girl" of thirty or so, wearing a canary yellow blouse scooped deeply to display a great deal of her head-sized breasts. Her long skirt was without flounces or adornment other than its positively manic striping.

He said, "At the bar."

"Hmm'?" She cocked her head on one side and tried to look sweet.

"Go to the counter, tell Ahdio I'm buying you one, and to look this way. I will nod."

"Nice man! Be right back."

"No. I drink here, you there."

"Oh."

Without further comment aside from a shrug that imparted massive movement to her blouse, she jiggled back to the counter. Strick saw her point, saw the big mail-coated man look at him. Strick held up one finger and nodded. So did the big man in the coat of linked chain. A moment later Ouleh was making expostulatory noises and gestures while Ahdio headed for the corner table, bearing a blue-glazed mug. Strick heard the jing-jing of the armor as the other large man approached.

Is he the focus? Strick could not be sure. He read three separate spells in this place. Two involved Ahdio's assistants, the extra-homely woman and the young fellow with the limp. The other was in back, and seemed to have to do with an animal.

Someone called, "Takin' that poor innocent stranger another mug o' cat-pee, Ahdio?"

"Nah," the dive's proprietor called back, turning his head that way. "Sweetboy Special is what's in your cup, Tervy. Newcomers get the good stuff." Arrived at Strick's table, he went on in a lower voice: "Ouleh said you said you'd buy her one and would nod to prove it. Overhung Ouleh's an old friend and this place's favorite blowze, but for all I know she told you to nod hello to me when I looked this way. Brought you one, though."

Strick decided to stand. Patrons stared. They seldom saw a man as big as Ahdiovizun, even one an inch or so shorter.

"She told it right. And she's to stay over there. I have a message for you." When the other man instantly shifted the mug to his left hand, Strick backed a pace. "Easy. I just came here from Firaqa. Name's Strick. Along the way I met a young man and woman. Boy and a girl, maybe. He asked me to tell you that the big red cat with them followed them—even out across the desert—and to swear that he did *not* take it."

Ahdio stared for a moment, then smiled. "You get the next one," he said, and drank half the contents of the cup in his left hand. "Dark fellow, hawkish nose, medium height and wiry? Wearing anything unusual?"

"Knives."

Ahdio laughed. "That's Hansey! Thanks, uh, Strick. I've been wondering about Notable. Hanse is the first person that cat ever took to. Be damned. Where was this?"

"Hey Ahdio, how about onea them sausages over here?"

Ahdio glanced that way. "Suck your finger, Harmy! This is an old war crony. Throde? Sausage for Harmocohl. Oh, and fill a cup for Ouleh before she stares a hole in my back."

"Up in Maidenhead Wood, other side of the desert," Strick told him. "A day or two this side of Firaqa. They were headed there."

"They were? You know, I've never even met anyone from up there. You just arrive, Strick? Moving to Sanctuary? Got a place to stay?"

"Aye."

Ahdio grinned. "All three. All right. I won't ask any more. Thanks again. You're not staying here in the Maze?"

"No."

"Thought not. The cat look all right?"

"Large and well-fed. Stared at me the whole time we tocked."

"That's Notable!" Ahdio nodded, beaming. "Uh—Strick. Because you bought Ouleh one, Avenestra will be over here next. She's a mighty unhappy little girl, and taking too much mouth from too many of the boys here. You did Hanse and me a favor. Wish you'd do her one. They'd leave her alone when she's with a man as big as you—who is also an old war crony of mine," he added, with a new grin. "Maybe just talk with her a while, or just let her talk. She's all right. Mixed up pretty bad. A round for you both is on me."

"All right. Give her what she wants and suggest that she bring it over here with a mug of something weak for me. Ahdio: any men in here looking for work? Anybody you trust?"

Ahdio smiled. "That narrows the choices! What kind of work? Beg pardon, but you look like a weapon-man to me."

"No. Need a guard, when I open a shop. And a—oh, a lackey who knows Sanctuary and can look and act decent."

"I'll give it some thought and tell you later, Strick. Oh— and thanks, for all of it. The girl too, I mean."

Strick nodded.

Ahdio returned to the counter. Strick didn't see what he did, but a few moments later a girl—this one really was, an angular girl in her mid-teens—was moving toward his table. Her black singlet fitted her like a coat of paint above a violet skirt slit up both sides to her big black belt. Looked as if she had a waist measurement to match her age and a chest maybe eight inches larger. She bore two mugs. Someone said something she didn't like and someone else slapped her bottom and that quickly she turned to dump the contents of one of the mugs down his front. Men laughed, but not that one, and two big men converged on the trouble spot.

The man in the soaked tunic, on his feet with his hand
raised to slap her less intimately but more painfully, glanced
up to his left. Massive chest and scintillant mail, chin at a
level with his eyebrows. Then up to his right. Big broad chest
and arms in an undyed tunic big enough to fit him twice, and
a chin on a level with his eyelashes. The butt-slapper sat
down.

"When a girl wants her tail slapped, Saz, that's one thing.
When you know she doesn't, that's another. You want to
stay?"

Saz nodded. Ahdio nodded. "Throde! Saz needs one, and
so does my old war crony—oh *no!* Now Avvie, damn it, why'd
you go and do that? You have two mugs—why'd you have to
throw the *qualis* on him 'stead of the beer?"

That brought more laughter, while both Saz and Avenestra
kept their heads down. Ahdio said something, and Strick did,
and the girl went to sit with Ahdio's old war crony.

Conversation began slowly. He knew at once that Avenestra was unhappy and defensive. She kept darting curious/
suspicious looks at him from black eyes under jet brows that
indicated her hair had help in being gold-blond. She glugged
her qualis, set the cup down rather sharply, and stared at him.
He signed for more. It came. He told her little and said none
of the things a male might be expected to say to a female in
her apparent profession. He asked questions and shrugged
when she didn't answer or was evasive. He even said "Sorry;
not prying," a couple of times, and he did not ask her age. He
studied her, but looked away when she acted uncomfortable.
He did learn that Avenestra was infatuated with Ahdio, and
that the homely woman was his wife. Never mind his age;
he'd been kind to Avenestra. She told Strick what qualis was
and assured him he would like it; she offered him a taste. He
shook his head and she knocked back the expensive wine. He
signed for another round.

Avenestra put her gaunt-faced head on one side. "You trying to get me drunk?"

"No. You had your limit?"

"You rich?"

He shook his head. "Are you an orphan, Avenestra?"

Her eyes clouded. "How'd you know? Oh, Ahdio told
you!"

"No. If I'd known I wouldn't have asked, believe me."

"Why should I believe you?"

"Because you know you can and because I don't want a damned thing from you."

"Huh! That's a first."

He said nothing and neither did she. She drank and let him see that her cup was empty. He looked at the empty mug, looked at her, and signed for another. Again she put her head on one side and gave him that dark, dark suspicious look.

"You're hardly drinkin' anyth' but you keep or'erin' f'me. You sure you not tryina get me drunk?"

"Do you need help?"

Avenestra put her head down and wept for the next ten minutes.

Strick sat silently. He did not touch her. Ahdio's wife came, but Strick raised a finger to his lips. He gave her money. "Tell Ahdio to tell Cusharlain." She did not understand, but gave him his difference and went away. *Good woman, spell or no,* Strick thought, while Avenestra kept weeping. After another five or eight minutes she raised her head, looking horrible and pitiful. She watched him thrust a big hand down into the outsize neck of his tunic and come out with a white cloth. He handed it to her.

"Wha'm I sposed to do wi' this?"

"Wipe your eyes and face, and blow."

She sat staring, blinking, oozing kohl from her eyes. Then she wiped her face and eyes, and blew. She looked at the kerchief and shook her head.

"Avenestra: let's go."

"Wan' 'nother cup first."

"If you have another qualis you won't be able to go."

"So?" She made a feisty face and used a matching voice: "You *said* you didn't *want* anything from me."

"So you'll be here, drunk and unable to wock, and then what?"

She didn't have to translate his "wock" to "walk." She wept for ten more minutes. After that, they left. Ahdio watched. His fingers were crossed.

The Golden Lizard was hardly golden and hardly comparable to the Golden Oasis, but it was not a hole and aye, a room was available. No eyebrow was raised when Strick laid down coins for two days and three candles, and took a candle and a silent Avenestra, her legs almost functioning, upstairs. He was careful to secure the door and inspect the window. He turned to the girl slouching unprettily on the edge of the bed.

"Avenestra, I want you to give me something."

"Uh-huh. How you wan' it?"

"No, I mean an object. Something of yours. A coin. Anything."

"Huh! Think you're that good? You give *me* someth'."

He handed her a silver coin. "That's yours. I want nothing for it."

She stared at it, held it up closer, stared, and slid off the bed. Sitting on the floor, she wept for the next ten or so minutes. When at last she looked up, he bade her use his kerchief. She did. He repeated his request. She stared, head on one side. At last, wriggling loosely, she gave him her broad black belt.

"Thank you." He squatted and put his hands on her narrow and meatless shoulders. "You think fondly of Ahdio as an uncle. Since you have no reason to drink, you just stopped."

"You," she advised, "are so full of shit your blue eyes are turning brown."

Grinning helplessly, he whipped back the tired old spread and inspected the bed. He found nothing alive. He picked up the slumping girl with preposterous ease, and stretched her on the bed. He took off his weapons belt, thinking about the new armband he'd been forced to buy. He sat on the floor with his back against the wall. The candle he set to one side.

When Avenestra awoke five or so hours later, headachy as always, he was not in the room. The silver coin was. She was certain that she had done nothing for it. And she remembered what he had told her. *Crazy,* she thought, and was thinking fondly of that nice fatherly Ahdio when she slipped back into sleep.

Cusharlain arrived in the common room of the Golden Oasis shortly after noon and Esaria shortly after that. She was bright and summery and pretty in a long sky-blue dress cut dazzlingly low. She was also babbly, and her cousin put a hand over her mouth.

"I have two good prospects as places of business *and* lodgings, Strick, and Ahdio suggested four names. A fifth he is not totally certain about. Said he had seven, but you specified decent *and* honest. You can interview them where and when you wish. Unh! Stop licking my palm, brat!"

"Let's go look," Strick said. "Stop giggling, Esaria, and you may come along with the big boys."

They went. Along the way Esaria told them how miserable her mother was because of the new bosom-displaying style.

"Beard of Ils!" Cusharlain said. "With those melons? She should be pleased and proud to display all that bounty of the gods, much less half!"

"You don't understand, Second Cousin. *Never* tell her I told you, but mother has a large hairy mole rather high up on her left, uh, bounty. Right on top. That's why she has stayed covered to the collarbones, always. Now—either she reveals it, or everyone whose opinion she cherishes will sneer at her for being so ridiculously out of style."

Cusharlain laughed. Strick did not, and Esaria noticed. She took his arm and snugged it to her. Her bodyguard ambled along behind, aware that he was smaller than Strick.

By midafternoon that quiet man with the accent had leased three rooms, two upstairs over the ground-floor one, and had optioned another. His shop and dwelling were on the street called Straight, between Chokeway and the Processional and thus not at all far from the Golden Oasis. By the following afternoon, with the help of Cusharlain and an eager Esaria, he had acquired most of the furnishings he needed.

He paid Cusharlain and returned Esaria's hug.

"I will visit Sly's tonight and *observe* the men Ahdio recommends," he told her cousin. "But as to Harmocohl: no, in advance."

"Surely I can be trusted by now, Strick. You have a carpet, drapes, some chairs and a desk, and beds. What sort of *shop* is this to be? What do you plan to do here?"

"Help people," Strick told him, and after a while Cusharlain went his way, having learned no more. Strick turned to Esaria.

"Esaria: you must get your mother here as soon as you can. I don't care how many bodyguards she brings. You've just got to get her here."

She looked at him. "It isn't going to do me any good to ask why, is it?"

"Not yet. Try."

"Try! I'll *do* it! Are you going to take me to that dreadful dive back in the Maze?"

"A bunny in the lions' lair! Never!"

"What about to bed? Are you ever going to take me to bed?"

He repeated his previous utterance.

No, Strick was told, Avenestra was not in the Golden Lizard. No, she had not drunk anything and she had not stayed the second night. But she had been in four times, asking after him. She had bidden the proprietor mention . . . Uncle Ahdio?

Strick smiled, paid for two more days/nights and made his thoughtful way back to the Golden O. There he was confronted by a certain caravan guard. Solemnly Fulcris turned up the sword-arm sleeve of his tunic.

"The wound is fine," he said. "And by the very beard of Yaguixana, I'd wager there will be no scar, either!"

"Told you, Fulcris. I know a good wound when I see one. What are your plans for—"

"It's not going to be that easy, my friend. What did you do? What have you done?"

"In addition to which," a new voice asked, *"what are you,* Strick?"

Strick looked at him, eyes large. "Hello, Ahdio."

"You might as well call me Uncle Ahdio. Avenestra does. And now I have a non-drinker cluttering up my place!"

Strick didn't laugh. "You know what I am, Ahdio. Just understand this: It is what Sanctuary needs most. It's all white."

"All, Strick? Always?"

Strick met his eyes and put force into his gaze. "All, Ahdio, always. It's a vow—and don't question me that way again."

Ahdio returned the gaze, his head moving almost imperceptibly in the mere hint of a nod. "I believe you. I even apologize."

Strick smiled and squeezed his arm, while their exchanged look lengthened.

"Do . . . do I dare ask?" Fulcris asked nervously.

"Fulcris my friend, I will tell you. Not just now. I repeat, though: what are you going to do? Stay? Go? Find work here, or on the next caravan out?"

"I will tell you," Fulcris said with dignity, "but not just now." And he turned and walked away.

"That's interesting," Ahdio said. When Strick said nothing

but only gave him a questioning look, he said, "He's the fifth man. The one I told Cusharlain I couldn't be sure about because he isn't a Sanctuarite and I don't know enough about him."

Strick smiled and looked at the door that had closed on Fulcris. "I do," he said, so quietly. "Proud fellow, isn't he!"

"Um. That's three of us. Strick—you said 'you know' when I asked what you are . . ."

Strick looked at him again, into the other big man's eyes. "Aye. Three spells in your place, none dark—though I can't be sure about the cat I've never seen. I doubted coincidence."

"You can . . . see spells?!"

Strick nodded. "Usually. Often, anyhow. Not always. It's an ability."

"God—it's a *talent!* A marvelous talent!"

"No, Ahdio. An ability. I paid. I paid for all of it."

Ahdio met the gaze of those large blue eyes for quite some time before he said, "I won't ask, Strick."

"Good. I won't either. Tell Avenestra she has a room at the Lizard tonight and tomorrow night."

"I'll tell her. And I won't ask, Strick."

The man named Frax arrived clean and military-looking for his interview. He had been a palace guard. Then the Beysins came. Now Beysibs guarded the palace. Frax had yet to find employment. Strick sat thinking about that for a while, chewing the inside of his lip. Suddenly he stared past Frax, his eyes going wide. He had not finished his "Look out!" when Frax had spun to face the door, crouching, poised. Each fist had grown a dagger. He saw nothing; no one and no menace.

"You're hired," Strick said, and Frax turned to find him still seated comfortably. "A partition will divide the room downstairs: an entry hall and your room. Your bed will be in it, and your belongings. You'll consider yourself on duty at all times, starting on the morrow. What payment did you receive, as palace guardsman?"

Still in partial shock, Frax told him.

"Hmp! The Prince is no less important than I am—yet. Same wage, Frax."

"You—that was a trick! You tested—"

Frax blinked down at the swordpoint at his chest. His new

employer had stood and drawn and set it there as fast and smoothly as any man Frax had ever seen.

"You had to be almost as good as I am, Frax," he said in that equable way, eyes large and serene. "I won't be wearing a sword." And Strick swung the sword up and back, touched his shoulder with it, and sheathed without glancing down. "Do you know anything about a sort of over-age street urchin named Wintsenay?"

"Not much, Swordmaster. He's a—"

"You definitely are not to call me that, Frax! We'll—" He paused, listening, and smiled. "I have a guest, Frax. If I'm lucky, two guests. In the morning, Frax?"

Frax was nodding, working at finding a respectful title for his astonishing employer, when Esaria bubbled into the room.

"I eluded my 'escort' for once! Hurry, Strick," she said, and, triumphantly: "Mothahhh awaits your pleasure in the Golden O!"

Strick smiled. "Good. My guardian Frax will accompany you." He unbuckled his weapons belt and passed it to the other man. "Hand me one of your daggers, Frax; there's a good one in that sheath. Frax will escort you, Noble Shafralaina, and will escort your mother back. *This* is my place of business."

"I will do anything for you, Lord Strick!"

"Do not call me lord and do not be silly, Avenestra. Your infatuation with Ahdio is ended and so is your nightly drunkenness, that's all. You are right back where you were. An orphan of fifteen who hangs about a low tavern every night and survives by selling her body—for what little poor men can afford to pay! It's a rotten life and will only rot you. Besides, there is the trade, or reverse effect. The Price. What effect is your new craving for sweets going to have on the body you peddle?"

Avenestra looked at the floor and began leaking tears. "What—what else can I d-do-o?"

"What would you like to do? Think, girl! For once, think!"

"B-b-be you-you-ourss!"

Strick slapped the desk cover, a huge piece of deep blue velvet trailing gold tassels on her side. "My dotter, you mean."

"Daughter? Uh—"

"Look at me and consider my age and forget the other, Avneh!"

She did look at him, from unkohled eyes all soft and misted with tears that traced glistening tracks down her gaunt cheeks. She bit her lip. She nodded.

"What—what does your daught—your *dotter* do?"

"Strangely enough, she is called niece rather than dotter, calls me Uncle Strick, and lives in the room across the corridor. I am helping to relocate the present tenant. My niece learns decent behavior and decent things to do, wears decent clothing, and will I hope become aide and receptionist."

"I—I—I don't even know what that means . . ."

"In the meanwhile, she markets for me and cooks for me."

"Oh, oh M-Mother Shipri—yes, yes, I will cook for you!"

Strick smiled. "My niece also stops watering this nice carpet with so many tears."

She smiled. "Oh my lor—Uncle Strick! How did you come by your ability?"

"The power of the Ring of Foogalooganooga, far west of Firaqa, Avenestra. Wints!"

The door opened and a thin man appeared. He was freshly barbered and shaven, wearing a nice new tunic of Croyite blue. "Sir?"

"Take my *niece* around to a few places and introduce her, Wints. You and she will be buying some food. At Kalen's, tell him she is to have a tunic from the same bolt as yours. White broidery at the neck and—umm. Length just above the knees. Avneh: it is *not* to be tight!"

"Y-ess, Uncle," she said, trying not to weep in her joy.

"All right then, be on your way—what's all that damned noise!" Then, "Easy, Wints. Don't be so fast to draw that dagger!" Strick strode to the door and stared at the stairwell. "Frax! What's all that n—oh, Noble Shafralain. Come in. My aide and my niece were just leaving. Wints: despite his stride and fiercely determined look, this man and I are friends."

He gestured. Wide of eye, Wintsenay and Avenestra departed while the silken-tunicked nobleman strode into the room that Strick called his "shop." Shafralain paused to regard the other man, who was most unusually attired. Strick's calf-length tunic of medium blue and oddly, unfashionably *matching* leggings made him seem less big and yet more imposing, in a different way. A matching skullcap, encompassing most of his head, had replaced the odd leathern cap of the same design.

"What *are* you, Strick? First I saw a big man with a sword and few words. Another caravan guard, I thought, probably looking for mercenary employment. Then I discovered you had character and consideration—and silver. In my home I was struck by your comportment—aye, and deportment: the manners of a man well born. Nonetheless I was nervous about my daughter's uh seeming fondness for you. Yet Cusharlain assured me that you were not encouraging her; strange way for a man to behave, with a highborn girl who shows him attention! Soon I learned from her that you had taken these rooms, in a good location, and purchased furniture. Next I discovered that you have real money; we share a banker, Strick. Ah, don't look that way! He is close-mouthed as he should be; it is just that I am one of his partners. Now my wife—gods of my fathers, Strick! What *are* you?"

"Sit down, Noble," Strick said, as he did so. "It's no secret, now: I am open for business. I recognize most spells, and I possess a smallish ability to *redirect* . . . problems. Call it an ability to cast minor spells. I also have rules. I help people, but by what most would call 'white magic' only. I will have nothing to do with the other kind, but would fight it."

"That is the most I have ever heard you say!" Shafralain had slid down into the comfortable chair across the handsomely draped desk from the quiet man. "Whence . . . whence came this *ability?*"

"From Ferrillan, far north of Firaqa. From a woman now dead. I am unbound by gods and locale, or by spells or antispells. Partners with my moneyhandler, eh?"

"Never mind that. The unsightly mole on my wife's . . . chest has been there for over ten years. Now it has vanished without a trace, because she came to see you. She is ecstatic—and she says you did not even touch her."

"Not quite true," Strick told him. "I did see the mole, and later I did put my hands on her shoulders. It was sufficient."

Shafralain shook his head. "Such power—and can you heal? Are you a physician-mage, is that it?"

"Not really. Can't raise the dead and wouldn't strike dead an enemy of yours, not for all your fortune. Couldn't heal a dagger wound in your belly either, Shafralain."

Shafralain made a face at the image that brought to mind.

"My lady wife is the happiest of women, and yet you took from her a single piece of silver. Now—"

"No. I asked for something of value, in advance, and a silver coin was what she—my third client here—chose to give me. Another gave me water and wine; another a worthless belt. But it was of value to her, you see."

"Now my wife tells me I should give you a hundred more!"

"I have what I want of her and of you, Shafralain," Strick said, omitting the other man's title for the second time. "How many of high station has she told?" He smiled. "I hope she exaggerates the amount paid but not my ability! Because of her, others will come. I will have my hundred pieces of silver! But—is she totally happy? There is always another Price; a Trade. I paid mine. A person who was infatuated with one much older and driven to drunkenness now has a craving for sweets that will become trouble. Fulcris's wound healed swiftly without a scar. I had only a little to do with that, but he will have some small complaint by now. The reverse effect; the Price."

Shafralain stared. "Expimilia's tooth! You are telling me that the suddenly painful tooth my wife had to have drawn is an additional price she paid for your help?"

"Probably. It was not in front, I hope. Ah, good. Doesn't show? Good. Has she any other recent complaint?" When the other man shook his head, Strick shrugged. "The painful abcess was probably the Price, then. Not a terrible one. That is beyond my control. It might have been gentler, and it could have been worse. Still, some people prefer the original problem to the Price."

Shafralain sat studying him. "I am not sure I believe all you say, Strick. Easy to admit that I'd like to! White magic only, eh?"

Quietly and in an equable tone, staring, Strick said, "Snarl and sneer at street urchins, Noble Shafralain, but do not question me."

Shafralain stiffened and his knuckles paled as he gripped the arms of the comfortable chair Strick provided for his visitors. Strick's eyes never wavered from the nobleman's stare. At last Shafralain's hands and body loosened.

"Strick, my family existed in ancient Ilsig since before Ranke was. My family has been here since Ils the All-seeing led my people out of the Queen's Mountains and here to Sanctuary. The city of the children of Ils has been beset by blood-lusting Rankans and weavers of the darkest spells. For a time it seemed that the All-father had turned our city over to His son, the Nameless One who is patron of shadows and thieves. For a time some of us thought we saw promise in the young prince whom the emperor—the murdered emperor, now—sent out from Ranke. He is no Ilsig, but damn it we thought he was a man. Now we have the sea people. New conquerors. And that same young prince, who has a Rankan wife, consorts openly with one of those . . . creatures."

He came to painful pause rather than a halt, but Strick said, "All this I know, Aral Shafralain t'Ilsig."

Shafralain nodded. "I said that I want to believe you, Strick. White Magic is the Old way. We need it. Sanctuary needs hope." Abruptly he rose. "I was not questioning you, my touchy friend. I love Sanctuary and hope you do."

Strick rose. "My vow is long since made, Shafralain, and bound about. I am what I say. A minor weaver of spells; spells for good and that only."

"You said that you paid a price," Shafralain said, after gazing at him for a time. "I would dare ask what price you paid for your . . . abilities. A tooth?"

Strick shook his head. He reached up and brushed his hand over his skullcap, wiping it backward from his head. Shafralain stared at the other man's head, and at last he nodded. He extended his hand. Strick took it, and again their gazes met. Then Shafralain departed amid a rustle of silk. The big man carefully replaced his skullcap.

Noble Shafralain could guess at the rest of the Price Strick had paid for the ability, but probably would not. Strick didn't care.

His name was Gonfred and he was a goldsmith with a reputation for honesty. No shavings, no scrapings or drippings remained in his possession when he worked with the gold of others. He hiccoughed as he entered Strick's shop and again by the time he was seated and laying a silver coin on the desk's blue cloth.

"Is this of value to you, Gonfred?"

The goldsmith gazed at him, smiled shyly, and added another silver coin. And he hiccoughed.

"How long have you had the hiccups, Gonfred?"

"Six days. I work with my ha-uh!-hands. Can't work."

"I want you to sit back and take about three deep breaths. Hold the third as long as you possibly can. If you hiccup during that process, do it again. Avenestra!"

Sucking up great breaths, Gonfred saw the blue-tunicked young girl who appeared. "Sir!"

"Please fetch an ounce of Saracsaboona for this honest goldsmith, with two ounces of water."

She departed. Gonfred hiccoughed and started the deep breathing again. He succeeded in holding the third. Avenestra returned from the adjoining room. In both hands she bore a goblet of translucent green glass. It contained an ounce of ordinary wine, an ounce of water, and an ounce of saffron water for color. She set it before Strick. Taking it in both hands, he rose and came around to the seated goldsmith. Gonfred accepted it and looked questioning; he was still holding, barely.

"Let the breath out," he was told. "Drink, and try to do it in such a way that it all goes down at a gulp."

When Gonfred took the goblet, gasping, Strick put his hands on the seated man's shoulders. "Your hiccups are going, Gonfred . . ."

Hurriedly Gonfred knocked back the contents of the goblet. He gasped some more, watching the other man return to his chair behind the cloth-draped desk.

"Your hiccups are gone, Gonfred my friend. There is always a trade, a Price beyond this silver, over which I have no control. If it is unbearable, return."

Gonfred sat staring. His hiccoughs were gone. "*Thank you, Spellmaster!*" He was at the door when he turned, paced back to the desk, and retrieved both silver coins. In their place he laid down a plain, drilled disk of pure gold. Then he departed.

He entered carrying a sack. His name was Jakob and he was called Blind Jakob. Strick's face was sad as he watched Wints guide the fruit pedlar to the chair. Jakob's hand found the desk and he set the sack upon it.

"I am Strick, Jakob, and I have fear that I cannot help you."

"It—it is—you think it is permanent, sir?" The blind man looked stricken. "Ah gods. But it is so troublesome—so embarrassing."

Strick blinked. "Embarrassing?"

"The roiling inside is bad enough, but when I break wind in public, particularly when a woman is examining my fruits . . ."

Strick clamped both hands over his mouth to hold back all sound of laughter. The poor fellow was accustomed to his true affliction. But gas *disturbed* him; it was socially embarrassing! Strick rose and moved around the desk.

"I am coming to put my hands on you, Jakob. Give me something of value."

The blind man leaned a little forward to touch the sack. "Three people have insisted on buying those in the past hour, sir. They are the most valuable I have had in a long while."

Strick's hands were on him, now. He was relieved to feel no death here, and he knew at once that the offering was of value to this man. Then he felt the tension, and was sure that Jakob's gas was not dietary. He must be careful. This man did not live or work in a truly dangerous area. Yet relieve him of all tension and he might be left so complacent that he really would be in the danger that now he mostly imagined. Strick did what he could, to the extent he dared.

"Your gas is gone, Jakob my friend, save when you over-indulge in food or drink. Radishes and cucumbers are your enemies, Jakob. Mind now, there is always a trade, a Price beyond this sack, and over that I have no control. If it is unbearable, return."

Jakob arose, made his request and heard it granted, and traced out the lines of the other man's face with his fingers. He departed with his sack, now empty. The two muskmelons were superb, indeed things of value.

"Bad breath, yes. Would you open your mouth and let me see the source, please?" Bent close to look, Strick was half overcome by the foul odor that was his client's complaint. He turned his head aside, took a deep breath, and looked closely into that mouth. He straightened. Shaking his head, he went to give Wints quiet instructions. Strick returned to stand over this friend of Shafralain, looked sternly down at him.

"Noble Volmas, you must have more love for both gods and self. The gods gave you those teeth. You have not cleaned them for years. Do so, man! In the meanwhile—ah, thank you, Wintsenay. In the meanwhile, Noble, take this cup. Note the five seeds in its bottom. The cup also contains salt water. Aye, make a face—and drink! See that you swallow the seed. The Seeds of Malasaconooga are the source of my abilities."

Strick remained standing, sternly watching, while the poor fellow drank off the salt water. Finished, he made choking noises and a dreadful face. A stern Strick held out his hand for the cup. He peered within. A seed remained. He heaved a mighty sigh, sent it back to be filled with water, and gave the finely dressed man with the great belly even sterner instructions. The noble drank. The fifth seed went down.

"Now. That foul breath that has cost you friends and alienated your wife is not gone, but will go, steadily. I am only a maker of small white spells, Noble, and sometimes I must have help. Keep that cup. Use it. Clean your teeth twice daily, after you eat. Get in there with cloth and soap. Yes, it will taste terrible; you've been told there is a Price here, beyond those ten silver coins you claim to find dear. After you have cleaned, add a *goodly* measure of salt to that cup, fill with water-not-wine, and *rinse*. You need not drink. Swirl it about in your mouth and spit, until all is gone. *Remember* all this! It is important. If in two weeks your breath is not improved fivehold, return to me."

After Volmas had left, Strick stood shaking his head. *Charlatan,* he told himself. Yet he had done good for everyone who had to come in contact with that stupid swine, to whom ten pieces of silver were as naught. That cup was one he had never liked, and he had known he'd find a use for some of the seeds from blind Jakob's melons!

"My dear, you are under a spell. I cannot see whose, and I am sorry. You need the aid of powers beyond mine. Go to Enas Yorl. Here now, take back your gold. I have not earned it. If he does not or will not help, return and we will *try.*"

Smoke of the Flame, he thought in anger and true pain, watching her unhappy departure. *Abhorrent black magic again. After two weeks here I have done so little for these poor pitiful people with their misery and their wicked sorcerers!*

• • •

The lady of wealth was forty-eight and showing about one gray hair for every six black. The dyes she had tried made an ugly mess, deadening her hair. He considered her, her vanity, and her offer of three golden disks bearing a likeness of the new Emperor.

"It is a natural process, Lady Amaya. The problem is that presently it's streaky. If it grayed faster, or went white, you would be both beautiful *and* striking."

"Oh—oh my."

She went away and he waited an hour before sending her golden coins to her.

She returned next day. "Show me silver," she said, setting a largeish clinky bag of purple cloth on his desk, and he showed her. He also "cheated." She did look magnificent with silver hair, and he added a small spell so that she and her vanity agreed with the fact.

"Oh! Oh my!" she said, staring at the mirror, turning her head this way and that. "Oh, Spellweaver! You are a genius! My husband will love it and all the girls will—oh my. What shall I tell them?"

"That you have been dyeing it for two years or so, and are *so* happy to be over your vanity!"

Amaya laughed in delight. "A genius! They will be filled with both shame *and* envy!"

Within the next two weeks he had five requests for silver hair, although none of these others, of varying stations in life, gave him fifty pieces of silver. Not to mention the chain of gold Amaya's husband sent as "token of his pleasure."

"So. It's been a month, and you are staying busy. Tell me about your day," Esaria said, looking so bright and sunny across the little table from him. They were taking dinner in the Golden O, while her guard and Frax sat across the room, visiting. He wore his odd blue "uniform," including the plain gold disk on a gold chain about his neck.

He spoke to the pepper pot with which he toyed. "I was asked for a love potion. She said she just knew he was fond of her but when he's up close he loses ardor, unto aloofness. I gave her what she needed. A vial of colored wotter with a bit of wine and camomile for aroma, and soap made green by simple herbal coloring. I bade her bathe daily and well, putting a bit of each into the bath wotter and drying thoroughly."

Esaria looked very skeptical indeed. "That's a love potion?!"

"It is what she needs. She stinks. If he doesn't respond to her better aroma, someone will; she's attractive. For that I earned two coppers. Stop laughing, brat. My business is help for the people. I had to turn away a clubfoot. I can do nothing about that—by the Flame, how I wish I could! A former client returned. Looked good: I had indeed removed his acne, but his Price took the form of diarrhea he could not bear. I removed the spell and returned his two coppers. So—he has acne and a settled stomach." Strick shrugged. "He's seventeen. The acne will go. Mine did."

"So has *most* of mine," she said. "But at this rate you could starve!"

He shook his head. "Hardly. A certain friend of your mother's is very sensitive about her scraggly hair. I put a little spell on it *and* made her promise to wash it at least every other day. For that, she left fourteen silver Imperials—old Imperials. Said it is her magic number."

"Is it?"

He smiled. "No. Must be mine, though," and they chuckled together. "Too, a messenger arrived from Volmas. His message was a nice fat gold piece."

"Is *that* what happened to his foul breath! Ah, my hero!" Clasping her hands under her chin, she gazed at him. "What else, Hero of the People?"

"I spelled a wart off a finger. *Ten* coppers! Accepted a sack of decent wine for still another head of silver hair. I think it was more than she could afford, at age thirty. A woman asked me to cast a spell on her neighbor, who is after her husband. Third request for punitive spells this week. I refuse them all. The very next client asked me to make her more attractive to her husband. See the difference in the minds of the two individuals? I told her she would be, as soon as she gets him to come to me. The spell, you see, needs to be on him, so that he perceives her as more attractive!"

"How lovely! You might put one on a certain man for me," she said, tracing a finger idly along his forearm.

"If you were more attractive no one in Sanctuary could stand it," he said, and rushed on before she could say what he did not want to hear. "This is interesting. The man and the woman came together. Their neighbor's dog barks every night and disturbs their sleep and that of their infant. He said he wanted the dog dead and I told him no. He came back with almost a command: 'At least punish my neighbor! The swine sleeps right through that beast's noise!'" Strick sighed. "That was tempting!"

"I should think so! Sounds like justice to me," Esaria said.

"True. But it's beyond what I will do. When he settled down and she begged for any sort of relief, I promised that the dog would not bother their sleep again."

"Oh how wonderful, Strick!" She squeezed his arm. "You put a sleeping spell on them?—or one on their ears?"

"No! Never that; I couldn't make such a spell selective. They could perish in their sleep because they heard nothing. No, but if you'd like to take a little ride with me 'morrow afternoon, we will visit their neighbor's dog. Simple: I merely see to it that he makes no sound between late twilight and dawn."

She laughed aloud. "How marvelous! And yes, I'd love to go!" She squeezed his arm at the elbow. After a few moments she sobered: "Oh. But suppose someone tried to break in at the home of the dog's owner? Won't you have done bad along with the good?" Now her leg had found his, under the table.

"A dog that barks at night without real cause is of no value, and better off on a farm someplace. Besides, its owner sleeps right on, remember? Else he'd have got rid of the dog long ago. Or become its master as well as merely owner."

"Ah. I should have known better than to question you. Oh Strick you're so wise and so sensitive! You care so, about people!"

Strick responded to compliments no better than most, and chose not to respond to that. "Do you know someone called Chenaya?"

"Yes. Uh—not well. I am not interested in knowing her well."

"Um. Neither is much of anyone else, apparently. Came in yesterday. First she challenged Frax and sneered at him, then made a sexual suggestion to Wints and then a nasty remark, said another nasty to Avneh and came swaggering in. Reminds me of an adolescent boy with a lot to prove. Challenged me —not to a passage at arms, I mean, just by remarks and attitude. A thoroughly poison personality. She had persuaded herself to come, but had trouble stating her problem. A very, very defensive . . . person. Demanded to know the source of my ability. I told her the emerald Eye of Agromoto and—"

"That's not what you told me!"

"No, but it's what I thought of yesterday; today I told a fellow it came from the Hoary Head of the Hawk of Horus. I asked this Chenaya for something of value and she slapped down a dagger. Nice sticker, with a jewel or two. She wondered aloud what's under my cap and I only stared, waiting. She kept hedging and meandering verbally. I made the signal for Wints to interrupt and tell me someone was waiting. 'Get out of here, lackey!' she snapped at him, and I quietly told her that I would give orders to my people, thanks, and never to hers. She glowered for a while, then looked away, mentioned needing privacy, and told me what she perceives as her problem."

Strick paused to shake his head. "'I'd like to—to do better with people,' she said. 'No one—I mean, some people don't uh er seem to uh like me.'"

Esaria made a nasty noise.

He went on: "At last she'd got it out, but she continued looking at the wall. Embarrassed and defensive. Ready to challenge, snap back, fight, argue. What a rotten job her parents did with her; how defensive and unhappy she is! I told her that I could help her, but that she would not like the solution —and only her gods could know what the Price might be! She looked at me, then, and I thought how sad it is that she has such genuinely pretty eyes."

He shook his head. "'What would you do that would be so terrible?' she wanted to know, and I told her: Lock your tongue. Render you unable to speak. That and some real counseling."

Esaria giggled.

"Her glare got worse," he said, ignoring her. "She called me charlatan, snatched up the dagger, and stalked to the door. That didn't surprise me; it just saddened me. *Then* she surprised me: she turned back and made a sexual suggestion. I said no. Unfortunately she demanded a reason. I told her I did not find her sexually attractive. I don't, and stop looking that way. She seems bent on couching every male in the city—as if, Wints says, her creator mandated it. Not this one. I am more than disinterested: The idea is abhorrent."

"Glad to hear it," Esaria said. "Does that vow encompass all women?"

He shook his head and leaned back, smiling to cover discomfort. "No. Just Chenaya, girls such as Avneh, and the daughters of wealthy noblemen."

"Bigot!"

In his mind Strick identified his bankers as the Pearl One and the Gold One. Amaya was the wife of the Pearl One with the simple name: Renn. The Gold One was Melarshain— probably another ancient Ilsig and relative. After three months in Sanctuary, the quiet man had a considerable amount on deposit with each; far more than the pearls and gold that had established his credit here. It was Melarshain who asked him to come in this afternoon for a "discussion." Without asking questions, Strick went. First he changed clothes.

The floor on which he paced into the chamber was of rich tile, alternating a warm russet with a nicely contrasting pale cream yellow. Handsomely painted scenes decorated the walls; one centered around an intricately fitted mosaic. Entering with his lightweight beige cloak flapping at his ankles, Strick saw that the furnishings were designed simultaneously for show and for comfort—rich comfort.

He was surprised at the collection of men who awaited him, but did not show it. They showed their surprise that he did not wear the "Strick uniform" of unfashionably long tunic over unfashionably matching blue leggings. Today he boldly displayed large bare calves and big bare arms in the undyed tunic with the extra-short sleeves and extra-large opening at the neck. He had chosen to appear as colorless as he had been when he arrived in Sanctuary, three months agone. The cloak, however, was no inexpensive garment.

"So the moneyhandlers of Sanctuary are not enemies, hmm?" he asked, looking blandly at Renn. And at Volmas, and Shafralain, and another man he did not know, and then at Melarshain. "A moment, please." He turned back to the doorway. "Fulcris? It seems that I have not been invited here to be murdered after all. Come and take this, will you, and find some aide of Melarshain's to go down and tell Frax he can relax his guard."

While five men of wealth sat staring, an armed man Shafralain recognized came into the chamber. He wore a blue tunic with darker bands at hems and over both shoulders. Without so much as a glance at them, he accepted the weapons belt Strick unbuckled, and took it away.

Strick turned to face the seated men, who were staring and exchanging looks of surprise or worse. These five represented a fifth of the wealth of Sanctuary. Strick nodded to them, and sat. He gazed at Melarshain with a mildly questioning look and an expectant air.

"This is Noble Izamel, Strick."

"Hello, Noble Izamel. You probably know why you are here. Melarshain, I have come as asked. Tell me why."

Izamel, a quite old man around whose skull remained only a halo of white hair, chuckled. "I have been told considerable about you, but I had not realized how direct you would be, Spellmaster."

"I am in the company of wealthy men who can afford an afternoon off. I am a working man who can ill afford the luxury."

"You are hardly a poor man, sir."

"I did not say that I was poor, Noble. Since it is you who speaks and not my moneyholder Melarshain who invited me, I repeat to you: I have come as asked. Tell me why."

Melarshain glanced at Renn, but it was Shafralain who made an impatient gesture and rose. He paced as he spoke.

"We are men who love Sanctuary. We believe that you do. We have heard that you consider leaving."

Strick's face was open, his eyes large. He said nothing. He had started the rumor.

"You have done good in Sanctuary; for Sanctuary," Shafralain resumed, when it became obvious that Strick would not comment. "For four of us here directly, but what is more important, for the city. For the people. For us of Ilsig, for Rankans—even the Beys. We wish you to remain, Strick."

"I am moving into the city from my villa, sir," Izamel said. "The villa is for sale. We wish you to purchase it."

"You . . . flatter and please me," Strick said, even more quietly than usual. "Too, I appreciate bluntness, Noble Izamel. Yet while I have prospered here, I am sure I cannot afford your villa."

At last Melarshain got himself together. "Strick, what you see here is a new cartel. We have discussed. The five of us love Sanctuary and welcome another who has only her good in mind. We propose to loan you the money to purchase the villa of Noble Izamel, at no interest, and to sell you as well an interest in the glass manufactory two of us own. You may specify the terms."

Strick looked about at them. The ancient aristocracy and wealth of ancient, long-dead Ilsig. Five men who genuinely cared. Cared. These were Ilsigi—Wrigglies, to some who did not care. He saw five men with their arms outstretched to a foreigner who had come to act as advocate for the people—for their people.

"You seek to whelm me, and you succeed. In fact, you quite overwhelm me. I have not seen your villa, Izamel, but I accept. Yet we all know that I am nothing if I do not continue to see anyone and everyone who comes to me." He looked at Shafralain. "You know part of the Price I paid, my friend. The other part is that I Care. I must. I Care, unto agony. This is not always what I have been. There was a time when I cared about nothing save me. I was a swordman. Then I made a bargain, and I made the demanded trade, paid the Price." He paused, looked away from their eyes. "I may have been happier before. . . . But there is no going back. This is what I am. I accept your offer, provided you realize that I must maintain my shop in an accessible area, with my same people."

"We had thought that you would move the—the shop to the villa, Spellmaster." That was Renn, moneyhandler.

"No. I am not the toy of Sanctuary's aristocracy. I am all people's advocate." In a low, low voice he added, "I have to be."

Melarshain only glanced at the others. "Then we accept that, Spellmaster. The chances are excellent that we insist on, say, two more bodyguards. You employ them; we shall pay them."

"No. I pay my people well. They are loyal to me. I shall not have them loyal to you."

Shafralain said, "Still the mistrustful swordsman, Strick?"

"Who am I to dispute the judgment of Noble Shafralain?"

Volmas and Izamel laughed aloud, in chorus.

Strick rose. "The loan will be open-ended. I wish to pay interest; one-half the going rate for such men as you. Prepare the documents. Renn: I wish one of my pearls back. The other goes to Volmas as down payment. And gentlemen, gentlemen all: I wish to see the Prince."

Good then, Strick thought as he walked back to his shop. *Now it's time to begin work toward my true purpose in Sanctuary.*

AFTERWORD

C. J. Cherryh

I have two sayings about *Thieves' World:* one of which is that we live there. It's amazing how the writers, sitting at one restaurant table, tend to sound like the council-in-the-warehouse.

> ASPRIN/JUBAL/HAKIEM: Well, I think we have to get a consensus here.
> CHERRYH/ISCHADE/STILCHO: Look, I haven't forgotten the ten bodies that got dumped on my doorstep. I can't stand still for that. It's a question of professional pride.
> ABBEY/MOLIN/ILLYRA/WALEGRIN: We want the streets quiet.
> MORRIS/TEMPUS/CRIT: Hell, it's just a couple of buildings we want to take out.
> OFFUTT/SHADOWSPAWN: Can I take care of Haught?
> ASPRIN/JUBAL/HAKIEM/ *(as appalled silence falls at nearby table)* Hey, those people are *looking* at us.

The other maxim (one Asprin is fond of quoting) is that you write your first *Thieves' World* story for pay. You write your second for revenge.

I got into this project as a result of a panel at a convention, in which the remarks from one end and the other of the table ran:

> ASPRIN: I asked C. J. here to write for *Thieves' World* and she turned me down.
> CHERRYH: You did not.
> ASPRIN: *(feigning puzzlement)* I didn't?
> CHERRYH: You never did.
> ASPRIN: *(more and more innocent)* I thought I did.
> CHERRYH: Never.
> ASPRIN: *(with predatory smile, playing to two hundred witnesses)* Hey, C. J., how would you like to write for *Thieves' World?*

As neat an ambush as any in Sanctuary. *Thieves' World* was already a couple of volumes along, and dropping in on a town with this much going on in it is a ticklish business. So I played my opening gambit very carefully, determined to offend no one.

After alienating the gods of Ranke and Sanctuary, Shadowspawn, and Enas Yorl, as well as the clientele of the Vulgar Unicorn, and discovering there was war brewing in town, all in my opening story, most of my characters decided to withdraw to somewhere less trafficked for the second round. Mradhon Vis went to Downwind, where absolutely nothing could go wrong, right?

Wrong. It turns out Tempus is moving into this side of town and Stepsons are riding back and forth through Downwind like mad, feuding with the hawkmasks, two of which, thanks to a gift from Asprin, are mine.

We don't plan these things. We just write our pieces and we try to mind our own business until someone drops a real mess in our laps, whereupon we sit in our living rooms like Ischade ticking off the town madmen on her fingers and deciding that she has quite well had it—

You get the picture. Live and let live is not quite the motto of the town; and any time you become tempted to let a round pass, you realize that no one else is going to pass, that your people are going to be sitting targets, and you are going to have to make some preemptive strikes or discover yourself in an insoluble mess.

Then there are the phone calls.

MORRIS/TEMPUS/ROXANE: Look, there's this little matter I couldn't get taken care of. . . . Could you get rid of the demon?

DUANE/HARRAN: Can Ischade go to hell?

CHERRYH/ISCHADE: Maybe we could silt in the harbor?

PAXSON/LALO: I don't know, the painting just sort of grew on me.

Writing is a profession practiced in locked rooms, in manic solitude. At least we try, between ringing telephones and solicitors at the door. Rarely do writers get the chance to practice their art in groups, or to write each others' characters, or interfere in each others' plots and plans; so part of the success of *Thieves' World* is that it's a challenge and a new kind of art form for the writers. Asprin and Abbey have invented an entirely new literary form, and an environment which has regularly surprised even the seasoned participants, who, you would imagine, ought to know what is going on and what turns the story will take.

Well, the honest truth is that we have very little idea what will happen. Unplanned war breaks out in the streets. It lurches and falters in settlements, just the way it does in real life, my friends, because certain people in it have to get certain things or believe there is a way out, or they go on fighting. Feuds break out between characters and resolve themselves the way they do in life—with some change in both characters. Characters mutate and grow and turn out to have apsects that surprise even their creator. Moria of the streets has become Moria the Rankene lady; Mor-am is in dire straits and may never recover—or may, who knows, end up well off?

What snags us into this madness? It's those phone calls which arrive and inform you that Ischade has gone to hell, but will be back in time to meet schedule in your section, or that tell you there's something nasty lying in your back garden, or that Strat has this terrible compulsion to come back to Ischade's house even knowing what she is.

We have our peculiar rhythms, too. Morris always moves first; she sends me what she's done, and *then* I know what I'm going to do. I am occasionally tempted to ask her where she gets her ideas, because try as I will to get started, nothing happens for me until I hear from Morris. Duane and I occasionally discuss things. And Abbey and Asprin and I. And Abbey and Asprin and everybody else, some of whom probably consult with each other and don't tell me or Morris or Duane. As in real-world politics, *we* don't know all the alliances that exist in this town.

Then the organization happens. Abbey and Asprin fling themselves under the wheels of the juggernaut, writing last, bringing the whole scheming mass of us to coherency and making it sound as if we had always known what we were doing and where it was going, all of which is illusion. Usually we know the season of the year, and the situation at the start. Period. The rest works by rumor and inspiration.

Revenge is part of what makes it work. And partnerships and pair-ups. Writers arc a curious lot, with expertise in the eclectic and the esoteric: You want to know how Minoan plumbing worked? Ask me. You want to know something medical? Ask Duane. Hittites? Ask Morris. And so on and so on. Together we make quite an encyclopaedia. And remember —we have to write everyone else's characters, sometimes from the inside, with all their opinions and their expertise— soldiers and wizards and kings and blacksmiths and thieves, oh, yes, thieves. There are only a couple of professions I can think of where you need to know how to pick a lock or jimmy a window: one is writing. Likewise we have to know what a legislative session sounds like or what goes on behind the closed doors of a head of state's office, or inside the head of a painter or a doctor. All of which means that we have to learn something as we go, because we don't know who we may suddenly need to write from the inside, or when we will need the skills of a mountain climber or a sailor. *Some* of those phone calls we make are fast exchanges of technical information, whether or not, for instance, Sanctuary has a well-developed glass industry, and what technological advances it implies, how hot a fire has to get, how pure the glass can be, what a glassblower's tools are made of and whether this might imply some military development as well that we might wish not to let happen— also what oil they burn and where it comes from and what trade routes, and how they light their rooms and what provision there is in town for firefighting.

"Well," I say, looking at the White Foal River, "that looks like a fault line to me. Has this place ever had earthquakes?"

"Sure looks suspicious," says someone with geological expertise.

"Wait a minute," says Asprin, with the evident feeling that things are slipping out of control.

Being The Authority, he informs us that whatever it is, it is quiescent and will remain that way.

Across the table, several writers exchange thoughtful looks. Now, none of us would violate that rule. After all, The Authority could toss us out. On the other hand, recall that this particular assembly of individuals can pick locks, plumb Minoan buildings, set bones, and negotiate a ceasefire. So can Asprin, who built this place, and who probably knows more about its underpinnings than we do; and Abbey, who has connections to the gods, is already thinking of ways to head this off which are capable of distracting all of us.

Not a good idea, we decide.

Later.

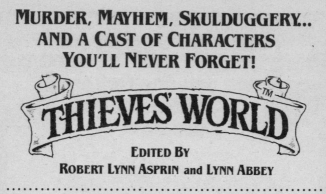